DARKMIRROR

AGENCY

Hell's Belle

Marie Castle

Bella
BOOKS

2013

Bella Books, Inc.
P.O. Box 10543
Tallahassee, FL 32302

Printed in the United States of America on acid-free paper.

First Bella Books Edition 2013

Editor: Katherine V. Forrest
Cover Designed by: KIARO Creative Ltd.

ISBN: 978-1-59493-333-2

About the Author

Marie Castle lives in a little town in Mississippi once called Gandsi-Zion for the train stop that ran between the Civil War-era Zion Seminary and the Gulf and Ship Island depot. There, she practices Practical Romanticism (her term for being single). She has been known to dance in her socks when no one is around and does foolish things on a regular basis merely because she can. She welcomes feedback and can be contacted through her Facebook page.

Disclaimer

The events and characters in this novel are all fictional. Any similarity to persons still living, dead, or otherwise engaged is coincidental. The same holds true for the history related herein, with two exceptions. Tragically, Hattiesburg's landmark drive-in theater did recently burn. However, neither the author nor our intrepid heroine were connected to this in any fashion. Secondly, the author does indeed often wonder if her cat is possessed by some dark power. But as the cat swears her innocence, it seems only time will tell.

Author's Note

To borrow a quote from one of Cate's friends, "In the South, a story never starts where it should. Ask a man why he killed his neighbor, and he might start by saying, 'Well, I had Cream of Wheat for breakfast, then put on my favorite flannel shirt...' An hour later, he'll get to the point." And that, dear reader, is why this story begins three decades in the past...because it is told by a Southern woman with the traditional penchant for the long-winded version. Even if this is a very untraditional story.

—M

PROLOGUE

The Past

Evie ran as if the demons of hell were chasing her, because if they weren't, they soon would be. She'd hidden her flame-red hair and bright green eyes underneath a dark, hooded cloak and walked with lowered head at a painfully slow pace until reaching the long-forgotten entrance. Now, she was alone in the labyrinth of tunnels that would lead to a gate similar to the one that had brought her here to Denoir, the first of Hell's seven realms. It had taken weeks of sending out just the whisper of her power in a subtle search to locate an unguarded gate. Yet, it would take Denoir's prince mere minutes to discover her escape and send his dogs searching. But they wouldn't find her before she reached her destination, and then it would be too late.

It might have taken the dark faction months to open the gate that had brought her here. But as a guardian, she was gifted with the power to open and close them at will. She'd fought and nearly defeated the faction, but the Lord and Prince of this realm had been another matter. Like her, he guarded the gates that led in and out of his world very closely. The opening of one had drawn his attention, and so he'd captured her...claimed her...before she could escape home.

That was three months ago. Now she was alone, running, listening to the sounds of her soft shoes scuffling on the rough stone floor. Haunted by even the echo of her breath rushing in and out. It was reckless to run so quickly in the pitch black, but a torch would have aroused suspicion, and using power to form a ball of light might be felt. But light wasn't needed, because the darkness was no longer empty. She was so near the gate now, and the power of it sang to her. A soft sigh of relief barely passed her lips.

Freedom.

It would take mere seconds to open, pass through, and close the gate again. Her power—her salvation and her damnation. For as a guardian, she had the power to unleash Hell on Earth. A great power, and an even greater responsibility. With enough power, anyone could open a gate for moments. But if a guardian willed it, one could be opened for hours, days, perhaps even an eternity. Masses of the lower-level demon scavengers could roam a green Earth or any of the other realms, sucking the life from anything too weak to protect itself. And that was the best-case scenario.

When the faction had been unable to simply steal her power, they'd tried to force her to their will. They hadn't succeeded. Neither had the Prince, though his methods had been much different. But that would have changed very soon. With each passing day, her secret had become more difficult to hide. So she ran, not just for herself, but for the child she felt growing within her. The child whose life would be bartered for its mother's power…or used against its father. She had seen that future and would not allow it to be. She would not wait and be forced to choose between the lives of her entire world or the life of one so precious.

Her heartbeat pounded loudly against the eerie silence of ancient stone walls. What a surprise to find the very thing she sought located below the Prince's dungeons—in essence, below his very nose. She stopped beside a crack in the tunnel wall barely large enough to slide through. Long ago, it might have been a doorway, but the entrance had been filled with stones until it now seemed as one with its surroundings. Only someone who felt *The Lira*—the song of power—would know what was there. Evie took a moment to catch her breath then began to work her way through.

Moments later, she stepped into a vast room, empty of everything but cobwebs and dust. The ghostly-white threads luminesced, seeming to sway as winds of power flowed from the darkness. Like a curtain separated by an unseen hand, they opened and closed gracefully as she passed through.

A welcoming.

The far wall seemed untouched by time. No webs. No dust. Just a slab of black stone polished to a mirrored sheen, faintly illuminated by the glowing threads. The wall and the gate were one and the same, and they were massive. A smaller, man-sized arch was etched into the stone underneath another, much larger arch that encompassed most of the wall.

The magic in the air changed. Someone had noticed her absence, and large whips of searching power were lashing out. Evie's already great sense of urgency increased…yet, she stood still, the mirror's reflection holding her attention. The woman looking back at her had a mass of wild red curls and haunted jade eyes. It was her, and it wasn't. That woman looked ready to break, which meant it couldn't be Eleanor Victoria Delacy. Evie was not the sort of woman who fell apart. She was a hunter, trained by the Guild's masters themselves. She was a Guardian. Most importantly, she was a Delacy, heir to thousands of years of magical knowledge.

Shrugging off her doubts, she placed her right hand on her abdomen then closed her eyes and focused. She barely felt the pain as she cut her finger with the small silver knife she'd stolen two weeks ago. Like tears, crimson drops of blood flowed before being quickly smeared onto the stone, connecting her to the mirror. She willed the gate open, and it obeyed. The solid blackness rippled like living water. Another moment, another measure of power, and the portal's destination was set. Then she stepped through, one hand on her abdomen and the other at her neck, wrapped around the only thing she had taken of her lover's—his medallion.

A vision came in the void between worlds. Or rather, it was The Vision, the one that would change everything. The shock of it nearly broke her focused hold on the gate's end point. In that moment where there is only nothingness, it tested her abilities to absorb the images into a mind no longer in possession of a body. There was no air. No light. No being. Only a fragmented glimpse of the future. Her child, a daughter, would have power. Power greater than her mother's. Power, perhaps, greater than that of the dark demon with midnight hair and fiery blue eyes who would never know he'd stolen her heart…and given her a child.

Then she was through. And maybe, right before she closed the gate, it was the echoed cry of her stolen heart that shook the still rippling, black-mirrored wall of the cavern she'd landed in. Or maybe it was the cry of another heart in a world that she could never return to. The words, *Forgive me*, echoed in her mind. But were they her thoughts…or another's?

She would never know.

CHAPTER ONE

"For every face that you see, there are hundreds more hiding just beneath the surface."

—*Illusions: A Magic User's Guide*

Present Day - Day One

I muttered, "Shit," plus a few other words my Aunt Helena would consider unladylike under my breath as I watched the supposedly human embezzler I'd been sent to retrieve gleefully playing black-magic dodgeball with a pair of miserable rats. I was too far away to hear their squeals, but the look on Bob's face (that was my bag-and-tag's name) was giving me the willies. Of course, my aunt would probably also consider crouching in a gravel parking lot and peering through a dusty warehouse window improper behavior for a Southern belle. But then again, she usually made exceptions for anything I did when working as a runner for our agency, The Darkmirror. My aunt, a semiretired professor, had hit the lecture circuit years ago in her capacity as a Demonology expert. Often out of the country, she didn't have much to do with the business these days. When my mom disappeared three years ago, that left me in charge. Most days, being the boss was nice. But on days like today, it just meant I had no one but myself to blame for this mess. Well, almost no one.

I was more than willing to blame my latest clients who had insisted that this was a simple job: Track down and bring in one

Bob Rainey, the Blood-Kin's stupid but human accountant. That would be the not-so-human accountant standing in the middle of the building, watching the warehouse's front and back doors. Or maybe it was more truthful to say that he wasn't human anymore. The smell of death and decay leaking out of the open window meant that whatever that was in there, it wasn't alive. *The lights are on, but Bob's not home.* Which was good. I wouldn't have to worry about the Kin killing my catch after I handed him over. He was already dead… or as close to dead as a walking corpse could be.

The photo I'd received showed a middle-aged white male with glasses and a clean-shaven head. That didn't jibe with the badly done toupee and gold bling Bob now sported. If not for the expensive suit, I would've suspected some sort of Bob Rainey doppelganger. It wouldn't be the first time. *But if the suit fits…*

And it most certainly did. It was the kind that had an Italian name and cost more than a fashion model's nose job. I'd been briefly romanced by a player and had learned two important things. How to recognize the cut of an expensive suit was one of them. No one puts a suit that pricey on someone else, especially not someone who smelled like they'd been dug up and microwaved.

Suit. Toupee. Gold chains. All were at odds with Bob's empty face and the ball of black-magic resting in his hand. I looked again at the photo. It was a match. That was Mr. Bob Rainey, CPA, and the guy who'd stolen ten million from the Kin, New Orleans' own Vampire Mafia. Or at least, it was Bob's body. From the smell, I'd say his soul was long gone.

The fee for this job was going *way* up.

I should've known something was amiss when the vamp's man-of-business, Benito Carmel, called this morning. The Kin didn't normally farm out these things. Still, it was May. Nightfall would come slowly in the Deep South. A smart thief could take a long lunch, hop an international flight, and be halfway to China before it was dark enough for the fanged ones to walk the streets. Which was why I'd started to wonder when the tracking had been so easy. Ten minutes with a scrying crystal and atlas had led to this warehouse in Gulfport, an hour and a half from the Kin's home in New Orleans and only forty minutes from my town of Gandsai. Bob should've been headed for the airport or, at the least, bought some time by shelling out a couple hundred bucks for an amulet that warded against location spells. That was what I (or anyone else concerned with dying) would've done.

I'd parked my beat-up work truck two streets over and walked to the back of the building. I could feel the noonday sun beating down. The sky was a cloudless blue, and the temp was already climbing. But the heat worked in my favor. It was Sunday, so many of the warehouse's windows had been left open. Without the ventilation, Monday's workers would've walked into a concrete and steel oven.

A trail of sweat streamed down my back. Some days my body craved the heat. But today wasn't one of them. Thankfully, I'd worn jeans and a tank top instead of leather. Leather would protect you in a fight but it wouldn't matter if you died of heatstroke before the first punch flew. For the same reason, I'd pulled my raven-black hair into a braid.

I used my palm to remove dirt from the windowpane, wiped the grime on my faded jeans, and briefly noted my reflection. The mirrored woman's light-blue eyes looked worried…and tired. The dark smudges under those eyes were from a month of nightmare-interrupted sleep. I ignored her worry and the foreboding sense those shadowy dreams had evoked, instead looking past my reflection to assess the warehouse's layout. There was one main door with a center aisle wide enough to allow the two forklifts parked at the front to pass each other. To each side was aisle after aisle of stacked building supplies. Not surprising, considering the building was part of a boat builder's shipyard.

I was climbing through another window farther down, out of Bob's sight, when I heard the gravel at the warehouse's front crunch. A door slammed, and I moved quickly inside. If Bob had a partner, I wanted to catch them both. It was doubtful the miserly vamps would increase my fee, but I was a classic overachiever…when I wasn't majorly screwing something up. My business partner, Mynx, said it was a yin-yang thing. And I agreed. Like clockwork, at least once a week, life always came full circle to bite me in the ass.

Once inside, I paused, letting my eyes adjust. There was fluorescent lighting high in the rafters, but as this was a clandestine meeting, it hadn't been turned on. Dust motes swirled in the sunlight coming from both high and low windows. Sawdust covered the floor, its scent nicer than the sickly-sweet, rotten meat smell drifting from Bob's direction.

While I worked my way through aisle after aisle of timber and God knows what else, I double-checked my weapons. They were the standard stun guns that most runners carried when dealing with humans. It was illegal to use magic against a human, unless they were also armed. That was one of the many rules the government had established to help the humans feel safe after the Supernatural community had popped out of the proverbial closet. Still, that particular rule no longer applied here.

The stunners were holstered in a leather harness that ran across my shoulders and back, leaving the guns beneath my arms. In my utility belt I had an assortment of charms. And attached at my right hip was my whip, real silver woven into its black leather braid. The whip was great for intimidating Weres. But for Bob? It was doubtful either weapon would help. And I couldn't be sure of my charms. I'd never used one on someone who was already dead. And, unfortunately, I'd left my more deadly knives, sword, and silver-tipped throwing stars at home. I'd thought bringing those to retrieve a human was overkill—a decision I was already regretting.

That left me with only one viable option: My own, innate magic. My family was comprised of generational witches, dealing mostly with earth and energy magic. I had those abilities, though they needed refining. Plus, I had a little something extra.

I'd nearly reached Bob when I heard muffled voices. I carefully looked around the metal shelf separating us. A tall figure was taking a briefcase from my target. No matter how hard I looked, the figure's face was hazy. *A distortion charm.* A well-made and very illegal one. Not that these two were concerned with obeying the law.

The distorted man almost appeared to be wearing a cloak, but that couldn't be, not in this Mississippi heat. For a moment, his guise slipped, showing a twisted, gnarled face.

"You work for me," the distorted figure growled.

"Maybe today," Bob said, "but only because my master wishes it. You've been gone a long time, Nicodemus. Things change." He paused. "Allegiances change." Bob's reply was slurred. That was good. Very good. No matter how powerful the possessing spirit, dead bodies still broke down. A slow tongue meant Bob's other muscles would also be slower and less accurate.

I inched closer, barely hearing the distorted man snarl, "The pendulum swings both ways, my friend." He sneered. "Soon it will swing again in my favor. You'd do well to remember your loyalties."

I frowned. This sounded like more than missing money. The cold, hard knot forming in the pit of my stomach echoed my thoughts.

I could've walked away. They weren't aware of my presence, and I was ill-prepared for this fight. Every instinct I had said go. Everything my family had taught me about picking my battles seconded that. But there comes a time in life when you have to do the wrong thing for all the right reasons.

Or maybe I was just in the mood to do something really, really stupid.

Usually the criminals I'm hired to retrieve at least do me the courtesy of waiting until I announce something cliché like "Reach for the sky" before fighting. I've been told that I have a deceptively innocent face and that my five feet five stature is *not* intimidating. But I've always thought it was my sweet, Southern drawl that did it. As my Nana says, "A pretty face and charming disposition go a long way to disarming a man." Although, come to think of it, I've never determined whether or not I was supposed to take that literally. Whatever the cause, most don't believe I'm there for them…until a knife pressed to their ribs drives home the point.

But I guess my mystery man and Bob were in a hurry, because I'd barely stepped into the open when Bob said, "Someone's here." The distorted man's hooded head jerked in my direction. I had a moment to note that I had been wrong. The cloak *was* real and not part of the illusion. Then I was dodging as Bob—who I was beginning to think deserved a more villainous name—threw a ball of black-magic at me. I skidded behind a heavily laden shelf, and the ball whooshed by with a dark chill, narrowly missing my ear. My enspelled earrings sparked, reacting to its magic.

I moved again, ducking behind a crate of nails just as another ball flew past, smashing into a stack of timber behind me. Wood sizzled, smelling of acid rot as black-magic consumed the planks. I raised my head then quickly dropped again. I didn't need my eyes to locate Bob. His evil aura and revolting smell were strong enough to paint a bull's-eye at midnight. But with his distortion amulet, my mystery man could be anywhere—a sniper waiting for a chance to pull the black-magic trigger.

Or not.

Movement on my right drew my attention. The distorted man was slowly and confidently walking out with the briefcase. On my left, Bob was forming another of those deadly balls. I shuddered. Bob

Rainey had the same sadistically happy expression he'd worn when playing with the rats. The distorted man said, "Meet me, Sarkoph, when this is done, but take another body. That one has outlived its usefulness." He stepped into the sunshine streaming through a high window. Again, I glimpsed a gnarled, twisted face, but this time, sharp, red-brown teeth and black lifeless eyes were also discernable. He turned back to say more, and his features were once again like that of the hooded reaper, only blackness where a face should've been. "And leave no trace of this one. We are too close now for mistakes. Fail, and I'll make sure your true master, not that bitch you serve, executes your punishment."

Bob or Sarkoph or whoever he was (well, I had wanted a more villainous name) simply said, "It shall be done, my lord Nicodemus." He spat out the title.

Wait, did he say dispose of? I was suddenly furious, my previous caution washed away. It would take more than a stiff-limbed accountant with demonic powers to finish me. And if they thought anything less, they were in for a surprise. Mr. Monkey-Suit and his fake hair were about to find out that I was descended from a long line of ass-kickers.

My breathing slowed. I focused on the fire flowing through my veins. I'd promised my mother never to call the flames outside of our family home. It wasn't a power witches had. It wasn't even a power guardians had. My mother had said if the wrong person found out, there'd be hell to pay.

However, things change. My mom wasn't around to care about a promise made years ago. And even if she were, Evie Delacy had been the one to teach me that sometimes to survive you had to break the rules. This was a matter of survival. There would be no containing a demon-possessed body. One way or another, Bob Rainey's dark rider had to go.

Two orbs then a slight pause looked to be this thing called Sarkoph's pattern. With only seconds before the next attack, I came out blazing, literally. I threw a ball of bright green earth-magic at the distorted man. It clipped his shoulder, eliciting a muffled curse. Then he was gone, fleeing into the brightness of a spring day. The door closed with a click. And Sarkoph and I were alone in the half-light.

From the corner of my eye I saw Sarkoph prepare his throw. Pulling on my innate magic, I twisted, letting the forbidden fire run down my black and silver whip. The flying leather coiled around his hand, and I pulled. His magic flew right, splattering with a loud *boom* on something metallic. Ears ringing, I barely heard Sarkoph's pained cry as fire seared his wrist. Who knew the dead could feel pain?

I certainly hadn't, but it was useful information. I might not be able to destroy his body, but I could make it a highly uncomfortable residence. A little voice in my head said that was a bad idea. But I wasn't listening. It was the best idea I had, so it would have to do. I felt the pain in my own arm. Blood dripped warm and slick from where his last shot had grazed me. Though small, the cut felt like it was simultaneously being melted and frozen. Magic that corrupt was poisonous, even to the one wielding it. The wound needed to be cleansed soon, or things would get nasty.

I needed this fight to end...and quickly. I looked at Sarkoph. It hadn't occurred to him that I was within reaching distance. I needed to act before that fact smacked us both in the face. This close, his cologne, eau de decay, was horrific, making the urge to gag mind-blowing. And his appearance didn't help. Bob's facial muscles were loose, jowls sagging, all visible skin a purplish white. Even if I hadn't crashed the party, the spirit would've needed to abandon his body soon.

Sarkoph was trying to pry my whip from his wrist, but as long as I kept my flames steady, he couldn't get a good grip without scorching his fingers. But controlling my fire was difficult, another reason to hurry. I dug deep, pulling fire into my left hand.

I was about to do something really dumb...and really, really stinky.

Stepping forward, I dragged Bob's smelly, rotting corpse closer, dry heaving as we came nose to nose. His eyes widened, hands rising to stop me, but I was already shoving fire straight into his chest. Sarkoph's eyes rolled back. His nails dug into my forearms, his magic-coated fingertips scorching my skin before his grip slackened and his hands fell away. For a second, my flames danced on his chest. I kept pushing, willing them to go deeper. The spirit resisted. His body sagged, his weight pulling on my whip. Then the resistance slipped away. Like a ship gliding through water, the fire pushed into and through him, forcing the possessing entity out.

With a surge, the wall I'd been pushing against simply dissolved, and I nearly fell on top of Bob's corpse, managing at the last moment to throw myself backward. I landed on my ass in the sawdust and sat there for a second, disbelieving what I'd done. Then I jumped up. Confused, I found myself suddenly standing over an unmoving, lifeless, decaying lump with a very pissed-off mass of darkness hissing and hovering above it.

There wasn't a curse word big enough for this.

I'd never used my fire against something living or, in Sarkoph's case, something dead but with a body capable of independent thought. (I wouldn't say intelligent. He had, after all, stolen from the Vamps.) It shouldn't have worked like this—exorcism was not one of my powers—but the magic had heeded my request…just not in the manner I'd expected.

Using my fire, I quickly drew three of the four protection wards. They shimmered red in the air. Against a full blast of black-magic, three wards wouldn't hold as well as four, but they'd have to do. I wasn't about to turn my back to draw the last corner. Hopefully, with my fire's boost, they'd keep me from being possessed until I could banish this demon. And I was sure now that he was a demon or, at the least, one of their lower-level cousins. A bodiless spirit, Sarkoph's true power came through possession, meaning he was vulnerable until he made himself a new host by forcing someone's soul out. Unfortunately, I was now the most convenient Motel 6.

Time. I needed some to think of a banishment. "So, tell me, why didn't you run?" I asked, slowly dragging my feet through the floor's sawdust. I wasn't really expecting a reply, just hoping to occupy the spirit while it tried to process my question. *No way was Aunt Helena going to believe this.* "That was an awful lot of money. You could be on a beach somewhere, sipping margaritas."

Only the oldest spirits could speak outside a body, so I was surprised when the darkness that was Sarkoph did, his deep grating words barely understandable. "Know…runner come…always send powerful ones." The dark mass vibrated, expanding and contracting with each word. Tendrils of demonic power began to test my wards. I kept moving. "Make runner mine. Money good…body better. This one…smells."

I snorted, stifling a sarcastic retort. *Smells* was a definite understatement, but criticizing the vocabulary of something trying to possess me seemed unwise. I moved further, never turning my back, adding what earth-magic I could to strengthen my defenses, racking my brain for something…anything.

"Think…man dead," he continued. "Bloods get their stealer…not chase runner." His dark power clashed with my weakening shield, sparking green and black. I would've been worried to hear his plans for me, but adrenaline, pain, and magic were all I could feel. I gritted my teeth, focusing more energy into the wards. *Just a few minutes more.*

"I'm sorry," I said, "but the Vacancy sign is off. You'll have to take your stench and bad taste in men's hair accessories somewhere else." I'd pitched my taunt, hoping he'd bite, and wasn't disappointed. But apparently Sarkoph had a quick learning curve, because his words were becoming clearer. Not good. I was sure adapting quickly was listed in *Fighting Evil for Dummies* as a big no-no.

"You are not…my choice. But I…do much…your body." Definitely a he. The words might be garbled, but the tone was precise. If this thing could form a face, it would've sported a big, lecherous grin. I'd now made a half circle and could see where his previous blasts had landed. I'd once seen a comedian burst a watermelon with a sledgehammer. That had been less messy but likely what would've happened to my head if he'd hit me as intended. I shuddered, stopping to push more power into my wards. Sensing my fear, Sarkoph pushed back.

We stood like that in the sunshine, battling with will and magic for what felt like forever but was probably only moments. Or rather, I was standing. The darkness was doing an ominous hover that could've put the best yenta to shame. In my mind, the spinning wheels ground to a sudden stop as a memory pulled the brake.

The only banishment I knew was a simple charm we witchy-children were taught while others learned nursery rhymes. When I made it out of this, I promised to read the texts Aunt Helena was always trying to force feed me. Okay, well, I'd probably only skim through half of them, but I'd definitely read at least one—whichever one had the most pictures.

More sparks flew as Sarkoph battered my wards in earnest. I clenched my jaw, squared my shoulders against the rising pain, and took another step. "Didn't your mama teach you how to treat a lady?" I was talking now more out of instinct than anything else. Certain now that the spirit was male, my natural reaction was to treat him like I would any overbearing man who'd stepped on my toes—with a swift kick in the remember-your-manners shins. And the first lesson of reminding a man about proper etiquette was to mention his mama. Though, as his next words came, I thought that lesson might not apply here.

"I ate…the one who birthed me."

I shivered at its emotionless tone and slowly dragged onward. "*That* was a mental image I could've done without." My hands moved, drawing power from the earth like shimmering, green droplets of water that hung briefly in the air before flowing into my body.

Sarkoph didn't appear to rotate, but I felt him watching me, his confusion almost palatable. He rumbled, "Worry not small one…I will treat your body…with great care. Give unto me…and your death will *hold little pain*." He drew the last words out, but I only half-noticed, barely listening as I began the spell. For extra insurance, I pulled more magic from the earth. Streaks of green power flowed like ivy vines over my protections. I called what flames I could. It hurt. I was channeling two magics that shouldn't have been able to exist side by side. Fire scorched Earth. Earth suffocated Fire. But strangely enough, here I was. It was a unique gift that might just save my life—if it didn't kill me first.

Soon, there was a massive ball of red fire crisscrossed with bright green lines churning in my hand. The charge of channeling so much magic was exhilarating…and dangerously addictive. In my mind, I saw the image I must present. My bright blue eyes would be glowing. A few raven strands of hair had worked their way free and floated upward in the red and green magical currents now snapping around me. My body felt weightless, only my tiptoes touching the ground. And everything in the room—from the steel shelves, wooden crates, and sawdust-covered floor to the dirty glass windows—everything suddenly seemed brighter, as if the essence of life glowed from within them.

That essence was the truest form of earth-magic. It was akin to the magic of the soul, something white witches were forbidden to harness. I was desperate, but not enough to pay the price such magic required. *Well, almost everything glowed.* My eyesight receded to the mind's eye, where the universe's magical planes become visible in all their glory. As this happened, the building and its contents took a depth and range of spectrum that the human eye cannot comprehend. Everything but Sarkoph became brighter, more beautiful. The demon darkened, becoming a black void that cringed from the light.

Soulless.

I didn't even dare think the term. Such creatures were stories, invented to scare witchy children. I had to focus on the physical. The real. Things I could vanquish in the daylight. As it was, this was going to be close.

Just as my wards fell, I threw my fireball, moving quickly backward. For once, my aim was true. The fire landed on the line I'd painstakingly drawn while dragging my boots through the sawdust. Sarkoph released an unholy screech as the magic followed my command, curving to become a circle. Then the swirling flames flowed upward, becoming a half sphere, completely enclosing his dark mass. Fire was energy, and the energy of my circle arched downward through the concrete, forming a half-unseen but no less impenetrable sphere. The magic called, ringing through me, seeping into my bones.

Oh, yes, Sarkoph was good and fucked.

As I chanted, his screeching increased, the pressure of it so fierce that my nose began to bleed. Hands pressed to my ears, I shouted, feeding my words to the fire. "As Above, So Below. Darkness to Darkness must go." Sarkoph's screams became impossibly louder. I continued, knowing the words flowed out, even if I couldn't hear them. I made it to the next to last line, "We consecrate this land," then went blank. *What were the words?* Shit, I couldn't remember. *Maybe it wouldn't matter.* Right. When had I ever been that lucky?

Blood dripping down my lips and chin, I repeated the chant three times. As the words ended, the circle began to shrink, slowly at first, then faster, collapsing inward. I released my vision from the mind's eye. The magic was becoming too painful to view with such clarity. Even with the limitations of normal sight, it was an eyeball-searing visage. Like a collapsing star, Sarkoph's darkness drew in on itself, the fire pressing him tighter and tighter.

My hands stayed over my ears, but that didn't keep them from popping as the air shifted. One by one, the warehouse's windows slammed shut. The fiery sphere began to rotate, slowly then faster and faster, consuming the building's oxygen as it burned hotter, then hotter still, nearly blazing white. I stumbled backward, gasping for breath. Heat drew the skin on my face tight. There was a low roaring like a train. *This was wrong. So wrong.* I'd never been present at a banishing. Few had. But I'd read enough to know this wasn't how it worked. The circle should've stayed the same size, transporting the spirit simply and quickly to the Otherworld.

I had a sinking feeling that Sarkoph wasn't the only one who was fucked.

I backed into a steel shelf. Eyes locked on the sphere, I raised my hands, feeling for something sturdy. *There!* I grasped the shelving's supports. My survival instincts screamed, *Run!* But I stood transfixed.

And within seconds, it was too late.

A new, heavy gravity formed at the sphere's heart. My feet began sliding as the sawdust was dragged into the flames. The burning sphere's draw grew exponentially. Bob's abandoned corpse inched toward the fire.

A sudden gale began as the room's air was drawn into the sphere. Small whirlwinds whipped my hair and clothes. Despite the circle's heat, I began to shiver. I attempted to slow my breathing, trying not to hyperventilate in the suddenly oxygen-deprived air. Nails and other bits pinged as they became mini missiles, tossed by the rushing air. There was a flash of pain as something sharp nicked my cheek, passing on its journey to the fiery oblivion. It should've hurt more, but everything was beginning to go numb. And that was a very bad thing.

I was going into shock, my limbs weakening with the lack of air. I held on with everything I had. Sarkoph's earsplitting wails had nearly stopped. But there was the new sound of metal creaking as the heavy shelves bent toward the imploding circle. As if through a dark tunnel, black spots formed on the outer edges of my vision, expanding, coalescing into a whirlpool of darkness with only flames visible at its heart. Knees weak, my sweaty hands bore more and more weight.

Just as Bob's thousand-dollar shoes slid into the fire, my fingers slipped. I collapsed to the floor, reaching backward. But I was lighter than Bob's corpse. And within those few seconds, I'd already been pulled several feet. I stared in abject horror at the flaming sphere, now no larger than a beach ball, hovering inches above the ground. That might not sound big enough to eat a man, but that was exactly what it was doing. Inch by inch, it consumed Bob's body.

And I was dessert.

I forgot to breathe. Not that there was much air. My mind dimly registered the warm leather wrapped around my arm. It was such a habit to retrieve and wrap the whip around my forearm after use that I didn't even remember pulling it from Bob's corpse. Exhausted limbs fumbled, throwing it at anything that would hold. The braid caught on something behind me, tugging at my grip. I wrapped the leather around my wrist just as it snapped tight. My body jerked forward, yanking my arm painfully over my head. My scream was drowned out by the fire's roar and the crash of metal falling from all sides. The heat scorching through my boots was almost as unbearable as the force that threatened to pull my shoulder from its socket. My pants came fast and shallow. My vision went dark, and I fought to stay conscious.

As I hung there, body nearly lifted from the ground by the unrelenting suction, I was certain that, like Grendel, my muscles would tear, ripping my arm free, leaving my body to be consumed by Sarkoph's blazing sphere. My eyes closed, giving in to the fatigue that suffused my body. Then, like a candle suddenly snuffed out, it ended.

The magic in the room shifted. I cracked my eyes. The sphere was…I wasn't quite sure what description fit. Devoured, sucked in, collapsed, consumed? Within the few seconds that I'd looked away, the fire and Sarkoph's darkness had shrunk to the size of a quarter. Like an eerie, demonic eye, a flaming red dot with a fathomless black pupil hovered in the air.

Then it winked out of existence.

Without warning, the vacuum vanished. Air rushed into the building. "Uff," I rasped, my body hitting the ground. Objects flying toward the black hole's maw dropped with the unmistakable *clang* of metal hitting concrete. On autopilot, my boots dug into the hard floor, now bare of sawdust. I slid up enough to release my bruised wrist from its braided noose and gasped as blood flowed into my numb hand, shooting pain throughout the limb. I closed my eyes, gulping air before finally releasing a large breath of relief. Little spots flickered against my lids, a reminder of the sphere's brightness. Ears buzzing, my panting sounded overly loud in the sudden silence.

The smell of burned flesh was stifling, but I lay there, too exhausted to move. I may have lost consciousness, or maybe I simply dozed for a time. Perhaps it was my imagination or a dream, but I saw myself briefly as a man in a far-off land, standing in a tower watching a dark, desert sky as a black ball coated in fire flashed across the horizon.

When I finally got to my feet, I stood dumbstruck. I wasn't sure what I'd expected, but definitely not a mini black hole. Had I just cast him into the shadowed void between worlds? Mother of the Moon, that was some messed-up shit.

"Somebody's got some 'splaining to do." My best Ricky Ricardo impression echoed in the now quiet room as I dried the sweat and dust off my face with my shirt. I'd learned that spell when I was four. Who in the hell would teach a spell like that to kids?

If I had learned only one thing from this mess, it was that my kids would stick to reading *Mother Goose*. No witchy texts for the Delacy brats. Not until they were middle-aged, and maybe not even then. Although, if my future children were destined to be half the little hellion my mother had said I was, I would not be popping any out.

My adrenaline was long gone, and though my mind and body had shut down for a time, I wasn't rested. But at least I felt more human. I looked at what was left of Bob and this time I did vomit. Everything below his upper thighs was missing. There weren't even ashes where his legs had been. Hands on my knees, I took several deep breaths, pushing from my mind the realization of what could have been if something had gone differently.

Muscles protesting, I stood tall, wiping the bile from my lips before taking inventory. All that was left of our battle was the scent of sulfur, three-fourths of a dead body, a wrecked building, an injured witch, a crater in the floor, and, somewhere soon, some very angry vampires. The last was just a guess. I'd checked Bob's poorly parked car on the way in for the money. And there wasn't room in his suit for a giant wad of cash. No, Bob's embezzled funds were most certainly in the distorted man's briefcase.

Speaking of dead men, I was so *not* touching that body. Bad enough that his unique odor du jour was never going to come out of my nostrils. I stomped out to my truck for work gloves, a tarp, a first-aid kit, and a bottle of water. Today was too damn hot for this.

On the way out, I passed the forklifts. My gaze moved from the machinery to the dead man and back again. Bob, even missing part of his legs, was hefty. On a good day, with a little magical help, I could handle that. But right now, I was beyond tired. Of course I'd never driven one of these things. But there was a first time for everything. There was nothing funny about this situation, but as I returned and began pulling the lift's levers, I found myself smiling.

All in all, it had been a good day.

* * *

Denoir, Hours Later

Falcon was surveying the battlements when Vanguard, his oldest friend and the only one he trusted with his search, approached. He noted that the other man's short-cut hair, the same midnight black as his own, now had one white streak. Vanguard's expression was unreadable.

"My Prince." Vanguard dropped to one knee. "I have news, but not of the sort you may be expecting."

Falcon cast a shadow spell around them to avoid prying eyes and ears. "Speak, my friend," he said as they made their way back to the main hall. "Do not stand on ceremony. I can tell your journey has been difficult."

Despite the magick's protection, Vanguard leaned close, nearly whispering his report. "Hours ago, the scouts manning the towers near the wasteland saw something fly across the sky. It flamed like a star, but there was blackness at its heart. My Lord," Vanguard said slowly, "it was The Betrayer's soulless, and it was covered in hellfire." He paused, adding carefully, "Your fire."

"No, I have no—" Falcon stopped, his expression darkening as he came to the same conclusion as his old friend.

"There is more, my Prince," Vanguard said urgently. "The scouts tried to track the soulless. They followed his trail, finding bits of odd metal, glass…and this." He passed his Prince a sliver of bloodstained wood. "It is from a tree that grows in the Overworld." He had made many trips to the realm called Earth and was familiar with such trees. The demons' keen noses easily detected the blood—demon mixed with something else—that lay under the scent of smoke and scorched wood.

"Where is the soulless now?" Falcon asked.

"Fled," Vanguard shook his head, "to another world. Perhaps back to his master." He had ridden hard to arrive so quickly. His tired face could not hide his worry. There was only one reason why the Betrayer's soulless would walk in the Overworld. And it did not bode well for any of them.

When they reached the hall, Falcon dismissed his friend to care for his own needs. Standing as he was by the inner wall, the prince and lord of this land could see his people as they went about their lives. Which of them plotted against him and those he held dear? For surely, someone *must* have helped the Betrayer send his soulless to the Overworld. He was still hidden within his spell when the first of only two women who could see through his shadow-cast approached.

"My son."

Although Falcon felt little relief these days, his mother's soft voice still gave a small measure of comfort. "Mother." He nodded respectfully, unsurprised by her approach. The Queen's spies were vast. Blue eyes, so like his own, looked back at him from beneath short, silver hair. "You are aware?"

"Yes, I believe I was informed just prior to you. Although," she cast the exiting Vanguard, whose looks were almost a mirror-image of Falcon's, a disapproving glance, "I would have chosen a more discreet manner than your cousin." It went without saying that even here the other Demon Lords had eyes. Falcon was secure in his magick's protection, but it was always best to act with caution. He nodded again, acknowledging her rebuke. She continued, "I have sent word to the Council. They will dispatch a Draig."

"Which one?" He hadn't heard tell of this species in centuries.

"The only one." She turned and walked away.

Not surprising. As Queen, she always had the last word. He'd learned over the years that some things were the same with women, no matter the species. Only one female, the same contentedly pacing by his side, had ever let him have the last word. A draig was good, but he wanted his own eyes. While extremely powerful, the species had once been their ancient enemies. This one might have its own objectives. Falcon ruffled Wrin's fur once before sending her on her task. *Watch and wait, my friend. Intervene only if the draig fails.* He lowered the piece of bloodstained wood. Her eyes flashed red with hellfire as she took in the scent. Then she was gone, traveling to a world he could no longer enter.

CHAPTER TWO

"And Hansel and Gretel thanked the nice witch for their gingerbread snacks and returned home to their mother and father. When the witch opened a Sweets shop in town, they were soon her favorite customers."
—Excerpt from *The New Politically Correct Fairytales*

Day Two

The phone rang. Loudly. With a jarring start I awoke, grumpy, disoriented, and grabbing for the papers attached to my forehead. I'd been having a wonderful dream that I now couldn't remember. Good dreams had been in short supply lately, so though I was supposed to be reviewing the papers that had become my pillow (and subsequent headdress), I wasn't happy about having my midmorning nap interrupted. I picked up the phone and hearing the dial tone slammed it down again. I took a sip of chai tea, grimaced at its chilly, over-steeped flavor, and listened as Mynx in the outer office answered the call. The clock said I'd slept almost an hour.

The night had been long. I'd arrived home to find Aunt Helena back early for an extended visit. She'd patched up my arm (jabbing me with needle and thread more than I thought necessary), removed a few splinters from my nicked cheek, given me a long, loud lecture about the dangers of leaping before looking (especially if I was going to bound in head first), then taken a look at Bob's body. His missing legs had elicited a raised brow, but for once she'd been blissfully silent.

I'd then called and explained to a coldly polite Carmel the day's events. We'd come to a win-win agreement. Or rather, it was win-win for the Kin. I'd be paid for bagging Bob's body as previously agreed upon. But if I figured out where the money went, there would be a substantial bonus...more so if the money was recovered. Not that the latter would happen. Ill-gotten gains tended to burn a hole in a man's pocket, as well as his soul. But if I found Sarkoph's accomplice, Nicodemus, the Vamps would owe me a favor. And that was worth more than money in the bank. Most importantly, while I was working for them, the undead wouldn't be out for my blood. And if I didn't find Nicky-boy and the money? Well, the vamps weren't out of anything but my original fee.

After our talk, I'd waited patiently for Carmel's cleanup crew. I really didn't want to know how or why they'd had an ambulance complete with stretchers and body bags ready to go in record time. Before they'd arrived, I'd done a quick search of the remains, turning up car keys, several gold chains, and a black medallion with a strangely familiar golden sun design.

I couldn't place the design but knew it was demon made. Hopefully, Aunt Helena would know what it was. Given the day's heat and Bob's near incineration, the medallion had been surprisingly cool to the touch, only warming with my body heat. Every other piece of metal on the corpse, including his car keys, had been soaked in evil magic, requiring a good cleansing before their return to his family. *Everything* but the medallion. It had been free of tainted magic. And considering where I'd found it, that shouldn't have been possible.

The metal disc now sat on my desk. I ran my fingers over its blazing sun. My gut said the demon had stolen it—the most unlikely and irrational of possibilities. But I had an unshakable belief that it belonged to someone else, someone more powerful. I'd return it to the Kin after I had some answers. If the piece was important, its owner would come looking.

And I didn't want it in my possession when that happened.

I'd started reinforcing the house's wards before the ambulance's dust had even settled, not stopping until I was certain they would halt anything short of an atomic bomb. Call it another gut feeling, but I knew a storm was on the horizon. A big one. And I planned to have a pair of waders and a Delacy-sized ark handy. Though maybe

I'd overdone it. I'd been low on power from the day's fight. A nap and some herbal tea had helped. But by the time I'd crawled into bed at dawn, I'd been blissfully numb from the strain of using so much magic.

And that's where I should've stayed—in bed, sleeping. But no, I was reviewing the notes my aunt had made on the state of Bob's body. From the level of decay and black-magic saturation, Aunt Helena estimated that Bob had been dead for nearly a week before he'd absconded with the Kin's money. A nice trick, but a pain in my ass nonetheless.

I'd already put the word out that I was looking for a character named Nicodemus but knew I'd probably have as much luck following the paper trail, which meant I needed to investigate everything Sarkoph had done as Bob. And if that didn't lead anywhere, I'd go over the week before and determine how the CPA was targeted. That was a hell of a lot of paper to go through. Did I mention that I *really* hated paperwork, dealing with pencil-pushing vampires...and Mondays? The devil could keep them all. Their only redeeming quality was the satisfaction one received from putting them in an industrial-sized shredder and hitting *puree*.

This time when my phone rang, I didn't jump. I heard Mynx say the call was for me, but I must've still been sleep-fogged because I sat there rubbing the phone against my temple, staring unseeing at my nearby tank of magical piranha...mind simply wandering...not realizing that she'd already transferred the call.

"Lace? You there?" The smooth bass brought me to my senses. I moved the phone back to my ear. "You must be on a case. I can hear the wheels in your head moving from here."

"Luke?" Voice scratchy from lack of sleep, I stuttered then laughed. It had been awhile but I'd know that voice anywhere. Our romantic relationship had ended three years ago, but we were still friends...although not through any real effort on my end. Like a good Southern boy, Lucas Deveroux felt responsible for all the women he knew and called to check in regularly. Mynx said he wanted to rekindle our relationship, but I disagreed. Lucas simply had a soft heart and an overactive sense of obligation. He was also a cop, which made him all the more protective.

I disregarded the "Lace." I'd given up years ago asking Luke to stop using that silly nickname. For some reason, he thought butchering my last name was cute, especially since I wasn't exactly a lace and roses kind of girl. I asked, "Hey, how are things going? How's your mama?" I'd skipped yesterday's bi-monthly Sunday tea with Mamie Deveroux to track down Bob. I cradled the phone against my shoulder and grabbed another sip of chai.

"Mam's good. It's you I was worried about." Luke cleared his throat. There was a significant pause before he spoke again. "I ran into your old pal Jupiter down on Bourbon."

I hadn't seen Jupiter Jones in weeks. Possibly the darkest-skinned African-American I'd ever met, he looked to have been carved directly from a slab of ebony. Jup played the trumpet for the tourists who flooded New Orleans. Human, as far as I could tell, he always knew what was happening with everyone, human and Sup alike. I could hear Luke breathing, hesitating. He'd never really cared for my friends, especially those with a Y-chromosome, and though the man was old enough to be my grandfather, that included Jup. So why would Luke call me about seeing the trumpeter? Surely I would've heard if something had happened to the old man. I leaned forward. "Luke, Jup's not sick or anything?"

"No, the old man's fit as a fiddle and as ornery as ever." I released a breath and relaxed back in my chair. "Jones said to tell you to be careful. He said and I quote, 'That girl has a heap of trouble heading her way.'"

I set my teacup down with a thump. The old man was never wrong. Still, Luke had never given stock to his warnings. If my ex was calling to pass the message, Jup had made *some* impression.

Before I could offer assurances, he continued, "You do know, Cate, that you can call me if you're in trouble?"

Eyes misting, I spoke softly, "I know." I leaned my head back, suddenly exhausted. They were getting easier, but interactions with Lucas were still emotionally draining. Although we were no longer together, in a way I still loved him. My walking away had hurt us both. Luke hadn't understood, and I couldn't explain. That hadn't changed, which put a strain on our continued friendship. Because of this, his offer, which I knew he'd stand behind come hell or high water, was no small thing. Trying to keep my voice steady, I continued, "I'm okay right now, Lucas. But thank you. You know I'll call if there's a need." The words seemed so inadequate to express how I felt. But some things couldn't be said without changing *everything*.

Luke again cleared his throat. "I've moved up in the Pack, Lace. If you need us, the wolves will be there." He was promising the Pack's protection—an offer my ex really couldn't make. Still, I had no doubt that he and his friends would come if called.

"You always were a sucker for a damsel in distress, Deveroux." He chuckled at my reference to our first meeting. I tried to put a smile in my voice. "Don't worry. If I get in over my head, you can throw me a life preserver. But if I catch you doing CPR on me, your furry ass is toast." His deep laugh as we disconnected brought a true smile to my face. Even so, I was worried. What did Jupiter know that I didn't?

And how much was it going to cost me to find out?

* * *

Day Three

"Catherine Eleanor Delacy, you get your butt right back here!"

My left eye twitched. Aunt Helena's voice was usually slow, sweet, and full of that Southern drawl that always seemed to charm men, especially men who didn't know better than to be charmed by a Southern woman with a legendary temper. But on days like today, when her mood was boiling, my aunt's voice could compete with a banshee's wail. And I mean that literally. I'd seen my aunt's banshee secretary, Elvira, cringe in the face of her boss's vocal intensity. Not surprisingly, Elvira had stayed in Europe for a "vacation." The woman had probably jumped at the opportunity to have an ocean between herself and her sometimes cranky boss.

"I've gotta run, Auntie. I'll be back by ten," I yelled over my shoulder, bumping the foyer table while rushing to the front door. I grabbed for a toppling vase, barely making sure it was steady before exiting, not waiting for a reply.

I was of a like mind with Elvira. Distance really did make the heart grow fonder. And it didn't hurt the ears none, either. Which was why I'd headed for the door the minute Aunt Helena had started yelling about how *that* advertisement—the one I'd successfully hidden from her until she'd picked up a paper in town—would endanger the family. Her argument would've worked, except I knew when my aunt said "family" she meant me. There was no family.

Nana was on a endless RV tour of the country. My Grams, my great-grandmother who'd lived next door and helped raise me, had passed away over five years ago, two years after we'd lost my grandpa who I'd been especially close to. I had more than one fond memory of him teaching me to parallel park that old unwieldy '83 Silverado, which was now my work truck. And Aunt Helena was only home a few weeks out of the year. Even our closest neighbor, Dr. Wellsy, who was like an adopted uncle to me, was away guest-teaching at a university in Virginia. I got in my rebuilt yellow Jeep, Susie, and headed down the long gravel drive, turning north once I hit the highway.

Only Mynx lived full-time with me in the Delacys' ancestral home, an old, sprawling two-story farmhouse. Hundreds of years older than the rest of us, Mynx was a Delacy in name and heart, if not blood. And with her own unique abilities, the green-eyed brunette was more than capable of protecting herself. And my mom...I pushed down my grief. We didn't know where she was, which meant she was probably dead. I knew my mother—she would've gone through hell to get home to us. That was what Delacys did.

The truth was that my aunt thought advertising that our agency was now taking Supernatural cases made me a target. But she was wrong. We already had ties to the Supernatural community, and it was these ties and not a small piece of print that had brought me Sunday's run.

It had been less than two days since I'd made my deal with Carmel to locate his bosses' missing money. I was meeting a possible lead at Mag's, a bar on the outskirts of Hattiesburg (The Burg), Mississippi. The Burg and New Orleans (NOLA) were about three hours apart. Luckily, my home in Gandsai, Miss. was smack-dab between the two. It was good that I had an appointment, because just walking outside wouldn't have been enough to escape Aunt Helena's temper.

At that thought, I glanced in my rearview mirror, but there was only an empty stretch of blacktop. The old farmhouse was miles away. Until the Supernatural's governing body, the Council, had told the world about us, most Sups had moved from city to city to hide their longer lifespan. Our house and the long number of generations raised there were a testament to my family's ability to blend in over the years. The space had often been lonely, but I had to admit that the house's white clapboards and green roof made a charming picture. Charming and expensive. And now mine. Keeping up a house that size cost more than I could make taking on your average cases, which was another reason for my recent advertisement.

My ancestral home was far enough southwest of The Burg to still be in a rural wooded area. Gandsai was private enough for a witch's needs but close enough to neighbors to satisfy the town gossips. Yet the house wasn't so far from NOLA or The Burg that a client couldn't drive out, which was why the faxed request, from a Council operative no less, had come as a surprise.

All I knew was that I was to meet the Council's local sheriff, Josephine Fera, for a retainer and further details. There'd been no phone number, so I couldn't call to decline. The fax said simply that it involved a man named Nicodemus and that I'd want the case. Presumptuous. The message had intrigued me, especially the mention of Nicky-boy. Never one to stand up a lady, I'd thought it best to make an appearance. Or so I'd tell my aunt…when I eventually told her my meeting had been with a Council operative. I smirked as the wind blew in the Jeep's open doors, whipping little tendrils of black hair about my face. Maybe for once my family's emphasis on good manners would play in my favor.

The Sheriffs, once called Guild Masters, had been leaders of a particular group, like a Were Clan's Alpha. They'd changed their name right along with the Council, who'd originally been called the Guild Council. With the new name had come new job specs. Now anyone powerful—and crazy—enough to run roughshod over their district's Sups could apply. I'd never met Fera, but I'd heard she was part Fae, part maverick, and all immortal. But while there were perks to working for the Council, a great deal of their operatives, even the not-so-mortal, tended to live a shorter than normal lifespan.

So immortal or no, Fera didn't have time to waste. And neither did I. But if I was lucky, the sheriff would know where a hooded man with fugly teeth and no fashion sense might stash a pile of the bloodsuckers' mob money. That, and a free dinner, might be worth an hour of my time.

CHAPTER THREE

"When in doubt, don't stick it out. They might just bite it off."
—101 Ways to Deal With Weres

A glorious crimson and gold sunset was fading into a dark night as I pulled into Mag's. The breezy ride had made me appreciate the black leather jacket and jeans I'd worn to blend with the biker crowd, but as I exited the Jeep the cracked asphalt under my boots reflected enough heat to make sweat bead, dripping between my breasts. Compared to Sunday's fiery battle, this heat was nothing. Still, I was glad that the modern miracle of A/C was only a few feet away.

Resisting the temptation to hurry, I strolled. Assessing. Fera might be a potential client, and Mag's might be a public place, but the instincts I'd honed over the years didn't distinguish between Chuck E. Cheese's and a war zone. To drop your guard was to get smacked between the eyes, especially if you were at the former. Those little kids with mallets could be real bastards.

The lot was empty of people but full of motorcycles, cars and pickups. My Susie was the only bright spot in the sea of black, chrome, and blue, dust-covered Harleys and Chevys. If the number of vehicles was any evidence, Mag's was hopping.

Built from gray, weathered boards that most likely dated to the bar's opening in the '70s, the only exception was the nice side deck that had been added since my last visit. It was a beautiful night to sit outside. Too bad Fera had specified as discreet a meeting as possible. To that end, I took a moment to ensure my jacket still concealed my weapons. I was licensed to carry the stunners. But the whip on my hip and short sword sheathed in line with my spine weren't exactly legal or illegal. Either way, a woman carrying weapons—other than those used for deer or raccoon hunting—was enough of a novelty in rural Miss. to draw attention. Attention Sheriff Fera didn't want. Although, and I grinned at this thought, anyone, woman or man, would draw attention if they walked into a bar carrying my small arsenal. Considering this was a business meeting, it was probably overkill. But I wasn't comfortable going unarmed, especially after the Kin's job had turned into such a mess. Satisfied that everything was hidden, I pulled open the dented wooden door.

The bar was dim and smoky. Maybe the smoking ban didn't reach this far outside the city. Or more likely, no one cared. Straight ahead, a dark polished bar rested against the rear wall. Green felt pool tables were on my right with booths and dining tables to my left. As I headed for a booth, I exchanged a brief nod with three Weres and a gremlin playing pool with the bikers and wannabe cowboys that crowded the place. I couldn't help but grin at the number of eager women in denim and cowboy hats crowding the men, unaware that they were being drawn in by the Weres' pheromones, like moths to a sexed-up flame.

I kept walking, leaving everyone to their fun. The Weres looked friendly enough, and the phers wouldn't make anyone do anything they didn't want. The "moths" might go down singed, but everyone would walk away happy. Besides, lycanthropy was almost never transmitted sexually. So as of yet, the Council hadn't banned Were to non-Were intercourse. Still, if you were an unattached man or woman, it was good to keep an eye on an unmated Were. They were notoriously horny bastards, especially the women.

I should know, I used to date one.

Uh…I mean, I used to date Luke, who was definitely male. But I'd been around a few female Weres and knew they put out as much if not more phers. I'd also learned that Weres were cautious, which was why I wasn't worried. The scent of my whip's silver worked better than hanging a NOT AVAILABLE sign around my neck.

I picked the darkest corner and settled in, back to the wall. The seat's springs had long since given up, and the menu was only a plastic-covered piece of paper, but the jukebox was state of the art, an old Willie Nelson song carrying well over the chatter. What the place lacked in décor it made up with atmosphere. The walls were covered in a mixture of hunting trophies, old posters and framed black-and-white photos. I liked the way a picture of Elvis had been placed next to a stuffed wide-mouth bass so that they seemed to watch the pool players. The place was charming…in a sort of homey way.

As if conjured by my thoughts, the hair on the back of my neck rose. The players weren't the only ones being watched. I hid my face behind the menu, closed my eyes, and opened my mind enough to do a deep search. I found nothing. But the Fae was here. Or at least someone of power was. Watching. Waiting. I searched again but couldn't pinpoint anything. It was one heck of a spell that could hide from my mind's eye. Of course, I could be paranoid. Maybe Fera was just fashionably late.

The instant I put the menu down, a tan, bleached-blonde in a black *Mag's* tank and jeans strolled over. "Hi, hon," she said. "I'm Jimmi Mae Travers, the bar's owner. We're a waitress short tonight, so I'm doing double-duty. What can I getcha?" She had the smoker's voice and laugh lines of someone in their early forties…and the breast implants of someone making good money. She also had a touch of magic. The slight smell of earth gave her away as a non-practicing witch. Wicca had made earth-magic cool again. Now it was unusual to find one with real magic not practicing. But some people simply didn't know or want the power that was within them.

"Bless your heart." I gave her my friendliest smile. "I worked as a waitress for a bit during college. It's hard enough without being shorthanded." I didn't mention that it was only a two-day undercover job to determine if the owner was cheating on his wife. That was one job I'd actually gotten a bonus for getting fired. "I'll take the spicy chicken club, hot fries extra hot and a tea."

Jimmi Mae smiled back. "Let me know if you need a job. We're hiring." Just as she turned to walk away, the room's magic shifted and a tall woman slid into the booth's other seat.

The stranger smiled, lightly drawling, "Sorry, sugar, but our Catie girl's about to have her hands full."

I arched my brows, smirking inwardly. This had to be Fera. If she wanted to pretend we were old friends and she was simply another belle out on the town, that was fine by me. It was her dime. I couldn't help but grin at Jimmi Mae's double take. The elf was stealthy. If I hadn't felt Fera's cloaking spell drop, I'd have my mouth hanging open, too. But her dramatic entrance begged the question: Why did the Council need my help when they had such skilled operatives?

After taking Fera's order, Jimmi Mae walked to the bar, muttering about getting her eyes checked. The cheap vinyl squeaked as I slouched back. "We need to work on your definition of discreet." I smiled, only half-joking.

Nodding, Fera watched me with amber-colored eyes. "I'll add it to my list." Her smile was friendly enough but wary, too. I couldn't tell if her ears were pointed behind the hair that flowed down her back and around her face, but I did see the gold glitter of earrings. It took a moment to determine her hair color. It looked sandy brown, but strands of red, gold, and even a few black made random appearances. I blinked. For a second, her hair had taken on a spotted texture. *Must be the lighting*.

I'd been expecting either a stiff suit or a femme fatale with leather and daggers. What I'd gotten was a gypsy in modern clothes. Dressed in capris, flip-flops and a black T, her outfit appeared casual, but it didn't hide a trained fighter's muscle tone. She didn't wear any makeup. But then she really didn't need any. Her golden skin glowed, making me envious. My skin, always a light-olive, darkened when I got hot or flushed but never really tanned. Still, it could be worse. Thankfully, the Delacy freckles had skipped me right along with the red hair.

We made idle chitchat until Jimmi Mae dropped off our drinks. Then Fera slid a brown file folder across the table. "Your boy Nicodemus has been busy."

I casually flipped open the folder, nearly choking on my tea as my mind temporarily shut down. Five pictures. Blood. Death. Sacrifice. I recognized the setup but kept my face blank. Young women with open glassy eyes lay in a perfect circle of their own blood. Ritualistic symbols were etched in blood and stone around the circle, their counterparts cut into the bodies. A senseless waste of life.

I snapped the folder shut, looking up. My eyes locked with amber ones that seemed ancient. I took a slow sip of tea. The chilly beverage felt good against my suddenly dry throat. Fera sipped her own drink before continuing, "Our operatives followed a tip to the first body about five months ago, right after the Winter Solstice." Her voice was pitched low, but it was hard to imagine that anything could be heard over the bar's increasing noise. The darker the night grew, the faster the place was filling up. It seemed so wrong to be speaking of death and violence while life was going on as usual around us. John Mellencamp's "Hurts So Good" was blasting in the background, and we were talking about human sacrifice.

Fera watched me and the darkened windows before sliding a manila envelope across. I opened it to see a healthy wad of cash. She looked me in the eye. "I need your help, Cate."

I leaned back, returning her stare. "Really? And why would I want to risk my ass by getting entangled in a Council mess?" I put the envelope down, tapping it with one finger. "Money's nice. But there are other jobs out there." I'd decided to take the case the minute I'd seen the pictures. She knew I would. I could see it in her eyes. But I wasn't going in without knowing why. Why me? Why pick a no-name runner of questionable magical abilities? It didn't make sense. I'd already walked into one trap this week. Unlike my business partner, Mynx, I didn't have any lives to spare.

Fera's face was grim. "You're already involved. Everyone knows you're looking for Nicodemus for the Kin. Our sources tell us he's behind this."

"I was hired to find the money, not the man. And I can walk away as easily as not." The ominous conversation I'd overhead between Nicodemus and Sarkoph said she was right and the former was involved. But that wasn't reason enough for the Council to call on me. Determined, I placed my hands on the table and half-stood.

"Wait." Fera raised her voice slightly.

She still seemed calm, but I sensed her unease and wondered what she feared. It certainly wasn't me. I gave her an expectant look.

She sighed. "I won't mislead you. This is a dangerous mission that would normally be given to a team of operatives. However, I'm no longer sure who I can trust. And it's no secret that there's no love lost between you and the Council. You're the last person anyone would expect us to ask for help."

I grinned. It wasn't as if I'd egged the Council headquarters, but since my mom's disappearance I'd gone out of my way to make life difficult for them in other, more subtle ways.

Fera continued, "But more than that, I worked with your mother years ago." She took another long drink then stared at me, lips set tightly. "I trust Evie Delacy with my life. I'm hoping I can trust her daughter, as well. Because I think it's my life and everyone else's on the line this time."

I fell back into the seat. Finally, a measure of truth. But I was more caught by her use of the present tense in reference to my mother. Leaving that for later, I said, "Okay, so assuming I'm in, I want to know *everything* you know. This isn't just some serial killer run amok. These symbols," I pulled a photo forward, pointing to a demon sign marring the lifeless body of a young brunette with gray cloudy eyes, "are archaic. Few know them. Even fewer would use them." Fera nodded. "But your guardian operatives would have already told you that."

Smiling, she simply arched a brow, but there was a flicker of something in her eyes. Cocking my head, I reassessed. "Or don't you have any?" My shot in the dark paid off when her body stilled. Damn, so they didn't have any guardians, at least not close by. That made my decision simple but complicated everything that would come after. "But you have witches that can sense gate activity and are trained in the ancient ways?" I knew the answer but asked anyway.

"Yes." On safer ground, Fera relaxed. "A few."

"So," I tapped the photo again, "you know those are rift bearers, meant to collect the energy that slices through space and time. Someone's trying to take a trip, and no one uses such dark magic to visit Disney World."

Amber eyes unblinking, she challenged, "Yeah, so what are we going to do about it?"

Her simple question was loaded with an eternity of possibilities. Knowing she wouldn't understand my answer, I remained silent, instead picking up my drink and crunching a piece of ice before looking again at the pictures of five girls who had been forced to watch their deaths come slowly. I knew what I was going to do. I was going to take her money and use some of it to buy earplugs before heading home. I would need every bit of help I could get.

Aunt Helena was *not* going to be happy.

Telling me she was certain she'd been followed, Fera barely touched her food, rushing to explain what they knew, which wasn't much. All the victims were Supernatural, but none were on the public list. And all disappeared weeks before their deaths.

There was one other detail. The Council had intel that a local occult group, led by Nicodemus, a rumored sorcerer, was believed to be behind the deaths. But Nicodemus was very careful. Every operative sent to infiltrate his group had disappeared, and after each sacrifice, the group left town. They'd been in the NOLA area, then the Gulf Coast, and were thought to be headed for The Burg, which was why the case had been given to Fera. The last girl had been killed in Gulfport only hours before I'd tracked Bob Rainey's demon-possessed corpse to that area. That removed any doubt. Her Nicodemus and mine had to be one and the same. I told Fera about my mystery man and Sarkoph's overheard conversation.

It didn't take much to open a gate, but the power needed to keep it open and tied to the right location was immense. Enough magic had been gathered for that, yet no gates had been opened. My guardian powers were still weak, but I'd have felt one open close by. And Fera's people were certain one hadn't been opened in NOLA or on the coast. So Nicodemus was building up to something. This much magic wasn't simply to bring one or two lower-level demons across. No, whatever he was up to could bring a city to its knees. The question was: Which one? There were gates in most major cities and a few, like my hometown, that were not so major.

We hammered out a few technical details, Fera always with one eye on the windows. Finally, she stepped from the booth, and I broke down. I'd almost decided not to ask about my mother, thinking it just a slip. But I couldn't *not* ask, not if there was the slimmest possibility that Fera might know something. My words practically spilled out.

"Sheriff, you said you 'trust Evie Delacy,' not 'trusted'." Fera's expression turned serious. "Do you have reason to believe my mother might be alive?" It was my turn to rush, not wanting to ask anything of anyone from the Council. They'd proved unhelpful, uncaring and untrustworthy in the past. But as we'd talked, I'd gained a measure of respect for Fera. When she wasn't all business, she'd been flirtatious and outrageous. The traits, at odds in most, worked for her. She was a person who took her responsibilities seriously, caring deeply for her friends. And it was apparent that my mother had been a friend.

Fera shook her head sadly. "There hasn't been any new information." She looked away briefly. "And I know the higher-ups conducted a search." She waved a hand, dismissing my next question. "I don't know why they didn't want you to know, maybe because Evie was retired. The policy is not to get involved if an agent isn't active or on assignment." Fera pushed back her multicolored mane. "I said 'trust' because my gut believes your mom is still alive. But don't let it get your hopes up, kid." Her expression became distant. "Because my heart thinks differently."

I was too busy trying not to choke on the lump in my throat to speak. Poised between staying and leaving, Fera hesitated, finally adding, "I can tell you this." Her eyes blazed. "She wasn't working for us when she vanished. I made sure of that." She turned to walk away then hesitated, adding softly, "Speak with Helena. Maybe knowing more about the months your mother was missing before you were born would help. Evie never talked about them, but if anyone knows anything, your aunt would."

The hand I'd raised to wave goodbye hung frozen in the air, her last words echoing in my ears.

My family had never mentioned a previous disappearance. *How could they keep something like that from me?* Part of me wanted to jump up, floor the gas home and confront my aunt, but I kept my butt plastered to the vinyl seat. They'd obviously had their reasons, which meant Aunt Helena wouldn't give up the details easily. This would take some planning. A frontal assault was suicide. My aunt could keep a secret better than a Capitol Hill call girl.

I'd have to ensure she didn't see it coming, which wouldn't be easy. It was always hard planning an ambush when the target generally knew you better than you knew yourself.

* * *

"Hey!" Puffing for breath, I ducked the sword that swung at my head, raising my own to block the next strike. "Watch it, I'm still convalescing." I'd made it home just in time to change clothes and join Mynx outside for our usual sparring session.

"You want to stop?" Mynx took a step back, lowering her sword, not even flushed.

We sparred several nights a week. Sometimes, when she was home, Aunt Helena would join us. But tonight my aunt was sorting through dusty books in an equally dusty NOLA library, probably as much to cool down as to research something, which was a good thing. My shoulder still ached from Sunday's bout with Sarkoph. Aunt Helena would've made me skip practice again.

"No." I gritted my teeth. "We've already missed one because of that last damn run. Let's just go a bit slower until I work the stiffness out."

We stood at the back garden's center. The night was quiet, the sounds of crickets and frogs muted by the wards that surrounded the house, front lawn and gardens. I'd always had more difficulty with my powers than was expected for a guardian. My grandparents had built me this area in Gram's garden. Generations past had trained inside, but with the Genesis, the term the Council used for their announcement of our existence, we were free to wield magic in the open. A wonderful but necessary gift, the outdoor, stone and earthen space was mostly fireproof. Plus, there was the added benefit of being more connected to my earth-magic while in the garden, which was large and naturally fenced for privacy with tall purple shrubs. There was earth, plants, water and wind chimes in abundance. What more could a witch want? My lonely heart had a suggestion, but it was just another thing I chose to ignore.

"All right." Mynx raised her sword. As her feet moved across the practice pad's cool outer square of gray weathered stones, the inner black ones glowed with glyphs of protection and power. Some were chiseled into the stone while others, like the rune for peace, shone from inside the hewn rock's heart. More symbols slowly lit as I followed, assuming the proper form.

We bowed and began again. Though I was hurting and slower than normal, I put my all into our match, only grunting occasionally as our blades connected, sending their aching vibrations into my sore muscles. Despite the pain, I desperately needed this. After Fera's departure, I'd stayed at the bar playing pool with the Weres, who'd turned out to be soldiers on leave from the local military base. I'd been upset, needing to blow off some steam…needing time to focus my mind away from Fera's last words. I'd purposefully subjected myself to the Weres' phers, not realizing how severe my reaction would be. I blushed, remembering. Hopefully, Mynx would attribute my flushed cheeks to the strain of deflecting her continuous lunges and strikes. Either way, she'd find out soon enough. Mynx would say I told you so…once she stopped laughing.

Forcing the memory aside, I tried to read Mynx's moves before they came—a nearly impossible task. The brunette had trained for centuries, first learning from then teaching generations of Delacys. Even though my hormones were through the roof, I didn't feel a twitch of attraction. Mynx had always been there, watching me grow. She was my sister of the heart. Not to belittle her attractiveness. Mynx, who was upping the ante by drawing green magic down her blade, was the definition of sex kitten. With long, wavy chocolate-brown hair and green eyes flashing in the moonlight, Mynx had the type of body women would sell their souls for. In fact, said body's former owner had probably done just that.

My eyes were dilated, my breath coming a little too quickly, so I wasn't surprised when Mynx stopped us for a breather. "Are you okay?" She eyed me with concern.

"I'm fine." I wiped my sweaty brow. "I spent a few hours playing pool with some horny Weres from Camp Shelby. Their call was especially…potent." I called my own magic to my blade, letting my fire demonstrate my good health.

"Did you?" She arched one perfectly sculpted brow.

"No." Teeth clenched, I growled the word. We'd had this discussion before. Mynx and I had different views on sex. I thought she had too much. She thought I had too little. "The worst of it will be gone in a few hours." *Hopefully*. I quickly changed subjects. "You know, oh wise one…" Mynx snorted, choking on a sip of water. I ignored her. "It's about time you started taking more runs on your own. For someone so old, you certainly know every new gadget." Her outraged cry at the word "old" was also ignored. "You should take the new infidelity case. Plus, I have something else that calls for your unique skills. Tell me: Have you ever met the Council's local sheriff, Josephine Fera?"

Mynx thought for a moment then shook her head. I gave her the details, including what I knew of Fera and my impression of her. I'd wondered more than once why Mynx wasn't a Council operative. She had more training and know-how than a hundred spooks. And she didn't have my distrust of the Council. But for some reason she was afraid to commit, which was why it had taken me years to get her to agree to a full partnership in the Darkmirror.

Explanation finished, we began again, coating our blades once more with magic, causing them to throw red and green sparks every time our magics crossed. Over the sound of clashing steel, I explained what Fera had said, only leaving out the bit about my mother's previous disappearance. As usual, Mynx had few comments. She always thought over things before speaking. That was why I trusted her opinion over anyone else's.

We grew quiet as we began to spar in earnest. We danced, our feet gliding over the now bright glyphs. Each symbol resonated, seeming to rise, hovering inches above the black and gray stones. Our movements became hypnotic, calming my mind and spirit, making my body's desires only a dull throb. I'd finally gotten my flames to stay where directed without conscious effort when the house wards shuddered. Having been on a magical lockdown for days, the wards were impassible to anyone but family. The wave vibrating through them was the equivalent of a unfamiliar Sup ringing the energy like a doorbell.

Since turning Bob's body over to the Kin and then Luke's call with Jupiter's warning, we'd only seen clients during daytime hours. Aunt Helena wouldn't need to buzz the wards, and we weren't expecting anyone else. Of course, the big bad probably wouldn't ring the bell.

Before Mynx could stop me, I turned, sword still flaming, and raced from the circle. Then again, I'd agreed to work for the Council, been hired by the notoriously in-house Kin, and been attacked by a toupee-wearing bean counter possessed by a demon that wasn't supposed to be on this side of the gates. It seemed to be a week for unlikely happenings.

In fact, I was almost eager to see what would come next.

CHAPTER FOUR

"Different can be good when it comes to sex, food or company, as long as different doesn't have its own set of sharp teeth. In that case, discretion would be the better part of valor."

—M. Delacy

Mynx arrived seconds before me. She was spry for someone who'd lived through the Civil War. The wards shimmered green with earth-magic, except where interspersed with blue, ley-line arches. A tall figure, half-shrouded in darkness, stood beyond the barrier's glow. As we approached, the figure stepped closer, materializing into a woman. The wards flickered, alternately revealing and shadowing her. At least six inches taller than me, she appeared unarmed.

My heart jumped while my stomach dropped, tightly stretching me in different directions. I'd never really noticed another woman's sex appeal, but she could sell it by the bushel. Every step closer disclosed more details. Close-fitting pants. Shirt cut into a slight V. Tight, slim muscles devoid of fat. Even with her unarmed and in modern clothing, I had the mental image of an Amazon warrior. And the effect she was having on my rising hormones was most assuredly coming from *her*, not her clothes. Of course, I had about a gallon of Were phers running through my system. An armadillo would look good at this point.

"Will you let me in, or should I pitch a tent?" Her husky, seemingly amused words carried through the night air, unhampered by the magical wall separating us. It was the sort of siren voice that once lured sailors to their deaths with promises of cool sheets, warm beds and dark liquors.

Mynx and I stepped closer. Unexpectedly, my magic surged, and I had to work hard to keep my fire from breaking loose. *That was odd.* Remembering the flames covering my sword, I dismissed them before our visitor could notice.

I took a deep breath, trying to calm my pounding heart. "That depends. Are you going to huff and puff and blow the wards down if we don't?" Hand on my hip, I gave her a cheeky smile, waving my sword for emphasis. I'd always found it best to fight fire with fire. Or in this case, sarcasm with sarcasm. 'Course, Aunt Helena would just say it was arrogant stupidity. And truthfully, I was probably being rude. I couldn't seem to—or maybe didn't want to—control myself. *Those damn Weres.* This had to be a result of my crazy, pher-induced hormones.

The Amazon looked briefly confused then smiled, flashing white teeth. "No, I suppose not. Unless, of course, you ask very nicely. Then I'd be obliged to force my way through and give you the pleasure of my company."

Mynx, standing back and to my right, snorted.

"Jacqueline Slone, at your service, m'lady." She gave a brief bow, which looked suspiciously unsarcastic.

Despite intentionally keeping my eyes above chest level, I still somehow noticed her high, firm breasts and fought to keep the flush out of my cheeks.

Jacq pulled a hologram badge from thin air, its design and name unmistakable. Fera had advised that there was one Council agent she trusted to help with the case, though she'd neglected to mention that "Jack" wasn't a he. Jacq had supposedly been on leave from the Council for years. (No one ever really left the Council.) Until now, she'd had no access to the investigation. Meaning, she couldn't be the one tipping off Nicodemus. Jacq was supposed to provide backup and a link to Fera since meeting with her again would be too suspicious. The badge, however, was not Council but NOLA SCU (Supernatural Crimes Unit). They were boys-in-blue with fangs and claws. This explained why she hadn't been active with the Council.

Big Brother didn't allow theirs to serve two masters. While working for the police, she would have no knowledge of Council matters.

"Okay, Detective. You're expected. Although if you'll give us more warning next time, we'll bathe before you arrive." I gestured to our sweaty clothes, or rather, my sweaty clothes. Mynx was as pristine as ever.

I stepped to the nearest blue arch. With a thought, *Sesame*, and a magical push, the green magic inside the arch dissipated. Jacq eyed us before stepping through. With our recent reinforcements, the wards were some of the strongest in the county. But if she wanted, with enough time and effort, Jacq could undoubtedly break an arch and leave. The wards were designed to keep people out, not in, and hadn't served that purpose since I was a kid. My family had placed the wards far away from the house so I'd have somewhere safe to play. My Grams had always had an inexplicable worry that I'd one day drown in the creek that curved around our property.

Jacq wore simple black shoes, gray trousers and a white, long-sleeved T. Her deep auburn hair fell just shy of her shoulders. Add in the gray eyes that missed nothing, and you had a poster child for lethal elegance. I, on the other hand, was a hot mess with flushed skin, damp cotton workout clothes that felt tight against my suddenly itchy skin, and sweat-drenched hair plastered to my neck. My self-effacing humor kicked in. It could be worse. I could've tripped and landed on my head at her feet.

"Please call me Jacq or Jacqueline. I'm not here in any official capacity. In fact, 'officially' I'm on vacation." Her husky voice was even more powerful without the wards' barrier. I shivered, blaming my damp clothes.

Fera had said "Jack" was a highly skilled operative—someone to be trusted. I wasn't so sure about trusting anyone from the Council. But the sheriff hadn't budged. Jacqueline Slone and the case were a package deal. I wasn't so naïve to believe that Fera couldn't find someone more qualified for this job. Her real reasons in choosing me were still unclear, but we three Delacys currently in residence were certain of one thing: Council operatives, past or present, always had ulterior motives. This woman was no exception. In the South we had a saying, "Keep your enemies close enough to spit at." I wouldn't be swapping spit with her, but I'd definitely be keeping Jacqueline Slone close.

And the more we knew about her, the better. As the woman in question brushed by, I breathed in her slightly musky sage and sandalwood scent. There was no earthy witch smell. No spring Fae smell. It wasn't quite like the Weres' animal musk. She stepped past Mynx, who shook her head. Even Mynx's more sensitive nose couldn't identify what manner of beast this woman was.

Mynx headed to bed while I led Jacq into the kitchen. Normally, I'd discuss business in the agency's offices, but they were beyond the wards. And after sunset I was staying within their protection, if possible.

There was something out there, in the dark, stalking me. I felt it. Waiting. For what, I didn't know, but I'd thought I'd seen red eyes peering at me from the dark woods the night before. Maybe that had been my imagination, but this feeling wasn't. I'd never had clear premonitions, but listening to my gut had saved my life more than once. And my gut said the smart thing to do was lock the doors, turn on the lights, and hide under the covers.

Never one to do the smart thing, I'd managed only one out of three.

The kitchen lights were dimmed, but moonlight shone through the windows, giving the room a warm glow. I offered Jacq a chair and busied myself with heating water for tea. Between my sweaty clothes and the A/C, I had goose bumps. While I worked, I turned my back, hiding my peaked nipples, uncomfortable with how attractive I found the other woman. The phers' effects would ease in a few hours. Until then, I'd deal with it.

Using a window's mirrored reflection, I watched Jacq stretch out long legs and lean back in a chair that allowed her to view the door, windows...and me. Thumbs tucked into her pockets, she stared boldly at my back. There were dark circles under her eyes. Perhaps I wasn't the only one who'd been having trouble sleeping. The possible similarity intrigued me.

"Will your partner be joining us?" Jacq asked quietly, her expression almost brooding.

I raised an eyebrow, wasting the look on the teakettle. Few knew that Mynx had finally accepted a full partnership in the business. And I'd never mentioned her during my meeting with Fera.

"No, but she'll help out if we run into more than we can handle." Jacq's eyebrows drew down, a frown forming at the corners of her mouth. Should I be offended or amused? I went with the latter, lightly saying, "Don't worry. I'm sure we can handle ourselves."

"I don't doubt it." Jacq smiled, laughing softly.

Something twisted in my gut, and I looked away, pulling down mugs, assembling a tea tray. *Damn phers.*

Her amusement disappeared. "But your partner may be our only help. I meant it when I said I wasn't here officially. I owe Jo a favor, and she's collecting." As I twisted, looking over my shoulder, my confusion evident, Jacq explained, "Guild Master Josephine Fera. Sheriff?" I nodded, understanding. "Neither of us, you and I, is officially on this case, because there is no case, or at least none on record. The Council wishes to keep this from the police and media. If we need help, it won't come from them."

I bit back a sarcastic comment. I knew the Council wouldn't bail me out. Why should it surprise me that they'd leave their own to flounder? Jacq seemed nice enough. No matter how tempting, I wasn't going to take my frustration out on her. Besides, we needed to focus on what we *could* do and not what we couldn't. It was late. We had details to discuss. Then I had a Council operative to shoo out the door. Before I could get us to the night's business, Jacq surprised me.

I could feel her eyes on my skin as she asked, "How did you hurt your arm?"

I looked down at the white bandage covering my nearly healed stitches. "A dead accountant with a hellish curve ball didn't want to go home to his mommy." I received another puzzled look. The old adage was correct—truth really was stranger than fiction. We had several minutes while the tea was steeping. "I need to run upstairs for a few." Pointing up, I turned around and leaned against the counter, facing her. The steaming kettle had warmed me, but it wasn't the reason for the flush in my cheeks. I still felt too grungy for entertaining guests. But more, I needed a minute alone.

Jacq gave me a slow smile, her eyes sweeping my body. If I didn't know better, I'd swear she was checking me out. My shivers returned. I resisted the urge to hug myself.

"Don't worry. I won't steal the silver." Her mouth joked, but her gray eyes said different. She'd seen my distrust.

Brushing aside the strange sadness that realization evoked, I laughed, passing her on my way out. As I headed through the archway, I tossed over my shoulder, "Oh, I know, Detective. Though

I believe you've forgotten where you are. Here the tea service is iron, the cutlery is steel, and the money is green. The only silver you're likely to find will be catfish scales." The echo of her soft laughter was still ringing in my ears as I bounded up the stairs, unsure if I was in more of a hurry to leave or to return.

As the shower heated, I used the bathroom's full-length mirror to look at my body. Had it truly been years since I'd taken more than a cursory glance? I'd been so busy—and if I was being honest, so numb to my own needs—that, with the exception of a few scattered dates, I hadn't cared about what I might present to the outside world. Oh, I cared about how people saw me when it related to my work. I'd dressed for battle, to intimidate, or to appear professional. But I hadn't wondered if someone found me attractive unless it was necessary for a run. Then I'd intentionally set out to do what needed to be done, promptly reverting back to simply being Cate once the mission was over. That sexy and beautiful woman who'd gone undercover had never been me but an artifice created through makeup, magic and the right clothes. I'd never presented my real face and body. And over the last few years, I'd never wondered if anyone found the real me as tempting as the illusion. Was it the phers or the woman downstairs that made tonight different?

Well, the real Cate Delacy was staring back at me. No artifice. No magic. Completely nude and unhidden from my prying eyes. I watched as the woman in the mirror ran her hands down her body. It wasn't a bad physique. Lean, but rounded at the butt and hips. Her breasts, cupped by slightly darker hands, were firm. Light blue eyes stared out of a face that seemed almost too sharp. Hands moved down to trace scars. One across a belly that was nearly too flat. Another that zigzagged across the left upper thigh. The pristine white bandage, contrasting so nicely with the darker skin, hid another scar soon to be added to the total. The reflected woman was in great shape, but she needed the few pounds lost during the last three years.

Was this the same face I'd had downstairs? Her cheeks were flushed, her nipples sharp from arousal. Was this brooding, hungry look present in her eyes when clothes covered her curves? Part of it could be the phers. Part of it could be the strange and novel attraction to a woman. But if I was honest with myself, I'd been like this—hungry—for a long time. Tonight's events hadn't started the fire. They'd merely fanned the flames. Maybe Mynx was right. Maybe I should've given in to my body's needs long ago.

The woman in the mirror shook her head, lips curving into an amused smile. We were in agreement. I'd never been able to separate intimacy, sex and love. It was too late to start now.

I looked again at that woman who was me but no longer recognizable. Her arms were toned from martial arts, sword drills, and occasionally kayaking the local creeks. The same was true for her legs. Each scar, a badge of honor. Her loose black hair began to curl wildly in the shower's humidity. I was happy with this body. She was strong, capable. Sexy, if she chose, which was good. This was my body for the next hundred and twenty years or so, assuming I lived to be a ripe old witch. But even with all those years to come, I didn't have time for this tonight.

Her hands again moved, traveling between her breasts, barely grazing her cleavage, moving over the tight abdomen, then along the inner edges of her thighs. Fortunately (or maybe unfortunately), I was in control tonight. The hands stopped, just short of their destination. The woman disappeared as the mirror fogged over, and I turned to enter the shower.

As I moved under the stinging spray, my mind kept returning to the mirrored woman's last glimpse and the amused smile lingering on her face. Like after Jup's warning, I had questions. Really they were the same questions with only a change of subject. My mind flashed again to that smile and her bright hungry eyes. What was it that the woman in the mirror knew that I didn't? And how much was it going to cost me to find out?

I had a feeling I wasn't going to like either answer.

I quickly rinsed off, changed into my favorite pair of frayed holey jeans and sage-green hoodie, and brushed my hair before knotting it into a chignon. I might not make the cover of *VQ*, the Vamp's fashion mag, but at least I smelled better.

There was something very disarming about Jacqueline Slone. But disarming didn't mean unarmed. I strapped a small knife above my right ankle. My libido might be on a pher-induced roller coaster, but that didn't make me stupid. Jacq didn't appear armed. But then, I'd taken a thorough look and never determined where she'd pulled that badge from.

On my way downstairs I stopped in my aunt's study for a copy of the case file and the medallion I'd taken off Bob's body. The kitchen was empty when I returned. Jacq had removed the tea ball from the kettle before it could become overly strong. Considerate, considering I'd deserted her for far longer than planned. I put the file and medallion on the tray and went in search of my errant guest.

My bare feet made little noise as I padded into our family den. I found Jacq there, standing by my Grams' old black piano, staring at the family photos spread across its top. She had picked up the cat. Hex purred contentedly as Jacq absentmindedly stroked her fur. Apparently even feline vessels of unholy power found this woman attractive. Jacq focused on a photo of me and my mom taken when I was five, her expression inscrutable. She gestured to the piano. "Do you play?"

"Very little, but my mother played beautifully." The words simply slipped out. I looked away, using the distraction of setting the tray on the scarred trunk we used as a coffee table to clear the sudden lump from my throat. I stood, my own mask firmly in place, saying lightly, "I see you've met Hexamina, Satan incarnate, evil sorceress, and all around bad kitty." I gestured to the cat, who was enjoying herself a little too much, before signaling Jacq to sit.

Jacq placed the cat on the floor. "She seems nice."

Aunt Helena would've found my snort of derision most unladylike but Jacq merely smiled. People thought we Delacys were joking when we commented about Hex being a vessel of unholy power, a hell-cat, evil spawn, etc. Eventually Jacqueline Slone would find out for herself. If she was lucky, all her limbs would still be attached after the epiphany.

We had an old cream-striped couch and two brown leather armchairs cozied around the brick fireplace. What the pieces lacked in beauty they more than made up with comfort. The only thing from this decade was the flat screen hanging over the fireplace and the nearby sound system. It was too hot a night for a fire, but the recessed lighting and café latte walls kept the atmosphere warm.

Jacq sat on the couch with one leg out along it and the other, crooked at the knee, resting on the couch cushions. I pulled a chair a little closer and sat.

While we drank orange spice tea I filled her in on everything from my fight with Bob to the five girls' disappearances and deaths. Viewing the photos, she wore a hardened cop's mask of cold professionalism.

I was surprised when she pointed at the rift bearers, saying, "That explains why Fera picked a guardian for this."

The fact that we were guardians was a closely kept secret. Jacq knew, too? Who else in the Council knew? And was it the result of my recent advertising? Now was not the time to ask. This woman had the type of poker face only someone who'd lived centuries could perfect. But I'd eventually learn to read her. And then I'd ask the questions battering at the locked doors in my mind.

Finally, we came to the black medallion. Brow creased, Jacq silently traced the gold and silver engravings, lost in thought. "This," she pointed to what looked like an ancient temple with a large moon hanging low over it, "could be for an Elite house. This one," she turned the medallion and ran her thumb across the other side's sun symbol, "looks familiar. It also represents an Elite house, but I cannot place it."

Only demon nobles were considered Elite. That meant it bore the symbols of two highborn demon families. There were several small magical surges as she checked the metal for residue. I knew what she would find.

"It could be a talisman," Jacq said. "They're homing beacons to help the Elite focus during gate travel. For more than that, you'll have to take it to a Demonology expert."

A talisman? That fit but didn't explain why it had been in Sarkoph's possession. "Thank you. Unfortunately, my Aunt Helena is stumped and she's an expert in most things demonic." I met Jacq's eyes over my tea, noticing little flecks of dark blue, nearly black, in the gray. After a moment, I realized I was staring, and the object of my fixed attention had noticed. Jacq met my gaze with a slight half-smile.

I busied myself refilling our empty teacups, continuing my explanation, "My aunt did email photos to a few colleagues. Maybe they can provide more information. I was just hoping for faster answers. Guess I'll have to practice patience."

"I'm sorry I couldn't offer more." Jacq gave me a full-blown smile.

For the second time today, I nearly choked on my drink. It wasn't right that this woman should look so good *and* have a dimple in one cheek. I barely avoided shooting an embarrassing stream of hot tea out my nose. Fortunately, when she leaned forward to return the medallion, the only liquid in my mouth was a healthy amount of drool. I caught a peek of cleavage and shifted uncomfortably in my chair, moving my eyes to where Jacq's hand rested on mine before we both pulled away. My skin *zinged* where our hands had brushed.

Was it magic, chemistry, or both? I hurried to finish my explanation, hoping she'd attribute my once again flushed skin to a fresh infusion of hot tea.

I said, "Oh, but you have. We hadn't considered the possibility. Maybe we'll know more when someone replies to my aunt's email. Until then, there's not much hope of solving this mystery." I tapped the metal still warm from her body. It felt nice resting in my palm, and I curled my fingers around it. I smiled into gray eyes, darkened nearly to black. "At least, not without catching a demon and tickle-torturing the information out of him." I tried for a moment of levity but had an ominous feeling as the words left my mouth. "And there never seems to be one of those around when you need 'em."

CHAPTER FIVE

"I thought it was true love? How could he go back to her?"

"Really, my dear, you're just an A-plus. Did you truly think he'd leave his O-neg wife for you?"

—*As the Blood Turns*, Nighttime's most popular Soap Opera

Day Four

"Mr. Richmond, please…" I passed the distraught man seated across from my old cherry desk a tissue. "Tell me how I can help." I kept my voice low, soothing, pushing my exhaustion away. It had been another long night. Due to the late hour, Jacq had made a good argument for crashing on our couch rather than make the drive back to her home near NOLA. She didn't seem the type to slit our throats in the night, so I'd been persuaded.

The pher-induced lust had left me achy, needy, and confused as hell. My sleep had been fitful…especially knowing the accidental object of my desire was just downstairs. I'd really needed sleep and knew, from years of going to bed alone, a quick cure. But I'd made no move to satisfy my body's demands, that sort of pleasure seeming hollow. Thankfully, the pher level had dropped during the night. And although I had a headache from lack of sleep, my body was almost my own again. I wasn't reacting to the middle-aged Mr. Richmond, which boded well for my next meeting with the tempting Jacqueline

Slone. I brought my thoughts back to Mr. Richmond, who was trying to quietly blow his nose.

He tucked the tissue away, focusing his red-rimmed eyes on me. His voice seemed calmer as he said, "My daughter Isabella called me last night." He passed me a picture of a pretty young brunette with her father's hazel eyes then clenched his hands. "She was upset. I didn't understand what she was saying. I told her to calm down and explain." His words were tumbling out. "Maybe if I'd just left then for Hattiesburg…" He shook his head as if forcing those thoughts away. "She said there wasn't enough time, asked me to pack. She was coming home. We'd leave together. She was so…scared." His voice slowed.

We both waited while his breath shuddered in and out. Finally he said, "I told her I would come get her, to wait there, but she kept saying she had to leave right then."

Mr. Richmond looked at his hands. My heart ached for him already, and we weren't through the entire story. I watched his hands clench and unclench.

"So I waited, but Isabella never made it home."

Just then, Mynx walked in with a tray loaded with my aunt's brown sugar pound cake and two steaming cups. Most people would consider ten in the morning too early for something so rich, but our family was a big believer in the Southern tradition of soothing grief (and every other ailment) with food. Fortunately, witches had high metabolisms. Mynx sat the tray down on a side table as I said, "Mr. Richmond, I'd like to introduce you to my distant cousin and business partner, Mynx Delacy." They'd met when he'd barged into our offices, but no formal introduction had been made. Mynx smiled slightly. Maybe it was from calling her a cousin when she was actually my ancestor's cat familiar…or maybe because I'd finally convinced her to take the more-than-deserved title of partner. Goddess knows we wouldn't make it around here without her. Now we just needed a new secretary.

As testament to his extreme distress, Mr. Richmond stared into his coffee, not sparing Mynx's gorgeous body a second glance. Mynx silently left, hopefully to go keep Jacq out of trouble. Our clients' cases were confidential. The last thing I needed was the law present. It didn't matter that she was out of uniform. A po-po could hide in a clown suit and the people in this area would still see a cop with a red nose and big shoes.

I picked up my tea, sipping my favorite spiced chai. We sat in silence while Mr. Richmond gathered his thoughts. I wanted to reassure him that there was nothing he could've done differently. Rushing to Hattiesburg wouldn't have halted his daughter's disappearance. But platitudes would have to wait. We hadn't reached the point where he'd trust my judgment. Plus, I had the sinking feeling that I needed to hear the rest of this tale.

Fera's case had been on my mind all morning. Nicodemus hadn't yet opened a gate, so he must need something. More power and another victim were the obvious answer. I'd been on the phone with my local contact at the PD to see if any girls were missing when Mynx had announced Mr. Richmond's arrival. There were no scheduled appointments for today, which was why my loosely knotted hair was still damp against my shirt. But when the panic-stricken father had told Mynx his daughter was missing, she'd shuffled him into my office. I was looking for a girl to go missing, and he had one. Mynx, like all the Delacys, didn't believe in coincidences.

After another moment, a steadier Mr. Richmond continued, "I waited, but Isabella never showed. I called her cell over and over with no answer. Part of me didn't want to leave in case she showed up. What if she'd forgotten her phone? I could pass her on the road and never realize it. I waited four hours, enough time for Isabella to get from her apartment in The Burg to our house in NOLA. I called her boyfriend, Kyle. He tends bar at a club in NOLA. Kyle was at work and hadn't heard from her. I couldn't wait anymore."

I jotted notes, nodding for him to continue.

"My daughter's a creature of habit. She always takes the same routes. I followed the roads, stopping every time I saw a car pulled over in either lane." He released a humorless laugh. "I ran across another girl my daughter's age whose car had broken down. I called her a tow, but I never saw my Iza. When I made it to her apartment, it was empty. Her car was there. Kyle arrived soon after with some of the club's bouncers, and they began to search for her." He paused, put aside his untouched coffee, looked at me then looked away.

Why the sudden hesitation? Undoubtedly everything he'd said so far had been true, but we were about to get into some difficult questions. I didn't like taking a job knowing only half the facts—case in point: Sunday's run for the Kin.

"Mr. Richmond, I understood that your daughter was upset and is now missing," I paused, waiting for his downcast eyes to meet mine.

"But what brings you to my agency instead of the police?" Clients usually came to me weeks after the PD had exhausted their own resources. It didn't bother me to be the second or third option. This was a poor area. No one wanted to pay a PI if the law would help them for free.

Before I could finish my question, I had a foreboding. Trouble was approaching. Just as Aunt Helena walked in, Mr. Richmond pulled a crumpled scrap of newspaper from his pocket. My stomach dropped, recognizing the ad as he placed it on my desk. The words "Now Taking Supernatural as well as Natural Cases" seemed to jump off the page, catching my aunt's eye. This was the ad we'd fought over yesterday, the version I'd neglected to mention placing in The Burg's paper.

Aunt Helena's easy smile faltered. She not-so-gently shooed Hex from a chair and gracefully sat. I would've felt sorry for the cat if she hadn't been evil incarnate. Other than to introduce herself and pat Mr. Richmond's knee, Aunt Helena was silent. Hex, on the other hand, protested her cruel treatment loudly as she stalked from the room. I waved for Mr. Richmond to continue.

"You see, my Iza has very unique abilities." His hands fisted. "The police wouldn't be able to help me. And even if they could, I'm not sure they'd bother."

I hid my frown. If I wasn't mistaken, the man sitting before me was human. I didn't sense even a smidgen of magical ability, but I wasn't surprised by his claim. The PD's Supernatural Crimes Units only handled magical cases against humans. If Isabella was Supernatural and missing she was the Council's responsibility. But obviously, her father had his reasons for not seeking their help. Reasons he finally looked ready to share.

Mr. Richmond said, "This has never been discussed outside our family. If Isabella's mother were still alive, she could explain better. My late wife was a Druid."

I raised my eyebrows. Druids were humans with a genetic twist that allowed them to connect to the most ancient of magics. Unfortunately, there were few left. The bloodlines had become so mixed with other mortals that those left had little or no power. An issue I understood well, as some said this was the reason there were now so few guardians.

I didn't need magic to know he wasn't lying. No one would willingly label themselves or their child a Druid. Druids were one of the few humans with powers. Because they were human *and* magical, they were outcasts, not fitting with either group. It wasn't a matter of being popular but having no structure to protect them. With their numbers few and scattered, they usually hid, pretending to be as powerless as other humans.

"Exactly what type of abilities does Isabella have?" I caught myself before saying, "did have." Usually, when pretty young girls went missing they didn't turn up, at least not alive. I didn't need a reminder, but if I did I had the macabre photos of five such girls filed in the drawer inches below my teacup. Still, I was firmly an optimist, at least when it came to other people's lives. I wanted myself and Mr. Richmond to believe she would be found alive.

His answer was barely a whisper. "Premonition. Very strong. Very clear. And the newspaper with your ad," he placed a finger on the ad in question, "was in my daughter's apartment, lying on the kitchen counter under her keys."

A ring of red fire had been drawn around the print. I looked at it more closely. Over the text had been written four, red letters, CATE.

He raised his head, his eyes blazing with certainty. "My daughter wanted me to come here, wanted me to meet you. I feel it in my soul. And so, Miss Delacy, here I am." There was silence as myself, my aunt, and Jacq, who had Mynx trying to stop her from entering the room, froze.

With difficulty, I tore my gaze from Mr. Richmond's and gestured for Mynx and Jacq to sit. It seemed Jacq would need to hear this after all.

Precognition. Holy mother of all that was sacred. The true power of premonition hadn't been seen in centuries. I met my aunt's eyes, reading her thoughts clearly. That explained why Isabella Richmond had been so upset. I could practically see it in my head. Most likely, Mr. Richmond's daughter had been picked to be the feature star in Nicodemus's next grisly scene. She had seen something, possibly everything, in a premonition, gotten scared and tried to run. But it was too late. Isabella was a resourceful girl though. I agreed with Mr. Richmond. She'd left her father a message. Why else would a college student circle an ad for a runner—one conveniently looking into a case regarding other magical girls? More importantly, why write my name, a name not listed in the ad, over it?

Mr. Richmond pleaded, "I'll pay you whatever it takes. Just bring my daughter back to me." He lowered his head to hide more tears. I got up, rushing around my desk to stop his jerky efforts to retrieve a checkbook.

"Mr. Richmond...Henry, please." I leaned against my desk, placing my hand on his shoulder. "We'll take the case, but consider the fees paid." I hadn't missed his frayed cuffs and scuffed work boots. Even if I weren't already being paid by both the Kin and the Council, I wouldn't have accepted this man's money. And if the case had been simply a missing girl with no magic, one who didn't have a possible connection to my other cases, I'd still have accepted. Maybe I felt a kinship to Isabella Richmond who'd also lost her mother. Or maybe I envied her for having the one thing that as a child I'd always wanted: a loving father. I never made promises I couldn't keep. I was going to make a promise now, and I'd raze the seven levels of Hell to honor it.

Mr. Richmond looked up. My eyes held his as I squatted, placing my warm hands over the cold ones still tightly clenching his checkbook. "We'll bring your daughter home. I swear it."

Mynx and Aunt Helen left to do their own things, but Jacq stayed. "Henry, this is my associate, Jacqueline Slone." I didn't dare say detective. He was worried enough. I hoped I wasn't lying when I added, "You can trust her with Isabella's secrets." I looked from the crying man to Jacq and found her watching me. I looked away quickly. "We're going to ask you a few questions now." I pulled a chair close to Henry and Jacq and sat, notepad in hand.

"Does anyone else know about Isabella's abilities?" Jacq asked.

"No," Henry said.

But that didn't mean much. It wasn't hard to know Isabella had power. I knew this like I knew Isabella's father had none. Magic users recognize each other, but it's nearly impossible to tell what someone's power does unless they're like Necromancers and give off the smell of their trade.

"But Kyle, Isabella's boyfriend, knew?" I asked.

"Yes," Henry said, "but they've been together since they were young. He wouldn't have done this."

"Of course," I said, not meaning a word. Lovers' quarrels had been known to get messy.

"We'll still want to speak with him," Jacq said.

This time I caught her looking at me, and she looked away. Something in that look made me wish I were again behind my desk.

"Yes, certainly," Henry said, nodding. His tears had dried, his hands steadying as he focused on our questions. He reached into his pocket. "Isabella's phone was by the paper. It has Kyle's number along with the names and numbers of her friends and teachers." He placed a small pink phone on my desk and smiled sadly. "She keeps her entire life in that thing."

After several general questions, Jacq asked, "Are Isabella's powers transferrable?"

I nodded, knowing where this was headed.

Henry cleared his throat. "I'm not certain I understand what you mean."

"Some powers are linked to the body," I explained, "others to the soul. Others still are a mystery. Is Isabella's premonition something someone could take into themselves and use?" Transference was one of the darkest magics, not to mention a really bad idea. If you don't believe me, just ask Hexamina. Yeah, that demon masquerading as my cat. Generations back, she'd been one of the most powerful sorceresses alive…until she'd gotten greedy and attempted to steal my ancestor Erin's powers. Thankfully something had gone wrong. Hex had trapped herself in the body of Erin's cat familiar, Mynx. Yes, the same Mynx that was my business partner and housemate. She'd ended up in the sorceress's body. For some reason, Mynx and Hex never aged. And so the Delacys were left with cat-sitting duty.

"I'm not sure." Henry shook his head. "My late wife always said her abilities were genetic." He looked at us expectantly.

"That's good." Jacq gave him an encouraging smile. "Without her body, Isabella's powers would soon fade after being taken. Possession spells and transference rituals take a great deal of power and effort, more than what someone would use for powers that would not last."

I momentarily met Jacq's gaze. We both knew there was more to it than that. Mortal, Isabella wouldn't survive an attempt to steal her powers. But her death could generate a lot of magic, even if it didn't give the recipient the power of premonition.

I asked Henry, "Why isn't Kyle with you this morning?" If my lover was missing and I thought someone knew something, I'd be tearing down their door. I looked to Jacq. I could practically see her reassurance, wrapping around her like a warm cloud before seeping into Henry. She looked up, again catching me staring. This time, I detected a glint of humor in her gray eyes. Maybe I was getting better at seeing past her cool exterior, or maybe she'd decided to let me in. My attention turned to Henry.

"I didn't tell him I was coming," he said flatly.

I frowned. Hadn't he just said he trusted Kyle?

Henry explained, "When Kyle was sixteen, he was in an accident. His parents were killed, and he nearly died. During surgery he was accidentally given blood tainted with the Lycan-virus. He's a Were. So were the men he brought with him. They looked almost wild when they heard she was gone. I stayed at Isabella's apartment hoping she might come back while they ran the streets, looking for her. Kyle returned to check in before running out again."

Weres and they hadn't been able to track Isabella? That eliminated random human violence. It would have taken someone with magical skill to hide their scent from a Were's nose.

Henry continued, "Kyle was never alone, and while I trust my daughter's boyfriend…" He met my gaze. "I don't know or trust his friends. I couldn't think of a way to explain why I needed to come here without revealing Isabella's secret."

We asked a few more questions then wrapped up. Every piece of information Mr. Richmond had shared made it clear: Isabella had been taken by someone off the grid. Someone with nothing to lose and no reason to play the game. Someone like Nicodemus. He and his followers needed power to open a darkmirror. And if Nicodemus had her, Isabella was the most powerful being taken thus far.

The gates to the Otherworld were currently shut, but our missing Druid could be the key to it all.

* * *

After Henry left, Jacq and I formed a plan. We'd try magic first. If that didn't work, we'd do some good old-fashioned legwork. We began in the agency's workroom scrying for Isabella. But instead of dropping on a spot the crystal danced over the map like a wind chime in a hurricane.

"Uggg." That was my fourth attempt, and I was beyond frustrated.

"Can I help?" Jacq asked. I jumped, nearly dropping the crystal. Completely focused, I'd forgotten that she was standing close, watching me. Even with the phers' decrease, her whiskey-smooth voice still sent shivers down my spine. "Are you cold?" This time I did drop the crystal as she touched me, sending a wave of hot magic *zinging* down my arm. I was already burning up inside, but probably not in the way she'd intended.

I rubbed my pleasantly tingling arm. "No, I mean yes." I looked up from the maps I'd spread across a massive metal table. Her smoky eyes, today almost a light gray-blue, watched me with amusement. She'd obviously borrowed the guest shower. Her straight auburn hair was damp, and she'd changed into a pair of black trousers, gray shirt and matching black vest. My khaki cargos and blue shirt with a golden sun didn't even compare.

I looked down. "You can help. I've upped the juice but keep getting the same result. Someone's using some serious magic to block Isabella's location. We need to try something else." I moved around the room gathering supplies, talking as I went. "The easiest spell to hide someone is a simple magical shield. It's easy to make, easy to break. Unfortunately, Isabella is being hidden by something more complicated, which takes her magical signature and distributes it into the ley-lines. Bits and pieces of the signature flow through the currents, causing the crystal to swing back and forth." I dumped my supplies on the table, and Jacq looked curiously at the items I'd gathered. "That's good in a way. Such a spell only works if a person is alive." At least I could tell Isabella's father she was still amongst the living.

"If not scrying, what do you wish to do?" Jacq tucked her hair behind a not-even-slightly-pointed ear. Likely not Fae, but she didn't seem surprised at my explanation of magical signatures, which meant she'd patiently let me explain something she already knew.

"With your help, I'll attempt to trace the signature back to its source. But at some point we may need to share magic."

Cheeks flushing, I turned back to the map and away from her piercing gaze. The sharing of magic was very intimate, requiring people to drop their guards and share their very nature. Jacq had to know this. Most magic users did. I kept my eyes diverted, explaining the process and side effects anyway. Still amped on lust phers was a bad time to do this but if it would get Isabella Richmond home safe, it was a risk I was willing to take. I wasn't the only one.

"Let's try it."

I blinked slowly, looking again at Jacq. Her expression was warily determined. The issue decided, I moved away, describing what and why as I closed the drapes and began to light candles. We'd do this now, before one or both of us came to our senses.

"The magical plane is bright. The less light to distract me from reaching it, the better. A candle is lit to each wind. To the North

Wind. To hasten the Journey." As I spoke, I placed each candle in a pre-prepared cradle in the room's corners, lighting them with a taper. Both the main and guest houses had been built so the corners coincided exactly with the four compass points. I lit a white candle. It was scentless, which wasn't the tradition. Then again, letting an outsider help was also a first. "To the East Wind, for clarity. May I not stray from the path." This candle was sky-blue, also scentless. Jacq's eyes followed my every step.

"To the South Wind, for strength to complete the necessary task." I would be leaning on Jacq's strength. This candle was tan with a strong sandalwood scent, tying her to the spell. I barely whispered the last words, but from her worried expression, I knew Jacq heard me say, "And to the West Wind, to light the way and bring me safely home through the darkness." With absolute certainty, I substituted a green sage candle for the usual clean-scented white one. The candles flickered, their scents merging, painting Jacq's skin in a rosy glow and haloing her hair. I didn't let my eyes linger, instead striding to the table and her side.

"Ready?" I held out my hand. This time, we wouldn't use the crystal. I would use the maps to focus my mind as it traveled through the streams of magic. Hopefully, I could track the signature threads to their true source by finding the strongest one. It might be a long, tiring search, forcing me to rely on Jacq to guide me back. In that regard, it was a very dangerous spell, a fact I'd intentionally left out.

"Yes." Jacq grabbed my hand, immediately bringing her tingling magic to where our palms joined. That magic, that strength, would be my focal point for return.

She would be my West Wind.

"One more thing." My tone was low and tight, deadly serious. I put my other hand on the map. "This hand stays here. I can find my way back without the extra connection, but it would be much harder."

Jacq nodded just once. Her worried words barely filtered in as I began the process of leaving my body. "If this is too much…"

My mind's eye rose, too far gone to stop and reassure her. Unlike when I'd looked at Sarkoph, I didn't halt my progression. As my consciousness continued up, flying beyond my body, I tightly chained my fire. We'd do this with my weaker earth-magic or not at all. Jacq was no beginner. Should I draw the other magic out, she would feel the difference. Plus, there was plenty to worry about without the possibility of unconsciously burning her hand off.

Using the maps as guide, my mind left my body, the house, even the county, traveling along the ley-lines, moving through magic roaring as wide as a river to lines barely trickling with power. No longer simply viewing the magical plane, I was part of it. Always glorious, it was the most spectacular, most freeing…most dangerous…of road trips. The thousands of variations of every color, brighter and more beautiful than the eye could comprehend, could be a deadly distraction.

The consciousness and body are irrevocably connected, unable to survive a lengthy separation. If one lost its way, the mind would stay here until the body eventually died, so I tried to hurry. But every thread led to a dead end. I stayed that way much longer than intended, unable to give up when the next piece of signature held such promise. I moved from one to another to another until I'd scoured the majority of ley-lines in The Burg, NOLA, and the coast. I didn't stop until I felt the string connecting me to my body faintly tug. Something, or someone, was calling me. My mind turned, looking at the swirling colors. So beautiful. So mesmerizing.

So deadly.

Everything began to blur in a kaleidoscope, impossibly more chaotic than normal. If I were on the physical plane, my vision would be hazy from weariness. I saw with a dawning horror the truth of my situation. I'd waited too long. Or nearly so.

My magic was taxed beyond its limits. I was weak, so weak. The link between my mind and body was steadily growing thinner. If I didn't hurry, it would continue shrinking until it snapped. Then both my mind and body would waste away.

I desperately searched for my way back, surfing the lines for what seemed like forever, trying to follow my own dim thread. The magical plane was ever-changing, its magic fluid. Landmarks didn't exist here, which was why it was unwise to take these journeys alone. I knew better than to disregard the rules. *Don't panic.* Stopping, I metaphorically took several deep breaths. Soaring above the plane, I pivoted in circles, looking for something tangible, something to lead me home again. I'd nearly given up hope when I spotted a splash of pulsating silver, shining true and pure even from a distance. There was something familiar about that magic.

Weaving through swirls of reds, blues, greens, so many other magics, I moved ever closer. Even far away, the silver magic prickled warm against skin I no longer had. The closer I came, the more my magic reacted. It was warm and welcoming. I began to tingle. I tried to be cautious, to approach the light slowly. But I was a drowning woman seeing a ray of sun pierce the dark waters. My need to survive took over, rushing my mind into the light without consent.

My consciousness returned to my body, and I gasped, eyes popping open, disoriented and dizzy from adjusting to so few colors, so little light.

"Careful, breathe slowly."

I looked into concerned eyes, glowing silver. Jacq held me close, speaking urgently but softly in my ear. *It was her.* Jacq had drawn me back. My hand was still gently cradled in hers. No longer at my side, she'd wedged herself between my body and the table, our bodies wrapping around each other. My other hand was still on the maps while her free arm circled my waist. And until I'd leaned back to see her face, my head had been tucked under her chin. I took another deep breath, realizing my knees had buckled, possibly hours ago. Jacq had been, and was still, supporting me.

"It's okay. You're safe," she murmured, releasing my hand to push my hair away from my face. Her glowing fingers moved, caressing over my cheek, leaving trails of hot magic behind. I couldn't look away from her eyes. Black with silver streaks, they held something I didn't want to consider.

Finally I broke eye contact, but the image of those glowing orbs, like silver lightning piercing a dark sky, lingered in my mind. I needed to pull myself together. I was practically clinging to the woman. Her hands moved to my waist, and before I could protest, Jacq carried me to a chair.

As she eased me down, I smiled up in thanks, taking the opportunity to study her. Jacq's mask of calm detachment had been replaced by genuine concern. I was too physically drained for the phers to matter, but a moment before as she'd held me close, I'd still noticed her warmth, her musky scent, her low, sensual voice. Okay, so this went beyond chemical lust. The sensations had been...nice. You heard me. Nice. That was my story, and I was sticking to it.

Jacq passed me a glass of water. I took a sip, joking, "Magic was a bust. Old-school it is."

She didn't respond, instead pulling up a chair. All I could see was the crown of her auburn head as she looked down, gently chafing my hands. Her knees felt comforting resting outside my own. My skin, now tingling as her hands rubbed mine, seemed dark against her pale rosiness. Jacq was no longer intentionally *zinging* me with her magic, but it continued to brush mine. In that moment before my consciousness had merged with my body, we'd connected, leaving me, and no doubt her too, with a strange sense of oneness that would eventually fade.

Or so I assumed. I was on unfamiliar ground. I'd done this many times with my family and never had this experience. I wasn't sure what to do, but touching seemed like a bad idea. I tried to pull away, but Jacq ignored my attempts to remove my hands from hers, simply saying, "You're freezing." I felt another *zing* of heat. This one left me feeling somewhat more energized as my body soaked it in. "You didn't mention how weak this would leave you. And," she nearly growled, "don't think that I don't know how dangerous that was." She let out an exasperated sigh.

Her eyes, once again gray, met mine. Her scolding wasn't as severe as Aunt Helena's would've been, but the emotion in those eyes... It was more effective than any lecture I'd ever received. I *had* been taking more risks lately—flying solo when it was easy to ask Mynx for help. I'd been unusually reckless, almost wild with the urge to stand on the edge of that cliff, and was at a loss to explain why, even to myself.

"I'll be fine." I managed to pull my hands free, tucking them under my armpits. "I'll take a warm shower and be as good as new. Then we need to check out Isabella's apartment and conduct interviews. The longer it takes to find her, the more danger she's in." I tried to stand but fell back.

Jacq looked me over with another frown. "No." She offered a hand, pulled me to my feet. "I'll go to town. We need to sweep Isabella's apartment anyway, and you're in no condition to use more magic. Why don't you stay here and track down the boyfriend."

"That's fine." I sighed, sitting back down. At her questioning look I explained, "You can go. I'll wait here until I have the power to open the wards." I hated to admit that my magic was that low, but I wasn't about to lie either.

"I'll help you into the house." She answered my unspoken question, "Mynx temporarily keyed me to the wards, so I could come and go without an escort."

Mynx didn't make rash decisions. How had Jacq earned her trust so quickly? I was consumed by irrational jealousy. Had Jacq charmed and been charmed by my beautiful friend? I looked away, trying to hide the foreign feelings, which faded as I saw a candle burned down to a small puddle of wax in the dim corner. It wasn't just cats and cat-women that were easily charmed by this woman. I'd made my own spur-of-the-moment decision, putting my life in her hands while traveling through the magical plane. And she'd proved herself worthy of that trust. But would she continue to do so?

As we walked the path leading from the agency offices to the main house, we revised our plan. Or rather, Jacq revised. I focused on placing one foot in front of the other. The stubborn woman wanted me to lean on her arm. And I was as determined to walk on my own. For the last three years I'd managed perfectly without having someone to walk me to my door. No point in getting comfortable any other way. The woman at my side would walk away when this case was over, and I'd still be here, walking this path alone, returning home.

* * *

After taking a scorching hot soak I felt nearly human. I wasn't sure when heat had become fuel. It'd happened so gradually over the last few years, generally only occurring a few days a month, that at first I'd barely noticed. But recently there'd been a big jump. Too bad this hadn't worked several days ago. Today at least I could charge my drained batteries.

I could survive without the heat, but I thrived with it, the absorbed energy speeding up my metabolism, healing me, satisfying a deep hunger I couldn't explain. It also helped metabolize the phers more quickly. When around the Weres, that was a bad thing—the increased metabolism also increasing my absorption rate. But when alone, it helped burn out the phers already in my system.

I headed back downstairs to begin my research. Luckily, Jacq had carried my laptop and files into the house, leaving them and Isabella's phone as requested on the kitchen counter. The hot water had helped, but I was still weak, making it unwise to venture to my office outside the wards' protection. The house was empty and quiet, though there was still a warm kettle on the stove and the lingering scent of sage and sandalwood in the air.

Before I started my calls, I looked over the background Henry had given me. Kyle was a student at Tulane and had been in a night class at the time of Isabella's call, leaving there to go to work, unaware of his girlfriend's disappearance until Henry's call.

I powered up Isabella's cell. First, I tried the mobile number, which went straight to voice mail. I thought about calling Luke but didn't know what type of Were Kyle was. There were hundreds scattered throughout this area. The chances were slim that Luke would know him. I dialed Kyle's work number. No way was he tending bar. I knew from experience: If someone you loved went missing, you didn't go back to business as usual the next day. But they might know how to find him.

A gruff voice answered, "Blue Moon Club." That surprised me. The Blue Moon was run by the Alpha of all the local Were Clans. If Kyle was working there, he wasn't any moon-howler but someone close to their leader.

"Yes, I'm looking for Kyle Thompson. Is he in?" I went for professional, but all I got for my trouble was a snarl. "Excuse me? I didn't catch that."

"Hold on, lady, I'll check." I held for ten minutes. I was about to hang up and call back when the call was transferred without warning. It rang and another voice answered.

"Yes?" The woman's musical voice was perfectly modulated. She didn't sound like a twenty-something male Were whose girlfriend had possibly been kidnapped by a sorcerer bent on world-domination (or something else as trite). I slapped my hand against the table. Knowing my luck, the snarling man had transferred me to a random stranger for shits and giggles.

"Hi, this is Cate Delacy. I'm looking for Kyle Thompson." There was silence on the line.

"Kyle's not here, right now." She stopped.

"It's urgent that I speak with him. Is there a better time I could call?" Again silence, this time too bare of sound. She'd put the phone on mute.

"Kyle's been detained on Pack business. He should be available tomorrow night. Be at the club at eleven." Her tone left no room for discussion.

Were the Alpha's people covering for Kyle? Or had Isabella's boyfriend found his own set of troubles? I gave my thanks, jotting down her directions.

I sat staring dumbly at my notes. Tomorrow was Thursday. I was going to walk into a nightclub full of hundreds of horny Weres putting out seas of lust pheromones, and there was no way that Detective Jacqueline Slone would sit this dance out.

I was so screwed.

* * *

Jacq returned as I was preparing dinner, dashing my dream of a little alone time…or so I told myself, ignoring the part of me that was happy to see her again. I'd sorted through Isabella's phone looking for red herrings. But nothing had seemed out of place. And there had been no connection to any of Bob's or the other girls' contacts. I'd called Jacq with the names, numbers and locations of everyone our missing girl had spoken with recently. Then I'd spent the afternoon poring over fact sheets on Bob Rainey and all the dead girls. I'd gone over every photo meticulously, staring at the mess until my eyes crossed.

I desperately needed to get away from all that death for a few hours. There was a comfy couch and a DVD waiting for me in the den. Until Jacq had shown up, I'd had the house to myself. My aunt had gone back to New Orleans to visit friends and wouldn't be back until tomorrow morning. I hadn't been alone with Aunt Helena since my meeting with Fera. I suspected she was avoiding me, maybe sensing my need to talk about my mother's previous disappearance. And Mynx was out, doing surveillance for her own run.

During our call, Jacq had said she'd return to compare notes, but when she hadn't arrived by dusk, I'd thought she'd gone back to NOLA. Her knock on the kitchen door nearly made me jump out of my skin. I reached to turn down the upbeat country station I'd been blasting while puttering around the kitchen and gestured for her to enter. The doors stayed unlocked when the wards were up. Anything that could get through our wards wouldn't be stopped by a bit of wood.

"Have you eaten?" I asked, removing my head from the fridge. I set my ingredients on the counter. Jacq, looking as alluring as ever in her now unbuttoned vest, was back in her usual chair. Had she been staring at my ass? Must be my imagination, because her eyes were fixed on the range top.

"No."

Uh-oh, one word answers were never good. Her expression was remote, but I detected a hopeful glint in her eyes. Poor woman. She was probably starving after traipsing all over The Burg.

"Would you like some dinner? I'm just putting together a quick salad. Nothing fancy." I pointed to the chicken left from lunch. My Grams would rise from her grave and beat me with her cane if I didn't offer food to a dinnertime guest. Jacq smiled at the offer. She thought I was being solicitous. She had no idea. It was purely self-preservation.

"You'd cook for me?" Her Cajun accent was stronger than usual.

My head tilted slightly. She sounded a bit smug, as if I'd just offered her all my worldly possessions. Maybe I had. Some of the more obscure species had some pretty strange practices.

"Well, *cook* might be an exaggeration. I'm simply reheating the chicken and putting everything in a bowl." I moved about the kitchen, throwing the chicken and a splash of water on the electric grill before piling the greens in two big bowls, topping them with nuts, berries, feta, and the now steaming chicken, finally drizzling everything with balsamic. I put the bowls down, turning to face her.

"Would you like to watch a movie with me?" Where had that come from? "I mean, we can talk over the case while we eat..." I stammered, unable to meet her eyes. "I'd planned to watch a movie, a dark comedy. Join me?"

Jacq smiled fully, that elusive dimple peeking out. "I'd love to." Her response was low, husky.

I shivered. It was good that I was done talking, because her smile left me suddenly breathless. I sucked in a much-needed breath, helpless to stop my own smile as we picked up our salads and moved into the other room. What can I say? I was easily pleased and, apparently, so was Jacq.

I was still smiling later as we finished talking business and put on the movie, *Army of Darkness*. Drinks in hand, we sat side by side on the couch, our bare feet propped up on the old trunk and a big bowl of popcorn between us. I'd known this woman for less than twenty-four hours and was now treating her like a long-lost friend. As we laughed at the main character's cheesy one-liners, I couldn't help but think that if crazy is as crazy does, then I might better check into an asylum. It wasn't the fact that I seemed to be going insane that worried me. It was that I really didn't care to stop.

* * *

Carlisle shivered in the dark. Already dead and coldblooded, it wasn't from the temperature. He'd never liked these clandestine meetings. He was a politician, not some military type to slither along in the shadows. To add insult, the demon lord's earthbound contact was always late. Nicodemus, as he called himself, liked to make an entrance. Although an abandoned building probably wasn't his preferred setting nor Carlisle and a few rodents his preferred audience. Concessions had to be made in the name of secrecy. But that would all end soon.

"Report!"

Carlisle jumped at Nicodemus's booming voice. He was an Immortal, for pity's sake, high-ranking in the house of Louisiana's Vampire King. But Carlisle's status didn't matter to Nicodemus. He and his distortion charm always got a sadistic enjoyment out of making everyone in his presence cower. Even with Carlisle's supernatural eyesight, he could barely discern the shadow passing through an outside streetlamp's glow. The spell was the best he'd ever seen, even hiding Nicodemus's body heat. Carlisle whirled to face the shadow, cringing at the two sets of red eyes blinking at him from the darkness. *Hellhounds.* He hated it when Nicodemus brought those beasts with him. Many times larger and more vicious than their Earthen counterparts, the hounds always looked half-starved, making them too hungry to be trusted.

"My spies followed Guild Master Fera to a local bar, where she met an independent runner." Carlisle sounded cool, collected. He'd had centuries to mask his fear, to connive his way into power. He wouldn't give it up so easily. "It appears the runner was hired to begin her own investigation. The name's Cate. My spies managed to get a cloth with her scent." He held up a bar napkin and large envelope. "The information is all here. The Guild Master appears to have stalled in her investigation, but the runner concerns me." He'd humor the weak Council's attempt to appear more mundane in public, but he refused to use the human titles, such as Sheriff, in private. Things would eventually return to the old ways, where the Blood took what and who they wanted. And the change couldn't happen soon enough for him.

"Good." Nicodemus came forward, taking the items. "See that the Guild Master's search continues to meet a dead end. My hounds will take care of the runner." Lowering the cloth, he let the beasts catch the runner's scent. Then he turned and disappeared, the hounds following behind. Even so, Nicodemus's last words hung in the air. "The gate will open soon. My master will come through with his legions. And when we remake this world, your reward will be great."

Carlisle shivered again…but not from the pleasure the words should have evoked. He questioned, not for the first time, making this deal with the devil.

CHAPTER SIX

"If you play with fire, you're gonna get burned. And if you play with Hellfire, you'll keep on burning. But oh the pleasure of the fall."

—Author Unknown

Day Five

I was in the kitchen cooking up suppression amulets while listening to the sounds of battle coming from the backyard. After yesterday's search for Isabella, my magic had been too low for even such a simple spell. I didn't want Jacq to know about my new weakness to the phers, so Mynx was again distracting our guest while I worked. Their sparring would also allow Mynx to evaluate Jacq's skills. Which would be important when we fought together...or if she ever turned on us. Something in me said the latter would never happen, but my more logical side was in control this morning.

Jacq and I were meeting Kyle at The Blue Moon tonight. Run by the Weres' leader, Grey Gryphon, it was a favorite hangout for anything that turned furry. With only a few nights to the next full moon, the place would be full of aggressive Weres looking for sex. The phers at Mag's were nothing compared to what would be circulating at Grey's. Without these amulets, I'd be a puddle of shivering, aching, gotta-fuck-someone's-brains-out need before I even made it in the door.

This spell didn't require a circle, so as I stirred it, I watched Mynx and Jacq spar. They were both dressed in dark workout clothes presumably from Mynx's closet. I'd never seen Jacq with luggage, and nothing of mine or my even more petite aunt would've fit our much taller guest. The black jeans and tank fit Jacq like they'd been made for her. The two moved in a synchronized ballet of swordplay so stunningly beautiful that I almost forgot to add the last ingredient: a drop of liquid Were pheromone. Even after I had set the spell into small wooden discs, I continued to watch.

The women appeared well-matched, but I sensed that one or both were holding back. The aggressive show, helped along by the phers, made my blood surge, but I also found it disheartening. The years of study necessary for this level of expertise would find me merely dust in my grave. While witches were long-lived, we weren't immortal.

Even now I was probably breathing more heavily than those two, though both were covered with a heavy sheen of sweat. Jacq's ivory skin glowed softly. I couldn't help but notice the strong arms that so masterfully parried Mynx's blade. Those arms had kept me standing yesterday while I'd conducted my searching spell. *If she had let me fall…* That thought stopped as something caught my attention. I narrowed my eyes, frowning as silver runes flashed in the sunlight, glinting off Jacq's sword. That wasn't one of ours, practice or otherwise. She hadn't brought spare clothes, but she'd brought a weapon? I grinned. At least she had her priorities straight.

I tucked the amulets away, taking a moment to think of our guest. Last night after the movie, I'd lingered. I'd been tired. Jacq had been tired. But it's good to get to know a person if they may someday be fighting at your back. Or at least that was the excuse I gave myself. So, we talked. Jacq was intelligent, charming, and had also been disillusioned with the Council's machinations for decades. No matter how many hints I dropped, she'd never disclosed her age or species. So it startled me when she shared her motives for leaving the Council.

Originally, she'd been undercover with the PD, working for the Council. After the Genesis, she'd seen an opportunity for the police to learn and had left to help start the first SCU. If she didn't turn out to be a spy, we might end up friends.

I was about to call a halt to the sparring when I felt the house's wards shudder. That happens sometimes when the military base's flyboys create a sonic boom. Sometimes the wards even drop for a millisecond. But the expected *boom* didn't follow.

There was a second shudder then a discordant sound like a bow pulled across an untuned fiddle. *Shit.* I wiped my dirty hands on a tea towel. That was the alarm, which meant someone was attacking the shield. At that moment Jacq glanced in my direction. Seeing me framed in the window, she mouthed, "Stay there." Then she and Mynx took off, running toward the disturbance.

Like hell I would. Did I look like a dog? If evil knocks on my door, I meet it—pink pajamas, bunny slippers, and all!

Of course, weapons would help. I looked around. I had none. I'd have to lose some time and head to the training room, which was in the wrong direction. I was almost to the kitchen door when a flash of metal caught my eye.

Yes!

For once, being absentminded worked in my favor. My practice sword still leaned against the doorjamb where I'd left it two nights ago. The sword's blade was dull, but it didn't have to be sharp to smack someone over the head.

The only question was who to hit first: Our uninvited guest trying to breach the wards or the high-handed guest about to defend them?

As I ran toward the front door, another longer louder shudder hit. Jacq and Mynx had to go around, giving me a chance to get there first. Though it would've been better if I weren't wearing slippers. Floppy ears and soft, no-traction bottoms were not sprinter-friendly. But of course if my aunt were to ask later, I'd state that I walked through the house with ladylike decorum. I'd claim I did not run with a sword (which, though dull for practice, is probably deemed more dangerous than scissors). I did not step on Hex's tail. And there was no need for me to curse a blue streak as my slippers did not slide on the hardwood floor. This did not cause me to bump into the buffet table holding Aunt Helen's favorite (now broken…possibly by the cat? At least, that's my story.) vase.

My ladylike stroll ended with me reaching the wards seconds before the others. Jacq scowled when she saw me, but perhaps her sense of self-preservation had finally kicked in because she didn't comment. We stood on the grass directly in front of our drive. As the alarm's cause became apparent, I was very glad to have parked Susie on this side of the swirling blue and green barrier. Three hellhounds were separated from us only by the magical wall. Two were hurling themselves against the wards like kamikaze battering rams. A much larger, third hound was sniffing around my old Silverado.

My jaw dropped, metaphorically. In reality, my teeth were clenched tightly together. Hellhounds were rare, usually staying in, well, Hell. Or rather they lived in the Otherworld, but Hell was much easier to say. A hound there served the same purpose as a hound here. The Demon Elite bred them for hunting. Only the Otherworld's game usually looked like prehistoric horrors. Consider the type of dogs necessary to take on something from the Mesozoic Era, and you would have a picture of Hell's hounds. Larger than the largest Great Dane with a pit bull's locking jaws and the magical ability to track their prey through any plane of existence, they would never be mistaken for anything from Earth. Did I mention their eyes glow an eerie, cliché red? Well, they did. No matter the hound or the location, one thing was always the same: Blood sport wasn't much fun when it was your blood they aimed to spill.

"Bad puppy!" I yelled as the hound sniffing my Chevy lifted a leg. It was nearly the size of a small pony. Knowing my luck, the flood of demonic pee about to erupt would do something weird—like melt rubber. This was a serious matter. I couldn't afford new tires right now, but Mynx and Jacq, both laughing loudly behind my back, obviously didn't see it that way.

I hopped on one foot then the other, removing my slippers. Noticing my footwear, the two laughed louder. I spared Mynx, who knew better, one glare. Then I gave her a wicked smile, immediately strangling her glee. Jacq, unsuspecting, continued to chuckle, the rich sound flowing free. If I had been in a better mood, I might've enjoyed how it made her eyes sparkle.

I again faced the hounds, hearing Mynx's, "Uh-oh," just as my magic whipped out. *Sesame*. One of the larger ley-line areas dropped, and I hurled one bunny slipper after another at the urinating mutt. It's a scientific fact: Bunny slippers make excellent distractions. Plus, the slippers would have to be thrown out anyway. For some unimaginable reason, they had little vase bits embedded in their bottoms.

"A little warning next time," Jacq complained as she and Mynx stepped forward to face the two hounds now barreling toward my opened door. Auburn hair glowing in the sunshine, Jacq eyed my sword then moved to stand between me and the wards. I didn't know if it was her natural protective instincts, if she saw my dull blade as insufficient, or if she simply doubted my battle skills. Whatever her reasoning, it only served to further piss me off.

"Certainly. The next time the big bad comes a knockin' and I decide to let them in, I'll be sure and send out a memo first."

I grew up in a house with four mother figures. My innocent act was flawless, but with sarcasm, there was always room for improvement.

Mynx only gave a Cheshire grin, happy to have the legendary Delacy temper directed at someone other than herself. But my glare must've needed work, because the harder I scowled, the more amused Jacq became.

I watched as each woman took a hound. Mine was still happily chewing Mr. Bunny's ears, so I raised the wards. It could stay on that side until we were ready for it. Although my dull sword might've been more effective at tripping the hounds than cutting them, I joined the fight.

The battle was a bloody thing of beauty. Time slowed. Our breathing evened, and the adrenaline flowed. I was oblivious to the sting of rocks cutting my bare feet or the warm sweat trickling down my back. There was only us three, floating across a sea of grass, determined to kill these nightmarish things.

Slash. Cut. Dodge. Thrust. The hounds were built for tracking, speed, and stamina. But they couldn't turn quickly. Within moments, both were seriously wounded. However, every wound healed, and they kept coming. As if by unspoken consensus, magic began to simultaneously run down our swords.

Mynx's magic glowed greenish-gold. Jacq's shimmered silver, like the runes now blazing from her sword. I used my weaker, green earth-magic. As I watched, every cut Jacq made glowed with the silver runes. Then those glowing glyphs slid into the hounds' bodies. Not only did those wounds not heal, they continued to grow as time progressed. The spell seemed familiar, but I couldn't remember from where. And there was no time to consider the missing memory.

One hound went down. Jacq stepped aside to finish it. Mynx had the other cornered. It fell, and she prepared to take its head. I turned my attention to locating the third.

Fighting in the daytime was always surreal. Blood and gore were meant for the dark of night. But that's not always how it goes. The grass beneath my feet was warm. The sky was bright with only a few nimbus clouds hanging against a blue horizon. The smell of May's early roses was in the air. Oh, and there was Death, Magic and Evil-Intent lurking. See? It doesn't sound right. And it didn't feel right.

Everything had ended too easily, but I couldn't pinpoint the cause of my unease. It was simply a bad feeling—a sudden heavy weight in my gut, a painful clutch at my heart.

I approached the wards, tracking the other women from the corner of my eye. The last hound was nowhere to be seen, which might explain my unrest, but the wooded area our drive cut through was quiet. Still. No giant monster creeping in the shadows. I turned back to the others.

At some point, Mynx had moved between me and her downed hound. I moved to keep them both in sight. Sunlight glinted off steel as she swung for its head. As the sword arced downward, the hound lunged. Maybe it had been playing possum. Maybe it had been truly dead and had reanimated.

Whatever its previous condition, it was now very much alive. The hound swerved her death stroke, its bulk ramming Mynx's side, knocking her off-balance. She fell, but I didn't have time to worry for anyone but myself as the hound headed directly for me. Hoping escape was its goal, I lunged sideways, opening a ward door with a thought. But the hound stopped only feet away, looking from me to the wards. It turned, rearing. Razor-sharp claws tore toward my breast. Eyes widening, I instinctively swung my sword to block but knew I was too slow.

This was so gonna hurt.

Suddenly I was pushed aside. Jacq cried out as she took my place. Momentarily dazed, I lay on my face then rolled about. My unmoving rescuer lay a length away. Dark red blood flowed onto the green grass from a slash in Jacq's side. Something inside me broke.

NO! I wasn't sure if my scream was in my head or aloud. I tore my eyes from the gruesome tableau to the more grim sight of a hound straddling Jacq, jaws ready to sink into a pale throat.

In my periphery, I saw an unarmed Mynx regain her feet. No time. By some miracle, my sword had landed only inches from my hand. But it would take too long to stand and stop the descending jaws. Acting on instinct, I grasped the familiar leather hilt and called my fire, picturing the form I needed. For once, my magic obeyed without hesitation, running down the blade. For a millisecond, my body and mind were frozen. I'd only ever thrown magic from my hands, never my blade. But this was the fastest way. No choice. It had to work. My blue eyes fixed on the hound's glowing red ones, and I let go.

Like a javelin, a spear of dancing red flames shot through the air, straight into the hound's gaping jaws. I'd aimed square between its eyes, but that would work. The hellhound's legs locked in death then began to collapse. Dropping my sword, I lunged to my feet and half-dragged, half-carried an unconscious Jacq away.

We collapsed in a heap near the crumbling corpse. Like my anger at the hound's actions, my fire raged on, consuming the dead beast. I breathed through my mouth, ignoring the nauseating scent of burning flesh. Holding Jacq between my spread legs, I cradled her to my chest, quickly beginning a healing chant.

I distantly saw Mynx sever the hound's smoldering head, ensuring it stayed dead this time. Though this healing wouldn't require my consciousness to leave my body, I was still vulnerable. Bloody sword in hand, Mynx took up a guard position, joining me in the chant. But she kept her distance, knowing the dangers of disrupting a healing.

Jacq. I ran my hand down her cool cheek. "Stupid, chivalrous woman." I had a moment to realize I'd said that aloud then I dropped into myself, seeking the healer within. My mind's eye rose, extending to where my body touched Jacq's, then further, scanning her. I released a mental sigh of relief. There were no internal injuries, only four bone-deep slashes. Beginning beside her left breast, they curved downward over her ribs and inward across her abdomen, stopping right above her navel.

The bleeding slowed as I poured magic in, knitting muscles, repairing cells. The wounds healed quickly—more so than my skills warranted. The list of Sups that healed this fast was short. But at this moment, I wasn't interested in another clue to Jacq's species but simply glad that no matter what she eventually revealed herself to be, our detective was obviously on that list. As the gushing blood slowed to a near trickle, her pulse steadied, then sped, her heart soon beating strongly against my palm where it lay just below her breast. I relaxed, taking my first deep breath since seeing Jacq's still form.

She would live.

Nearly finished, I took a moment to look past the bones and sinew and *truly* see my patient. If possible, Jacq was even more beautiful when viewed this way. As her magic flowed below and over her skin, she glowed softly with a silver so pure it was nearly white, its shine slowly intensifying as she recovered. And it wasn't alone. Currents of green earth and red fire magic whispered around us. Unbidden, the latter had risen, and I was too distracted to push it down again. My hands never strayed from Jacq's side, but as I watched, my fire—without my consent or control—made its own, less-noble intentions known.

A haze of green covered my hands, healing, while red ribbons of flame explored Jacq's body. Tracing a smooth collarbone. Twining around long limbs. Mapping strong planes of face and form. Sliding through silky hair. New and definitely not part of the healing process, I felt every fiery burst of power like an extension of my own hands… touching her…learning her…lov…No, I wouldn't even think it.

This was way beyond checking for harm. It went against my healer's oath, but I couldn't rein myself in. My head knew she was okay, but it was as if my magic needed its own reassurance.

Jacq's magic responded in kind, the silver glow rippling, sparking where our magic touched, as if she had her own fire burning deep. I held her in my arms and watched as our fires touched. Instead of raging against each other, consuming themselves in a blazing oblivion, they melted together, forming one whole. The nearly golden glow was so bright I averted my eyes. But sparing my sight did nothing for the rest of me.

I dimly heard Mynx shouting my name but couldn't respond. She stood near, unable to touch us for fear of making things worse. I wanted to reassure her, but the sensation of merging magic left me speechless. A hundred times stronger than yesterday's fleeting joining, it was an all-consuming rush beyond passion, beyond pleasure. Although there was plenty of that, as well.

The physical reaction was unimaginable. My breathing hitched. My heart pounded. Warmth streaked from my breasts to my groin, electricity flashing through me to Jacq and back again—a live wire arcing between us. As another powerful burst hit, my back arched, arms tightening convulsively. But even as my body drew Jacq closer, a small part of me tried to push her away.

It saw the magic. It felt the flames. And it knew a fear like no other.

And with good reason. Because stronger than the magic, more powerful than my body's reaction, was the sense of rightness. A frighteningly familiar feeling. That part of me that could still think, still feel, screamed, *No! No! No!* This couldn't be happening. Not now. Not with her.

And yet, it was.

An unconscious Jacq moaned. From pleasure? From pain? I wasn't sure. But if she was experiencing a tenth of what I was, then it was the former. I gasped, jerking my magic and consciousness back just as she awoke.

My eyes locked with ones gone completely silver with something unrecognizable. I blushed, understanding how our position appeared. At some point, we'd reclined on the warm lawn, my legs wrapping around hers. My head was tilted forward, hers back, cushioned between my achingly sensitive breasts. I took a deep breath, watching her pupils dilate. I could smell the copper of blood mixed with her unique sage-sandalwood scent, and it was disturbingly arousing.

Part of me wanted to stay there, in the bloody grass and sunshine, and hold her until the dark and cold forced us apart. So I did the only logical thing.

I ran.

I scrambled to disengage, standing quickly. Stone-faced, Mynx jabbed her crimson-stained blade in the grass and helped Jacq sit. I had trouble meeting either woman's eyes. "Stay." My voice was gruff, unintentionally expressing my own body's demands. I grimaced, realizing too late I'd also unintentionally repeated Jacq's earlier words.

Jacq snorted, "As my lady commands." The confident, almost sarcastic response didn't match the strained lines around her mouth.

I laughed. Something in my chest simultaneously eased and tightened. Humor was good, but the flutter her wording caused was not. Brushing it aside, I said, "Careful you don't look for trouble. Just ask this one." I nodded toward Mynx, who grunted in silent affirmation. "I can be a harsh taskmaster. Speaking of which, think you can stand with some help?" The gashes were barely bleeding, but Jacq was still too pale. I wasn't sure how much blood she'd already lost. If the old saying was true and blood really did make the grass grow, then to my disconcerted eye the red-black puddle spreading across the green lawn would keep us in fertilizer for a long time.

"Yes." Jacq nodded then groaned at the movement. As Mynx and I moved to lift her, our eyes met over her auburn head. Mynx's face was carefully bare, but I saw the concern in her eyes. I shook my head. If

I wasn't ready to talk about it to myself, I certainly wasn't ready to talk with someone else.

We carefully proceeded to carry Jacq to the house. But of course there is always a silver lining, which I managed to find as we settled our guest in the kitchen for a little Dr. Delacy home medicine. With an injured guest, two mutilated hellhound corpses on the front lawn, a blood trail drying in the sun, and general chaos abounding, it was unlikely that my aunt would notice the demise of her favorite vase... at least not any time soon.

CHAPTER SEVEN

"Many Magical creatures mate for life. Others cannot propagate until they find their biological match. See the mating dance of the elusive Brownie…"

—*Discovery Supernatural Channel*

Jacq might have been more comfortable in a guest room rather than leaning against the kitchen table, but lugging her upstairs was beyond us. By the time we dragged the injured, surprisingly heavy woman through the front hall, past the broken vase, and into the kitchen, I was out of breath. Mynx arched a brow at the porcelain jumble scattered across the hardwood floors, thankfully not saying a word at my muttered, "I know nothing. I see nothing."

I gazed at the blood slowly dripping onto the kitchen's brown tiles, trying not to let my anger show. Was I angry with myself for being careless or with Jacq for taking a blow meant for me? Probably both. Mynx took one look at my face and silently left the room. I knew without asking that the practical brunette was getting our bloody guest clean clothes.

Jacq looked from me to Mynx's retreating back and misunderstood. "Don't blame Mynx. This was my fault. Maybe if I'd been faster, more attentive." She huffed, roughly pushing a blood-splattered hand through her hair.

Needing to keep busy, I turned, becoming a whirlwind of motion as I gathered supplies. My words were clipped, my movements jerky as I pulled things from cabinets and drawers. "Absolutely. It's your fault you're a stubborn, chivalrous, brave, stupid woman who pushed me aside so that thing could maul you instead." A cabinet door banged as I closed it. "I blame you fully for getting between me and its claws. Claws, by the way, that wouldn't have gotten near me if I'd been more attentive." I shoved a drawer closed with my hip, setting the herbs I'd pulled from it on the counter. "So, of course that must also be your fault." Spinning around, I blew a strand of hair from my eyes, gesturing to her top, making an effort to calm down. "But what's done is done. Let me see how badly you're hurt."

Jacq crossed her arms, grimacing slightly. "The wound will heal on its own. There's no need…"

At my glower, her words petered out. I *knew* the wound would heal. I'd made certain of it. That wasn't good enough. I was weak, worried, and expecting a killer headache from using so much magic. None of which put me in the best mood.

"Count yourself blessed. I only want to clean and bandage it. If Aunt Helena were here, she'd be poking at you with a needle and thread. Of course if you'd rather wait for her tender care…" I waved my hand. Jacq's sudden, almost frightened expression was nearly laughable.

Before I could blink, she whipped the tattered shirt up, stopping just below her breasts. I sucked in a breath, stopping my hand before it reached to touch the angry slashes that ran around her ribs and over her stomach. I'd seen them with my magic. But it had been more an idea of a thing, not right there in black and white…or, in this case, crimson and rose. Luckily, the cuts no longer appeared as deep. Most of the blood seemed to be dripping from her clothes.

"Here." I handed her a clean tea towel from the counter. "Put pressure on it before I change my mind about those stitches." I turned to the sink to fill a bowl with warm water, herbs and salt to purify the wound. Vaguely hearing Mynx's return followed by the familiar *snick*, *snick* of a zipper, I studiously focused on my task, refusing to think about the woman undressing mere feet behind me.

Once I was finished filling two bowls, one with the solution and another with water, I turned back to find Jacq wearing another of Mynx's outfits. A harsh exhale whistled between my teeth and I put the bowls down hard, sloshing water onto the table. The pants were similar to what she'd worn earlier, but the top was much different. A charcoal sleeveless T with the bottom half cut off, it ended right below her breasts, exposing a great deal of hard, muscled midriff along with her wounds. Mynx had presumably left to dispose of the bloody clothes, leaving Jacq and me alone. Together. Like last night and the night before. But after our intimate moment on the lawn, this felt like so much more.

"Uh." Anger suddenly lost, I swallowed hard, not meeting Jacq's eyes. "Whenever you're ready." Gesturing to a kitchen chair, I wiped up my spill then turned to retrieve our old black doctor's bag. I'd intended for her to sit, so I could kneel at her feet and ply my angel-of-mercy skills. But Jacq had other plans. When I turned back, she was sitting on the table. I found myself standing between her spread legs. *When had this room gotten so small?*

Self-conscious, I wanted to move then apologize but did neither. Both would be admitting that Jacq made me uncomfortable. Instead, I moved closer, reaching around her body to soak my washcloth in the cleansing solution. I was so focused that Jacq's next words nearly made me jump.

"You look a bit flushed. Perhaps Helena should ensure you are well, also." Her words were low, serious, but there was something else there.

I looked up. Her eyes sparkled, but her lips were locked in a grim line. Was she teasing me? I couldn't tell. Looking back down, I took a deep breath and gave myself a pep talk. *It's just a bloody scratch, and she's just a woman...a really hot woman.* Literally.

"No, I'm fine. Probably too much sun." Swallowing, I stared, unseeing, at the torso before me. A torso giving off wave after wave of heat much stronger than yesterday's intentional *zings*. It poured off her body and seeped into mine. How had I not noticed this before? Some could be from exertion. But not all. I ran pretty hot due to my fire magic, but Jacq was several degrees hotter. In a way, it was a good thing. Like yesterday's bath, my body fed on that heat.

With my metabolism's sudden jump, the last phers burned from my system. Unfortunately, they'd already been so weak I couldn't blame the chemicals for my reaction during the healing. And I couldn't blame them for my reaction now.

We lapsed into a long silence. Jacq's body was tense, her eyes following me as I cleaned blood and sweat away from the wound, repeatedly reaching around her to dip the cloth into the herbed water. For balance, I placed my hand on Jacq's iron-hard thigh but quickly pulled back as her muscles jumped. Too late, her scorching heat had already sent delicious tingles racing up my arm.

I reached for the disinfectant, smelling her unique scent mix with the eye-watering punch of antiseptic. "Sorry, this is going to sting."

"It'll be all right, cher." Jacq spoke softly, her whiskey-rich voice lapsing into a surprisingly pleasant Cajun accent much stronger than yesterday's slip.

She didn't flinch as I applied the painful chemicals, though her knuckles went white as her hands gripped the old table's edge. As if in sympathy, a burning pain at my own side briefly flared. I frowned but dismissed the strange sensation, moving quickly onward. Jaw set, Jacq watched me with eyes smoky gray, flickering with some elusive emotion as I pried each bloody hand loose from the table. She opened her mouth to argue, but shut it again as I dipped each into the clean water before cupping her hot fingers and gently rubbing each bloody knuckle clean. Her fingers twitched in my grasp, and I pretended not to notice.

My braid had loosened during the battle. So as I worked I bent my head forward, letting my loose locks hide my own carousel of expressions. My brain and body were muddled. *Why was I still standing here? Why was I washing her hands?* She wasn't so helpless that she couldn't do this for herself. I didn't have an answer. For whatever reason, I had the nearly overwhelming urge to fit my hand into hers. *Were these feelings mutual? More so, did I want to act on them?* I briefly looked at Jacq. Her half-lidded eyes were nearly silver again. That answered one question.

Desire in a woman's eyes didn't look that different from a man's. Unless I was merely projecting my own desires onto the first available person in sight. It had been three lonely years. I could be tilting at windmills, seeing dragons of want in her when there were none. Whether real or simply a projection, the expression in those eyes left my emotions spinning. I peeked again at Jacq. She looked as if she wanted to consume me.

My heart jumped but the rest of me stood still. For a moment I was frozen, staring into Jacq's eyes. She didn't move or speak. I knew that look, that hunger. I'd seen it in my own eyes before, as recently as the night we'd met. It was the kind where one knew they would never partake of the pleasure they craved. And it was most definitely *not* my imagination. Coming to my senses, I released a mental sigh that was part regret, part relief. At least she knew better than to act on this.

I reluctantly placed Jacq's hands back on the table then moved a little closer, applying more pressure to the wound. Not realizing that Mynx was back, I was startled when she said, "I'm going to shower. I'll fix breakfast when I'm done so you two can clean up."

My mind momentarily blanked, thinking of hot water and warm flesh. I shook myself from those thoughts before I could add a face to the fantasy. The combination of adrenaline, phers, our near-miss and an extremely intimate magical joining had obviously robbed me of my wits and turned me into some mindless sex fiend. I looked up in time to see the exiting Mynx smile and pat Jacq on the shoulder, saying, "Be well."

"Hold this." I placed Jacq's hand on the gauze and quickly stepped outside the circle of her legs.

"I think that is the most Mynx has said since we met," Jacq said quietly.

Surprised, I half-choked, half-laughed before turning, searching the drawers for an Ace bandage. "You're right. She doesn't say much, but it's not necessary with us. We've known each other so long that we just know what the other's thinking. There's a level of trust there that few have." I couldn't see Jacq's face, so her next words surprised me.

"Trust, yes. But if you were my partner, I wouldn't let you stand so close to another…or hold another the way you held me earlier."

I blushed, thankful she couldn't see my face. That answered the question as to what she'd noticed. But surely, she didn't mean "partner" like it sounded. Just in case, I tried to explain without actually explaining.

"Mynx knows I'm a big girl, Detective, and can take care of myself. I trust her to do the same. Our relationship works well. I think this morning showed that. That trust and knowing that I can count on her to do her job are some of the reasons I made her a partner in the business."

Suddenly too warm, I paused, stripping off my sweater, revealing the pink T that matched my PJ bottoms, mulling over the shirt in my hands. Would spot remover work on hellhound gore? At least two globs of red and brown ooze marred the pink fuzz. "Besides, it's a family business. And Mynx is family. In fact, she helped raise me."

"You're not lovers?"

At the quiet, barely heard question, my shoulders tensed. My hand landed on the needed bandage, but I didn't turn, instead softly saying to the window, "No, not lovers. Mynx may not be my sister by blood, but she's my sister in every other way." Unable to avoid it any longer, I faced my patient.

Seeing the red fuzzy valentine monsters with heart antennae chasing bouncing pink hearts across my shirt's chest, Jacq's stiff, almost pained expression morphed into silent laughter. The monsters mimicked those in an animated kids' movie and were one of the reasons I loved this shirt so much. (Although I'd have to be tied down and tortured with a branding iron before I'd ever admit that aloud.)

"Hey, these were a gift from my aunt. If someone gives me a gift, I wear it. It's the 'nice' thing to do." I made air quotes, giving her a fake angry look before crossing my arms over my chest. "Plus, they're verrry comfortable."

"Oh no, don't misunderstand me. I like them verrry much."

Jacq's tone again had that thick accent. I suppressed a shiver that had nothing to do with the A/C.

"And you'd better call me Jacq. You wouldn't want me to develop a 'complex'." She made her own air quotes then shrugged, adding at my surprised look, "An immortal that refuses to change when the language does is quickly discovered."

"A complex, oh no." Hand on forehead, I faked a swoon. "Mustn't have that. Jacq, it is then." I couldn't help but smile. Momentarily at ease, I busied myself putting items back in their proper places. I said quickly, "Hold the gauze there a minute more. Once the bleeding stops, we'll wrap it." It wasn't necessary to wait, but though the tension of the moment was broken, I needed time to collect myself. I put up all the medical supplies but what was necessary to finish bandaging her side then dropped to my knees to scrub the bloody floor. Jacq looked like she wanted to protest but stopped herself.

Once again, I could feel her watching me work. Had I missed something? Her gaze suddenly seemed hotter, her hunger stronger. Confused, I swallowed hard and snuck a glance. Tense again, Jacq was coiled to spring from the table at any second. The room began to shrink once more. By the time I moved to finish bandaging her ribs, all traces of laughter were gone from Jacq's face, as well as my own. This time, I stood outside her right thigh and used butterfly strips to pull the wound together before taping the gauze in place, rushing, not letting even my trembling fingertips linger a second more than necessary.

Jacq sat quietly as I wrapped the bandage around and around, securing the gauze. On my last pass, I accidentally brushed the underside of a shockingly bare breast. At her quick hitch in breath, I looked up, seeing eyes completely silver with desire staring at my lips. There was no doubt about that look. Something had changed. She wouldn't be holding back any longer. I almost kicked myself for correcting her misunderstanding about Mynx, but I was incapable of intentionally misleading her. I hastily stepped back, leaving her to tuck in the bandage.

"Cate, wait." Jacq's voice was anxious.

I looked at her knees, not wanting to see those eyes…that face… or that body right now. She lifted a hand toward me.

"No, I can't do this." Trying to keep the panic from my voice, I took another step back, suddenly feeling claustrophobic. I skirted the table, heading for the door. I knew without looking that she had turned to watch my retreat. "I'm going to shower. I'm sure Mynx is out by now."

"Why?" The crack in Jacq's voice stopped me, but I still couldn't face her.

"Because I'm dirty and sweaty and smell like demonic dingoes." I intentionally misunderstood. Too bad my conscience wouldn't let me stop at that. "I'm sorry, if I misled you." I took a breath, letting it out slowly, my gaze staying on the open archway that led to the hall and freedom. A few feet had never seemed so far. I knew she could see my stiff shoulders and clenched fists, but I couldn't pretend that this didn't matter. And I couldn't walk away without saying one last thing. "I'm not myself right now."

Inexplicably, there were tears in my eyes…and maybe also in my voice. I didn't know if they were tears of frustration, apology, or something else. I had the overwhelming urge to trust her. To stay and explain the phers' effects and that the signals I was sending couldn't be real. To explain that I'd never before been attracted to a woman. To explain that I was scared by the connection we'd shared as our magic merged. To explain that I would never settle for anything less than growing old together, and she would never grow old. There was much that I wanted to say, maybe needed to say. Instead, I walked away.

I didn't need eyes in the back of my head to know that Jacq sat, motionless, watching me go. Just past the door, outside her line of vision, I stopped to wipe away my tears, not wanting to explain to Mynx why I was crying, especially since I couldn't explain it to myself. My moment's hesitation was the only reason I heard her last, whispered words, "If you're not you, then who are you?"

I wish I knew.

* * *

Three Years Ago

The spell wasn't complicated. *But the cost?* It was more than I was willing to pay. So I had changed it. Rearranging spells was dangerous, but with time and patience it could be done. Too bad I had neither. Magic was at its highest today of all days. There wouldn't be another equinox or solstice for months. I was desperate.

It had to be today.

I stood in my veil and white dress in a circle of green magic deep in the woods, looking down at my altar. The candles. The knife. Everything was prepared. It had been a wonderful ceremony, but something had been wrong. Maybe I'd noticed my mother's absence more because most of the faces had been unfamiliar. My new husband was still at the reception, smiling, greeting those strangers. In a few minutes they would notice my absence. It was dangerous to hurry, but grief had numbed my mind and removed any caution I might have felt.

I began the chant, twisting here and there the changed words. The spell required a person to give blood freely and suffer greatly. This person was not meant to be the spell's conductor, but I couldn't ask another to make this sacrifice.

Hissing with pain, I sliced one wrist then the other—shallow wounds meant to bleed but not kill. If I was dead I couldn't complete my task. My spine stiffened as blood flowed into the ceremonial bowl and the true pain began. I tightened my grip on the altar, standing straight. Whips of magic swirled in the air, licking at my skin with dark red tongues…pulling at my pinned black tresses…caressing me with icy fire that seared my muscles and sizzled my bones.

With every second, my agony grew tenfold. I locked my jaw, swallowing a scream. Red covered my sight. *Was there blood in my eyes or was this the spell?* No matter. It was too late to go back. All that was left was to keep my eyes open and wait for the vision.

I suddenly felt exhausted. *My strength…where…why?* The dim words moved slowly through my mind. Then I understood. The cuts were deepening. *This was wrong.* There was too much blood, too much pain. The bowl was nearly full, its blood dark red like the spell's magic. The spell was exacting a higher price as my penalty for changing what had been written.

I clung to the altar as my knees weakened and my ears roared. If the price was higher so would be the reward. That was the law. Debts must be paid. The magic owed me. And I'd be damned if I would quit without collecting.

I held on, repeating the spell until my tongue became too thick. My flowing blood slowed to a trickle. *But was I healing or had I no more blood to give?* My arms became weak, my heavy eyes closing. Hazy images formed in my mind. Another minute and they would be clear. This was the answer I so desperately sought.

But time had run out.

My weakened limbs gave way. "*No!*" I clutched at the altar. It was no use. My bloody fingers slipped. I reached deep inside for strength, magic, anything to stand a few moments more. At the desperate call, something inside me unlocked. Strength and power flooded in… seconds too late. I tumbled backward, breaking my circle.

As if dreaming, I watched from outside my body as I fell, my head hitting the soft ground with a loud *thump*. My white lacy sleeve caught on the altar and the wooden table fell toward me. A sudden miraculous wind pushed it aside a heartbeat before it could land on my head. The bowl hung in the air for an impossible moment before its collected blood rained down on me. My last thought before the dreams began was that I had failed.

I awoke six days later still wearing my wedding dress, though its once pristine whiteness had been dyed a dark red pattern that seemed to shift when viewed from the corner of the eye. It wasn't until that moment when I awoke and saw my family and new husband, Lucas, all sitting by my bedside, watching me anxiously, faces haggard and eyes bloodshot from worry and tears, that I knew I had been wrong. The price had been paid and a gift given. I remembered little of what

I had seen, but it was enough to know this: I had changed. What I knew of the world had changed. And my life and the lives of those I loved would never be the same again.

I would never be the same again.

CHAPTER EIGHT

"Southern hospitality is best served with coffee and pound cake, but Krispy Kremes will do in a pinch."
—Gwendolyn (Nana) Alecé Delacy

It was well past ten when we pulled up to The Blue Moon Club in New Orleans. I'd met Jacq at her home, and we'd ridden in silence while the radio quietly played old rock ballads. There was too much that couldn't be said. So while my body sat in the car with my Council-assigned babysitter, my mind went over the day's events.

After my shower, I'd been both relieved and disappointed to go downstairs and find Jacq already gone. She'd merely left a note with directions to her home. We'd agreed the night before to meet there and ride to the club together. I'd immediately gone to clean up the shattered vase but had found it once again whole and in its rightful place. Mynx had denied the miracle, so it hadn't been difficult to guess who had saved me from a long lecture.

Throughout breakfast, my freshly returned aunt gave me strange looks. Mynx had filled Aunt Helena in on the battle royal with the hounds, but she wouldn't have said anything about my interactions with Jacq. Even when I was a child, Mynx had safeguarded my secrets. Aunt Helena was either waiting for the other shoe to drop or she sensed my turbulent emotions. My money was on both. That woman was either an empath…or she had a damnably reliant crystal ball.

I'd spent the morning cleaning up our lawn then checked outside the wards for the third hound, but all that remained was one saliva-soaked floppy ear from a slipper. The afternoon was spent shaking down every shady contact I had in The Burg, looking for more information on Nicodemus. Either no one knew anything or they were running scared.

I'd swung by Isabella's apartment. As expected, I'd found the same thing Jacq had. Nothing. The place had been wiped clean of all magic, including Isabella's. There was only faded Were musk and an overwhelming sense of sadness, as if the walls had been painted with buckets of grief. I hadn't been inclined to linger. I'd spoken with Isabella's neighbors and called her few friends. All had painted her as a sweet, shy girl. By rights, she should've had more friends than the few listed in her cell. But I understood all too well. Isabella had been hiding her magic all her life. That made it hard to make connections. Seeing bits of the past, future or present undoubtedly compounded the difficulty.

I'd returned home with enough time to shower, dress in my favorite faded jeans and tight light green sleeveless shirt. Its gold-threaded streaks looked clubby but actually contained several protective spells. The shirt ended right above my navel, leaving its piercing visible. I'd changed out my normal everyday stud with a golden phoenix. Maybe it was the fire or maybe the symbolism. For whatever reason, I'd always liked this bird that rose from its ashes.

I was more discreet with my weapons. If the bouncers—who were bound to be Weres—scented silver, both Jacq and I would be searched. I'd explained this last night. Jacq had cheekily replied that she wouldn't bring a weapon. I hadn't believed her for a second. However, she was welcome to walk into the lion's den unarmed. If her ass got mauled, I could always resuscitate her long enough to say "I told you so."

I'd settled on silver-coated knives in synthetic sheaths tucked into each light brown leather ass-kicker boot. The sheaths were tight enough that the scent of silver wouldn't escape. The draw wouldn't be as fast as a well-oiled leather sheath. But they'd have to do. Leather breathes, and the body-heated oil would carry the scent of silver to a Were's nose better than a homing pigeon.

At the last minute I'd activated four suppression amulets, tucking them into a belt made of hollow antique brass medallions that draped around my hips. Each medallion was actually a well-disguised pouch

containing titanium throwing stars and a few inactive amulets—
amongst other things.

A pair of enspelled jade earrings completed my outfit. I'd never
had much patience for makeup. That's why my nicer pieces held
complexion charms. This one would provide a deep red lipstick, a hint
of blush and smoky eye shadow. I could kick butt all night long and
my mascara would never run. As an added bonus, the jade brought
out the gold in my eyes. A quick look in the mirror confirmed that
between my shirt and the earrings, my eyes were a swirling blue-
green. I'd twisted my hair into several small braids, which I'd worked
into an intricate knot at my nape. The wind whipping through the
Jeep's open doors would make a mess of anything loose.

I'd left two hours early, driven Susie into the heart of New Orleans,
and walked up and down Bourbon Street, checking the tourist
haunts and locals' bars for Jupiter Jones. But I never saw him. It was
a Thursday night. The musician might've stayed home. However,
within ten minutes, Jup would've known that I was looking for him.
Nothing happened in New Orleans that he didn't know it. But when
he wanted to hide, he did a damn good job of it. And apparently he'd
wanted to tonight. After one more quick loop around, I'd left to meet
Jacq.

I pulled into a crushed seashell drive bordered by tall, green
hedges. The cottage-style house was rose colored with dark brown
shutters. Charming and unassuming, it seemed at odds with its
mysterious, compelling owner.

Jacq, leaning against a sporty silver Corvette's hood, was waiting
for me. Parking just beyond the security light, I cut the engine and
pretended to look for something in my glove compartment while
examining her from the shadowed darkness. I'd had time to deal with
my earlier reactions, making that moment my first time to see Jacq
with eyes clear of confusion and phers.

Only one word did her justice: Wowza. Don't be surprised.
Women think other women look good even when lust isn't involved.
And boy, did Jacq look good.

She was no longer an Amazon. Tonight's outfit screamed
gunslinger, even though there were no telltale bulges. She wore
high black boots and a floor-length charcoal coat that matched her
trousers. The coat was open, showing a deep blue silk shirt with a
high collar that caressed her neck. Several undone buttons revealed
a hint of cleavage. Her eyes, no longer smoky, were fathomless pools

of that deep, deep blue. She had a black necklace with a barely visible silver medallion nesting between her breasts.

My eyes had caught on that flash of silver. Even without the phers' influence and our magical joining, there was still a strong attraction that was all me. That realization had shaken me. I'd shifted uncomfortably in the seat before pocketing my keys and leaving the Jeep.

"Cate." Jacq's husky whisper, too close to my left ear, broke my train of thought. "Our escort's here."

We stood on the club's second floor—a blue-and-silver decorated loft with lots of private rooms for "meetings." I looked to see a tall female Were approaching. She had chestnut hair and was dressed in a slimming wine-colored suit. The look was a little too *Charlie's Angels* for my taste. But it worked for her.

"Miss Delacy?"

I recognized that musical voice from yesterday's call. Strikingly beautiful with high cheekbones and chocolate eyes, the woman looked familiar, but I couldn't place her. "Yes?" My tone was neutral, my face blank.

Although the meeting was set in the Alpha's territory, only Kyle had been mentioned. The woman had said nothing of involving the Alpha, but she was dressed too nicely for anything else. Either something had changed, or I'd been intentionally misled. Likely the latter. Jacq must've been of a like mind, because her face was again masked, this time with congeniality. The woman's next words confirmed my assumptions.

"I'm Becca. The Alpha will see you now." She gestured to a half-hidden staircase in the corner. Becca led, and we followed. I'd thought this trip was going to be a bust. But if the Alpha was involved, then something big was up.

We were stopped at the top by several Weres who did a quick pat down and amulet scan. Either they didn't notice the knives in my boots or disregarded them as insignificant. The Weres were confident that no one would attack in the middle of their Alpha's stronghold. That would cost them someday. My suppression amulets and complexion charm registered as mundane on their scanner, and we were allowed past. I was surprised to see that Jacq, good to her word, was indeed unarmed.

The third level was more open with brighter lighting, dark cherry hardwood floors, and high ceilings. As we passed through several large rooms, all continuing the red theme with dark rosewood furnishings and a light rose-colored wallpaper, it became evident that the blue theme marked the club area and the red the Alpha's personal space. Surprisingly, the different tones didn't clash. The heat, chatter and music from downstairs could barely be felt through the thick walls. I breathed a sigh of relief as the suppression amulets again overwhelmed the phers that had soaked into my system as we'd passed through the Were-crammed club.

Moving down a long hall, we passed several closed doors. At the end, we reached a large room and what must be the lion's den…or rather, the tiger's. According to Luke, that was the Were Clan leader's other form. As expected, the man himself sat casually on a deep mahogany leather sofa. However, the figure to his right, occupying a smaller matching love seat, was a shock. Jacq bumped my back as my feet refused to move.

"Cate?" Jacq's soft inquiry in my ear brought me to my senses. I subtly shook my head and tried to mask my confusion. We moved farther into the room.

"Miss Delacy," the Alpha said, "I'm Grey Gryphon, Alpha over this territory's Were-Beasts. I believe you know my second, Lucas Deveroux, Alpha of the Wolf Clan." He gestured to an unsmiling Luke, who didn't look at all surprised to see me.

Six months ago, Luke had been fourth in his clan. He'd been a busy boy. I nearly laughed, remembering Luke's assertion that he had "moved up in the Pack." What an understatement. He'd become the m'f'ing head honcho. Why had he left that information out? We were friends. He knew I'd be proud of his accomplishments. Didn't he?

"And this is my consort, Abigail," Grey said.

I tore my gaze from Luke to the beautiful redhead sitting to his left. Dressed comfortably in light purple leggings and a darker purple peasant-style pullover, the loose clothes didn't hide her rosy glow or pregnant bulge. Abigail returned our nods with a smile, flashing white teeth and two dainty fangs. Weres didn't have fangs in human form. And those incisors were too small for the Blood. That left all manner of things (with very sharp teeth) that go bump in the night. But that was a question for another day. From their joined hands and soft smiles, theirs was obviously what my beloved Grams would've called a "love-match."

Both men looked comfortable in dress shirts with rolled up sleeves and open collars. Grey wore khakis with a white shirt that offset his chin-length copper hair. He had a ruddy complexion and bright gold eyes that didn't miss a single detail. I surreptitiously peeked at Luke as we moved to the offered mint-colored armchairs.

Compared to Grey, Luke looked more human, if that could be said of a werewolf. He wore a navy dress shirt. One ankle was crossed over a gun-metal-colored trouser-clad knee. His once unruly sandy brown hair was now a no-nonsense military buzz. Gone was the mischievous grin, but the dark blue eyes were the same. Even dressed up, he still had the rough-and-ready cowboy air that had first caught my attention.

As we were getting settled, I took a moment to search my inner psyche. While I was surprised to see Luke here, my attraction to him was gone and had been for a long time. I'd moved on. We'd been friends and interacted for the last three years without issue. Why should this be any different? It shouldn't, and it wouldn't. Or so I hoped.

We exchanged formal greetings, Jacq making her introductions. The Weres definitely knew of her, but it was unclear as to whether they'd met before. Finally, we got down to business. "We came to speak with Kyle Thompson," Jacq said. So my detective had also noticed an absence in our happy little greeting party.

Everyone looked to Grey, who rumbled, "That's why you're here. But first, my second has advised me, Miss Delacy, that you will likely be armed."

Mated pairs were notoriously protective. A pair expecting kits? Even more so. Threats, intended or otherwise, were dealt with swiftly and mercilessly. Luke fidgeted in his seat before stilling. Good, the wolf knew the position he'd placed me in. Just because I understood his obligation to his Alpha didn't make his stewing in his own guilt any less enjoyable. (I was emotionally sadistic that way.)

I met Grey's gold eyes. "My apologies, Alpha. I had no idea that I would be meeting yourself or your consort this evening. If it eases your mind," I said, meaning every word, "I will gladly relinquish what few weapons I have." No Were would engage in unprovoked violence in the presence of a pregnant female. I wouldn't need my weapons... as long as Abigail was near.

Grey held my eyes. I didn't look down, but after a long period I looked to the side. I wasn't one of his Weres to play dominance games. But neither was I stupid enough to challenge him in his own territory.

"Respect my home," he said, "and no harm will befall you while in my domain." There was a significant pause. "At least, for this evening. Even so, you may keep your weapons. Break my good faith," he spread his arms, "and you will be punished." A look passed between the two men, "Severely." It took a moment before I understood their silent communication. Grey had made Luke responsible for my behavior and possible punishment. Oh no, I was so not playing "spank the bad witch" with my ex. I shot daggers at Luke, who wore a completely neutral expression. I held my tongue, setting my shoulders. If they expected me to do something stupid, they were mistaken.

Grey turned to Jacq. "You need no such reassurance, Detective Slone. But I also trust that you will respect the rules of the Alpha's house."

"As long as no harm befalls myself or my companion, you have my pledge." Jacq's husky tones were solemn, but there was an underlying warning as she added, "For this eventide." Jeez, these people and their fancy speech. Somebody needed to give them a calendar. They'd obviously forgotten what century we were in.

I was pretty sure they'd just said "We'll behave for tonight, but tomorrow all bets are off." Hopefully, Grey's house rules were similar to mine: "Don't pee on the carpet. Don't mess with Grandpa's ashes. And don't kill each other before breakfast." Maybe there was a list tacked up somewhere. I'd hate to inadvertently break a rule and have our safe passage revoked.

"Now that you two have bonded, could you explain where Kyle is?" Despite my exasperation, my tone was respectful. Magical beings always had bigger pissing contests…even if they didn't have bigger everything else.

Abigail answered with a slight Irish brogue, "Kyle is below. His Beast has been agitated since Isabella was taken. My husband," she rolled her eyes at Grey, "would not allow him in my presence."

At that moment, Becca joined us with a tray of café au lait and pastries. Even moon-howlers knew the fine arts of Southern hospitality: food and coffee. She sat the tray down on a low table before serving us. When she was done, she pushed Luke over, squeezing in beside him. I couldn't help but notice that Luke treated Becca with brotherly affection. However, his seatmate seemed to have a different attitude. I smiled into my coffee cup. Some men were clueless.

"Isn't it unusual," I asked, my question muffled as I bit into a delicious chocolate-filled beignet, "for a Were to be unable to control his Beast?"

Becca picked up the tale. "Kyle proposed to Isabella Sunday night. Isabella had asked Kyle not to mention it as she wanted to tell her father herself when she went home this weekend. What is only known to the Pack is that Monday morning, with Isabella's permission of course, Kyle officially claimed her as mate. They had filed a petition to have her turned."

"Mated pairs are magically bonded," Abigail said, picking up the tale. "They're able to sense each other physically and emotionally. Although Kyle only placed his claim days ago, they have actually been bonded since they were young." Abigail's face showed her worry. "Kyle's been separated from his mate, and she's in danger. He has the overwhelming urge to go to Isabella…no matter what. If Kyle loses control, his Wolf will lay waste to anything in his way."

I nodded, understanding what they weren't saying. The spell hiding Isabella from scrying would also hide her from the mate-bond. Kyle had no way of connecting to her, of knowing she was safe. He would get progressively worse until Isabella was found…or died. If the bond was severed by death or if it took too long to locate Isabella, Kyle might go mad from heartbreak. It had happened. And when it did, it fell to that Were's Alpha to provide the Were a quick, merciful death.

Abigail looked to Grey. Deep sadness was evident in his eyes as he said, "I have chosen to authorize Kyle's request. Though not yet turned, Isabella is now Pack. She is ours to protect. To that end, I have charged my Second and Kyle's Alpha, Luke, and his Second, Becca, to assist you in your search."

Grey looked to Becca, and she again spoke. "There have been rumors. Missing students from Tulane. Kyle had informed us of this before Isabella's disappearance. Luke and I both left the force when he recently became Alpha and I his Second but we still have contacts. The disappearances are all human, so the New Orleans PD didn't think it was Supernatural related. However, Isabella recently toured the campus. She was transferring back home to be near her father and Kyle."

That was it. Rebecca Hartford was the name of Luke's partner on the force in The Burg. We'd never met, but I suspected why she seemed familiar. Time would tell if I was right. My mind hurried to process Becca's next words.

"Isabella told Kyle that as they moved through several active classes she got a bad feeling, like she was being watched. Her exact word was 'probed.' But their group was moving so quickly that she didn't catch the lecturer's name. Kyle feels guilty now for not asking for more information, and that guilt makes it that much harder for him to control his Beast."

"Are the missing students also female?" Jacq questioned. I twisted so I could see her.

"Male." Luke's reply was more an angry growl. "Five so far."

I frowned. It didn't fit. All our victims were girls with power who'd lived in The Burg, NOLA, and everywhere between. Only Isabella was in college. Nicodemus was new to the area. Was Tulane simply one of many places he picked his targets? And who had scanned Isabella? Nicodemus and his distortion amulet wouldn't pass too well in public. Most importantly, why did Luke sound like he was chewing on sandpaper?

"How long have they been missing?" I asked. "Have any of the boys or their bodies been found?"

Abigail flinched at the implications. Becca pulled out two folders. "We received this from our people in the PD." She passed one to each of us.

I looked from the files to the Weres to Jacq. The extra help was a good idea. I had an unsettling feeling that time was running out for Isabella, Kyle, and possibly these five boys.

If the Weres were in for a penny, they were in for a pound. And I could tell from their faces that they weren't planning on leaving the search to Jacq and me. If that was the case, the Weres needed to know what Nicodemus was capable of before committing themselves—the Council's directive be damned.

They say a picture is worth a thousand words. Well, I had five dead girls whose stories our new allies needed to hear…or rather see. And there was no time like the present.

"I'm going to need a laptop, Internet access, a printer, and about another gallon of that coffee. We've got lots to talk about. Then we need to speak with Kyle." I gestured at Jacq and myself. My demands seemed to shock everyone but Luke, who simply looked amused.

Using Grey's hardware, I accessed my home network and printed a file similar to the one I'd shown Jacq the night we'd met. We went over their information first. Five missing boys. All human, young, physically fit, and, like Kyle, orphans. The pieces were starting to come together in my mind, but I wasn't quite ready to share the dark thoughts now surfacing.

Grey was incensed to learn that several of the dead girls had been from his area. But none of the sacrifices had been Were, which could be the Council's reasoning for not notifying him. Or perhaps it was the leak they were concerned over. Maybe the Council believed a Were could be bought by Nicodemus. But I didn't. Weres were fiercely loyal to their Pack. One of theirs was in danger. They'd do nothing to jeopardize Isabella's rescue.

Once a Were gave away his heart, he couldn't take it back.

* * *

The club's dance floor was less crowded than when Jacq and I had arrived. Even though it was a few hours before closing, most people had to work come sunup. I'd come downstairs for a moment away. Earlier, this wouldn't have been the place to go to be alone. But with the reduced numbers, I was confident I could avoid playing a round of "Groping Miss Delacy." Truthfully, I love to dance but rarely have the opportunity. There was a brief time when Luke and I would go, but always to human establishments. The phers that hung in the air nearly as thickly as the cigarette smoke explained why we'd avoided this and other Were clubs.

Before our arrival, the Weres had given Kyle something to help him rest. His reaction had been stronger than expected, and he was out cold. Our talk would have to wait until the morning, meaning Jacq and I had been invited, persuasively, to stay. Soon enough I'd be worrying about what the sleeping arrangements were. But for now, I was alone. The music was fast. And the temptation was too great.

So I threw myself to the wolves, literally, joining the undulating bodies on the floor. Twisting, turning, gliding through an endless rush of faces, arms and legs. All sweat-slicked, glowing with a hundred different shades of blue cast by the ceiling's laser moon. For a fraction of a second, faces and limbs would pop into the light then blend back into the shadows. The crowd was mainly Weres, but there were humans and other magical creatures mixed in. Some danced together, while others like myself just roamed. It didn't matter that I didn't know the song. The quick pounding rhythm was the essence of life.

This time, the dance's effect was much stronger—maybe from the phers and heat, which my body was glorying in, like bathing in a rich sensual river of warm chocolate. From above, I saw my body moving through the others as I too lived that moment, feeling and seeing with new eyes. I was there within myself and without. Two spirits. One body. A body which was graceful again, barely brushing the swarming flesh as other dancers rolled through the room, rising with the rhythm. There was an unspoken boundary as that physical part of me moved through their wake. As we moved, even my brain let go, shutting down all but the most basic understandings. One made two. The heart, lost to the pulsating drum. The mind, tied by a thin thread.

Separate and together.

The music slowed, beginning the tumultuous strains of Texas's "The Hush." I was still two, feeling below and seeing from above. Warm hands encircled her/me from behind, settling on her/my hips as an elusive, musky scent came to our nose. And just like that, we were again one.

"Cate," Jacq said, her breath moist on my neck.

A ripple went through me. Part anticipation. Part dismay. When we had entered the club, I'd thought briefly about what it would feel like to be in Jacq's arms on the dance floor. It had been a dangerously appealing dream. Thankfully, we'd had a meeting to get to. Now my fantasy was being brought to life, and there was nowhere to run. We rocked gently, oblivious to the other dancers as her heat engulfed us.

The skin below my ear tingled, kissed by air so recently filling her lungs. My neck arched, unconsciously begging for even the briefest caress of lips, but no more words were spoken. Jacq pressed us tighter, so close that I felt all of her. Hardened nipples rubbed at my back, while the friction of silk trousers tormented my backside.

I relaxed into her body. It was safe to indulge this need. Nothing serious could happen while we were guests in another's house. My magic began to rise. Again my innate fire had been called forth without conscious effort or control. But I didn't push it away, tired of hiding from Jacq. She'd already saved my life twice. I could trust her with this much. I closed my eyes and opened my mind.

Hot magical fingers gently ran over her. Did they follow my desire or their own? I wasn't certain, and I no longer cared. A whisper of fire memorized a sharp cheekbone. Another tucked a lock of hair behind her ear. Yet another cupped a round buttock.

"What is this?" Jacq murmured in my ear. The music and dancers were still there, but it felt like we were alone in the dark—her words so clear that I could hear her breath hitch…feel her heart's solid thump against my back.

"I don't know. I've never…" I was breathless as her magic began its own exploration, a tingling, velvety soft tongue stroking down, journeying from my ear to the pulse at my neck. I leaned my head back on her shoulder, giving silent permission. This was different, yet the same as the healing—a slower burn but no less intense for its gradual ascent into ecstasy.

Jacq's hands, hot at my waist, guided us through the other dancers to the outer fringes. A magical mouth began to suck at my pulse point, and those fiery hands clenched, pulling me hard against her body. One large palm splayed across my bare belly, slightly tugging the golden phoenix in my navel. Jacq murmured what sounded like a plea for mercy against my neck, and magic shot from her fingertips, pulling something lower. I cried out, on the verge of an unexpected climax.

Then, suddenly, it all came crashing down.

For a moment I didn't realize that the hard grip on my right wrist—the same wrist which had been physically fisted at my side and magically running down my dance partner's back seconds before— was not that of said partner.

"What in the *hell* are you doing?" Hearing the harsh demand, I opened my eyes, blinking the haze away, recognizing my surroundings as one of the curtained alcoves that surrounded the dance floor. The strong grasp was released, and I rubbed my tender wrist. I was not a woman to be treated so callously. Passion quickly turned to anger. My face went red with fury, instead of desire. And the man before me hesitated, finally realizing his jeopardy.

"No, the question isn't 'What in the hell I'm doing?' but 'What in the hell are you doing, Lucas—" I stepped forward, poking him in the chest, "—Alexander," another step and another poke, "— Deveroux?'" Another sharp jab. He winced, stepping back with each poke. Following his retreat with slow, deliberate steps, I barely took a breath before growling, "I know your mama taught you better than to shove a lady into a dark room without her permission or request."

Like a good Southern boy, Luke looked pained at the mention of his mama. And well he should. I knew he'd been raised to know better. I may no longer be with her son, but I was still one of Mamie Deveroux's favorite visitors. One word to her about Luke's ill-treatment and she'd lay low the almighty Wolf Alpha.

Luke was giving me those puppy eyes. That had worked so well when we were together, but things had changed. I had changed. And I wasn't done just yet. This had been a long time coming. "But more importantly," I poked him once more for good measure, "you don't have the right to ask about what I do when you're not around." I didn't mention that I'd been the one to leave him. That seemed too low a blow with Jacq within earshot. And what was with Luke's sudden jealousy? Surely Mynx wasn't right…

I could feel Jacq at my back, but she kept silent, letting me fight this battle on my own—a point in her favor. For that I almost forgave her for telling me to stay in the kitchen during the hellhound attack. Almost. I made a concerted effort to calm down before I accidentally burned the place to the ground. Although I'd been unsuccessful in locating the Beast-Clan's good manners handbook, I was sure that torching the Alpha's nightclub was a big no-no. Weres were temperamental like that.

"Lace, look." Luke ran a hand over his short hair in frustration. "This isn't what you think." At my doubting look, he quickly reversed. "Well, maybe it's a little of that." Mynx was right. Damn her.

Jacq moved closer. I wanted so badly to lean into her, to seek comfort. But what I wanted wasn't necessarily what I needed. A confused frown formed on my face. I felt more than Jacq's presence. I felt *her*. I could sense her anger, her smoldering passion, and other, more elusive emotions. Strangely, I didn't feel Luke. Obviously I was not developing an empathic ability. So it must have something to do with our previous magical interactions. I focused solely on Luke. There would be time to explore this new ability later. Right now, I had bigger fish to fry. Though fortunately for the man standing before me, I only meant that figuratively.

"Look at yourself." Luke gestured at my pants. "The good detective there was putting off enough heat to draw security's attention. She was practically glowing with it." He gave Jacq an accusing look, evidently assuming the heat had all come from her. In our years together, I'd never shown him my fire. Partially because it was a secret, but mostly because my ex had this thing against magic. I didn't know why. All Weres were more or less anti-magic, but Luke was nearly fanatically so. Why he had wanted to date a witch had been beyond me, but since I'd been almost a magical dud, it hadn't mattered.

I looked at the two hand-shaped scorch marks Luke gestured to. Light brown, they stood out against my nearly white jeans. "You should see our healer, Lace. You've got to be burned." His voice was gentler, his expression concerned.

That lasted for all of five seconds.

Luke took a deep breath, nostrils flaring. His concern was quickly replaced with hard eyes and flat tight lips. Realizing what his more sensitive nose must have picked up, I blushed and crossed my arms. It was awkward enough standing around in wet panties without my ex getting a whiff of exactly *how* and to whom I'd been reacting.

Jacq jumped in, "There was never any danger. I felt Cate use her magic to shield herself and the club."

True, there was no danger. But Jacq must know I hadn't been— and wasn't now—shielding. There was no need. I'd consumed most of the heat. Now I felt both energized and sated, like a rabid football fan stuffed on Turkey day feels as the first televised game begins. I was glad she hadn't mentioned that my own fire had generated some of that heat. I felt guilty letting her take the blame, but that was information Luke didn't need. Sometimes Lucas Deveroux could be like a dog with a bone, never satisfied until he'd unearthed and buried every secret ten times over. Though I did feel a bit like finding a hole and crawling into it, I would not be letting anyone cover me in dirt for a long time yet.

Luke opened his mouth. I raised my hand, forestalling the comment I knew he was dying to make. He snapped his jaw shut with an audible *click*. I looked at him, thinking, my fingers drumming against my leg. Luke ground his teeth. Jacq politely coughed. Or was that a laugh? I stopped, keeping my expression neutral. I'd been rubbing the spot where her hands had, minutes ago, so visibly rested.

This wasn't a moment for sarcasm, so I kept my tone gracious. "Luke." At my soft words, the muscles in his jaw loosened. "I appreciate your concern." He almost smiled, but that disappeared as I added, "However, we have an agreement with Grey. Jacq and I won't do anything to endanger his club or its occupants this evening, at least nothing outside defending ourselves or each other." At Jacq's name, Luke crossed his arms, scowling. "And as far as I know, we haven't broken any rules. Have we?" Hands on my hips, I stared him down, arching a brow.

Luke mutely shook his head. The man had never been able to lie to me. I should've saved us all some trouble and just asked him years ago if he was still in love with me. I let out a resigned sigh. *And I bet that would've gone really well.*

Luke shoved his hands into his trouser pockets, giving me a pleading look. "Lace, I—"

"No." I raised my hand then moved it to rub the aching muscles in my neck. My system's constant battle with the phers was giving me a headache. "We'll talk, I promise. But not here. Not now. Another night, okay?" My urge to fight suddenly gone, I looked at Luke with tired eyes. Maybe I was being rude, but it no longer mattered. I was becoming lethargic, every limb a heavy weight. Heading to bed sounded good. Tomorrow was a new day. I didn't let my mind linger on the depressing thought that it would probably be full of the same old bullshit. We'd deal with that then. I'd had enough drama for tonight.

"Would you please ask Becca to show us to our rooms?" I asked.

Luke gave Jacq an uncertain look. Did he think the woman would maul me if he left us alone for two minutes? I should be so fortunate. I expected Luke to argue, as was his standard. But maybe he was changing. Or more likely, he knew when to cut and run. At my frustrated huff, he left.

I turned to Jacq, inexplicably nervous. She leaned against the wall, watching me with dark, hooded eyes. *That look.* It made me uneasy in ways I didn't fully comprehend. My mouth went dry, and my mind blanked. The silence was thick with things that needed to be said, but I didn't know where to start.

Jacq must have seen something of my hesitation because she stepped forward with hands out, dropping them before touching me. "I didn't mean for that to happen." Something twisted in my chest. "But I don't regret it."

I released a breath I hadn't realized I was holding. I didn't understand why that was so important. It just was. Standing only a foot away, Jacq tucked her thumbs into her pockets, hands flexing.

Stormy eyes bored into my soul. I recognized what she was feeling, because I was feeling it too. Something in us needed to touch the other, but we were both resisting.

"Let's sit for a moment." Legs suddenly weak, I moved to the alcove's black leather sofa. Jacq closed the velvet drapes halfway, muting the club's noise, before joining me.

Although we weren't touching, as I turned to face her I felt her heat. She'd left her jacket in the car and I could clearly see the strong tight muscles that had so recently held me close. I inhaled her scent. Sage, sandalwood, and now something else. My cheeks flooded again. Jacq smelled like me. No wonder Luke had been angry. Not only did I smell like wet woman, but the auburn-haired beauty before me smelled like my personal scent of oranges. There would've been no doubt how *long* and how *closely* we'd been touching for my smell to transfer to her.

I tried to mentally force the blood to my heart or brain, anywhere but my face. But at Jacq's husky, "You're beautiful when you blush," I felt the red in my cheeks grow impossibly deeper. Hellfire and brimstone, I hadn't blushed this badly since my mom, Nana and Aunt Helena had tried to give me the birds n' bees talk…all together… with diagrams. It was quite possibly the most embarrassing game of Pictionary I'd ever played.

"Thank you." I managed a smile. "Does that mean I'm not beautiful when I'm not red-faced?"

"I wouldn't know," Jacq teased. "I've yet to have the pleasure of seeing you any other way." I laughed.

Sitting here like this, teasing each other, it was hard to remember my reasons for keeping my distance, but I hadn't forgotten our dance and that I needed time to digest what had occurred. Maybe Jacq needed time, too, because she was neither the masked flirt hiding behind cold detachment that I'd first met nor this morning's bonfire of need. She seemed open, relaxed…and waiting.

But for what?

Taking my cue from her, I relaxed, laying my hands flat on my thighs, denying the urge to touch her, not quite meeting her eyes. This wasn't like me. I'd never blushed, stammered, or been shy around someone I was romantically interested in. That thought stopped me. When had this gone from a simple case of physical attraction (albeit an extremely strong one) to romantic interest? I wasn't sure. But sure as I knew my name, I knew that was what this was. I was very much interested in the woman sitting across from me. And this was the wrong time to be having such an epiphany, especially when the woman in question was trying to regain my attention.

"Cate, look at me…please." I squared my chin, raising my eyes. Jacq looked worried. I frowned. She *was* worried. I could feel it along with her continued desire. My connection to her emotions was weak but sensible.

"Why are you worried?" I blurted out, my mouth on autopilot. Gah, I wished (not for the first time) that tact were part of my personality. Was it too late to be mentally reprogrammed?

A slew of unknown emotions played across Jacq's features. With joy and reservation, she finally asked, "Do you want the long or the short answer?"

I couldn't help but laugh. "Short, please." Jacq looked both relieved and disappointed. "But only because Becca will be here soon. How about a rain check on the other?" In a way, that was a promise that there would be other days, other talks. That secret half-smile returned momentarily before her face turned serious, watching me.

"Certainly." Jacq released a quick breath. "The short answer. This thing between us," she gestured to our bodies, "it's intense, but it feels…natural…true? I'm not sure of the word you would use."

"Right. It feels right." I spoke softly, halfway closing my eyes, not wanting to see her rejection, but she nodded, smiling. In a way, it was a relief that she felt the same thing. But in another, it was a different sort of strain. It gave this between us hope. Potential. Possibility. Something that could never be. Maybe it was the masochist in me that kept me from stopping her explanation.

"I don't want to scare you away." Her words were truthful, but there was more she wasn't saying. I'd have to make time soon for that long version.

Jacq watched me expectantly. I recognized that look now. She expected me to run, hoped I wouldn't, and was preparing for the inevitable. How had we gotten here so fast? Luke and I had been together for months, maybe years, before I'd seen that look. Did that mean we were doomed to crash and burn at an even quicker pace? How I could hurt this strong and wonderful woman was beyond me. Yet that was the only future I could see. For us both.

"Jacqueline…Jacq."

Her smile was radiant, a flash of white teeth and that delectable dimple. What could I say to reassure her without making false promises? I bit my lip, plunging onward, forcefully keeping my head up and my eyes locked on her dark gray gaze.

"I've never felt this sort of attraction to a woman before." I took a deep breath. "And it scares me. In fact, I've never felt this sort of magical soul-deep connection with anyone. That scares me a thousand times more."

Her pupils widened. I could've lied. Probably should've. But lying seemed wrong. We were both in agreement that the thing between us felt right. I wanted to keep it that way. We might never have anything more between us than honesty.

I couldn't take that away, as well.

I took a quick breath, continuing, "But I'm not running. I can't guarantee I won't want to, but I plan on sticking around to figure out what this is." *For now.* It was true, I would never run. But I couldn't promise that I wouldn't someday *walk* away. I knew now that, if—or when—that day came, there would be more than a little hesitation in my step.

I wasn't sure which of us was more shocked by my words. I'd always been an extremely private person, never sharing much of myself, which had caused more than one fight between me and Luke. I hadn't planned to share so much this time. I just couldn't seem to stop. Giving in, I put my hand over hers where it rested across the sofa's top—purely to offer comfort.

Or so I told myself.

"Besides…" I waited for the eyes that had been looking at our joined hands to meet my own before smiling. "You owe me a new pair of jeans."

Jacq turned her palm over, grasping my fingers. I was getting used to the warmth that crept through my body at her touch. With the sharing of skin, her emotions became clearer. There was worry and a measure of contentedness. But things hadn't changed. I couldn't promise her anything beyond friendship. Even if something did develop between us romantically, one day she would have to leave—preferably before my hair turned gray and my bones brittle. Still, I was loath to say those words and ruin her current joy. Sometimes the truth, like bad-tasting medicine, was best given in small doses with lots of sweetness in between. No one had ever accused me of being sweet, but I could certainly attempt it.

That dimple peeked out again, and my hand, acting on its own, reached up, tucking a lock of auburn hair behind her ear. Ever since my magic had done the same, I'd been dying to let the silky strands run through my fingers. Those same traitorous digits momentarily lingered, finally pulling away.

I'd almost forgotten we were having a conversation until Jacq cheekily replied, "If I'm buying, do I get to choose? You did say that if someone gives you a gift, you wear it." Her voice got notably deeper. "That's the *nice* thing to do."

I shivered, managing not to blush, but by the look in her eyes, Jacq knew the effect she was having. How typical, my own words were coming back to bite me in the ass. "Um," I gulped, backtracking as swiftly as I could, "we'll have to see about that." We needed to have that talk…and soon. The dark light in her eyes said she was thinking about shopping—but for something other than jeans.

I hadn't needed a chaperone for a trip to the mall since I was fourteen. Her eyes said that was about to change.

CHAPTER NINE

"Dreams often tell us what may be. Nightmares often tell us what might have been. It is up to you to be able to tell the difference." 1687 A.D.

—Claire Jovet, friend to Jacqueline D Slone

Day Six

"That's the worst idea I've ever heard," Becca said the next morning, barring me from Kyle's door and the possibility of seeing him without Were backup. Practically poking me with her finger, Becca spit the hushed words into my face. "His Beast grows more restless. The Alpha has promised you safety. And while I wouldn't mind seeing you with a few bruises, I don't want Kyle to pay for it. If you're injured, Luke will have to kill him to honor Grey's promise. Do you want that on your conscience?"

Becca's anger had a bitter edge. I wanted to tell her she had nothing to worry about, but after Luke's showdown last night, I wasn't so sure. At least I was certain of my own feelings. His? Not so much.

I'd lain awake for a long time considering that very fact. Not the issue with Luke—the one with Kyle. I'd formed a plan. I simply needed the Weres to go along with it. It was doubtful that Isabella's fiancé had told his people about her premonitions. Henry Richmond had been unrelenting in his belief that only he and Kyle knew what

Isabella's abilities were. If no one knew, I wouldn't be the one to let the cat out, but I couldn't question him thoroughly if we were trying to step around that information.

With head cocked, I gave Becca my best crazy-lady look, resisting the urge to shake my finger back—she'd skipped breakfast. "That is not the worst idea you've ever heard. I'm sure you've watched reality television at least once." Her strangled laugh was a good start. My grandpa had always said, "Kill 'em with humor if you can't kill 'em with a knife to the gut," which could explain my twisted sense of humor. "And Kyle won't be an issue…if you'll give me permission to magic him."

Permission was important. The Pack was touchy about using magic on their people without it. It was okay for self-defense or law enforcement. Otherwise, it was dishonorable since most Weres couldn't harness their magic. It was like bringing a gun to a knife fight. No matter that most witches couldn't grow claws and fangs… and didn't have a couple hundred pounds of extra muscle at their disposal. Considering Kyle's incapacitated state, Becca's position as his superior in the Pack allowed her to say yea or nay.

"I can calm Kyle. It's a simple spell. If I put enough magic into it, the effects will last for two days. That buys us time to find Isabella." I looked into Becca's chocolate eyes. "I don't want to bring her home to find her fiancé dead. Let me do this."

"Fine." Her pretty voice wasn't so lovely coming through clenched teeth. "But one of us stays long enough for the spell to take effect."

"Okay, but I can't guarantee that the magic won't affect anyone else in the room."

Becca gave me a scorching glare then tossed her hair back. "I won't ask my men to expose themselves to the Moon knows what magical mumbo jumbo. I'll stay, but if I come out of there with green spots and donkey ears, then the minute you're out of the Alpha's territory your ass will be mine. Capisce?"

I muffled my laugh as a cough, nodding my assent. The image of a jackass with Becca's face was too much for me. She might not care for my company, but at this moment I almost liked hers. Almost.

I wheezed out, "Understood."

The ground the Blue Moon was built on sloped downward in the back, allowing for a basement with high windows still above ground level. That was where we were now. "After you." I looked at the door and swept my arm forward.

Becca gave me another glare. Since I didn't have a key, the sarcasm was obvious.

After undoing several deadbolts, Becca led me into the room. I immediately recognized Kyle from the photos in Isabella's phone. The face and body were the same, but the messy hair and haggard expression didn't match the carefree, laughing man Isabella had captured so well.

"Kyle?" Becca inquired softly. He turned. Magic, warm and caring, brushed my shoulder before flowing toward Kyle. Becca's powers of manipulation weren't all physical, but it seemed very innate and unrefined. She likely didn't realize she had—and used— magic. Combined with the power, the sound of her voice could be very soothing. While Becca approached Kyle and began speaking to him softly, I stepped into a corner and began my spell.

The spell *was* for peace. That was true. But there was also something extra. I opened my mind's eye, viewing the Weres. Becca's energy was light lavender. Her aura pulsed steadily like the ocean's waves. Magic rolled out as she spoke, washing over Kyle, hypnotic and calming, like a mother stroking her child's hair. I forced myself to look away, lest I get trapped in her spell.

Kyle's energy was dark yellow but didn't have Becca's consistency. Instead darker random bursts of color flashed out and then fell back inward, like solar flares. As I worked, tendrils of green earth-magic attached themselves to his aura. The energy's color didn't change, but the bursts gradually slowed, finally stopping completely, Kyle's agitated pacing stopped. Becca glanced at me briefly before guiding him to sit on the bed.

While I worked, I examined Kyle. A faint magical thread led away from him. Upon closer inspection, I saw not one but many. Different from the magical signatures I'd followed when searching for Isabella, these were two-way bonds. The stronger the bond: the thicker the thread. One such thread, part of the Pack bond, connected Kyle to Becca. It merged with the other threads that comprised his connection to the Pack. Each was slim and fragile, but together they bound Kyle to the Pack more securely than duct tape.

Several thick threads wove through the others. This would be the Pack's connection to Luke as the Wolf Alpha and Grey as the Clan Alpha. Half of these were blue, the others copper-red. There was also one very weak thread the same dark yellow as Kyle's aura. Stretched taut, it didn't resemble the rest. It had to be his bond to Isabella. But it was so weak. I studied it for several moments. Could I?

I thought so. Thanks to all the heat and the phers I'd absorbed on the dance floor the night before, I was ten times stronger today than two days ago. With only one string to follow, I could be quick, reducing the chance of growing too weak and becoming lost…even without Jacq on this side to ground me. Reckless? Maybe, but I made the choice without thought. After this spell, I would follow the thread.

As I worked, I studied Becca. Part of my spell was for clarity. It had helped me see the mating connection with Kyle as well as unintentionally revealing Becca. Technically, I wasn't spying. Some things were just hard to miss. Her aura reflected creativity, strength, great purpose—and hid a deep heart. There was promise of more, if I only looked a little deeper. But that would've been an intentional invasion. Besides, I'd seen what I needed to see. The Wolf Second had lots of potential.

This next part would have been more secure if Jacq were here. But I'd left her and Luke upstairs divvying up the assignments. So far, Luke had been on his best behavior, even managing a toothy smile when we'd joined him for breakfast. I was relatively certain that for an hour at least he and Jacq could manage not to kill each other.

I moved into the magical plane quickly. The feeling was similar to sky-diving—a great rush then a thrilling sense of weightlessness. But that overriding sense that the ground was rushing toward you was missing. Here, you could freefall for eternity…or until you died when the thread holding you to your body broke. Again the colors grew brighter, varied to a degree that the mind cannot comprehend. I found the thread I needed and began to skim along its path. The trip across the Mississippi and into my state named after the rich delta waters would've taken hours by car but was only minutes when flying through the magical plane. I headed north, passing Gandsai and the military base. Right outside The Burg, I hit a brick wall.

Or rather, I rammed some sort of shield. Made with magic, tainted with death, it blocked my progress. The impact addled my wits and numbed my spirit, leaving me a helpless fly in the spider's web. Cold fingers of dark magic twisted, seeking to drag me into the barrier, which began to open.

Still strong, my own thread, my link to the physical plane, instinctually reacted. For the first time ever, that connection yanked me back, ripping me from the dark web, hauling me in seconds the distance I'd previously traveled in minutes, forcing body and soul together like a rubber band, drawn tight, finally released. My consciousness roared in without preparation. I would've fallen, but strong arms grabbed me. I blinked several times, my mind's eye disappearing. Right before the colors diminished, I noticed a faint outline around Becca. A ghostly lavender—or was it blue?—thread waited to be born. I blinked again, and it was gone.

The arms holding me tightened, pulling me roughly to a hard chest. I smelled a familiar musky scent and wasn't surprised by Becca's angry look.

"What in the blue blazes were you doing, Lace?" Luke hissed from above my head as Jacq entered the room. Seeing me in Luke's arms, her expression completely shut down.

"I'm fine now, Lucas. You can let go." I tried to work my way free, but it was useless. The man had an iron grip. I could stand there, or I could make a scene. I stood there. As tempting as it was to elbow Luke in the ribs or give him a tongue-lashing—not of the variety the furry ones enjoyed—any aggression around Kyle could undo our recent efforts to calm him. I gentled my voice. "With Becca's permission, I was working some simple magic to ease Kyle. I simply overextended myself a bit." My words were meant for Luke, but it was Jacq's face I watched. It was important that she understand, but her expression didn't change. "My legs were momentarily weak, so thank you for catching me. But I'm fine now…really." There was more that I wanted to say, but I wouldn't be saying it in a room full of werewolves.

"We'll take it from here, Deveroux." Jacq's husky voice was all business. She gestured to a chair near Kyle. "Cate, if you'll sit, we'll begin the interview."

I watched, amused, as Jacq proceeded to push the others from the room. It took us several minutes (and a great deal of protesting from Luke) to make him and Becca leave. As Jacq escorted them out, I turned to Kyle.

He might be sitting placidly on the bed now, but he wouldn't stay like that. My spell had been to calm, but it was more akin to the magic used for my suppression amulets. It couldn't remove his Wolf's nature, which was to rage and search for his mate. The spell would only suppress that urge. It could be repeated once, maybe twice more, but it wasn't healthy to continually repress someone's spirit. Besides, no matter how strong or often the spell was performed, Kyle's Beast would eventually break out. His Wolf was part of who he was. That couldn't be closeted away forever.

Before we began, Jacq walked around the room, weaving intricate silver glyphs in the air before pushing them onto the walls and ceiling. I didn't understand their purpose until we began to talk. As the sound echoed off the walls, it became clear that she'd warded the room with silence. Although it took some getting used to, it was worth the confusion of hearing our voices bouncing around. Jacq assured us that even the listening devices we knew had to be there wouldn't work. Somewhere, right about now, Luke and Becca (who'd undoubtedly been hoping to listen in on our conversation) were getting really pissed. I stifled a laugh, knowing exactly the look that would be on Luke's face. Jacq must've mirrored my thoughts, because the cold, hurt look in her eyes was soon replaced by a warm twinkle.

The interview went quickly with Jacq asking most of the questions. Although I wasn't as weak as before, the trip had drained me more than I'd expected. I was still recovering from the backlash of hitting—and nearly succumbing to—that tainted, magical web. Like Henry Richmond, Kyle was adamant that no one knew about Isabella's premonitions, and he wanted to keep it that way. There was no guarantee that Isabella's powers would work once the Lycos virus changed her. Many in the Pack would have used that as an argument against conversion, wanting to exploit her abilities without making her Wolf, resulting in a dangerous future. Even if Grey granted Isabella a protected status, her lifespan would only be a portion of Kyle's. And human-to-Were parings were usually infertile, a nearly tragic outcome for the family-oriented Weres.

Kyle, too, thought Tulane was a link, but he couldn't understand why Isabella, who lived three hours away, had been targeted. He gave us a list of everyone he could think of that she had come in contact with while visiting the campus. It was a good start. Before we left, I wrapped a little more calming influence around him, pushing Kyle into a natural sleep that would do him more good than the drug-induced one he'd received the night before.

On our way out, I reexamined Jacq's silver glyphs, having been discreetly dissecting them throughout the interview. With the last glimpse, I felt certain that if necessary I could duplicate them. I already knew one room I'd be warding. And if I had my way, I'd put one permanently over a certain wolf's big mouth.

Silence truly was golden.

* * *

My Nana always said that I'm not afraid to make a fool of myself. She was right, and they had the video to prove it. It was this quirky part of my nature that now had me standing in my faded jeans and a borrowed dress shirt on the second floor of Tulane's Liberal Arts College in NOLA, hugging a man who looked at me with abject horror. My joyfully shouted "Wellsy!" was still echoing around the open-air lobby. Worse, at the noise at least thirty heads had turned to bear witness to my mortification. Thankfully, Becca had stepped away to find a vending machine.

I should've known when I spotted Dr. Wellsy, our neighbor and one of my aunt's oldest friends, and felt a spidey-tingle, that something was wrong. Stepping back, I dropped my arms. Wellsy cleared his throat.

"I'm sorry, Miss?" He looked at me blankly.

My face grew redder still. He didn't know me. How could this be? I had the right man. Even the strong smell of Old Spice was the same. I'd known Wellsy since I was young. A widower, he'd always been like a funny uncle bringing trinkets back from his travels for me and my aunt. His daughter, Loren, had been a good friend before she'd died several years ago. Even though he was nearly my Nana's age, his witch blood had kept him looking young. He'd been very supportive when my grandpa had died and had helped in the search for my mother.

"*Cate*. Cate Delacy." He shook his head. "Helena's niece?" It took a nerve-racking moment—where I contemplated the possibility of amnesia, brain injuries, evil twins and alien abductions—before recognition lit his brown eyes. While I was waiting, I noticed that in his year away guest teaching at a Virginia university, Dr. Wellsy had aged drastically. I'd seen him before he'd left to be nearer his grandchildren. His salt-and-pepper hair was now pure white. His tanned face looked lined and haggard, and his tall rangy frame was gaunt and stooped. I rubbed at the bumps rising on my arms from a sudden chill.

"Yes, Miss Delacy." His voice was slightly deeper than I recalled, but the charismatic smile was the same. I shivered as another cold draft hit. "My apologies. You may have heard about my recent accident. I have been experiencing some memory lapses." He turned toward the curving staircase that led to the first floor then turned back. "Please make my apologies to your aunt." He smiled again. This time, I smiled back. That warm and eager expression was the Wellsy I knew. "It has been too long since I've had a chat with a Delacy. Tell Helena I'll visit soon."

Maybe the accident was responsible for his overly formal speech, as well as the lack of recognition. I just nodded. There were several things I should've said, questions I wanted to ask, but I couldn't force anything past my lips. Something felt wrong. Maybe it was Wellsy or maybe the tuna salad I'd eaten. Either way, my stomach was churning. I was standing at the banister, watching him leisurely walk out the building's front doors, when Becca finally returned.

"Sorry, had to run up four flights of stairs to find a vending machine that wasn't empty. It's finals, and these collegians have gone sugar crazy!" With a laugh, she passed me one of the coveted sodas. Becca wasn't even panting. Anyone but a Were would've been out of breath after that trip. I absentmindedly took the offered drink but didn't open it. Something was bothering me and I couldn't quite grasp what it was.

"Someone you know?" Becca inquired. In a T-shirt and jeans with her hair pulled back, she looked all of eighteen. Contentedly crunching on a candy bar didn't help.

I frowned. "One of our neighbors. He was teaching in Virginia for the year. Richmond or something like that. He mentioned an accident and didn't seem to recognize me. What was he doing here?" I murmured, walking back to the office we'd just left. Becca followed. She wore a sour expression but was blissfully quiet. I needed some information and a minute to myself to think. The first was manageable, but the second wouldn't be happening any time soon.

I pushed the door open, moving from cold marble floors to plush carpet before stopping at the high counter. I asked the same blond grad student I'd spoken with before meeting the dean, "Do you know what Dr. Arno Wellsy is doing here?"

"Oh, sure." The perky young man was all smiles.

I thought I'd finally get a quick answer, then Becca stepped in behind me. Bam, he was smitten. I stifled the urge to roll my eyes.

This had been happening all day. Even in frayed jeans and a Greek KAT shirt, Becca was still a bombshell. A bombshell with a sense of irony that I appreciated. I wasn't sure which was more interesting—the fact that she'd been a member of a sorority or that she'd picked one whose mascot usually got eaten by the big bad wolf.

Of course, the grad student's drooling could've been caused by the phers. I couldn't be sure as I was still wearing last night's suppression amulets. I had absorbed enough pheromones for a week, and hanging out all day with a Were who was in lust with my ex wasn't helping. At my pointed stare, the young man wrenched his gaze away from my wolfy, sorority girl bloodhound. "Um, he's guest teaching a class on Tuesdays and Thursdays, International Politics and the Genesis Saga. Fascinating stuff. The class is booked solid with at least three dozen students auditing off-book."

I thanked the young man then dragged Becca away. All I got for my trouble was a dirty look (from him not her). Wellsy had been back in town since January at the least. He would've had to leave his guest post in Virginia early. Could that have been for health reasons? If so, then why was he teaching here and not at home resting? Nana was one of the best healers around. He could've come to us for help, but I knew he hadn't been at the homestead in months. I checked on his house weekly, like he'd requested. This was all very unusual.

Next, we went to the registrar's office where we finally hit pay dirt. Their system had been hacked months before. Originally, they'd suspected an enterprising student of padding his or her transcript, but the only data touched were family medical histories. The major privacy violation had drawn federal investigators, but they'd yet to catch the hacker. I'd asked for anything they could release regarding what the search had been targeting but had been stonewalled.

This at least explained how the boys were targeted, if not the girls. We'd already hit the campus with a vengeance, using Becca's nose and my magic to check everyone who might have ties to our missing people. We knew that Isabella was alive, so Becca was checking scents, looking to see if anyone had come in recent contact with the missing Druid. I'd been looking for the taint of dark magic. We'd just finished when I'd ran into Dr. Wellsy, which was good. I was magicked-out for the day.

I was also trying hard not to be disheartened. After all of that, Becca and I had found bupkis. Hopefully Luke, who was conducting similar interviews in NOLA before transporting Kyle (per my request) to Hattiesburg, and Jacq, headed to that same city for her own interviews, would come up with something when they spoke with the missing girls' families.

According to the registrar, no one had any classes together, but the mention of auditing had struck a chord. We were heading back to the car when I said, "Call Luke and see if any of the girls from NOLA were auditing, maybe unofficially, any classes either here or in The Burg? I'll call Jacq and have her check the girls from Mississippi. There probably won't be any paper trails, so they'll have to ask parents and friends." I snapped my fingers, adding one last thought. "Oh, and have Luke ask Kyle if Isabella knew Dr. Wellsy, Arno Wellsy. He taught at USM." The Liberal Arts wasn't huge. There was a very good chance that she'd taken one of his classes.

Becca gave me a strange look. "Why don't you call him yourself, *Lace*?" Her tone had turned cold. So the gloves had come off. Well, if she wanted to play it that way…

We were at the car. I rounded the hood and approached the passenger door, my tone scathing as I said, "One: Because I *don't* want to talk to him." I ticked the numbers off on my fingers. (Visual aids help when dealing with the simple minded.) "Two: Because you *do*." The third was the clincher. Hopefully, Becca would get the point without me having to shove it up her ass…because I was more than happy to oblige if she didn't.

I yanked open the car door. Sliding into the seat, I waited until Becca was behind the wheel and had turned to face me. Even with the windows rolled down, her red Mustang should've been steamy in the May sun, but her icy glare could've had icicles dripping off the black roll top. I watched her face, making sure she understood. "Three: Things have been pretty awkward between us since he saw Jacq and I making out last night." Well, that might be an exaggeration, but the idea was there. And that idea did it.

Her mouth formed a silent *O*. The car's temp seemed to rise by at least ten degrees. I couldn't have been blunter if I'd said, "Sic 'em girl." Now if the reluctant suitor would just cooperate, this Cupid could walk away without having to bloody her arrows.

Life was good.

CHAPTER TEN

"The term undead reflects your bias. We may be centuries old, but your perception of us should not be. We are simply the living-impaired…"

—Councilman Marton Sevres in his speech to Congress regarding equal rights for Vampires

"Oh, that is the last time I try to help you!" I slammed the door none too gently, following Becca into my house. The yelling and arm waving were probably over the top, but I'd been subjected to over an hour of musical soundtracks. It was either voice my distress or strangle her on the spot. I was leaning toward the latter.

Becca had wanted to stop at the Blue Moon so I could shower and change clothes. Again. It wasn't a hygiene issue. I'd showered that morning before we'd left the club. No, apparently I reeked of Old Spice and old man decay. I believe the female wolf's exact words were "death warmed over." I'd refused. I didn't smell it. Besides, I was wearing last night's jeans and a borrowed shirt already. I wasn't going to borrow someone's undies and another set of clothes. Her nose had suffered the trip, so apparently my ears and sanity had to as well.

I was already angry enough that Luke had decided to ride with Jacq to her house and borrow my Jeep for his drive to The Burg. The only reason I wasn't yelling at him was because he'd followed the other Weres transporting Kyle and not piled them all into my precious one. I'd checked before entering the house. The Jeep didn't reek of wild dog, which meant my ex got to live to see another day.

Jacq and Luke stepped out of the den. Jacq once again had her sword. She must've been concerned over the yelling. Hmm, there was a simple solution to my problem. No, it would be bad manners to have her behead Becca—not to mention messy. *Damn*. But that didn't mean I couldn't be a tiny bit vindictive. A sly smile curved my lips.

"Wha—umph," Luke's question was cut off as I shoved the no-longer-smirking Becca into his chest. Well, she deserved something. I mean, who really wants to listen to the entire soundtrack of *Oklahoma*? Twice? Really. Why would someone even have that in their car? Luke put his arms around Becca—who I was happy to note had a very unladylike squeal—to steady her. I wasn't sure which one looked more surprised.

"You want her? Take her. I wash my hands of this sadistic woman and her horrific musical tastes. Arggg!" I stomped around them and into the dining room, grabbing my detective's arm along the way, almost used to the *zing* that occurred whenever we touched. Becca was still cuddled up to a confused Luke's chest.

Jacq gave my half-grin a puzzled look. I wasn't faking the frustration, but who said I couldn't vent and do other things too? We were at the dining room's threshold when she said, "You smell strange." Eyebrows pinched together, her nose twitched.

"Arrhhhh!" Half-screaming, half-moaning, I dropped Jacq's arm, did an about-face, and stomped upstairs to shower.

"What'd I say?" Her words echoed in the den before she followed, reaching me just as I arrived at my partially open bedroom door. I bit back a curse as I entered. I could swear I'd shut that door before leaving yesterday. As expected, Hex's black kitty body was nesting right in the middle of my white satin comforter. And there were definite scratch marks running down my black cherry headboard and dresser. She'd had nearly twenty-four hours to wreak havoc. If you look up malicious in the dictionary, there'd be a picture of that whiskered sourpuss face.

"Out!" I pointed to the door then had to grab Jacq as she started to leave. I pulled her into the room, gentling my tone. "Sorry, not you." I smiled to remove the hurt from her eyes. "The cat." I gestured at the hell-spawn currently slinking out the door. "Hex might be trapped in an animal's body, but she always understands what people do and say." Expression serious, Jacq nodded. Fortunately, I'd already shared the story of Mynx and Hex's body-switch, so that statement didn't sound quite so crazy.

I half-pushed, half-pulled Jacq to the small love seat in the room's corner. The sides bore claw marks, but the actual seat looked okay. I rubbed my hands up and down her arms. "I'm sorry. I'm not angry at you." Releasing a frustrated growl, I stepped back, searching the room for something to do with my hands. She felt too good.

"Stay there while I find some clean clothes in this mess." The laundry hamper sitting beside my small writing desk had been tipped over, everything scattered. Hex knew what she was doing. My favorite silk pajamas and lace undies were the most mutilated. My oldest pair of sweats and the pants that I never wore because they were a size too big were undamaged.

I began to discard garments too ripped to keep, explaining, "For some reason, Hex doesn't bother anyone else. I'm the lucky one. She's been doing this to me since I was a kid." I stepped over and closed the door. "Only it was worse when I was younger because I was allergic to cats. She loved to sneak in here and roll in my bed, my clothes, anything she could get her furry paws on. I'd itch and sneeze and break out in hives. We'd wash and wash, but there was always something we missed."

I snuck a glance at Jacq, who was listening intently as she watched me work, her long firm legs outstretched, relaxed. "I grew out of the allergy, so she's mostly left me alone." I shook my head. "Who knows why she's mad at me now?" My mind flashed briefly to the hellhounds' attack and my stepping on her tail during my mad dash through the house. This was an extreme amount of damage for that slight infraction. "Maybe she's bored." I sighed. A melodramatic cat was too much to deal with right now. I was about to strip off the bedding when Jacq left her seat and stopped me.

"Let me help." She stilled my hand with hers. Again, I felt her warmth as our magics touched, tingling. She kept her hand, beginning to glow silver, on mine a moment before moving it over the bed. "It's not well known—and I would ask that you not share this—but I have some small power over energy, and energy is in everything."

Her voice was wonderful. I suddenly felt awful about becoming angry over her "you smell" comment. (Though in my defense, that was something you should never say to a Southern lady unless you followed it with the words "lovely," "delicious," or "like heaven in the moonlight.")

"About earlier," I said, watching as black hair slowly disappeared from the comforter. "According to Becca, I 'stunk up' her car. To retaliate, she drove me bonkers with every annoying show tune you can think of." I swear Jacq flinched at the words, *show tune*. "So maybe I'm a bit sensitive about the smell issue. I ran into our neighbor, Dr. Wellsy, hugged him, and some of his cologne must've rubbed off." Reminded, I turned away from the fascinating sight and pulled open my closet. Thankfully, that door had stayed closed.

"I'm going to grab a quick shower. I wouldn't want to continue to taint the sanctity of everyone's olfactory senses." My cheeky tone managed to get a laugh from Jacq. The sound shivered down my spine. *Damn, that woman was too sexy for her own good.*

"Well, it's not that you smell bad…exactly. But I much prefer your own smell of oranges and cinnamon to the scent of a Necromancer."

Jacq knew what I smelled like? As I searched the closet, I kept my back turned. I really had to work on this blushing thing. Hold up—necromancer? She must be mistaken. Wellsy was an earth witch. I pulled out a pair of navy workout pants, matching jacket, and white tank top.

"Jacq?" My voice was soft.

"Yes?" She glanced in my direction.

"I'm sorry I yelled at you." I tried to make her understand with my eyes. Becca had irritated me. Hex had angered me. But neither had hurt me. And I'd seen it in Jacq's eyes. My careless words had hurt her. My eyes said I'd never do it again. My mouth simply said, "I'll see you downstairs in a few. Don't exhaust your magic. If you get tired, leave the mess. I can wash that later, or I can always sleep in the guest room tonight." The bathroom door clicked shut behind me before she could respond.

But even through the closed door, I still heard Jacq's outraged shout, "Wait—if you have a guest room why did I have to sleep on that short lumpy couch two nights in a row?"

I simply walked farther into the bathroom. That was one question I wouldn't be answering any time soon.

* * *

My scream brought Jacq running. I barely grabbed the corner of my white towel before she barreled in. "Put that away before you poke someone's eye out." I gestured to the glowing silver sword that seemed to appear and disappear quite frequently.

I wasn't sure how the mischievous cat had done it, but Hex had somehow gotten something very slippery all over the floor. From the orange smell I suspected my bath lotion. I saw Jacq's mouth twitch. I'm sure I made a funny picture. Big bad runner, naked but for a towel, hanging on to the shower rail for dear life.

"Oh, go ahead and laugh. Just throw me a towel from that cabinet to put on this floor."

Jacq grabbed a towel and stepped forward. I started to protest. She'd slip too, and I couldn't catch her without losing the towel. Instead, the same silver glow emanated from Jacq's feet. As she approached, the slippery mess disappeared. She stopped a hairbreadth from my suddenly overly warm body. Jacq no longer looked amused.

"Allow me." Her husky voice was deep, almost raspy. Jacq gracefully dropped to one knee, keeping her smoky eyes glued to mine. In her position, she could've peeked beneath the towel. Hands full, I couldn't have stopped her. But her gaze stayed with mine. I'm not sure that I would've been so noble.

As I watched, Jacq lifted one of my feet then the other. Her hands again glowed as she cleaned not only the floor but also the bottoms of my feet. My magic followed her hot, tingling fingers as they caressed the soles of my feet, running gently over each toe before sliding up the backs of my calves. White-knuckled, I clutched the rail for support. From the very beginning, every time we'd touched, I'd tingled. Now I knew why. Her magic had always been brushing mine. This woman was a living, breathing form of electroshock sex therapy. And it might be worth a trip to the loony bin to have a couple thousand watts of that running through my system.

Watching my pupils dilate and my breathing get heavy, she whispered in my ear, "I'll wait for you." Something in her tone said she was talking about more than my quick shower. My eyes closed as I leaned against the shower door for support. I heard her shut the door firmly and felt her absence as the room's temperature returned to normal. I made my way to the bathtub.

With these weak legs, the shower was no longer an option.

CHAPTER ELEVEN

"Time is fluid. Scientists will give you a bunch of mumbo jumbo about how this deals with space and relativity, but all it really means is that, like water, the harder you try to hold on to time, the faster it runs through your fingers."

—From the personal diary of Cate Delacy Deveroux

After my bath I headed downstairs, passing through a bedroom that seemed like new. I didn't want to know how much magic Jacq had expended. When this was over, I'd bake her a cake to say thank you. Nothing says "Thanks for repairing the damage my evil cat inflicted" like chocolate icing. Even the clothes I'd discarded had been fixed. I couldn't help but notice—she'd left my favorite lacy undies (minus the claw marks) hanging on the inside door. The fact that I was now wearing said undies didn't mean a thing.

Probably the most impressive thing had been the anti-kitty, silver-glowing runes spread across my bedroom door's threshold. Of course, Jacq hadn't told me that's what they were. She didn't need to. When I'd exited the bathroom, the sight of my open bedroom door and a spitting-mad Hex stuck on the other side said it all. I could kiss the woman for that alone.

Because the den had been too small for our group, I'd come downstairs to find everyone relocated to our rarely used dining room. Aunt Helena had made it back from wherever she'd been today, but

Mynx had sent me a text saying she was on the trail of something hot and would be back late. That left us five in the dining room, which worked. Its dark paneled walls and hardwood floor suited the somber task.

Becca wasn't angry about being pushed into Luke. *No shocker there.* She gave me a halfhearted glare for his benefit, which I promptly ignored. I recounted my harrowing tale of tuneful torment with subsequent moaning, groaning and placating (with a home-baked cookie from my aunt) before getting down to business. We managed for about ten minutes until Discord Deveroux had to bring up Wellsy.

"I think your professor friend is right in the heart of it." Luke pointed to the information he and Jacq had collected this afternoon.

I gave him a dirty look. I hadn't had an opportunity to speak with my aunt regarding her friend, and Luke had just ruined my chance to bring up the subject gently.

"What professor friend?" Aunt Helena turned to me. "What is Lucas talking about, dear?"

I pulled my braid then stopped. It was a childhood habit my aunt would recognize. "I ran into Wellsy at Tulane. I was going to tell you, but someone," pointed eye-roll at Luke, "beat me to it. He's teaching a class there." I dropped my voice. "Aunt Helena, he's different. At first, he didn't recognize me. He looks older and," I looked at Jacq for confirmation, "smells of necromantic magic."

At Wellsy's name, Aunt Helena grew pale, but her color returned quickly as she forcefully said, "That doesn't mean anything. There are a hundred unrelated reasons why he would smell like that."

"Yes, there are. And that's why we're going to check all the professors who have connections to these girls." I pointed to a list we'd made. Luke had a point. Wellsy was indeed connected to Isabella and two of the other girls. They'd been his students years ago. However, once we'd started looking at the college angle, we'd found several of the girls had unofficially audited classes and had several professors in common.

Luke gave me a dirty look. If this was a police case, he'd be all for playing by the book. But this was Were business. He didn't fool me. I knew Luke didn't care about who was behind this. He figured if we had the where and when, we could go in, kick ass, and get names later. He'd always been a quick finish kind of man.

"Back to the where. I believe the last ritual will take place in The Burg or nearby. They won't want to move Isabella far." That's why I'd had Kyle moved to that city. We might not be able to track Isabella through her mate-bond, but being near her general location would strengthen the bond and help Kyle stay calm.

My statement got us back on track and we went over the Council's photos again, looking for common factors. Becca was silent for several minutes, but I could tell she had something on her mind. Finally, she cleared her throat. I raised my eyebrows. She looked first at me then Aunt Helena.

"Won't the ritual have to be done at a gate? And don't you know the locations for all of those? You guys didn't misplace one or anything?" She laughed slightly, but her voice was strained. I opened my mouth, shutting it again as she continued, "I mean, how many can there be in one city?"

I saw my aunt gear up to answer. Better her than me. I'd asked my mom the same questions at least a dozen times growing up. I didn't like the answer then. It wouldn't be any pleasanter now.

"What you have to understand," Aunt Helena said, "is that the gates are only for one-way travel. It's not like an open door where we can travel through either way. Gates work best going from gate to gate. They're easier to hold, and there's less chance that you'll be lost in the void." I doubted the others understood how horrible a concept "lost in the void" really was. "The other option is to set up a beacon or focal point on the receiving side. It's like a magical marker telling the gate where to deposit whoever's coming through. It's more risky and takes more power."

This explanation could get a bit long. I pulled up a chair and grabbed Jacq's wrist. We sat close together. I passed her a cookie. Becca and Luke joined us. The Weres looked like they wanted to take notes. I smiled around the chocolate chips. The Council kept information about the gates on a need to know basis, and they didn't think anyone needed to know. This was like finding out who really killed JFK.

In lecture mode, Aunt Helena continued, "There are only a few gates close by. We're tuned to them and know the minute a ritual is begun to open one. We don't think Nicodemus is willing to take that chance when he doesn't have to. All his group needs is a small focal point on this side to set a destination and a massive burst of power. The large gate is in Hell. Power can be stored and hidden on a greater level within living objects than within something inanimate. We believe Nicodemus is using the missing boys as vessels to hold the power he steals during his sacrifices. Because they were not born to it, they can't harness the power. Even chock- full of stolen magic, the boys provide less resistance than if he just kept all of the kidnapped girls alive until the day he opened the gate. From the amount of power he's amassing and his use of the missing boys, this seems like Nicodemus's plan."

Becca's mouth dropped open. I passed her a cookie. She took it automatically. "But the power, the sorcerer, everything is on this side?"

"I've got this," I said. Aunt Helena nodded and sat. I slid the plate of cookies her way. A teaspoon of sugar makes anything go down better. You can bet there were more than a few teaspoons in those cookies. It was a scientific fact—one I was counting on—that people couldn't fight if they had a cookie in their mouth. "Becca, think of it like a collect call where the sorcerer, in this case Nicodemus, accepts the charges. I know it seems bass-akwards." I scooted my chair away from my aunt as she tried to swat me. Technically, I wasn't cursing. I moved just a bit closer to a laughing Jacq, who was fortunate not to choke on her own cookie. Becca watched us three with fascinated eyes. I wasn't quite sure about Luke's expression. It looked remarkably like rancor.

Once out of harm's way, I continued, "The gate would be initiated on the other side then connected to Nicodemus's focal point. The entrance can be powered by either side. Nicodemus is the one collecting power, so he'll be the one to accept payment and be responsible for holding the gate open. If he can't deliver, the call gets disconnected, and the gate closes." I didn't add that the gate *always* takes payment. If Nicodemus couldn't provide enough power, the gate might decide to take him body and soul. Or it might decide to nab anybody who was in the wrong place at the wrong time…like a group of guardians, Weres, and other sundry folk who decided to crash the party-line.

I took another bite, using the gesture to hide my worry. I simply wouldn't let that happen.

* * *

I was waiting with tea and cocoa when Mynx finally dragged in. Luke had left with a half-asleep Becca hours ago, and my aunt had gone to bed. We still hadn't gotten an opportunity for a private talk, but I wasn't too worried. We were living in the same house for weeks yet. Aunt Helena couldn't avoid me forever.

My aunt might be steering clear of me, but I couldn't seem to get rid of Jacq. She'd yawned, said it was too late to drive home, and headed upstairs to the newly discovered guest room. That was at nine p.m., and she hadn't looked a bit sleepy. I didn't have a clue as to what the woman was up to.

That was three hours ago. I'd almost tiptoed upstairs twice and knocked on her door. It would've been nice to talk to her while I was waiting, but I wanted to speak to Mynx alone. Making good use of my time, I'd pulled my laptop into the kitchen to research Wellsy's accident. I'd found a six-month-old article from a Virginian paper and was reviewing a printout of it when Mynx arrived.

Mynx had spent the last few afternoons and nights on stakeout, and she looked it, with tired eyes and rumpled clothes. I owed her *big* for this and knew exactly how to balance the scales.

"Here." I passed her the cocoa. "Mini marshmallows. Nothing but the best for you." I smiled, trying to make my tone light. My body was still strung-out on phers. I'd kept the suppression amulets on, even during my bath, although now they were under my jacket, strung around my neck. The chemical levels were dropping, but being around Luke and Becca, who were both putting out phers, hadn't helped. The constant arousal was always there, even if the symptoms were suppressed, and it was wearing me out.

"We make a fine pair of bleary-eyed women." I gave Mynx a bigger, more genuine smile. She just grunted and smiled back before taking the cocoa and passing me an envelope from a familiar photo center. I sipped a simple Moroccan orange tea and browsed the photos. There were several of Fera and different men in locations around The Burg and outside a home that could be the sheriff's. I stopped briefly at a shot of a café. Fera was kissing Jacq's cheek. The next showed Jacq whispering in Fera's ear. Finally, there was one of them in a lover's embrace.

I curbed my sigh. It didn't matter. They were both immortals. I was a witch who'd be dead in a hundred and twenty years, if I was lucky enough to live that long. I didn't have a hold on the woman. I picked up the next photo, my hand barely shaking.

Mynx gave me a look. "I don't think they're lovers. They put on a show for this one." She pointed to a man wearing a fedora. "The Fae knew they were being watched."

Well, it was a damn good show. Actually, a damning show. I'd briefly considered that Jacq might be a player, an immortal amusing herself with a mortal fling, but that didn't fit the woman who'd put so much effort into undoing Hex's destruction of my bedroom. Even if she wasn't a player, I couldn't compete with the wildly appealing Fera. My thumb brushed a close-up of Jacq's face. The heat that was in her eyes when she gazed at me was absent.

I needed to know where we stood, if only for my peace of mind. *Nothing to do with the state of my heart.*

I flipped the photos to another man. The angular features, long fangs, and aristocratic look said Kin. He was speaking with the man in the fedora hat outside a familiar office. "The leak?" I pointed at the vamp.

"Yes," Mynx purred around her cocoa. "The men following the sheriff report to him. His name's Carlisle and you're going to find who he works for *very* interesting. What's this?" She pointed to the newspaper article on Wellsy's accident.

"*This*," I passed her the printout, "is something strange."

She looked at the newsprint. It had a photo of Wellsy, a mining guide named Peter Traylor, and another man, Domini Roskov. The photo had been taken only minutes after their rescue from a coal mine cave-in. The cause of the cave-in was still unknown. The woman that had gone into the mine with them, Jazmine Manizales, was presumed dead. "Wellsy's a professor. What was he doing in a coal mine?"

"I don't know." I looked at the picture. Something about the men's eyes seemed off. "One man's a guide, the other a financier. The woman was an illusionist. What were they all doing there?"

Mynx just shook her head. "Strange is right."

We sat for a few more minutes, making plans, the file and photos between us like a hot brand neither of us wanted to touch. Then Mynx went to bed. Unfortunately, I had a few more calls to make.

Midnight was regular business hours for the Blood-Kin.

* * *

"I know what you are," Jacq said softly.

The night was quiet. Her voice would carry far, and Cate, in the kitchen, was as close as a walk through the gardens. Through the swirling blue and green wall, gray eyes met glowing red ones. The hound raised its head from the ratty slipper it had been nuzzling before twitching its ears. Jacq squatted, their faces inches apart, separated only by the wards' magic. "I *know* you understand what I'm saying." The hound huffed, pushing hot air against the barrier before baring its teeth.

Jacq grinned back, nothing friendly in either's smile. Predator to predator, they eyed each other, coming to a silent understanding. Finally she rose. The hound laid its head back down, looking bored. "I don't know whose house you belong to, but I know you were not with the two that attacked, which is why I didn't bother to track you down before. So you will do me the courtesy of delivering a message."

The hound huffed again, but Jacq knew it would do as she'd asked. Its loyalty lay with its master, who would want to hear this. "Tell those you serve that I know they will come for her. But if Cate goes," she let her growing power shine through, the silver so bright and pure that for a moment the night seemed like day, "she must go *willingly*."

With that Jacq released her magic, letting it sink in again. The hound didn't bat an eye as the woman left, and it likely wouldn't. But while the demons might never fear such as her, Jacq had the feeling that they might soon learn to fear their wayward child. There was a reason—a very good one—why the demons had once enlisted her kind to care for their young.

And it had nothing to do with their flair for cleaning up dirty nappies.

* * *

Day Seven

"What are you hiding?"

At my words, Aunt Helena dropped her teacup. I jumped forward, grabbing it. She shouldn't have been so startled. This talk had been coming for a long time. Although maybe I should be surprised at how easy it was to arise early and catch her alone in the kitchen.

"Thank you." Aunt Helena took the proffered cup from my hand then turned to take another from the cabinet. I nodded in acceptance of her silent question. We'd have possibly the most important talk of my life over tea and toast. "What makes you think I'm hiding something?" She poured us each a cup of sweet chai with a dollop of milk.

"Aunt Helena, really…" I sighed, blowing at my steaming mug. "You practically run from the room every time we're alone." I looked at my aunt, and as always, sadness swept my heart. The jade eyes, the flame-red curls, the face…Aunt Helena was a true mirror image of her identical twin—my mother. It was like having my mom's specter standing a heartbreaking inch beyond my reach.

The knot growing in my stomach made my tone urgent. "Tell me about the first time my mother went missing…before I was born."

"How did you—" Jaw set, my aunt shook her head. "Never mind. It doesn't matter how you know." Anger flared in her eyes only to be swallowed by something much greater. Her gaze met mine. Grief, like a dark silent river, flowed within the jade depths. "I can't—" She choked on the words.

"You can," I urged. "*Please.*"

Aunt Helena looked away, shoulders slumping. There were dark circles under her eyes. Maybe my bad dreams had begun to spread to those around me.

I bit my cheek, watching my aunt's throat work and her breaths quicken. My own anxiety grew with each moment. Whatever this secret was, it was tearing my aunt up inside, which meant it had to be bad. Really, really bad.

Finally she murmured, "It's not my place to tell."

I reached across the table and took her hand. It seemed so fragile in my slightly darker one. "Maybe not." Aunt Helena's eyes lifted. "But you're the only one here, and I have a feeling that I need to know whatever it is that you fear telling me."

"Oh, sweetie." My aunt's eyes watered then overflowed. Maybe it was a chain reaction because I too began to cry as she continued. "I'm not afraid for me. Evie and I were never afraid for us. We just didn't want to hurt you." I opened my mouth to reassure her, but she rushed on. "Or put you in a position to be hurt. I've always felt guilty because I wasn't there that night. I was supposed to be. But your mother, she said things happened the way they were supposed to. Otherwise she wouldn't have had you, and you were her greatest joy."

I moved around the table to hug my aunt. As I knelt there, loosely holding her, Aunt Helena's eyes closed, tears leaking from beneath her lids. Her hand absently stroked my hair. After a few minutes, she said hoarsely, "You're right. For your own safety, the time has come for you to know this."

She took a few shuddering breaths then began. "Over thirty years ago, a rogue cult tried to open a darkmirror. By a chance of fate, your mother got there first. I was at a night class when the cult began their spell. I left immediately but had a blowout. I spelled the tire rather than waste time changing it. Even so, I arrived just as Evie opened the gate, creating an outgoing path so the cult couldn't create an incoming one. Things went terribly wrong." Her head shook in agitation. "And your mother and the cult members were sucked in. The house the gate was in collapsed. By the time I got to the mirror it was closed. And without knowing the destination, I couldn't follow."

As the story progressed, my eyes dried. I'd already cried so many tears. There really weren't that many left. But my aunt still wept an occasional silent tear, unburdening her soul and releasing years of bottled grief. Lost in memory, she seemed to forget that I was there. Aunt Helena had been so strong when my mother had disappeared three years ago for what I now knew was the second time. I'd always thought my aunt had grieved in private. I'd heard my Nana cry more than once behind her closed door. Goddess knows, I'd done the same. Now, I thought maybe Aunt Helena had never allowed herself the necessity of mourning. She and Nana thought I didn't know their traveling was cover for their continued search for my mother. Like me, both women had worked themselves to exhaustion looking.

We sat like that for a long time, Aunt Helena sharing what my mother had told her about her stay in Denoir, the first of Hell's realms, and the man she'd loved. When Mynx returned we helped my emotionally drained aunt upstairs. Maybe my face didn't reflect my emptiness, my shock. Or maybe Mynx saw from Aunt Helena's troubled state all she needed to. Whatever the reason, I was grateful that Mynx didn't ask any questions.

I tucked my pale aunt into bed and kissed her forehead, saying, "Sleep. Everything will be better tomorrow." If only I could believe my own words.

I closed the drapes against the hot noonday sun then closed her door tightly behind me. It should've felt strange to have our roles reversed. I should've been angry to hear my life's story told with details I'd never known and saddened to know a new side of my mother and not have her here to explain it. Maybe I should've felt all of those things. But at that exact moment, I couldn't feel anything. I was completely…and utterly…numb.

I'd been shocked to learn that my mother had been trapped in the Otherworld before I'd been born. My world had been rocked on its axis when I'd learned that she had loved a demon. And not just any demon, but one whose blood was my own.

My father had been a demon.

All these years, I'd joked about Hex being a hell-spawn when I was literally one. Or, at least, half of me was. That would've been enough to knock me to the floor, but the most overwhelming fact hadn't been my aunt's words. No, it had been the immense sense of déjà vu they had evoked.

Without a doubt, I knew details that Aunt Helena hadn't said. Likely couldn't have said. Like the fact that my father's hair would be the same raven black as my own. I scrubbed my hands over my face as I headed downstairs. I couldn't consider this. My mind emptied of everything but work. Perhaps it would have been better if I hadn't sent Jacq away this morning.

At this moment, the infuriating, smoldering detective would have been a welcome distraction.

I was still viewing the world with a dispassionate eye when Mynx and I left later that night. As the day had progressed, my numbness had grown, sinking deeper into my body and mind, chilling me until even my soul felt frozen. As the sun set, we drove toward The Burg. The thermometer registered ninety. But while the outside might be a steam box, inside I was so cold I almost asked Mynx to turn on the heater. But I stopped myself. No external heat would help this.

There would be no quick thaw for my soul, not even if heated by the fires of Hell. I released a mirthless laugh. Mynx gave me an inquiring look. She probably already knew as much or more than I did about the events leading to my birth. Still, I kept my own counsel.

Tonight was a night for revealing secrets, just not mine.

* * *

Carlisle couldn't believe his luck. No one needed his services tonight, not Nicodemus, the Council, or Louisiana's Vampire King. That left him free to serve the master he owed true allegiance to— himself.

He was barely in the door of his favorite club, Lady D's House of Delights, when the hottest babe in the place signaled she wanted to play. His fangs were straining at his gums, itching to pop out and sink into her throat, before the brunette—sleek in black leather boots, a kitty-cat mask, and the largest black whip he'd ever seen—even reached him. He usually wasn't a submissive…but for her, he'd make an exception. Besides, if things went too far, he could switch roles easily. Inhuman strength was one benefit of being a vampire.

She purred then crooked her finger. He followed as they made their way past a vamp woman tied with leather straps to an X. Another woman, part Fae, whipped her with a cat-of-nine-tails then fondled her bare breasts. The ball in the tied woman's mouth barely muffled her cries of pleasure. This was why he came to Lady D's. Vamps thrived on sex and blood. But Carlisle needed pain, too, and this was the place to find all three. Anything went here—as long as no one died. And he'd heard that rule could be broken if enough money changed hands. There was good reason why such a popular club was in an isolated section of the backwoods.

They passed more couples engaging in all manner of activities. Some were hetero, others same-sex, and some were of the magical variety where their sex was indistinguishable. A witch in a sex swing moaned as she was penetrated from both sides by two bulky male Weres. As Carlisle realized their destination, his blood—what little flowed in his veins—headed south. The extensive one-floor House had three public sections: Bar, Dance Club, and BDSM zone. Newer players warmed up in the first two before making their way to the third.

They were headed to a fourth, private area. He'd used the VIP section only once. It was usually for the more messy players. Carlisle didn't hesitate. The tight, leather-encased ass swaying in front of him was worth making a mess. She stopped at the giant bouncer and ran the handle of her whip down his chest before handing him something. The red rope was pulled back. She stepped into a dark hall, turned, and again crooked her finger.

Carlisle stepped into the darkness behind her. Nothing out there could compare to the pleasure he was about to experience with this vixen.

The club's heavy music dimmed, but there was music of another kind. The constant sounds of heavy, nearly violent fucking came from behind every black door they passed. The steady slap, slap... the wet slurp, slurp...the rich moans and groans...all were a sensual symphony to his ears. Added to this was the ripe smell of sex, strong like he'd just shoved his nose right between a woman's wet lower lips. He licked his own lips in anticipation. Maybe after he was done playing her bitch boy, he'd show her exactly where a vamp's fangs could go. It was enough to bring any warm-blooded male to his knees. Thankfully, he was cold-blooded and able to muster the strength to carry on.

He followed the *click*, *click* of her heels and the scent of woman in heat into the hall's last room. She began a slow tease of undressing him, starting with his silk tie and ending with his Italian designer boxers. She laid his thousand dollar suit carefully over a chair, but he didn't notice. She could have put it in a shredder for all he cared. He was in such a sensual haze that he barely registered the feel of rubber sheets against his back as she pushed him onto the bed.

In anticipation of sex, he'd fed well before coming to the club. His only concern now was the demanding pain in his groin. He didn't notice the magically reinforced titanium manacles being attached to his ankles and wrists. As he watched her in the room's mirrored ceiling, he had his first moment of unease. Claws that looked much too sharp extended from each fingertip. Even so, he didn't realize his mistake until she cupped his tight balls and those claws pricked him as she purred, "Now, tell me about Nicodemus."

CHAPTER TWELVE

"In the South, a story never starts where it should. Ask a man why he killed his neighbor, and he might start by saying, 'Well, I had Cream of Wheat for breakfast then put on my favorite flannel shirt…' An hour later, he'll get to the point. This is why you never ask a Southern man why he doesn't love you. The answer usually starts when he was five and continues on through every previous love."

—Becca Hartford

"Exactly why are we here when I shouldn't be seen with you two?" Fera asked, half-amused, half-irritated. She lounged beside Jacq on a white leather sofa similar to the one I occupied. Jacq, her usual masked expression in place, sat with arms crossed. I sensed her anger but couldn't tell if it was directed at me or Fera, whose feet were sprawled in Jacq's lap. Though I didn't appreciate Fera's relaxed pose, I was glad she hadn't chosen to lounge in the big white bed with gray satin sheets against the far wall.

"We're waiting," I answered. While my eyes stayed fixed on the floor, my thoughts returned to Jacq. If I'd been feeling anything, I might've been concerned at her distance. I might've been saddened to think she could be angry with me. But I was neither. Just like the mask on my own face, I was empty and cold inside.

Even though I'd gotten up early, Aunt Helena had slept in, so I hadn't confronted her until after breakfast. That meal had been so difficult I'd wanted desperately to go back to sleep. Not only had I gone to bed very late, but my sleep had been plagued with restless dreams ranging from the erotic to the horrifying. Then I had to sit across the table from Jacq, who'd stayed to eat with us. She had smiled the entire time. I'd tried to smile back, unsure how to act—unsure of what I'd seen in those photos. Those uncertainties had made me want to overreact. To avoid this I'd gone into professional mode. I'd given Jacq specific instructions about meeting me here tonight with Fera. Then I'd asked her, politely, to leave. I'd desperately needed some time to myself and time to speak with my aunt, but I'd given Jacq other less personal reasons—like the fact that I had calls to return. And surely she had things to do, too. I couldn't expect her to be attached to my hip twenty-four-seven.

At first, the obstinate woman wouldn't leave, arguing that there was still a third hound lurking around. Jacq had spotted its tracks repeatedly circling the house's wards and had presented two very tattered Mr. Bunny slippers as proof. They'd apparently been left at the entrance to the back gardens. I'd almost forgotten about that pesky urinating mutt. For some reason, thoughts of that demon hound didn't worry me, especially after seeing that it had returned my slippers. Just my luck, I'd finally found a dog that would fetch my shoes and it was more likely to break the house than be housebroken.

To reassure Jacq, I'd promised not to venture past the wards alone. The necessity of making such a promise irritated me. I might be younger, but I was also a capable warrior. The voice of reason had saved the good detective's bacon. I might have powers, but she didn't know about them. Mynx and I were coming to the club together, so it wasn't a hard promise to keep. But that hadn't made me any happier with the stubborn, chivalrous woman.

Now Jacq, Fera and I sat here in the club's little known upper level. This room was twice as large as the one below. A portion of the floor was rolled away to reveal a two-way mirror set in the ceiling of the room below. It was this room I was watching while analyzing the other women. Jacq kept eying the space beside me where Mynx should have been. Jacq thought I'd broken my promise and come alone.

She would see soon enough.

The room visible through the two-way glass was currently empty of all but a padded chair and a large, black-sheeted bed. The club's downstairs had been done in black. Few knew about the white rooms upstairs. The area where we were seated was for Lady D's more famous clientele's vice of voyeurism. And if the glass floor wasn't enough, there were four massive flat screens, one on each wall, showing live feed from the currently empty room. Each showed a different view of the room below. Sound was piped in, too. But currently everything was quiet, which was why I'd picked that room. It was the best insulated.

Lady D's House of Delights was the address Benito Carmel, the Blood-Kin's man-of-business, had given me when I'd called regarding our leak. Or rather, *his* leak. Carlisle not only worked for the Council but for Benito's boss, Louisiana's Vampire King. And the time Benito had advised was fast approaching. Earlier in the day, I'd called Darryl Quinton, the club's drag-queen owner, to let him know we were coming. He also happened to be the city's reigning Voodoo Queen, Lady D, and my good friend.

I'd been fortunate that of all the clubs in the area, the loose-lipped council agent frequented this one. Darryl and I went way back, to my days tracking down cheating spouses. He'd hired me to spy on a business/bed partner he'd suspected of skimming profits. I'd caught the crook with one hand in the cookie jar and the other up a skirt. Only one of those had been Darryl's, and it had been the wrong one. I'd given D the evidence and walked away. I wasn't sure what had happened to the man. And I didn't ask. I owed the club's owner more than I could repay. But more importantly, Voodoo was one of the few things that scared the bejeezus right out of me.

Even so, I'd liked Darryl and his alter-ego, Lady D, and later introduced him to my old friend, Buck LaRue. They'd been together ever since. We visited often, but it had been awhile since I'd entered the club. Whips and chains weren't my thing…unless I was the one wielding them.

"Waiting for what?" Fera asked impatiently, dragging me from my thoughts. I was saved from having to answer by Buck's entrance. He was the only man I knew who could wear black leather pants and a black T-shirt with a Stetson and cowboy boots. The man oozed sex appeal. Fera's tail practically wagged as she jerked her feet off Jacq's lap and moved closer to the other woman, making room on the couch. For a several-hundred-years-old woman, she sure was transparent. If I didn't already know she was Fae, I'd think she was a cat in heat like Mynx. Little did she realize that a woman would never turn Buck's head, which was a definite loss for the fairer sex. Buck's sexiness was matched only by his boyish charm. That second characteristic was responsible for the large tub of buttered popcorn he carried. You could trust Buck to turn anything into entertainment.

"Down girl," I said as Buck sat beside me, tipped back his cowboy hat, and began to launch popcorn into the air, catching it with his mouth. Fera watched avidly. Buck seemed clueless to her reaction. I smiled inwardly, knowing better. I might be numb inside, but my friend's antics chipped away at the ice covering my soul. Buck's mischievous streak was just another thing that made us such good friends. "His man will tear out your heart and eat it."

Buck laughed. "No, honey, you forget. Darryl feeds them their own hearts as he watches." He winked, popping another piece of popcorn before adding, "My sweetie's a vegetarian." Stuffed jaws working hard to chew his snack, he looked around at the different monitors, completely missing Jacq's amused and Fera's disappointed expressions. The latter was understandable. No one would ever think Buck was gay by looking at him. With a dark tan, sun-streaked hair and green eyes, he was a good ole—sexy as hell—country boy. I'd always thought Buck was what happened when you mixed the *Dukes of Hazzard* with *Queer Eye for the Straight Guy*. But Fera's reaction was nothing compared to what happened when people saw him and Darryl together. Buck was the perfect foil for his much darker lover.

I was still empty inside, but Buck's joy of life was always infectious. A small spark lit somewhere within me. And seeing Fera's attention shift so quickly had left me feeling something—perhaps, something more generous—toward Jacq, but it was hard to tell. The emotion was only a seed of something that would hopefully grow larger as the night progressed.

Jacq wasn't the type to let a lover stray. Whatever her relationship with Fera, it didn't include benefits of a sexual nature. I snuck a look at the woman in question. She'd worn cream pants and a matching sleeveless top that made her skin glow and her auburn hair look even darker. Her closed expression had opened slightly since Buck's entrance. She now watched me with half-lidded eyes. I quickly returned my gaze to my friend.

Leaning his muscular frame back and extending an arm over the couch top, Buck asked redundantly, "Has the show started yet?"

He still had the athletic build of the quarterback he'd once been. I inhaled his spicy cologne and moved until I leaned against his shoulder. Buck was like a brother to me. Being near him was always comforting. And I knew he enjoyed it, too. Outside of Buck's immediate family, I was the only person who could cuddle Lady D's man without ending up in traction.

"What show?" Fera wouldn't be stopped.

That little seed of hope inside me had managed to sprout, even in the icy plains of my heart. Where before I hadn't cared, now part of me wanted to hear Jacq's husky voice instead of Fera's sultry one. As I saw the vampire walk into the room below followed by Mynx in her black leather cat-suit, I thought I might hear my auburn-haired protector comment. Unfortunately, it was Fera who rounded on me.

"What in the *hell?* What is that vamp lackey, what's his name?" Fera snapped her fingers. "Carlisle. What's he doing here?" Her angry tone turned humorous as Mynx began to slowly undress the hypnotized man. "You better not have brought me to some sort of sex show without warning. I'd have dressed more appropriately."

Fera looked nice in black trousers and a gold shirt that brought out the gold in her many-hued hair, so I assumed "more appropriately" meant showing more skin. The question sounded rhetorical, so I didn't answer. That was a mistake, because then Fera's gaze shifted from the now nude man to my face. Even my numb emotions couldn't completely block my sense of propriety.

"Why is she blushing?" No longer inquisitive, Fera had the demanding voice of someone who had a mass of highly trained spooks at her beck and call.

What a perfect time for the playful Fera to disappear and the commanding sheriff to appear. I was about to tell her to piss off when Buck, in traditional Screw-You-LaRue fashion, chimed in. Too bad, it was always his friends that got screwed.

"The Ice Princess has always been a bit of a prude. Haven't you, sweetie?" He nudged my shoulder, not giving me a moment to answer—not that my doubly embarrassed mouth could. "She swore she wouldn't even have sex until she got married." He laughed. I cringed. "I bet Deveroux popped that cherry good when you and he—ow!"

Even my frozen soul knew better than to let him continue talking. Just as he was about to say "got hitched," I shifted, and my elbow *accidentally* ended up in his groin. My one-week marriage to Luke had been annulled years ago. If only I could wipe that mistake from everyone's minds as easily as it had been removed from the state's records.

"Shhh, listen." I pointed at the glass floor.

Mynx's, "Now, tell me about Nicodemus," filtered through the sound system. All eyes riveted to the scene unfolding below. The white room fell blissfully silent, the only questions coming from Mynx as she worked her other form of magic—the sort that only needed razor-sharp claws, pointy teeth and a smile that said she enjoyed her work. Part of it was the cat's instinct to play with her prey, but Mynx had once confessed that her natural urges had taken a much darker turn after entering Hexamina's body. I shuddered. Sometimes I wondered about the things Hex had done with that body to have torture feel so natural to the woman now abiding there.

It was a little disappointing how quickly everything went. The stoolie squealed like a girl. Then he told everything he knew, which wasn't much. Carlisle's job was to watch Fera and the Council and report back. He'd been the one to target Bob for possession but didn't know what the embezzled funds were being used for. He'd been told to pick someone with access to money and had chosen someone in-house to screw over his boss, Louisiana's Vampire King.

Carlisle confirmed Nicodemus was working for one of the Demon Lords but wasn't sure which one. Nicodemus had always worn his distortion cloak. According to Carlisle, no one knew Nicky-boy's true face. He'd simply shown up in town one day and started making friends. Carlisle thought he was the only one within the Council's circle but couldn't be sure.

Apparently, Nicodemus's demon master was preparing an army to cross over very soon from one of the Otherworld's seven levels. Like a B-movie, the traitorous Carlisle had been promised a place in the new world order. Most of this we'd already surmised. Confirmation was good but not why we were here.

Between screams, Carlisle finally gave up something useful. He didn't know the final sacrifice's location, but he confirmed Isabella was the intended victim. Nicodemus had used Carlisle's spies to scout her apartment. Carlisle had been the one to have Tulane's registrar hacked, personally picking the five boys based upon Nicodemus's specs: Orphans with a special blood type. Nicodemus hadn't specified male or female. The vamp just hated to waste good pussy. The blood requirement was mystifying. Why would it matter? The blood sucker now gnashing his teeth in desperation didn't know.

Blood was often used in the darker rituals, but the boys all had other links. Having them the same blood type would create a common chain, making them easier to control. But why stipulate this particularly rare type instead of a more common one? It limited Nicodemus's possible vessels, making his goal that much harder. I couldn't even begin to guess. Carlisle also gave up the last target's name. He'd been unable to find six human boys healthy enough in the school's current medical files. The last vessel was a woman and due to be snatched very soon.

"I have to go now, but don't worry, suga." Mynx ran the sharp tip of a claw down his cheek. "Someone will be along for you shortly."

Her words brought my attention from the bleeding, whimpering, but still intact (in all the areas he would consider vital) vampire to the woman now wiping her bloody hands clean on his tie. I frowned. I hadn't realized Mynx was so near her heat. Blood and pain didn't do it for her, but she wasn't immune to the phers floating around the club. It must've been extremely hard for her not to rush the interrogation and go play.

"What do you want me to do with him?"

At Buck's low question, I swung my eyes to him, noting that Fera was watching Mynx with a predatory gaze. I almost warned her away but stayed quiet. They were both big girls, and big girls could take care of themselves. "Cut out his tongue. Then give him to the Weres. The girl they targeted was mate to one of their wolves."

I released a long breath. I'd had enough blood for tonight. Lady D would probably do the deed herself, loving the opportunity to add a vamp tongue to her Voodoo pantry, assuming she didn't already have one. "Call Luke. He's their Alpha now and will know what to do." Isabella was in the hands of a demon lord's minion. The Weres would've been nicer to Carlisle if she were dead.

I ignored Buck's, "Ooo, Wolfie-boy's been busy."

"The tongue will grow back." Jacq's husky voice shivered down my spine, and that seed in me grew, its roots cracking the ice around my soul. Jacq no longer looked angry, and when her gaze met mine, it was alight with speculation. Her concept of what I was capable of had just been upgraded.

If only she knew.

"I know, but it'll be a day or more before he can speak. I don't want Carlisle talking to the Weres until we've grabbed the girl. Nicodemus could also have spies within the Clan." This was highly unlikely, but yesterday's trusting mood had crashed and burned the moment I found out my mother and aunt had deceived me my entire life about my father being a demon…about me being part demon. Aunt Helena hadn't mentioned my grandparents, but they had to have known. My sense of betrayal was all-encompassing. I paused, swiveling to Fera who'd picked up her cell. "What are you doing?" Like I didn't already know. My harsh tone struck her like a whip.

Her mouth said, "Calling my guys to pick up Nicodemus's next target," but her eyes said, "How dare you ask?"

Icy fury surged, cracking the ice around my soul further. Fortunately, Jacq, ever the diplomat, jumped in.

"We'll get her, Josephine. Your agent just admitted he may not be the only one of yours working for Nicodemus. Having the girl picked up might put her in more danger."

"Fine." Fera closed her cell with a loud snap. "If you no longer need me, I'm going downstairs."

"Fera?" I called. She stopped, turning abruptly, golden locks whipping around her head. Forcing my anger away, I reached under my white dress shirt and grabbed the envelope I'd tucked into my tight leather pants before throwing it to her. The envelope held the photos Mynx had taken of the men following Fera. "There are a few others that work for Carlisle, but please wait until we get Brittan before cleaning house." Brittan was the name of Nicodemus's last vessel.

Fera gave a salute then left, putting on a sensual strut. She was no mouse, but her swaying hips said that without question her purpose for the rest of the night was to find a kitty and play. Buck followed her out, cell phone in hand. Jacq didn't say a word, watching as I stepped to a hidden console, pulled aside a white panel, and began to push buttons.

One switch caused a light buttercup carpet to roll over the glass mirror, blending seamlessly with the rest of the floor. Another cut the video feed. Yet another doused the sound. I began working with the video equipment, jumping when Jacq spoke from above my left shoulder.

"What are you doing?" Her breath brushed my ear. She stood inches away, our bodies not touching, but I could feel her heat soaking into my back.

"I'm copying the video to a DVD then erasing it from the system's memory. Eventually, I may have to explain to the Council and Kin why one of theirs is dead." Any legalities regarding gaining a confession under extreme duress wouldn't apply here. Certain things were permissible with the undead. Not that something like this would ever end up in a human court of law. The Council and the Vamps had bloody appetites. They didn't care about methods, only results—something I'd never liked about either group. It was frightening to think that in this case I agreed with them.

I felt a kinship with Isabella Richmond. We were both women without mothers trying to deal with powers we didn't understand. To get her back, I'd do whatever it took. Since my mother's disappearance, I'd been bending and breaking the rules regularly. But soon a line would have to be drawn. The possibility of crossing that line didn't scare me so much as not recognizing it when the time came.

I pocketed the DVD and turned to Jacq, who nodded and moved to sit on the couch where Buck had been. She patted a cushion. "You never answered the earlier question."

Not the cherry-popping one. I could handle anything but a reference to Buck's ill-timed, less than tactful, unfinished statement. My eyes rolled skyward as I silently prayed, *Please don't let it have something to do with me, Luke and sex.* The goddess probably didn't hear too many prayers with the word "sex" included. Hopefully, she'd take notice.

"Which question?" Voice cracking, I moved to sit down. I'd been focused on getting through tonight. Now that the vampire's "interview" was over, I felt my lack of sleep. I inhaled Jacq's scent. Even though we hadn't been around each other all day, I fancied her musk still carried a hint of orange. I rested my head against the white cushions.

"You never said why you wanted Fera here tonight." Jacq's voice was low and smooth.

I shifted, stalling as I considered my answer. We both stretched out our feet. Jacq mimicked Buck's earlier posture, placing her arm across the couch top. Like with Buck, it was tempting to cuddle close. I hadn't been close to anyone for so long. And eventually your skin simply hungers for the contact of another's. I resisted my body's need, focusing on her question.

"Several reasons. Mynx wanted her here, and I thought it was worth taking the risk. Fera can see to having the leak taken care of personally, plus we had those photos of the man following her. This was the quickest, most discreet way to pass them along."

Jacq frowned. She didn't buy my story. It was all true. Mynx did want Fera here, though I didn't know why. But I'd left out the most important part. I wanted to see Jacq and Fera together, to judge for myself if there was anything between them. I closed my eyes and temporarily called a halt to my internal conflict. Barely voicing aloud something my mind didn't want to consider, I said softly, "And I wanted her to know that I'm changing the rules."

"How so?" Jacq's voice was just as soft.

"We can't do this alone. We need help." I scooted a little closer, allowing myself to lean against her muscled shoulder. She murmured her assent. My earlier state of numbness aside, I wasn't the Ice Princess Buck had called me. My confession at age seven that I would someday freeze my heart so it could never be broken had earned me the moniker. I'd given up that dream a long time ago, but the nickname had stuck.

The day's events had affected me, proving that even a frozen heart bleeds, so surely it was okay to seek a little comfort. Maybe I wasn't the only one who felt that way, because Jacq silently pulled me closer, wrapped her arm around my shoulder, and eased her taller frame down so that her head rested against mine. Without effort, I let myself drift into sleep. Maybe I could think of a new dream.

It was too late to keep my heart on ice, anyway.

CHAPTER THIRTEEN

"Tonight on Springer: Gnomes and the women who love them. We'll begin with Sheryl. She's been having an affair with her lawn gnome for nearly five years. Sheryl, tell us, when did you first realize you were attracted to pointy-hatted men?"

"Come on, suga. It's time for you to take Miss Hot Stuff and go on home." A large hand gently shook my shoulder. "Unless, of course, you and her want to climb on up in that big bed there." I recognized the deep voice but still awoke disoriented. It had been a long time since I'd slept so peacefully. "Lady D don't mind none if y'all stay over."

I opened my eyes to find luscious chocolate irises and thick lashes staring back at me. I smiled, feeling not quite as cold inside. It truly was a shame that Darryl played for the other team. With his light brown skin, big eyes and slender swimmer's build, he'd made more than one woman swoon—in and out of drag. I stretched leisurely then looked at D. She was always stunning, and tonight was no exception. She wore a chic deep aqua pantsuit with her straight black hair pulled back at the neck. Lady D didn't perform much anymore. Yet, even without the dress and heavy makeup, she had a level of class and attitude that screamed *runway*. Her pale pink lips stretched into a wide smile. Sometimes D knew what I was thinking before I did.

"Where are Mynx and the others?" I asked, more out of curiosity than concern. I thought I knew where my business partner was, but like peeking under a bandage, I had a morbid urge to confirm the facts.

"The kitty has done run off with the wild one. An' a fine pair they make." D's voice came from beside the hidden video console.

I loved how Darryl and Lady D's personalities differed so. Darryl had the cultured tones of New England, where he'd been raised. Lady D was Southern drama to the core. *Wild one?* That must be Fera. An apt description. The look in her eyes as she'd left had most definitely been wild. I opened my mouth to comment but was interrupted as a woman with a Nordic accent called from the doorway, "Catherine Delacy, what trouble have you gotten yourself into this time?"

"Serena?" Turning, I blinked sleep out of my eyes, watching as the Vampire Queen of Mississippi strode into the room. Tall and pale blond, she resembled the Viking she had once been. She also happened to be Lady D's business partner and sister to Seth, Louisiana's Vampire King—Carlisle's master and Benito Carmel's boss. Her brother's right hand, Serena was the one Seth called upon when he suspected their own of disloyalty.

"What makes you think I've gotten into any trouble?" I asked innocently.

"Call it a preemptive prediction," Serena said knowingly. She smiled wide, showing large fangs. They didn't call Serena the Queen of Secrets for nothing.

"For your information," I said cockily, "except for the hellhounds and demon-possessed accountant, I've gone over a week without incident." Serena blinked black eyes at me. "Truly, my life is rather boring." I held the video disc of tonight's events in front of my face in play defense.

Serena snatched the disc away, growling, "Cate, this is serious business." She could've taken the memories of Carlisle's confession from my mind, but this way was easier for us both.

I sobered. "Believe me, I know." Our eyes met. "You'll be there?"

"Yes," Serena said staunchly. "I'll back you when the fight comes. All you need do is whistle." Puckering her lips, Serena rumpled my hair as she headed to the room's small bar.

Finger-combing my mussed hair out of my eyes, I glared at Serena's back before turning to D, who watched me absently, as if listening to something I couldn't hear. Her expression said trouble was brewing. I knew better than to ask questions I didn't want answered. The ominous feeling in my gut combined with the look on D's face said that was the case with my next question, but I trudged on. "D, if Mynx went with the sheriff, where's Detective Slone, the auburn-haired woman that came with Fera?"

D took his drink from Serena. "Miss Hot Stuff is downstairs with the wolves. I figure she and the boy have a lot to talk about. If you hurry on down, you might can stop their come-to-Jesus-meetin'."

At her words, I jumped up and rushed across the room. But instead of heading to the door, I barreled into D. She stumbled backward under my momentum, nearly spilling her brandy.

"D," I pulled her face to mine, laying a smacking-loud, slobbering kiss on her cheek, "have I told you lately how good a friend you are to me?" The ice inside was still melting. I suddenly felt giddy. Spring was coming.

The voice that spoke out of D's face was Darryl's deep bass. "I know, sweetie, but you'd better go on and save those two from themselves."

And I knew exactly which two he meant. Luke and Jacq. No matter the persona, Lady D or Darryl, s/he had always called Luke boy—even on our wedding day, which should've told me something. I laid another loud kiss on D's other cheek before doing a one-eighty and bolting for the door. I had to see a man about a horse. Or, at least, the back half of one.

"Hey," Serena shouted, "where's *my* hug?"

Over my shoulder, I gave her the finger. "Consider that an IOU." Serena's laugh chased me out the door.

I flew down the stairs, my sense of urgency increasing. By the time I reached the bottom, I was running. "Mother of—" The access panel's red light refused to change no matter how many times I swiped my card. I took a deep breath and tried again. *Green light. Go! No, no go.* I barely stopped myself from yanking open the door. That ominous, foreboding feeling had returned. Once I stepped past this door, everything in my life would change forever.

Never one to back away from the future, I forced myself to slow down, only cracking the door, allowing my eyes to adjust to the dimmer light. A few feet away, directly across from me, was the room where Carlisle had been restrained. I wasn't breathing hard from the run, but the words coming from behind that partially open black door were enough to give me palpitations.

"I don't believe it," Jacq said, her husky voice seething with anger. "Your mark isn't upon her. I would have sensed it, just like any magical creature that approaches her would. If. It. Were. There."

A quick survey of the hall revealed two Weres standing guard nearby. One to my left, farther away, was watching the hall's main entrance. The other, to my right, guarded the door I needed to enter. Although I hadn't heard Luke speak yet, he had to be the other half of Jacq's conversation.

The Were guards might be standing outside a human's range, but moon-howlers had excellent hearing. They were only pretending not to listen. Unfortunately, the closest guard—and the only one facing me—was an ashen Becca. In a traditional little black dress, pearls and heels, she looked dressed for a romantic night out. The slightly rumpled dress and smeared lipstick didn't match her clenched fists, set jaw and glistening eyes.

"I'm telling you," Luke shouted, "that Catherine Eleanor Delacy is my goddamn wife, and you'd better keep your paws off her."

He didn't. No, he did. I momentarily bowed my head in disbelief. When I looked up, a tear was slowly trailing down Becca's cheek. I stood motionless. Weres didn't cry, not over gunshot wounds or broken bones. When we'd first met at the Blue Moon Club, Becca's familiarity had triggered a memory. Becca's tears did the same, resurrecting a memory from deep in the back of my mind. Heartache was the only thing that could make a Were cry.

Becca was in love with Luke. The same Luke who was claiming *we* were still married. Whether he knew it or not, he'd just drop-kicked her heart.

The other Were, back turned to us, couldn't see her grief. No one would bear witness but me, and I was the one who needed to see. My eyes were riveted to that shimmering droplet of salty water. Forget me. Forget Jacq. Forget Luke, even. All that mattered was that lone tear and what it represented. The worst part was the reality that, more than my big-mouthed ex, I was responsible. I'd pushed her into Luke's arms, literally. I'd shown her the light at the end of the tunnel. And like a bad cartoon, that light had turned into a locomotive and run her over. I'd helped her love life become a big steaming pile of train wreckage.

I hadn't made a sound, but Becca's head turned in my direction, acknowledging my presence, her eyes accusing me of a crime I couldn't deny. I quietly stepped out of the stairwell. Becca roughly brushed the tear aside. The other Were shifted, looking at us, but Becca shook her head once, and he turned away. I stared at Becca, trying to form a plan that wouldn't come.

Seeing her pain was almost enough to melt the remaining ice within me. Fury, burning both hot and cold, filled me. I was angry at myself. I was angry at Luke. Most importantly, I was resolved. I would fix this. And I'd have to hurry, because Jacq's next words elicited an angry growl that said blood was about to be spilled.

"I've never touched someone that was another's." Jacq paused, letting Luke think he'd gotten his way before she pulled the rug. "But Cate doesn't look at me with the eyes of a married woman. This thing between us is bigger than you, Wolf, and you're not going to stop me from giving the lady any pleasure she requires."

A frightening thrill ran through me. I shivered, pushing it aside, too worried to consider Jacq's intentions. She had no idea how low she'd hit Luke. There were no sounds of furniture breaking or fists flying, but they couldn't be far off.

Luke's snarling reply was lost as I whispered to Becca, "Don't enter until I call for you." The words were little more than a breath forced through clenched teeth, but Becca's jaw tightened. She'd heard. Still, I asked, "Do you understand?" Her slight nod was barely perceptible in the hall's dim light.

The other Were stood motionless. I didn't bother with him. Becca treated me like I wasn't a threat. Until he saw something to conflict with that judgment, he'd do the same. Besides, Becca was Second. If she told the other Were not to enter, he had to obey.

That explained why he didn't stop me but not why Becca had agreed to my request. I had no authority over the Weres. Maybe she had more faith in me than I had in myself. More likely, she was too upset to care. I was confident that both wolves would stay on this side of the door as long as they didn't believe their Alpha was in danger. Or until Luke called. As I pulled the door open, my smile was grim. Lucas Deveroux wouldn't get that chance.

Few people knew that Lady D's was built on a ley-line nexus. Where else would a Voodoo Queen build her mini empire? I drew on the lines to reinforce my own magic. If I was willing to use my fire, this wouldn't have been necessary, but I'd been burning hotter and hotter the last few days. Partially from the phers. Partially from the heat I'd gotten from Jacq and the Blue Moon. And partially from something inside myself that was growing stronger. It was that last part that kept me using only ley-line and earth-magic for this tête-à-tête. I might want to fry Luke's ass but not literally so. There would be other days for that.

I eased into the room and shut the door. For the safety of the House's customers, these doors didn't lock. Would I trust the Weres to stay out? No. If there were any witnesses to what was about to happen, their Alpha would have to challenge me to save face. Or have the pack view Luke as weak. Then he would have to kill me quickly to prove he was still strong enough to hold the wolves together or have them turn on him. Both of those options would really, really suck. Needless to say, Luke and I would have to be alone for this meeting.

My fury was great and growing more so by every minute and every asinine, possessive word still pouring from Luke's mouth. But if I were to be honest, I'd have to admit that I didn't want to stop the angry tide. It felt damn good. Even so, I was fully aware of what I was doing. And more than anyone else, I knew what the consequences would be. Still, I stepped into the room and didn't look back.

The door closed behind me with a barely audible click, and I began my wards. They simmered blue in the air before attaching to the door. Beside my barrier glyphs was my own glowing version of Jacq's sound ward. No one would be coming into this room without a serious magical kick, and nothing said would be getting out, at least not through the walls or door. I intentionally missed warding the ceiling's microphones.

I never heard what Jacq said in response to Luke's snarls, but I could tell she hadn't been shocked by the word "wife." Maybe she was preparing to make me a widow. If she was a tenth as angry as I was, it was a definite possibility.

Then again, angry might've been an understatement. My blood was boiling, and my heart was still just icy enough to not worry about the feelings of the man I now marched toward. I barely noticed that the traitorous Council agent, Carlisle, and the bloody sheets had been removed. My focus was on the dumb shit with his back to the door. *Tsk. Tsk.* Rule one of survival was to keep all possible entrances in your line of vision. Rule two was never turn your back on your enemy. Rule three was don't piss off your ex-wife. We were more or less zero for three. I might not be Lucas Deveroux's enemy, but at the moment I certainly wasn't feeling very friendly toward him.

This wasn't how I'd planned to end the evening. Secretly I'd hoped to find Mynx right about the relationship between Jacq and Fera, then take a spin on the dance floor with the dimpled detective. With that possibility in mind I'd worn dancing shoes, which were much quieter than my boots. But if Luke had been paying attention to anything besides his own hurt pride, his keen senses would've caught the soft scuffle against concrete. Or my heavy, angry breaths. Or the *clack clack* as my teeth ground together. If this had been anywhere and anyone else, I would've been more careful in stalking my prey, but I was angry, unconcerned with being subtle, and unconsciously wanting Luke to turn around and see the wrath he had wrought. I grimaced at his lack of attention. It would get him killed one day. He should've at least noticed the small echoes as every sound bounced off the new wards.

Thankfully, Jacq hadn't gotten so caught up in the argument. Her skin nearly blazing silver with magic, her eyes almost white with wild fire, she stopped, her mouth still open, ready to reply to the insult Luke was snarling about "balls" and "penises." Like lightning, her storm-filled, nearly desperate gaze flashed to me.

I knew what she saw. Taking advantage of the temporary battle-reprieve, I'd worn my hair down. As my temper escalated, my magical control unraveled, resulting in glowing light blue eyes haloed by little locks of wavy hair that rose, moving of their own accord in the still air. This powerful display was well beyond what Jacq had seen during the hellhound battle. There was surprise and desire in her eyes. I almost laughed. She thought my magic was hot.

She had no idea.

Luke's back was turned, but I knew his reaction would be more extreme. I'd always been so careful, never letting my magic fully out of its cage in his presence. Why? I'd asked myself that time and again. Maybe I just didn't want to see the rejection in his eyes. That, too, was a mistake. A male Were's nature was to dominate and protect. Luke would've respected me for being stronger than him, but he wouldn't have wanted me for a mate. I'd tried to be something I wasn't, and he'd wanted to be with a woman that didn't really exist. It was a mistake I'd sworn not to repeat.

Flames of lust flickered in Jacq's eyes, replacing the desperation. That half-smile curved, and that dimple peeked out. Those beautiful reflections of how she felt would be gone soon, possibly for forever, and I wanted to enjoy the last, brief sight. Time had run out for us. I tried to return her smile but the muscles in my irate face wouldn't stretch right. My eyes rolled skyward in a silent plea before I mouthed, "Go."

It pained me to ask, especially when faced with the sudden hurt filling her eyes. I pointed upward. Hopefully, she understood. Though she was no Were, Luke would still consider Jacq a witness. If she stayed, he would have to kill us both or risk his own death. And Jacq? She might not forgive me for making her leave.

Damned if I do. Damned if I don't. But at least, this way, Detective Jacqueline Slone would live to see another day. As far as plans went, it was a pretty shitty one, but it was the best I had.

Jacq stepped past Luke, making her way to the door where I'd set the wards so she could pass through. He attempted to grab her shoulder, but Jacq brushed him away. Seething, Luke turned to follow, saying, "We're not done here." And that's when I acted.

Fire dripped from my fingers like little droplets of lava until I reined it in. Even so, my hands were still scorching hot when I reached up and grabbed Luke's ear. The Beast-Clan were extremely strong and pain resistant, but like all men, they had pressure points. And most notably, I'd learned that move from my ex's spitfire of a mama, Mamie Deveroux. She'd raised five Werewolf sons and was a fount of information on dealing with any sort of beastie boy.

"What the f—" Luke spun around, jerking his head down to relieve the pressure created by my tight burning pinch. I pivoted around his body, moving at three times my normal speed thanks to magic and phers. I wasn't faster than a Were, but as anticipated, Luke was slow to react. He was used to his mama pulling that trick and had trained himself not to fight back. No good Southern boy ever raises a hand to his mother…at least, not more than once.

We were face-to-face before he even said the third word. Or rather, I was face to chest. Still holding his left ear, I grasped his right shoulder with my other burning hand.

To an outsider, it might have looked like a dance. My hand caressing the side of his face. The other balanced on his shoulder. We were standing there like lovers about to embrace when the door clicked, and I knew Jacq was gone. That was what I'd been waiting for.

Scalding hot pressure at just the right point on Luke's shoulder forced him to his knees. His eyes met mine then grew big. He was easily four times stronger than I, but shock held him motionless. Fear did the same for me. For a moment I didn't breathe. It wasn't Luke or even what I'd just done that frightened me. Though maybe both should have. No, something dark, something definitely worth fearing, was growing in me. Not anger. Not the numbing ice. Much worse, it was a darkness—a powerful, sentient entity—within my own soul. One that was flooding me with a dark joy at the sight of this strong man at my feet.

For a millisecond, I let my mind gaze inside trying to locate and understand this unsettling presence. Sensing my awareness, it softly brushed against the walls of my soul, the sensation like an unfurling of wings inside my skin. I shivered, and it retreated back to a black corner, watching me from the pitch dark with glowing eyes.

I was me, but I was also this thing inside of me when I ordered, "KNEEL." My voice boomed in the warded room, echoing several times. Luke's midnight-blue eyes widened as green whips of earth-magic lashed out, binding his legs to the ground, his arms to his sides, and his jaw together. He was lucky that I hadn't used my fire. My dark side wanted to see it lick across his skin as he screamed in pain. But that wasn't me, and I was still in control...more or less. Like this, Luke could neither speak nor move. But the betrayed, angry expression on his face spoke volumes. In my heart, I wept.

With one word, I'd lost the man I'd once considered my best friend. Even my walking away from our marriage hadn't done this kind of damage. I took several deep breaths. There were things that needed to be said and things that couldn't be said. I had to make sure we were both coherent enough to get through this without mixing the two.

Inside, I screamed at Luke for making Becca cry. I could forgive his foolish behavior to myself and Jacq. We were strong. As was Becca. But a strong woman's heart was no less tender. Sometimes, it simply took longer to break. I understood Becca's hurt more than she or Luke could ever know, but I bit my cheek to keep those words inside. It wasn't my right to expose another woman's pain. Still, there was something I could say. Something that needed to be said.

I looked at Luke. He was straining against the magical bonds, muscles bulging under a hunter-green shirt. Like Becca, he was dressed nicely...though he'd missed a few buttons. Had Luke and

Becca been on a date? That would compound Becca's hurt and my own castigation. I bit my lip, holding in an apology. Luke was the wrong person for it. And the right person would probably take a fist to the face before she'd take an apology from me. I released a mental sigh. It was too late for what-ifs. The only thing to do was to go forward. Luke's struggling hadn't ceased, but his head tilted back, eyes following the pass of emotions on my face.

I pulled the padded chair in front of him and sat. Crossing my legs, I folded my hands over my knees and returned his gaze. "I will say this once." I held up my index finger. "Then never again. We will not speak of this outside this room." The angry, hungry darkness in me further retreated. I could now sympathize with the hurt and confusion in his eyes. But sympathy didn't get either of us off the hook for the mess we'd made. I softened my voice, adding a sense of urgency. I could only hope he understood. "It's important, Luke, that no one else know this." If possible, he looked a millimeter less angry. However, his confusion increased.

Sighing, I blew a flying lock of hair from my eyes. "We don't have time for complicated explanations. You'll just have to trust me." His expression was dubious but intent. At least he was listening, if involuntarily, which was the only way we would ever have this talk. The sound wards meant my magical gag wasn't necessary, but if I knew Lucas Deveroux—and I did—it was the only way I was going to get a word in edgewise. His jaw was already twitching, trying to force out words (most likely of the cursing variety). A thump sounded nearby as someone pounded at the door.

Interesting. Sound could enter but not leave? No matter. The Weres could sense their Alpha's agitation, but they couldn't know exactly what was happening. For the sake of appearances, Becca was probably making a halfhearted effort to break down the door. But the wards were holding strong. They'd have to smash the thing to splinters, and even that probably wouldn't be enough. I turned back to Luke. My stomach flipped once with worry. Not about Becca. There was plenty of time there. So, why this sudden sense of urgency?

I felt it then. Luke's Wolf had been rising gradually since his confrontation with Jacq. His dark blue eyes had a feral glow, confirming that when she'd left he hadn't stopped the progression. *Lovely. Just lovely.* I had maybe a minute before I lost his attention. Now I had to put what I couldn't say in three years into sixty seconds? No pressure there.

I'd never fully explained to Luke why I'd left our marriage. Maybe that was another of my mistakes. But sometimes to speak of the future was to change it. And the future I'd seen for him needed to happen…for both our sakes. I'd been wrong earlier—I would be sharing secrets tonight. The time had come for me to share one with my ex. We'd simply have to take the risk that the future would still happen as it should. Because I was pretty sure it was going to be real screwy if I didn't.

"Luke, Luke?" I waited for his eyes to focus again on my face. He was forcing his Wolf away, and it was costing him. I mentally girded my loins and continued, "I love you. I've always loved you." I didn't stop at his look of surprise and increased confusion. "But you were always meant for another. I saw it, Wolf." I ran my fingertips across a cheek bristling with the start of fur, rubbing the smear of lipstick from his lips out of habit. "And I left." I swallowed past the lump in my throat, taking my hand away to wipe my own tears, watching his change slow. *Good, he was listening.*

"I loved you, but I walked away from our marriage. And it hurt. It hurt me deeply to do it, knowing that I'd hurt you…knowing that I might lose you as a friend forever." His change hadn't fully stopped, but the feral look had been replaced with one of great sadness. Tears spilled from his beautiful half-man, half-wolf eyes. For me? For him? If he hurt like I did, then they were for us both and what might've been. I'd thought Luke was fighting for me to assuage his ego. I'd been wrong…and selfish, thinking I was the only one still hurting. All this time, he'd been hurting, too.

More silent tears dripped down my cheeks, and I didn't wipe them away. There would be time for grief later. Luke's shift was still progressing. He might have gone too far to stop, though his slowing the process had bought us precious time. His jaw elongated, brown hair slowly flowing over his skin. It was now or never. "I loved you, but not the way you needed. I did it so you wouldn't be stuck in a half-love with me when you have a true love and a true mate waiting for you." I pointed to the door, which rattled as Becca and the other Were threw themselves against it.

I placed both feet firmly on the ground, leaned forward, and whispered. Even with the wards to protect against eavesdropping, this was something that should only be said in hushed tones. "The spell I conducted on the day of our wedding was for a vision." I let out an empty laugh. "But I got more than I bargained for. I lost six days of my life to the magic, but I received what some would consider a great gift in return. I saw our future together when I was in that coma." I resisted the urge to reach out and comfort him again. This was going to be hard for Luke to hear. It was certainly hard for me to say. But we needed the clean break that we'd both denied ourselves for far too long. "If we had stayed married, we would never have had children, and we both would've been miserable." He shook his head. "Yes, Luke, eventually we would've realized that you'd bound yourself irrevocably to the wrong woman." The mixture of shock, confusion and disbelief on his face said that he didn't understand. But that was okay. I couldn't force-feed it to him. Or at least, not any more than I was already doing having him bound and gagged on his knees. It wasn't like I could drill a hole in his skull and cram the thoughts in, though the idea had crossed my mind.

I was nearly calm now that I'd said my piece. The fearful, hungry power inside me receded further. It felt as if the Universe had suddenly jumped back on the right track. I laughed, brushing the back of my hand across my face to wipe away the remaining tears before doing the same for Luke. I sniffled. "You're an ass, Lucas Deveroux, and I've half-a-mind to let D really make you into one." He began to struggle in earnest. We both knew D could make good on my threat…or do much, much worse, if she desired. "But I won't." Luke stopped. I couldn't speak for the wolf-man before me, but I was emotionally exhausted. "You're a blind fool, though." Yep, that was all I'd got. Three years to say what I thought, and that was it. Seriously anticlimactic.

I leaned back and smiled a wide, true smile. "But be sure and use a breath mint before you go after the girl, unless she's the kind that likes the smell of raw meat." I could actually smell the steak dinner on his breath. That wasn't my sort of thing. But if the smell of sex coating his skin was a good indicator, wolfy females dug it.

I got up and looked down at Luke. He had a good heart, even if he did have a pig's head. I just hoped he figured out sooner, rather than later, where to put that heart.

I dropped the sound ward first. "Becca?" I spoke softly, keeping my gaze locked with Luke's. The fires of hell were still burning in my eyes, and I wanted that sight to be the memory he most kept of me. Even after all the mush I'd just shared, I still hoped that after tonight he wouldn't remember me so much as an old love or friend but as a formidable opponent he should think twice before challenging.

"Yes?" The pounding stopped.

"Come take your Alpha home. He looks tired." I leaned close to Luke, who'd finally stopped his shift halfway. Impressive. My face beside his half-man, half-wolf one, I spoke quietly into his now pointed ear so that only he and I heard my whispered, "And Lucas, don't be mistaken. There'll one day be a Delacy-Deveroux Clan, just not in our generation. So go make beautiful babies. My daughter will someday need a strong mate."

I kissed his furry cheek goodbye then dropped his bonds and the door's wards as I softly uttered a sleeping spell.

I left the room with a much lighter—but slightly chilly around the edges—heart. Maybe I wasn't the only one. Or maybe Luke wanted to rip out my entrails. The wolfish grin on his face as he drifted into dreams on the cold concrete could've gone either way.

* * *

Nicodemus hadn't worried at first when Sarkoph didn't return. The lesser-demon had been caged in hell for eons. He was wont to satisfy a few carnal pleasures. Nicodemus drummed his long sharp nails on the arm of the small throne he'd erected. But then he'd sent his dogs after that runner, and they too hadn't returned.

It wasn't until his middle brother, Artus, had heard the girl's name, Cate, that they'd realized. The same girl he'd left the demon to handle was the one they'd sent the hounds after. The sheriff's new runner wasn't dead, and his dogs of war were missing. Added to that was the fact that she was a Delacy. That name left a foul taste in his mouth. It didn't take a smart man to recognize what had happened. He hadn't been a "man" in centuries, but his brilliance far surpassed human realms of intelligence.

The girl was more than a nuisance now. *She was a liability.* Nicodemus and his brothers had come too far to allow anyone to stop them. Their lord would walk the green hills again, and the lord's loyal servants would sit at his right hand and glory in the destruction that fell upon all who opposed their master. Then they would have the power to achieve their true goal.

But first, he had to tie up some loose ends.

Nicodemus looked to his brothers. One of them would just have to take care of the runner, this Delacy. It was a pity. She was such a pretty girl. So full of life. Too bad he was going to suck it right out of her. No matter, it'd been centuries since he'd actually had a heart to care. His fingers continued to drum. The *click, click, click* amused him and made the humans he had chained to feed his continued thirst jump in fear. Nicodemus smiled in anticipation, revealing long, brown teeth.

There would be no more interference. He snapped his fingers. Titus, his youngest brother stepped forward. "Yes, Nicodemus." Titus bowed his head, waiting for his eldest brother's orders.

"It is time to retrieve the next vessel. Take the nesreterka," Nicodemus commanded.

Titus again bowed before leaving. He was followed by three lumbering beasts that resembled a creature the humans should be thankful had long been extinct on this plane called Earth.

"Come." Nicodemus gestured to Artus. They were followed by their servants and more beasts. The former were only empty human shells, kept alive by the mercy of his power. "It is time to…How do the humans say it? Ah, yes…make some sheep's clothes."

CHAPTER FOURTEEN

"Stun guns make great party favors."
—Cate Delacy

I rushed upstairs. The two-way mirror was once again exposed, but the room was empty. Luckily, there was no video record of my confrontation with Luke. Even with the exposed view into the room below, only Buck, Lady D, Serena or Jacq could've seen what had occurred. Few people had access to the upper rooms unless they were in use, and none but ours was booked for the evening. If those four had seen, they wouldn't say a word. Even Buck. He was human, but life with a Voodoo queen had a way of educating a man.

But I didn't think anyone had stuck around to view the fireworks because I had to go through the entire upper level and half of the downstairs to find my friends. Finally, I found Lady D and her lover on the dance floor. D told me to look for "Miss Hot Stuff" by her car, if I wanted to go home. Or I could take one of the young studs dancing around us upstairs and spend the night. There would be no taking myself home. Mynx's SUV was in the lot, but I didn't have the keys. And hotwiring a car with magic usually didn't end well. So it was catch a ride with Jacq, accept Lady D's hospitality, or possibly turn my business partner's car into an incendiary device. All three could end with a bang.

I looked briefly at the muscular, sweaty men grinding away on the floor. The image was superimposed over by the memory of Jacq's eyes, desperate and blazing with magic. An easy choice. I headed outside. Jacq was waiting with arms crossed, leaning against her silver car's low hood. She didn't say a word as I approached, the unlocking car's beep and the club's muffled music and faint laughter the only sounds breaking the empty night.

Jacq's silence continued on the drive to Gandsai. I didn't blame her for being angry, didn't even try to dissuade her as we rolled through pine-bordered empty back roads, stopping once for a group of deer to bound across the blacktop. I simply laid my head back and closed my eyes. It was well past two a.m. when we stopped in front of the wards, which were locked down tight.

We sat there for a minute, looking at the silent house and starry sky, the Corvette's engine purring in the dark. Then Jacq turned off the car. I put my hand on the latch then stopped, turning toward the motionless auburn-haired beauty. I could let her walk away. For both our sakes, I should do just that. But something in me wouldn't allow it.

My hand fell to my lap.

"Please," I placed my hand over Jacq's where it gripped the gear shift, "stay." Her muscles leapt, but she only blinked, clenched her jaw, and looked away. I removed my hand but made no effort to leave. Somehow I knew that if I let her go now, when we met again in the morning something would have irrevocably changed. I racked my brain for some argument, some explanation. If the brooding woman sitting across from me had been sulking, this would be easy. She'd get angry then get over it. I'd been around Luke plenty when he was in a sulk and knew the signs. This was different, which both relieved and worried me.

Jacq was processing, weighing what she knew, making a decision. Such adult behavior was refreshing…and frightening. I knew once her mind was made, hell or high water wouldn't change it. My heart twisted. *Was that panic?* I didn't like how another's choices could so affect my emotions, but it was too late to change that. At least for now. I could deal with my wonky, calamitous heart later. At this moment I needed Jacq to hear the facts before she set her feet onto a path of no return. If only I could again feel what she was feeling.

Closing my eyes, I sought the connection we'd had at The Blue Moon. It was weak but there. I tried to bolster it using my own internal magic, unsure if it would work. I felt her hurt, her confusion…her deep longing. I nearly sighed, understanding the last emotion well. Then my mind was catapulted out, tossed over a wall that hadn't been there moments before. My eyes popped open.

Jacq sat gazing at the shadowed woods, seemingly unaware of my brief intrusion into her psyche. But I swore I saw her lips twitch. I closed my eyes again, focusing. Yes, this connection was like my magic but different. And like magic, it could be shielded against. I was familiar with the concept, having once trained with Serena, but my skills were beyond rusty. I felt the barrier's edges. Jacq *was* blocking me, erecting a wall to protect her mind…and maybe her heart. Well, we'd simply do this the old-fashioned way.

While Jacq considered whatever it was that had her so deep in thought, I considered her. Her profile was shadowed—the wards' swirling blues and greens hiding her expression. If I could see her eyes this very moment, what emotions would I see? Anger? Sadness? Despair? Part of me wanted to know. Part of me didn't.

We sat there in silence for several minutes. I leaned my seat back, closing my eyes. If need be, I would sleep in the car.

I'd just settled in for the long haul when she twisted toward me, grabbed my shirt, and pulled me over the console. I squawked. It was a terribly unladylike sound. But, hey, she surprised me. I thought she was leaning in for a kiss, but she pulled me tightly to her chest. I'll admit to being a wee bit disappointed in receiving only a hug. Still, Jacq's heat, her scent and the feel of her strong arms around me were intoxicating.

I'd just started to enjoy myself when she pulled away, releasing me in a flop back into the passenger seat. Dazed, I didn't even hear Jacq exit the car. I sat there, lost in the pleasant sensation of her body pressed to mine. Jacq had never once spoken, but she hadn't thrown me out. She'd hugged me, and she was coming into the house. It was definitely a step in the right direction.

Through the windshield I looked at the woman who'd so recently taken a predominant spot in my own thoughts. She stood by the wards, both hands tucked into her trouser pockets, the magic's light haloing her body and hiding her features. *Once again, waiting for me.*

I moved mechanically from the car. Jacq quietly walked beside me toward the dark house. If only I could believe that the hug had solved all our problems, but Jacq's thoughts were now hidden behind a curtain of seriousness that said otherwise. As I opened a ward door, it hit me.

I really missed that one dimple.

Our feet crunched over the gravel drive, and I asked, "Would you like some cocoa?" I needed something to keep me awake or I'd never make it through this. And I could bribe her with mini-marshmallows. I was old-school. Bribery was always a good idea. Unless it involved vampire hookers, a wad of hundreds, and a federal judge. Then bribery was a bad idea. A very, very bad idea. But unless there was a hooker hiding in the pantry, we were safe. At least, for the night.

"Yes." Jacq's whiskey-smooth voice was hesitant.

We moved into the kitchen. Like the night we'd met, Jacq sat at the table, watching me. Had that been only four days ago? I shook my head in wonder. So much had happened since then. While I warmed the milk, I laid down a set of photos identical to the ones I'd given Fera. They were of Fera and the men who had been following her. They also included the picture of Jacq and Fera kissing. This wasn't to put Jacq on the defensive (the skeletons in my closet were much larger—and more hairy—than hers). I wanted to clear the air. Even if Mynx was right and they didn't mean anything, I'd been spying on Jacq. Although unintentional, it made me feel guilty. And I had enough that I deserved to feel guilty about without adding this.

Jacq straightened, browsing the photos silently. "How long has Mynx been following Fera?" Her voice was barely above a whisper.

Aunt Helena was likely upstairs, sleeping soundly, but I knew that Jacq was being quiet more to set the tone for our discussion than for fear that we'd awaken my aunt. After this evening's events, my heart wanted to treat Jacq with kid gloves. Maybe she needed to do the same for me.

I stirred the milk and watched her in the window's reflection. "Since Fera gave me the case. She was certain someone was following her. Nicodemus has been so careful, always one step ahead of the Council—I knew she had to be right. After our meeting, anyone following Fera would have known my face, so I asked Mynx to do the honors while we continued our end, searching for Isabella. My gut said catching Fera's tail would lead us to Nicodemus faster than anything else considering how well he hides his tracks. It hasn't yet but I'm hopeful. Mynx's surveillance led her to Carlisle and his helpers, and Carlisle's given us the location of Nicodemus's next vessel, Brittan. Nicodemus will put someone to watch Brittan before grabbing her. We follow that person back to him."

Jacq smiled, but looked puzzled. "It's a good plan, but how did Mynx breach Fera's anti-locator spells? The sheriff is very good at what she does."

"A modified GPS tracker. It didn't so much breach the spell as go around it. Mynx is *also* very good at what she does." I smiled but it slipped away as I added, "Since my mom's disappearance we all carry one." Mine was currently attached to a suppression amulet strung around my neck. It rested near the cold spot that was my heart.

"Mynx won't catch Fera a second time," Jacq challenged lightly.

Remembering D's declaration that the two had run off together, I murmured to the milk, "Perhaps Fera's already good and caught."

"Perhaps, but not by me," Jacq said very seriously, watching me intently. "About this…" She pointed to the photo of her and Fera kissing. "It isn't what it looks like. We knew we were being watched and tried to be discreet in our exchange of information."

"I know. I figured that out when Fera ran after Mynx faster than a redneck going to a mud flap sale." I added the sugar and cocoa to the now steaming milk, ignoring her snorted laugh. "Anyway, you don't owe me an explanation. We've danced and, as my late-Grams might've said, 'exchanged long looks.' But I don't have any hold on you." I stirred the cocoa then turned to face her. It was imperative that Jacq understand. Every woman has her pride. I'd recently brought mine out and dusted it off, but it was too soon to see how well it would hold up under a full-blown assault. I leaned back against the counter, bracing my hands on the cool tile.

"It matters what you think about this." Jacq gestured at the empty air between us. "You're right, we don't have a hold on each other, but…" She paused. "When this is over, I hope…" She stopped again and cleared her throat. For the first time since I'd met the thrilling, often infuriating detective, there was a slight flush to her cheeks that had nothing to do with exercise and good health. I frowned. Could she be sick?

"Do you have a fever?" I stepped to Jacq and felt her forehead. She was awfully hot. Realizing what I'd done, I dropped my hand and stepped back. The woman didn't need mothering. Still, she had a way of neutralizing my good sense.

"No," Jacq growled softly, and a shiver ran down my spine.

I stepped farther back, bumping into the stove. The smell of warm milk and sweet chocolate roused me. I turned and lowered the stove's temp, half-smiling as Jacq let out a loud breath.

She said, "I'm not sick…I'm nervous. You, cher, don't have the patent on blushing…just yet," she teased.

From over my shoulder, I mock glared at her. The resulting smile and one obstinate dimple took any sting out of the comment. Then I realized what she'd said.

"*Nervous?*" I squeaked, spinning to face her, suddenly smiling at the humor of it. I couldn't resist teasing back. "Are you sure? I don't usually make people nervous unless I have a knife to their throat or a Taser to their balls." I had to stop a little thrill as I considered why I might make her nervous. Jacq's confession was confusing. But more confusing was my reaction. It had changed drastically in the last few days. The fact that I no longer cared as much about my previous objections was sobering, and I forced myself to hold tighter to those reasons. I'd almost forgotten that there could never be anything beyond friendship between us. A warm smile and a hot body wouldn't remove the fact that I wanted love and a future that couldn't happen with an immortal. But I couldn't resist one more humorous poke at the big bad blushing policewoman. "And I haven't pulled any weapons on you since the night we met."

Jacq chuckled. "Cate?"

"Hmm?" I cut the heat off and turned again to look at her. All traces of laughter were gone.

"You're very distracting."

My eyebrows rose. "I try my best." We smiled. I grabbed two ceramic mugs.

"You're distracting, but I haven't forgotten what I wanted to say."

The words were low. A sudden shiver of anticipation ran throughout me. I met Jacq's eyes. Everything was forgotten but the pure longing there.

"When this is all over, I hope you'll have a hold on me and me on you." She leaned toward me, trying to bridge the gap between us yet fighting to allow me the distance I needed. I found myself holding my breath, waiting for the words I saw forming on her lips. "What I'm trying to say is that I want to date you."

"You want to *date* me?" My voice was soft, my shock so great that I nearly whispered.

My low words seemed to hang in the air. The house shifted, creaking in the silence that followed. I wasn't sure what I'd been expecting, but that wasn't it. The fires of hell or a row with my ex-husband might not have been able to melt my frozen soul and warm my cold heart, but five minutes with Jacq was moving me from icicles to puddles. There was nearly none of that cold shell, which had been protecting me, left. And this woman's words had just caused another piece to break away.

"Don't sound so surprised." Jacq smiled. This time the smile reached her smoky eyes, transforming the shy suitor into the confident, flirtatious immortal I'd first met. She stood, inching closer with each spoken word. "You're beautiful...smart...and drive everyone around you nuts." She stopped less than a foot away. At my look, she grinned and leaned toward me. "I mean that in a good way, cher. Why? Isn't date the proper term?"

I shook my head mutely.

"We could go out. Dinner? I know you like to dance." Jacq's smile widened, crinkling her eyes.

At each offer, another chink in my frigid armor fell. We were suddenly standing too close, her heat and scent wrapping around me. I grabbed the cocoa and cups, sidling to the sink. I poured the hot liquid, put the cups down, then rinsed away the drops that my shaking hands had spilled, putting off my response for as long as possible.

The woman was bloody asking me out.

I bit my bottom lip then turned to Jacq, passing a steaming mug. She stood near the stove, staring at me. Waiting. *Always waiting.* I looked into her eyes and nearly drowned in the rioting emotions, finally free, reflected therein. Lost, I set the mug down on the counter before I spilled it and ended the night with one more embarrassment.

"No. Yes. I mean..." Stammering, I turned back to the sink, not able to look at her. Her thoughts were so often hidden. Now Jacq's stark honesty, her earnest eagerness, were difficult to see. I felt like someone living in a clouded world experiencing her first sunny day. I was in need of some sunshades. *Or Slone shades.* I almost giggled at the absurdity, my mind retreating to a safer, more surreal place. But as much as I wanted, it couldn't stay there. I forced myself to consider her question.

We were from two very different worlds. How could someone like me pair with someone like her? It no longer seemed important that she was a woman when there were much larger issues. Like the fact that when I eventually became a silver-haired woman dying in my bed, Jacq would still look as young and beautiful as she did today. The idea of her sitting beside me, holding my withered, frail hand in her young, strong one as I passed into the next life was more than I could bear.

"How old are you, Jacqueline Slone, peacemaker, Council operative...mystery extraordinaire?" Trying for humor, I forced the words past a tight throat and looked at her. Jacq's lips parted in surprise. It was a small opening but enough to draw my eyes for a moment. Even when my heart was breaking, I found her attractive. When she finally answered, it was my turn to be taken aback.

Jacq watched me with worried eyes. "I was born over six hundred years ago."

I sucked in a breath. That was much older than I'd expected.

Only the truth would do, but it still hurt to say out loud. Saying the words made them more real. "I'm twenty-nine. I'll live to be about a hundred and fifty...assuming some lucky bail jumper or evil overlord wannabe like Nicodemus doesn't take me out before then." I turned my face toward the window. Tears threatened to bubble over. *Why was I crying?* We'd met only days ago. Yet, all the pain from the day that had been hidden in my icy fortress—the sorrow of hurting Luke, the desolation of learning so much had been hidden from me by the women I'd trusted most—all of it threatened to pour out. "I can't offer you anything *but* a date." My voice barely hinted at the moisture building in my eyes.

Jacq moved until she stood beside me. Laying her hand over mine, she leaned forward until she could see my face. I didn't recognize the emotion brimming in her eyes. Her voice was soft but strong, "There's no guarantee I'll live forever or that you won't live longer. That doesn't matter right now. I've been alone for centuries."

I looked at her. Jacq smiled, but it didn't remove the sadness in her eyes. I felt our connection again. It had grown, and with that growth part of her sadness had become my own. I was willing to bear more, if she was willing to share. It wasn't good to be alone for so long. Three years had been hard on me. How hard must it be to endure more than three hundred? Her next words echoed my thoughts.

"Forever's not everything the romantics make it to be. Besides..." Jacq grabbed my hand, pulling it to her lips for a chaste kiss. The warm tingle as her magic brushed the skin above my knuckles was becoming a wonderfully pleasant craving. "I'm asking for only one night." She paused, clasping my hand between hers. "We'll decide what comes after."

With her words, the last piece of ice defending my heart shattered. It started with one tear. Then another. Soon, I began to cry in earnest. The crying gradually became large, racking, breath-stealing sobs. Porcelain clinked as Jacq moved our cocoa away from the counter's edge. Then her warm arms encircled me, muffling my cries against her shoulder, ruining her beautiful cream top. That thought made me cry harder.

"Shh, Cate." Jacq made soft cooing noises. "If the thought of dating me upsets you so, I won't ask again."

"No!" My muffled protest was ardent.

Jacq lifted my chin, brushing aside the tears that continued to fall. "Then why?" Her words were soft but thick as she ran a soothing hand up and down my back. Her own eyes were now glistening.

Please don't let me make her cry. I would come completely unglued if that happened. "Can we just say that I've had a shitty day and leave it at that?" The pain was washing away with the tears, and I didn't want to bring it back by sharing all the sordid details. I tried for a smile, which I almost felt. It must have worked because Jacq laughed softly.

"Yes, we can leave it at that…for now. But I hope one day, you'll tell me."

I nodded, releasing a massive yawn. I wasn't going to make it through that talk about me, Luke, and our marriage tonight. Tears still flowed down my cheeks. I swiped them away but they kept coming. I was too blasted tired to turn the spigots off. Too tired to even feel embarrassed. The river of tears would either have to run its course or run dry, whichever came first.

"Come on. You're exhausted." Jacq put her arms around my waist and began to guide me out of the kitchen. "Let me help you upstairs."

I should have protested, but I was feeling wobbly. "What about your cocoa?" My mind was becoming muddled, but this seemed vaguely important.

"We'll have cocoa another night." She half-carried me up the stairs.

My legs felt leaden. I was crashing in the worst way. "Oookay. We'll have it when I bake your cake." We were nearly to my room, but I didn't care anymore. It was nice and warm against her side.

"You're going to bake me a cake?" Jacq's voice was surprised and excited.

Food must really do it for her. I almost groaned at the thought of what I could do with her and a bowl of chocolate icing. Too bad I was so tired. "Yes, a big chocolate one," my words were slightly garbled, "to say thank you for keeping the cat out of my bed."

She pulled back my white comforter then eased me out of my leather pants and boots and onto the mattress. As she turned away, I had one coherent thought. I didn't want to be alone tonight. "Jacq?"

"Yes, cher?" Voice hushed, she stood at the threshold. I looked at her with slitted eyes. In the dark, she was only a vague silhouette. A silhouette that glowed faintly.

"Stay." I scooted over, patting the empty spot. "Stay with me." There was power in a word, and like earlier this evening, I would change the course of my life with only one: "Please." My drawl, which thickened when I was tired or excited, stretched the word into a near moan.

"Always, all you ever have to do is ask," Jacq whispered as she moved back into the room.

I blinked twice, trying to comprehend what she'd meant, but it was too much for my tired mind to grasp. As she came to me, she loosened the cream top, then her pants, laying both over the suede love seat. I could just make out a pair of rose-colored tight-cut boy shorts and matching sleeveless shell. I turned on my side, and Jacq slipped in behind me. Her arm wrapped snuggly around my stomach. We fit together perfectly. I began to drift in the warm cocoon of tingles created as her body touched mine nearly from top to bottom.

"Jacq?" I barely breathed her name, feeling more than hearing her hummed reply. My voice drifted in and out. "You said one night?" I could manage that. It wasn't like a person could lose their heart in that span of time anyway.

Her lips brushed my neck before answering, "Yes, cher, one night. One date." Her breath fluttered my hair as she rested her head behind mine. "One chance."

I smiled, feeling a fraction lighter. The last tear I'd cry tonight trickled down my cheek. Just as I fell asleep, I gave her my answer. "Okay, it's a date." I drifted into dreams with the sound of her still whispering something that sounded suspiciously like French in my ear.

CHAPTER FIFTEEN

"If at first you don't succeed, shoot the man that got in your way. Then try, try again."

—Iris (Risa) Legion

Day Eight

I arched, muscles straining, stretching. My arms spread through the sheets, but they were cool and empty. Had it been another dream? No. I turned my head and breathed deep. The scent of sage and sandalwood lingered, trapped in the pillow's cotton, along with a head-shaped indention, confirming my memories. I rolled over, stretching again. The sun was bright even behind the closed golden drapes. It was time to get up. The last part of the evening was hazy, but I clearly remembered agreeing to go on a date with Jacq.

I pushed my face into the pillow, muffling my groan. Why had I agreed to that? A date would only be trouble. I'd already hurt Luke. I didn't need anyone else's feelings on my conscience. Not that I was so wonderful that after one date she'd fall madly in love with me. No, when all was said and done, she'd walk away, and life here would continue on like it always had. I rolled off the bed and my feet hit the old hardwood's chill, my thoughts far colder.

I took a quick shower, braided my hair, and returned a missed call from Mynx. Then I dressed for war. Mynx and Fera were headed to locate and observe Brittan, Nicodemus's next target. Jacq and I would join them later. We didn't expect Nicodemus to try and grab Brittan for another few days, but I wanted all bases covered. There would be someone watching the girl twenty-four-seven. In no shape or form was Brittan to be involved. But I did wish for a way to lure Nicodemus out. A fight on his turf was not appealing. I'd been on the receiving end of too many traps lately. There had to be a way to turn the tables.

There were a slew of hours between now and the meet with Mynx, so it wasn't necessary to run around my house with whip, sword and stun guns. But I had *that* feeling again. Trouble was on the way, and I wanted to be prepared.

I stepped out of my bedroom and immediately collided with a wet, towel-clad Jacq. The woman was built like a brick house. I hit her solid frame and bounced backward. At my startled "Uff," she grabbed me with one arm. Fortunately, the other kept her towel firmly closed. When I'd been thinking about turning tables, I hadn't meant seeing Jacq in a bath cloth-draped position similar to the one she'd caught me in two days ago. Don't get me wrong—I wasn't complaining. Her nearly black wet hair was slicked back from her face. I took one deep breath of her delicious smell, felt her damp heat seeping into my light green cargo pants and matching T-shirt, then stepped back.

"I—" I said.

"Sorry—" Jacq said.

We laughed. "You first." I pointed at Jacq who, for once, looked completely open. The shields that hid her from the world were missing. Maybe she took them off when she removed her clothes. Like a good little scientist my mind wanted to experiment with that hypothesis. I immediately shut my Dr. Frankendelacy mode down.

"The guest bathroom isn't connected to the guest room." Jacq shrugged then grabbed for the slipping towel.

I lived here, so that wasn't news to me. Yet, it had never occurred to me that she'd be walking in a towel from the bathroom down the hall to the guest room—a room I'd originally neglected to tell her about since it was right beside my own.

"Okay," I replied automatically, distracted by a lone drop of water journeying across her bare collarbone before streaking slowly toward the hidden valley between her breasts. I abruptly turned on my heel, heading for the stairs. I had a sudden craving for a glass of cool, clear water.

"Cate?" Jacq's query was soft, but in my absentmindedness I spun around sharply. Too sharply. My heel caught in the upturned edge of a new rug Aunt Helena had sent home from her travels. My excuse: I was only half-awake and moving slower than normal. Although sometimes clumsy, I generally had quick reflexes and wouldn't have tumbled down the stairway, but Jacq didn't know that. Before I could blink, she'd used her supernatural speed to span the distance, again pulling me close to her chest.

"You keep doing that." My face was pressed tightly to her neck, my nose brushing the spot where jaw met ear, my voice muffled. *Don't look down. Don't look down.* It was hard to repeat my mental mantra and talk too, but I managed. "And you've lost your towel." I didn't need to see her to know this. I could feel the now unhindered heat and moisture from her bare skin soaking my own. With my boots' added height, we were nearly breast to breast. Pointed nipples begged for attention by rubbing against me in a decidedly unholy manner. Her other arm, now free of constraining a towel, wrapped tightly around my waist. I had to force myself not to moan in pleasure as warm, magical tingles moved across my skin.

"Doing what?" Jacq murmured. Warm lips pushed my hair aside, brushing a kiss against my temple. I shivered, barely maintaining my train of thought.

"Rescuing me. You seem to have a bad habit of rescuing me." I continued on, valiantly ignoring the lips now moving downward, toward my ear. "Not that I mind, but it's enough to give a girl a complex." Gentle teeth scraped the sensitive spot behind my earlobe, and my words ended on a moan. I clutched at her shoulders, my knees unexpectedly weak. The woman made me melt. It was inconceivable.

We'd never even kissed.

Jacq's husky whisper interrupted my mental rant. "Cate?" Her grasp tightened. "I'd like…" I was already nodding. I wasn't sure what she was asking, but it was a good bet that I would like it, too.

"CATE?" I jerked my head back, locking eyes with Jacq. Her pupils widened, her lips moving, but that wasn't her voice calling my name. Jacq's frightened, surprised expression at the sound of my aunt yelling up the stairs would've been funny had I not been wearing its twin. I had to resist the instant urge to jump out of her arms and race to the other end of the hall.

I stood my ground only because the stairs took a ninety-degree turn halfway up, so Aunt Helena couldn't see me in the arms of a naked woman. My aunt was pretty open-minded, but she was also big on propriety. I was sure she'd consider it improper, unladylike, and an excellent example of poor judgment to be embracing a dripping, birthday suit-clad woman in the hallway. Those sorts of things were supposed to happen behind closed doors, like the one we were currently on the wrong side of. "You've got guests," Aunt Helena yelled, but more quietly this time.

The wards hadn't sounded a warning, but my own internal alarms were ringing. I wasn't expecting anyone. Apparently, along with everything else, this was a week for unexpected guests.

"Be right down!" I shouted over my shoulder, scrambling to answer before my aunt marched up the stairs. At a much lower volume, I spoke to Jacq, whose composure had quickly returned. Her amused smile made me regret the interruption. "No wonder Lady D calls you Miss Hot Stuff." At her look of consternation, I smiled. "If you dress quickly, you might just have an opportunity to rescue me again." I felt her begin to pull away. My eyes widened. "Not so fast!" I grabbed her tighter, but this was assuredly more desperation than desire. "I'm going to close my eyes and hold onto the rail here," I patted the wooden banister that led down the stairs, "while you grab your towel. Tell me when you're decent." I closed my eyes, waiting for her signal.

Seconds later, Jacq softly laughed. "I'm *decent*." At her not-so-subtle innuendo, I snorted, opening one eye. As Jacq turned and walked away, I noticed the edges of a tattoo on her left shoulder, rising above the white towel. One golden, flaming wing rippled as her muscles moved before she ducked through her door.

I turned and headed downstairs, humming a happy tune and wondering what would happen if I stole every towel from the guest bath and hid them somewhere very dark, very distant and very, very much *not* here.

I was still mulling over that brief glimpse of tattoo ink when I walked into the den. I'd caught the musky scent of animal before I was even halfway down the stairs. Fortunately, the suppression amulets were part of my daily weapons array now. I was barely in the room when a tall man with strangely colored hair snarled, "What did you do to the Wolf Alpha?"

I didn't know the voice, but I recognized the Were as the one who'd been with Becca the night before. Pretty boy was trying to be frightening. In the last seven days, I'd dealt with the walking-dead, burned a hellhound to a crisp, learned I was half-demon, found out that my own family had hidden that fact from me all my life, watched a vampire be tortured, and dealt with a jealous, angry werewolf ex-husband. On a fright scale of one to ten, this boy was a minus three. He'd have to try harder. The moon-howlers were in my territory now.

And I was in no mood to play.

I surveyed the room. Becca was there, dressed in another nice suit with a skirt that showed a goodly amount of leg. With the Were from the night before was a woman who could be his twin. Both wore black military fatigues, had dark eyes, dark skin and black and white hair that blended to form a strangely appealing dark gray. Their exotic coloring, sculpted faces and muscled frames made them beautiful, but it was the beauty of a predator about to snap its prey's neck. Last night I'd assumed he was Wolf, but his smell and look were all wrong. My guess was Tiger Clan.

Face carefully blank, I turned to Becca, speaking formally. "I acknowledge the Wolf Second and welcome her own as my guests." She nodded, accepting the greeting. As the most senior Clan representative, Pack law dictated I address Becca first. Tiger boy was either testing me or trying to make me screw up. And more than that, they were hoping I'd lie. Weres could smell a lie, which was how they'd know that I was telling the truth—or mostly so—when I added, "In reference to her Were's question, I saved the Alpha's life."

"Explain yourself." Becca's musical voice was harsh, though her eyes were empty of all emotion.

I sighed. I had been doing a lot of that lately. "You were just picking up the vamp that targeted Isabella, so I understand why you and Luke wouldn't know Lady D's rules."

The female tiger sucked in a breath. Apparently they'd neglected to share a detail or two with the rest of the posse. To react that way, she'd have to be very familiar with the place.

"Rule three of the House is that there will be absolutely no shifting on the premises. The penalty is dismemberment or death, depending upon the Voodoo Queen's mood."

The female tiger nodded in confirmation.

"Lucas didn't know that," Becca said. "And how would the Queen know if he shifted? Luke was in a secure room."

I might have to rethink Becca's goal with this meeting. She wasn't pulling any punches, but that was okay. I'd prepared for this.

I gestured for them to sit and moved to grab the tray Aunt Helena had left on a side table. As I poured from the insulated carafe, the tension in the air was thick enough to cut with a knife. I set the cups down on the old scarred trunk along with bowls of cream and sugar. Fortunately, I knew the Beast-Clan's secret weakness.

"Krispy Kreme?" I offered them each a doughnut, taking a chocolate-covered custard-filled one for myself. Weres never could resist sugar. They each took two or three and a coffee before I continued in terms they could understand. "It doesn't matter if you know the rules or not. The House is the Voodoo Queen's territory. The laws have to be enforced. Ignorance is no excuse." All three nodded, understanding. "Besides, there has never been any love lost between Lady D and Lucas. She would never cut him slack simply because he's my friend."

This time only Becca nodded. So Luke had told her about the bad blood between him and Darryl. I'd never learned the cause, but I wasn't about to ask in front of gruff and grim, the tiger twins.

"That still doesn't explain how the Queen would know," the female tiger said, slowly licking icing off her fingers. She probably thought that was sexy. Ha, this tiger was a pale imitation compared to the woman currently dressing upstairs.

"Lady D knows everything that happens in her House." At their disbelieving looks, I considered telling them about the video and two-way mirror then thought better of it. The info would get back to Luke. If he thought D had witnessed our spat, things would go badly for us all. I tried a different tactic. "It was D who told me Luke and Jacq were about to rumble. It's part of her magic. Believe me when I say she would've known." Again all true. The tigers' flinch at the word "magic" was barely perceptible. I was happy to see that Becca didn't react. Maybe my attempts to calm Kyle had also, in a roundabout way, eased her own fears of the magical arts.

But Becca did flinch at the male Were's next words: "The Wolf Alpha claimed you as mate."

As fate would have it, that was the moment Jacq walked into the room. She sat on the arm of my chair, close enough to present a unified front...and close enough for me to smell her comforting scent. This could be very good or very bad timing. I chose to make it good. I'd only agreed to one date, singular, but she still needed to hear this.

My words were slow and very clear. "'Wife.' Luke said I was his wife. Our very brief marriage—emphasis on brief—was annulled three years ago." I looked each Were in the eye. The Clan didn't need to know that I'd been in a coma for six out of the seven days of that ill-fated marriage. From the way I was sitting, I couldn't see Jacq's face, but during my explanation she'd laid an arm casually across the back of my chair, brushing my neck. After my statement, her arm relaxed, but with Becca's next words, it again tightened.

More softly, Becca said, "No, Rom's right. Earlier, Luke claimed you as mate. That began the argument."

Jacq's body went very still. I'd guessed that Luke had said something like that but hoped I was wrong. Becca's hesitant tone caught the female tiger, who turned to look at her. The last thing I wanted was for Becca to look weak in front of the other Weres. They didn't have to be from the same clan to break into a bloody dominance game. I liked Becca. But I liked the state of my den more. And Were disputes usually ended with broken furniture and bloodstained carpet. Their broken bones would heal, my furniture would not. There was blood in the water, and all I could do was pinch my nose and cannonball in.

"Well, it takes two to tango," I said. "No offense, but I'm not in the mood to dance with the wolves." No one even cracked a smile. *Gee, tough crowd.* I added more formally, "I hereby renounce any claim to the Wolf-Clan's Alpha. Luke will have to find another mate—this woman isn't willing."

Jacq and Becca never moved, but I sensed their tension ease. Did they really think that after all this—after three years—that I'd want to be mate to Luke? I kept my body perfectly relaxed, despite wanting to sink my nails into something. The Weres were too tuned into body language for me to appear as anything but calm and confident. But real soon, I was going to get these ladies alone and explain a few things.

Our talk progressed well from there. The tension ebbed further when my aunt joined us. The male tiger offered to give up his seat, but Aunt Helena just pulled up the piano stool. The tiger went up a notch in my opinion. He was still a sneaky bastard for trying to get me to break Were protocol. But he was a sneaky bastard with manners.

We plied the tigers, whose names I learned were Risa and Romulus Legion (indeed they were twins), with caffeine and sugar until they were finally convinced of two things. One: I was not Pack material. Two: Luke would soon awaken refreshed, unharmed…and single. Then the tigers sheepishly confessed that they weren't actually here to hassle me about the previous night. That was simply a bonus. I say sheepishly only because Aunt Helena was in the room. She could've made Attila the Hun feel like he was confessing a bathroom accident to his first-grade teacher.

Before the pissing contest had begun, Jacq had filled Luke and Becca in on our interrogation of Carlisle, Nicky-boy's vamp inside the Council. In Luke's stead, Becca had reported back to Grey, who'd sent his tigers as more backup.

Risa and Rom had only recently moved into Grey's territory. They hadn't even finished unpacking before being told to stick to me like glue. This was their first assignment, and their new leader had sent these two, magic-shy Weres after a demon lord's sorcerer? *Who had they majorly pissed off?* Both tigers assured us that they were skilled fighters in human and beast form. One look at their bodies had me convinced. Like Jacq, they had a sleek, dangerous air.

Aunt Helena had gone upstairs. Jacq and I were walking the tigers to the door when it burst open. Mynx and Fera roared in, dragging along a loudly protesting and strikingly pretty young woman. Her disordered blond hair had one blue stripe down the side. Like a woman after my own heart, she wore a pair of holey faded jeans and an oxford shirt with her sleeves rolled up.

"Settle down! We just saved your bloody behind. How about a little gratitude?" Fera shouted. In her agitation, her normal drawl had switched to a very Old World accent. I'd never seen Fera lose her cool. The blonde had my immediate respect.

"I'll show you gratitude." The young woman yanked her wrist from Fera's grasp, twisted, and rammed her palm into Mynx's nose. Mynx had blocked hundreds of moves like that over the years, but with her hands full trying to restrain her attacker's other arm, she was helpless to protect herself.

Mynx howled. Risa, a few steps behind me, said, "Oh, that had to hurt." Blood gushed from Mynx's nose. I'd seen her receive much worse and wasn't concerned, but Fera dropped all pretense of controlling the blonde and turned to Mynx.

"That would be Brittan," I muttered.

Fera and Mynx had the door blocked, so Brittan charged forward, not looking back. On the frontline, I braced to meet her. But Jacq, leaning against the kitchen archway, wrapped both arms around my waist and pulled me close. "Oh, no you don't," she murmured in my hair. "I didn't save you from a hellhound and a tumble down the stairs just to let you get trampled by a feisty grad student with a killer right hook."

I didn't protest her grip because it felt nice, and I didn't protest her preventing me from stopping the infuriated blond linebacker rushing down my hallway because it didn't matter. Brittan wouldn't get far. She was headed straight for our new allies. Besides, the tigers had eaten all the doughnuts. They needed to earn their keep.

Brittan ran by, smashing right into Risa's chest. "What the hell?" Rom cried. He looked from the bleeding Mynx at the open door to his sister, who was holding on to a surprisingly quiet Brittan. The young woman was breathing heavily, unwittingly sucking in great gulps of air thick with phers, which were growing thicker as Risa reacted to her charge. Just great. I needed more sexual tension in this house like I needed a demon invasion. At that thought, my gut gave a funny twist, which I blamed on too many doughnuts.

"Hold on, little one," Risa said. "What's your trouble?" Her deep voice was surprisingly gentle considering that not long ago she'd growled at me over the last sprinkle-covered Krispy Kreme.

"Little? Look who's talking Goliath." Brittan tried to pull away, scowling, "Let go. I need to reach the police. I was assaulted." True, the struggling Brittan, dwarfed by the tall Risa, wasn't little. She was roughly my height.

Risa's arms tightened, nostrils flaring, scenting the crimson blood staining Brittan's torn sleeve. "Who assaulted you?" Ooo, that doughnut growl was back. Risa's teeth gnashed, facial bones shifting under her skin.

At my waist, Jacq's hand clenched. I was unworried. My eager gaze pinged from court to court.

Unaware of her danger, Brittan flippantly replied, "What does it matter to you? I don't care if you're the defender of the weak and helpless and secretly wear tights and a cape under your," she looked down, a bit surprised. "BDUs." She glared at the tiger. "I'm perfectly capable of taking care of myself." *Where had I heard that before?*

She pushed against Risa's chest, but the tiger didn't budge, instead taking her own deep calming breaths. Brittan's words would've been more impressive if she hadn't been stuck in the arms of said defender. But though her hands were free, surprisingly the protesting woman hadn't tried any of those self-defense moves on her keeper. Smart girl. While Mynx and Fera were fast and deadly, they were still civilized. With bulging muscles and bloodlust in her eyes, Risa looked like a female Rambo. She might not be the big bad wolf, but I bet she still ate little girls for breakfast.

Fera stepped forward. "Honey, we are the police. I tried to tell you." She grinned. "You'd think the metal bars afforded a clue." The look in Fera's eyes was definitely pissed, but her voice was calm, even amused.

Brittan leaned back in her captor's arms, glaring over her shoulder at anyone within range. "For all I know, you stole that ride. Let me see some ID."

Fera sighed. "Jacq, show her your badge. I seem to have left mine in my other pants." Fera and Mynx flushed.

I grinned, making a note to ask the two exactly where the good law-woman's pants were. Jacq pulled out her badge and flashed the hologram to everyone in the room. This somewhat pacified Brittan.

Brittan's eyes were still suspicious, but at least she no longer looked like she wanted to deck someone. Risa could've released her, but the tiger had yet to loosen her grip.

No one spoke, so Fera resumed her tale, gesturing toward Brittan. "The vampire fingered her as the sorcerer's next target. We were going to watch, protect her from a distance, but they moved up their schedule. We pulled up and nearly hit her," she pointed at Brittan, who was listening with rapt ears, "and her toy-sized scooter."

"It's called a moped. Jeez, what century are you from? And what are you talking about? Sorcerer? Are you on something? You know you're not supposed to eat the 'shrums that grow on those cow patties, right?" Brittan gave Fera the classic eye-roll and hair-toss. A blonde in action was a beautiful thing.

Fera didn't miss a beat. "The fifteenth century. Scooter, schmooter. It doesn't matter what the bloody thing is called. It would still have been a pancake if I'd run it over. And I would never eat anything that grows on shit. Anywho, the girl pulled out into traffic like the demons of hell were after her. I don't know if they were demons, but they were definitely big and ugly. I swerved and hit one. There was also one scary-looking dude hot on her trail."

Everyone opened their mouths, but Mynx waved her hand, answering the unasked question in a slightly nasal tone. "They weren't Weres or hellhounds but something much bigger and meaner. I've never seen anything like them. They were almost reptilian with no fur and slitted eyes. You should see what they did to Fera's cruiser."

Fera visibly flinched, and Mynx rubbed her arm. Ouch, running into a demonic beastie would be hard to explain to any insurance adjuster, even a Council one. "Fera said they looked like miniature blue T-Rexes, but we've been calling them raptors because they seem to hunt in packs."

Aunt Helena popped down the stairs. Like hot potatoes, Jacq's hands dropped from my waist. I grinned. The twinkle-toed po-po didn't feel so amorous when the family unit was around.

I eyed Mynx's puffy nose even as Aunt Helena took in our unexpected, bleeding guest, saying in a tone that brooked no argument, "Everybody to the kitchen. Now." More gently, she said, "Come child," grabbing from Risa's arms a Brittan whose sarcasm had fled upon seeing the older, much smaller woman bossing around the seemingly giant warriors. Charge in tow, Aunt Helena stalked through the group, not waiting for anyone to follow.

We were a tight fit, but all managed to move into the bright, airy room. I grabbed an ice pack and a tea towel, passed them to Mynx then moved toward the coffeemaker as Aunt Helena grabbed her black bag and headed for Brittan.

But we all stopped and stood still when Fera said, "Coffee's good. I figure we have a few hours to kill before those raptor marauders follow the blonde one's scent right to your doorstep." Fera smiled, shaking her cup in my general direction. "Cream and sugar, please." Her charming, carefree self was back and in fine form.

I just shook my head and moved to finish my task. It would be a miracle if that woman didn't give us all whiplash.

* * *

"I'm going to need a sword."

I'd just finished looking through our weapons stash when Brittan approached with her request. I looked up from the steel blade that I was wiping down. Freshly showered, Brittan looked earnest and more than a little pissed. My first response was to tell her no, but I hesitated. I understood her insistence. Technically, it was her butt we were protecting. From the stormy looks passing between her and Risa, it was obvious they'd already had a similar discussion.

"Do you know how to use a sword?" I gestured to the row I'd picked through. Earlier, we'd played a game of *I'll show you mine if you show me yours.* As it turned out, the tigers had been packing an impressive amount of firepower. Silly me, thinking "didn't have time to unpack from the move" included the grenades and semi-automatics. I was pretty sure one or two of the weapons they were carrying were illegal in this country.

I'd never thought of Becca as a fighter, but she'd also had a healthy amount of guns and battle gear. She'd changed out of her nice suit and into leather almost eagerly. The Wolf Second was spoiling for a fight. It was too bad that Luke was still conked out. I was pretty sure that if he saw how hot Becca looked in the tight black leather pants, vest and guns, he'd have her wedded, bedded and with cub before she could click the safety off.

However, even with all of those guns, knives, grenades and one flame-thrower (thankfully empty of gas), none of the Weres had swords, and they didn't seem convinced that their larger munitions wouldn't work on the demonic beasts we continued to call raptors for lack of a better word. After some persuasion—and much cajoling with sugary snacks—they'd agreed to use the swords...but only if their guns failed to perform. They might not be shooting blanks, but I'd assured them that if the raptors were anything like the hellhounds, nothing short of a rocket launcher would do. When I'd asked if they had one of those packed away, the twins had given me a funny look. Rom had answered in all seriousness that they'd left it at home. He'd also added, with a smirk, that they'd be sure to bring it next visit. I'd made a mental note to buy more doughnuts, just in case.

"I can use a sword...probably better than Twiddledum and Twiddledee over there." Brittan gestured at the tigers, who were looking at a rough map Jacq had drawn of the house and surrounding area. There was enough time to relocate, but if we went into the city, the raptors and the sorcerer leading them would follow. A few well-placed calls had found that the raptors had been spotted several times and that Fera was right.

They were headed this way.

The Council's spinners had quickly attributed the accidents to a pack of wild dogs straying into the road. The Council could get away with that because humans only saw what they wanted to see. But for once, I was glad for the Council's PR machine. People had a tendency to do stupid things when they were scared, which was why we were staying put. The raptors were now making their way here through the sparsely populated woods. The last thing we needed was for them to follow us into the city and cause widespread panic.

But we also couldn't stay holed up inside the house, nice and comfy, while the raptors rammed themselves to death on the wards. There were too many attackers for the shielding to handle. If they acted en masse, the wards would eventually fail, and there was no way I was letting those things inside to dig up my garden and get more blood all over the grass. It took forever to clean up the gore made by only two hellhounds.

But the selfish need to preserve my yard wasn't my main reason for taking the fight to our enemies. Our goal was to have Brittan and Aunt Helena stay within the wards, safe, while we went to meet the "marauders."

I slid my now gleaming sword into its sheath, laid it across a nearby chair, and pulled one of my favorite blades from the rack. It was the perfect length for someone my height. It also wasn't a practice weapon. I passed Brittan the sword, doubting my sanity. "Let me see you use it. But *try* not to bust my nose—I don't heal as quickly as Mynx. And the blade's sharp, so don't cut yourself. Blood stains the floors…and I hate to clean."

Brittan smiled, chagrined. We'd been ribbing her for bloodying her would-be savior. But I wasn't joking. I was all cleaned out. I might just leave the next person to bleed on my floors to die there. A shiver ran down my spine, and I swung my blade, trying to warm up.

"I'll be gentle, but I make no promises regarding anyone else." Brittan watched Risa with a gleam in her eye. It was the kind of gleam that said she was looking for a tussle.

I smiled, remembering. I'd looked in my bathroom mirror the night I'd met Jacq and seen that same look in my own eyes.

"Here." Reaching into my shirt, I pulled an active suppression amulet from around my neck and threw it to Brittan. She caught it midair, nearly dropping the wooden disk as she immediately felt its effects. "I wouldn't want you to lose because you were distracted." At her questioning look, I quickly explained the Weres' phers. She gave me a grateful smile and put the amulet around her neck, tucking it under the blue T she'd borrowed from me. Its color nearly matched her streaked hair.

We took off our shoes. I removed my gun harness, hooked it on the chair, and patted my pockets. Normally full of amulets and throwing stars, they were currently empty, which was a good thing. If I took a tumble, sharp discs slicing into my flesh wouldn't be too comfortable. A quick final check showed that except for the amulets I was magic-less…at least externally. We moved to the indoor sparring mats.

* * *

My mother had taught me to never underestimate an opponent. It seemed that I needed a refresher, because Brittan caught me off guard with her skill and speed. We circled each other, almost gently testing the other's defenses. Things quickly sped up as I realized her proficiency. Parry. Thrust. Lunge. I would advance. She would advance. The fighting began more like a warmup with neither of us sweating. Then it changed…As if a switch had been flipped, Brittan suddenly became fearsome. I'd been expecting it. The blonde had something to prove, and people with a cause were often dangerous in their single-mindedness.

Brittan stalked me around the floor, her face grim. Our swords clashed with more and more force. We both grunted as one blow's jarring power went up our arms. After narrowly redirecting a quick thrust, I realized too late that it was merely a feint. My right arm overextended. Brittan stepped in close, reversing her sword's direction, moving the blade vertical. She brought her hilt down on my wrist, pulling the punch at the last second. The blow wasn't hard, but it hit a nerve perfectly. My hand went numb, and my sword dropped with a muffled clang. At the same time she caught me with a leg sweep, knocking me off balance. I landed in an inelegant heap, my bottom breaking my fall. For a moment, I lay there, strangely pleased and unsurprised by the turn of events.

"That was a cheap shot." I rubbed my hand and smiled.

It was a good move, and we both knew it. No traditional sensei would've allowed it, but when it came to survival, those who fought dirty were—as my mom would say—less likely to pull a Humpty Dumpty and need putting together again. I liked this girl more and more. Brittan simply shrugged and smiled back.

Rom and Risa were talking to Jacq, who was openly watching me. Raising her eyebrows, she looked at my wrist. I shook my head.

Brittan looked from Jacq to the twins, whose strangely colored heads were still bent over their map, and finally to me.

"So you and the detective…you're an item?"

Brit's question surprised me. I couldn't read my own feelings, but apparently someone who'd known me for less than two hours could. Was it any wonder my jealous ex had gone ballistic on Jacq the night before?

I sighed. How could I explain something I didn't know? "You're going to have to take a rain check on the answer to that. It's time to go." I stood, rubbing my aching backside, and moved off the mats. "Rematch another day?"

"It's a deal." Brittan smiled. "But just so you know, I won't go so easy on you next time."

I looked at her for a moment, narrowing my eyes. She had a street fighter's gumption and a samurai's sleek efficiency. And after our initial explanation of the situation, she hadn't seemed too freaked out. I let my magic barely peek past my shields, scanning her. Magic faintly *buzzed* around her as if she were almost something but not quite. *Curiouser and curiouser.*

"At least it wasn't your nose," Mynx said with a grin. She and Fera had returned during the match. Her voice had already lost its nasal quality.

"Hearty-har-har-har." I stuck my tongue out. "Maybe I should've been more specific in my list of 'don'ts.' If I'd said, 'don't throw me on my ass,' then I'd be okay." My tone *may* not have reflected my enthusiasm at Mynx's reminder.

"No, then she would've thrown you on your head." Mynx tapped her chin. "Actually, that might have worked better…considering how hard it is."

Laughing, I moved to where I'd left my weapons. Traveling light, I looked fondly at my utility belt but left it in the chair. Then I pulled the spare sword from its sheath, checked its blade and balance once more, before encasing it again. I had barely fastened the sword's harness around my waist when Jacq approached.

"Are you all right?" Her voice was as whiskey-smooth as ever, but her eyes twinkled and her lips twitched. She was dying to laugh but was restraining herself. *Someone was learning.* Smiling in thanks, I grabbed her offered towel and wiped the sweat from my neck. Jacq smiled back.

"It's nothing that a hot soak later won't fix." At her smoldering look, I added with a cheeky grin, "Alone." I waited for my heart to speed up and my face to flush, but Jacq's subsequent laugh only brought a warm sensation to my chest. When had we become so comfortable that I could tease her about sex without blushing? I wasn't sure, but it was nice. I'd never really indulged in this light-hearted, innuendo-filled banter. It healed something inside me. Something I hadn't realized was broken.

Warmth *zinged* across my aching rear. "Cut that out!" Jumping in unexpected pleasure, I slapped at Jacq's roaming hand. Looking to see if anyone had noticed, I caught Mynx's eye. She winked. This time, I did blush.

But Jacq was unrepentant. She leaned down, whispering in my ear, "I just want to make you feel…" She hesitated, and my mind reeled, mentally finishing her sentence a dozen times over. Her breath was warm on my ear as she added, "ready…for what's coming."

"I am," I said, referring to the upcoming fight. I turned, brushing her warm arm with my hand. Each time our magic touched, I could feel her. I knew the desire and affection showing in Jacq's eyes were more than skin-deep…and that her worry for me was a dangerous distraction. "Thank you. I'm less sore already." My hand momentarily lingered, held by her fingers. Then Risa called her name, and Jacq turned away.

I moved to the tack area, grabbed a spare sheath that slung across the back, then headed toward Brittan, who was sipping water and staring pensively at the sword in her hand. Risa glared at us from across the room.

"You might want to put that up before you're tempted to gut a certain tiger." Brittan tried to pass me the sword, but I held up my hand. "No, put it in the sheath and put it on. I made a promise." I passed her the leather sheath then helped her adjust the straps. "You've more than proved your skill with a blade." She looked surprised…and embarrassed. *Had no one ever complimented her skill?* Before Brittan could misunderstand, I added, "But this doesn't change anything. I need you to stay inside." At her exasperated look, I continued, "It's going to be a magic free-for-all out there. Not to mention the Weres with their dumb-ass pistols."

Her eyes glazed, as if she'd heard it all before. No doubt she had. Risa had been dogging her steps for hours. "I can hold my own."

I cinched up another strap then gave her a once-over. Brittan had pulled her hair back into a ponytail. Her jeans had been ripped in a fashionable way, but the holes also allowed more freedom of movement. *Clever.*

I laughed softly. "Trust me, I know. You just finished kicking my ass, remember?" I rubbed my backside with an exaggerated grimace. She laughed too, and we shared a smile. Brittan had a nice smile. I could see why Risa was so taken. I didn't have lustful feelings for her, but I felt a connection. Like I'd felt to Becca and even hearing about Isabella Richmond.

A low growl came from the corner. Oh yeah, Risa was a goner. Brittan gave her a look of pure consternation. No doubt Brittan had been told she would be a liability in a fight. And she would. I couldn't sugarcoat that. The others would be busy protecting the Weres from the sorcerer's magic. They couldn't also protect Brittan. But she didn't need to hear that again. She was a fighter. A survivor, if I wasn't mistaken. She needed a goal. A purpose. She needed a reason to stay inside that didn't have to do with her own safety. I had that feeling again—as if this was going to change everything—but I carried on, unable to see how a few words might affect anything more than a hurt girl's spirit.

Smiling, I turned Brittan toward a mirror we used when weight training, hoping I had read my audience correctly. "How's that look?" My change of subject threw her. Confused, Brittan sheathed then unsheathed the sword, testing its resistance. She nodded her approval then began to undo the straps. My hands stilled hers. I redid the buckles. "Keep it. The sword, the sheath—they're yours."

"I couldn't." Brittan sighed, pulling the harness over her head. "I won't owe anyone, anything."

The *again* was left unspoken, but I heard it, nevertheless.

Everyone has a security blanket. They just came in different forms. I could tell Brittan wanted to keep the sword. She *needed* to keep it. But she wasn't going to allow herself to. And I wouldn't force her. I'd been in her shoes once. Brittan held the sword out, balanced across her palms.

"Why would you give something like this to someone you'd just met?"

I took the sheathed weapon and examined the leather, sliding the shining blade out. "You know, my grandfather made this case." After all these years, the brown hide was still smooth and supple. "His brother forged and folded the steel. It was necessary in those days." The flawless blade—still strong and sharp—felt nearly weightless. "It was hard to explain the purchase of swords in the post-Civil War period. They were good men who worked hard and lived long lives." The runes etched into the steel were still clear, untouched by time. Her brows drew down at the timeframe. "Witches live long lives. Our generations are more spread out than those of humans. But to answer your question...this has been in my family for a long time. It's precious. Some might consider it valuable. But it's still just a thing, and that's never worth more than a life. My mother taught me that." I pushed the sword back into its home, passing it back as I'd received it—balanced across my palms. I held it there, waiting for its new owner to take possession.

Brittan looked at it with dark, doubtful eyes. I continued, "A thing is just a thing. A gift is just a gift. And one is not necessarily the other. A person doesn't need a reason to give the latter. And there doesn't have to be strings attached or debts owed with the giving." They were words I'd heard often but only now understood. "But if you want to consider it something more, then consider it payment. I'll give you something precious, if you'll use it to protect something I consider far more valuable."

"Payment for what...to protect my own hide? I'd do that freely." Brittan's lips joked, but her eyes were wary as they moved from the sword to something behind me and back again. The mirror showed Risa slipping guns away into places I couldn't fathom a harness fitting.

I chuckled. "That too. But no, I want you to keep an eye on Aunt Helena. She'll never admit it, but she worries when I'm involved in anything more dangerous than a game of tic-tac-toe. So this next twenty-four, forty-eight hours is going to be hell on her. Keep her safe. Keep her occupied. Most especially, keep her inside the wards, and these are yours. Do you believe it a fair exchange?" I smiled, but my voice was deep and serious.

Brittan stood there for several moments, looking from me to the weapon in my hands to the activity behind us, and then out the sliding glass doors leading to the garden, finally saying, "Let's see. You want me to stick around this house for the next day or two with a bunch of hot, sweaty muscle-bound types, let your aunt stuff me with home cooking, and play with all your cool weapons, one of which you're giving me?"

I nodded several times sharply, returning her sudden impish grin. *Uh-oh. What had I gotten myself into?*

Brittan snatched the sword from my hand and slung it over her head so quickly I thought she might pull something. "Call me Brit."

"Okay, Brit. Does that mean you'll take the job?" I held out my hand.

"Throw in free Wi-Fi and a massage, and you've got a deal." She grabbed my hand, pumping it up and down.

I retrieved my hand, laughed and stuck my thumbs in my pockets. "The Wi-Fi I can do. You're on your own for the rest." A glance over my shoulder showed that Risa's patience had run out. I began to make a fast exit, but Brittan's hand on my elbow stopped me. I turned, looking at her expectantly.

"And Cate, thanks."

I heard the catch in her throat before her hand dropped. I just nodded and walked away as Risa stalked toward us. It was time to head outside anyway.

All of us but Aunt Helena and Brit left the house. When we reached the wards, I removed my suppression amulets and passed them to Mynx, who took the discs without a word. Although diminished, I could still feel the phers influence. But once the battle began, I'd be able to focus past my body's needs.

Jacq opened a ward door, and we stepped through. The pines around the house stood like shadowy, silent sentries. It was another bright, hot day with an endless blue sky. Was it any wonder that we had so many demons running around? They probably felt at home. Mississippi in May was as hot as hell—with seventy percent humidity added in for good measure. I took a deep breath of fresh, muggy air, sweet with honeysuckle and felt the heat making me stronger.

Goddess, I loved this state.

CHAPTER SIXTEEN

"Magic can bond like blood. Blood can bond like magic. The two together can create a conduit for untold power…or chaos, depending upon your perspective."

—Phoenix D'Artanian, former leader of the Draig

For the second time in less than a week, I was looking at a dead man who didn't know when to just lie down and let the nice people cover him in dirt.

The raptors had been early. We'd barely finished tromping through the woods to the desired spot before they arrived. I'd picked this clearing because it was in a direct path to the ward doors but also because it was beside the creek that twisted around our property before finally feeding into a large pond beyond the back gardens.

There would be a lot of magic flying, including my fire. Maybe that sounds surprising, considering I would be fighting alongside Fera and the Weres, but I'd been thinking for months that it was time to stop hiding. Learning about my family's deception and my demon father had been the last straw. Of course, that didn't mean I was ready to walk down NOLA's streets juggling fireballs and spouting Demonish. I'd be cautious and not make things easy for the Council. Or in this case, I'd wait until I was far away from the others before calling the flames. But I'd been born with these powers for a reason.

It was time that I put them to good use.

So, with fire and the magic spheres everyone would be tossing (well, everyone but the Weres), we had to be careful. The recent heat had parched the ground cover. The clearing was easily double the length of a football field, with the creek another few hundred yards away through a dense section of pine, oak and scraggly bushes. Close enough that water could be magically diverted to extinguish any out-of-control blazes. I didn't plan to beat these guys just to lose the house in a forest fire.

The raptors emerged from the dark woods, hurtling toward us at a phenomenal speed, and we divided up. One immortal with each Were. Each pair would take on a raptor. In truth, I was worried about the Weres, especially Becca. They had no way to protect against magic, which left Jacq, Mynx and Fera handicapped. They would have to fight and keep an eye on our allies. Fera had suggested having the Weres run in circles so the others could pick off the raptors as they gave chase. While joking, it was her way of telling the Weres that they'd either be an asset or a liability. Only time would determine which.

The approaching raptors slowed, but even from a distance I could see the intelligence in their eyes. Mynx had been right when she'd called them reptilian. They had wrinkled bluish-gray hides and ran on two legs with wide, sweeping tails for balance. There were only holes where their ears should have been. If not for their blue color, I would've thought they were animatronics from that movie about cloned dinosaurs run amok. I had just enough time to note that their long snouts held row after row of sharp, jagged teeth. Then they were upon us.

I headed toward the man following the raptors. One of the blue reptiles moved to intercept, and Jacq pushed it from my path with a pulse of silver magic. She nodded as I passed before turning her attention back to the creature who was now heading for Rom. Jacq didn't like that I was taking on the man, a sorcerer, alone, but this was my house…my territory. *Mine.* I would always be at the forefront when protecting it. Still, I didn't relish the thought of dying—not for a house, not for territory…not even for honor. Which was just another reason I hadn't become one of the honor-equals-life Weres. If I got in over my head, I'd say "Fuck honor" and run. Unless, of course, I was in the company of my aunt. Then I'd keep my comments to myself and run. Until then, I had a job to do.

I set my sights on the sorcerer. He stood near the wood's edge, tossing black-magic from behind his monsters. I dodged a black orb and pulled my sword, calling the flames. As I left the others behind, I heard the rapid *pop, pop, pop* of automatic gunfire then cursing. A louder rumble sounded, and for a moment I thought Rom had been holding out on me about the rocket launcher. Then I realized it was thunder.

A storm was approaching. In the last ten minutes, the temperature had dropped by at least ten degrees. Dodging blast after black-magic blast, I moved quickly. Tall grass whipped against my knees. Patches of sweet clover crushed beneath my feet. All the while, I never took my eyes off the lean, sandy-haired man's broken, red-brown smile. Lightning flashed in the distance, but I didn't spare the sky a glance. I'd learned my lesson during the hellhound battle about turning your attention from an enemy.

Of course, I didn't have to look to know certain things. The sudden cease in gunfire and Rom's repeated shouts of "God damn it!" painted a pretty good picture. The tigers had finally figured out that lead projectiles didn't do shit against Otherworld creatures. Jacq had temporarily spelled their swords with her deadly silver runes, so if the tigers bothered to use their "big-ass" knives as Risa put it, they'd at least do some damage.

Twenty yards from my goal I slowed, sauntering closer to my enemy, still dodging an occasional black orb. This one was strong. Much stronger than Sarkoph, he seemed to have an endless supply of the blasted things. During my zigzag across the meadow, I'd counted ten aimed at myself, several narrowly missing, and I'd heard the others shout as black missiles rained down.

From Fera's description, we were certain this sorcerer wasn't Nicodemus, which meant we needed him alive so he could lead us back to Nicky-boy, Isabella and the missing boys. The most harmless in appearance, I had taken the job of distracting the unknown sorcerer until the rest of my group could defeat the raptors and magically circle him. But as I got closer it looked like capturing him alive would be impossible.

He was already dead.

The smell hit me just as I recognized his face, confirming one of my worst fears. Suddenly aware of the threat my nearness posed, he turned to face me. I stopped only a few feet away. We stood under a pine's boughs, the first at the mouth of a trail that led to the creek. I raised my sword, giving a salute. Then I said calmly, not letting my distress show, "Hello, Peter. It's nice to finally meet you."

Less than thirty-six hours ago, I'd stared at a picture of this man standing beside Wellsy. This sorcerer's connection to our neighbor and family friend was too much to be ignored. Peter's empty black eyes swiveled in my direction, black-magic ball in his hand all but forgotten. I stifled a shudder and smiled. "That is your name, isn't it?" I stepped around him carefully, keeping my distance. I'd cast all four wards of protection on myself, with fire magic no less. But that didn't mean I would give him a free shot. Besides, the wards were situated slightly beyond my body, leaving some big gaps.

Peter warily eyed the fiery tears falling from my blade to the grass. His neck turned nearly one hundred and eighty degrees, following my movement. Oh yeah, he was well past the benchmark for creepiness and about to round the corner toward putrefying. If I hadn't already noticed the rotting clothes, atrophied muscles and purplish skin, the neck contortions would've been a dead giveaway. Not even the most accomplished yogi could twist his head on his spine until his nose sat between his shoulder blades. That wasn't human.

And Peter Traylor had been human. I'd pulled up his bio along with that of the other man and woman who'd been with Wellsy in that coal mine. Traylor had a wife and a son and was an employee of the Virginia Tourism Board. He'd disappeared right after the photo had been taken. The newspaper had gotten those details right, but someone had been wrong when they'd said that he'd been alive after climbing out of that collapsed shaft. Those eyes were as dead and soulless now as they'd been in that photo. Eyes just like those of the two men pictured beside him—the men who'd also escaped that mine, one of which had been our neighbor, Wellsy.

If eyes were the windows to the soul, how could I have missed the hollow where Wellsy's spirit should've been? The difference had been there for me to see when I'd bumped into him at Tulane. I could have slapped myself. I hadn't wanted to see the man for what he was: A shell. A shell housing a hungry darkness bent on destruction. A lot like the one getting ready to kick my ass if I didn't pay attention.

"Peter's out for a bit. You may call me Titus." His words had a very odd accent that I couldn't quite place. He smiled. The smile and tone might've once been considered charming. But death, undeath, or whatever existence he currently inhabited had changed that. His gums were so shriveled that his teeth resembled pikes, tall and jagged, rising from a bloody, muddied battlefield, and the voice was hollow and flat, wheezing from lungs decayed from lack of use. He lifted his legs, turning, but like a marionette whose strings were being pulled, his other parts did not follow.

"Titus it is then." I nodded slightly, never taking my eyes from his.

Titus's movements were slow, below human standards. Fera had said he was fast, and I didn't doubt it. He was playing weak, judging his prey, waiting for the right moment to strike. But I'd seen too many Louisiana gators lunge from seemingly calm bayou waters to fall for that trick. And the analogy fit. With his stiff features, dark unblinking eyes, and sharp teeth, the Peter puppet resembled a cold calculating croc. I couldn't help but think of the crocodile from *Peter Pan* who'd always been accompanied by the foreshadowing *ticktock* of a clock, which was a true comparison. His appearance here and now meant time was running out for us all.

Titus, tired of waiting for a response, haphazardly tossed the black-magic sphere over his shoulder. I heard a shriek and snarl as the volley struck its mark but didn't dare look. Titus's dark magic began to coalesce again, this time elongating into a sword. He didn't stop forming the undulating, black weapon until it was at least six inches longer than the steel gripped in my own hands.

"Oh my, mine's bigger," he said drolly.

I snorted. Apparently, even dead men had penis envy. "Yes, but do you know how to use it?" I stepped back into a classic defensive stance, body turned, left foot forward. Titus mirrored my actions. His words were confident. So were mine. But we were both cautious. Our weapons would do more than cut each other, and we knew it.

"It's been awhile, I'll admit. But they say it's like riding a cycle. You climb back on and start pumping."

Titus's sexual threats didn't create the distraction he'd anticipated. I kept one eye on his weapon and the other on his eyes, standing my ground. There was one thing I was certain of: this man's plumbing hadn't worked in a long time.

The storm's first arbitrary winds blew the strong odor of rotting flesh in my face, and I nearly choked, bile rising in my throat. Death didn't mix well with the smell of clean pine and sweet honeysuckle.

Just as the first fat drop of rain landed on my cheek, Titus leapt forward, his sword slashing at my head. I sidestepped, countering.

Black-magic slid against my flaming steel, its cold chill whooshing past my right bicep. My injury from my bout with Sarkoph flared, a deep, pulsating ache. Darkness called to darkness, even if it was only the memory of darkness contained in a fresh scar.

Titus's momentum carried him past, and I pivoted, continuing my blade's motion. He continued on, going for my back. Two could play at that. It was bad form to attack a man from behind, but we weren't exactly fighting by the rules. I did a half-turn, slicing my blade around in a shoulder-high, two-handed arc, keeping it close to my body for better control. He was quick, but speed without restraint was a liability.

Titus's stolen body had overcompensated for the stiff muscles with deteriorating joints that flopped like rubber. To keep all his body parts going in the same direction at the same time, he had to turn wide, putting him still facing away from me when I struck. At the last moment, I extended the blade, cutting through his shirt. He hadn't anticipated my speed, and the lapse cost him. I smelled burnt meat and scorched wool.

My hungry fire had bitten him.

Little wisps of smoke rose as licks of flame continued to move over his back. There was no flinch—no reaction—to the small, carnivorous fires that I'd intentionally transferred to him. Long dead, this one didn't feel pain, but I was willing to bet he'd be more careful from here on.

Titus twisted around, bending nearly backward, his sword flashing out at an impossible angle. I stepped back, knocking his blade aside with a downward sweep. Sparks flew as our magic clashed. Everywhere they landed, tiny embers glowed. A few in the dry pine needles. One on his left shoulder. Others spread out in an occasional patch of tall grass.

Thunder sounded closer. More rain fell. The water didn't put the tiny flames out, but neither did they grow. Titus hit me harder. Harder again. My arms strained to hold back the escalating onslaught. Sweat burned my eyes. I blinked it away, focusing on other senses. Beneath the sounds of battle, I heard rushing water. Then it made sense. I was being forced down the old path to the creek. Titus thought to douse my fire with a dunking.

We were getting farther and farther away. Too far to call for help, and I was being pushed farther still. Penned in on both sides by dense woods. Water at my back. Sorcerer at my front. *Piece of cake.*

I gritted my teeth, raising my sword to block another bone-shattering blow. Maybe I was in over my head, but I'd had time to consider this fight. More time than I'd had for any of my previous run-ins with the demonic. I, too, could be a devious devil when I put my mind to it.

As we moved, I saw the embers follow and smiled in gruesome satisfaction. Titus could roll us both over Niagara Falls in a barrel if he wanted. It wouldn't change a thing. More raindrops fell, this time steadily, plopping as they hit the ground. Titus smiled in joy then confusion, noticing my unconcerned expression.

That's right. I didn't care if we got a little wet. In fact, I was counting on it. This was one fire that liked to swim.

As Titus steadily pushed me back, I began to pull my magic in. My sword's flames died slowly. When the last fiery tear fell he shrieked in triumph, charging forward, thinking I was finally weakening. And in truth I was, but we weren't done just yet. Dirty blond hair darkened with water matted to Titus's forehead, but contrary to logic, as the rain came down, the little ember on his shoulder started to grow. Fireless, I parried his last lunge with nothing but Damascus steel and determination.

At the creek's edge, my feet slipped on the wet rocks and I stumbled backward into the water. It flowed cold and heavy into my boots, weighing my feet down as they slid on the sandy bottom. I kept moving until the water reached my knees, blinking as rain ran into my eyes, plastering my escaped locks to my neck and face. Titus stood on the bank, a half-ring of fiery embers surging, growing mere feet behind him.

"End of the line, girl." He took a step forward.

My first ward fizzled out. I took another step back. The second ward dropped. Titus's smile grew. The fear on my face was real. This was going to be close. If I was wrong, I was dead. I stepped again, this time sideways. The cold water was rising, pulling stronger as the storm flooded in. Nearly waist-deep now, I fought to keep my footing. Any deeper and I wouldn't be able to fight the current. I took another step, careful to stay parallel with the bank, putting distance between myself and the dead man. My third ward popped and disappeared.

Thunder pealed loud overhead. Lightning cracked close by, and I barely heard Titus say, "So, the only question now is how to best amuse ourselves. Nicodemus doesn't care what condition he receives you in…alive…dead…*sane*." He paused. "So long as he has a taste." With each word, he came farther into the water. "And it may be hours before my nesreterka finish your friends. My brother's not the only one who's hungry." A long, black tongue swept across purple lips and broken teeth. "So how best to spend our time, hmm?" As Titus spoke, he waved his magical sword like a baton. I had to hide my smile as the growing embers behind him flowed back and forth, following his unintended conducting.

I held my last ward with will alone…waiting. I should've known he'd want to talk. They *always* wanted to talk. I inched away. The ring of embers was almost to the water's edge.

"You know," I said, "I don't remember receiving an invitation to this party. Could you have the wrong girl? You were chasing a blonde, remember?" I took another half-step. "Completely understandable—I hear they're more fun."

"No, we have the right girl." Titus stepped closer, the water now nearly to his knees. "Nicodemus wants you, Cate Delacy. It was my good fortune that your people grabbed my brother's vessel. Two birds with one stone, eh?"

His use of my name made the hairs on the back of my neck rise. "I'm really not one for travel. Why should I go?" My voice trembled. Shivering, I wiped the now pouring rain from my eyes before wrapping my arm around myself. I wasn't exactly faking. This damn creek was getting colder by the minute. Without my fire to warm me, I was chilled to the marrow.

Titus took another step forward. A new light entered his eyes and his demeanor did an about-face. "Come," he said almost gently, holding out a hand. "We'll join my brothers and servants. You'll be a queen amongst our people."

As if. I'd been trying to cut the man to bits only minutes before. Now he thought I'd go with him willingly? We women really needed to do something about this rumor that double X chromosomes engineered fickleness. It obviously led to some sort of male-induced insanity.

My fourth ward dropped.

With that last shred of protection gone, I began to shiver uncontrollably. Strange, the water had been warm this time last year. No doubt the evil man standing only six feet away, nearly to his waist in water, had something to do with the unusual temperature.

As he edged forward, I gathered all my courage, standing my ground.

Five feet. Four.

Too close. Too close. I took a deep breath, sliding one foot back. "These nesreterka, they're your pets?"

At my change of subject, Titus's expression was puzzled, but his weapon began to decrease in size. Since it was a metaphysical rather than physical appendage, the miraculous shrinkage likely had more to do with my helpless posture than our frigid bath.

"Mindless creatures from the Illtrath plane. They live only to breed and hunt. They do as they're told, nothing more." Titus's eyes said, *unlike some*. He took another step forward. A red wave slowly crested behind him, the embers plopping one by one into the water.

I blinked more rain from my eyes and dropped my sword into the creek with a splash. "I ask because I always wanted a pet, but it took years before my mom would get me one." I lowered my voice to the sexy drawl I'd used more than once to mesmerize. Becca wasn't the only one who could use her mouth to good advantage. More plops blended in with the sound of heavy rainfall as wave after wave of embers flowed into the water. *Goddess bless. There were so many.* Hundreds more than I'd anticipated. There would be some explaining to do when this was over.

I began to discreetly inch away from Titus and toward the bank. "Have you ever watched that movie, *Gremlins*?" I knew Titus wouldn't have, but I needed to temporarily distract him. Having him search Peter Traylor's stolen memories should do it. Titus stood completely still, listening. I spoke slowly, keeping my eyes locked with his.

Four feet. Nearly five.

Like a snake charmer, I played my pipes for the cobra. "Well, I finally got a pet one year…a birthday gift. But unlike a gremlin, its rule wasn't about when you fed it…only how much." Water rushed against the back of my legs with an ever-increasing force, and I had to fight to remain standing. It was hard to keep my voice low and steady when my teeth wanted to chatter. "You see, the boralis are a lot like fire. They tend to grow and spread if you give them too much, and they're *very* fond of biting the hand that feeds them."

I saw the moment he realized what I was talking about. Even in the seven levels of Hell, those little buggers were well-known. Titus's eyes widened in rage, magic flashing outward. I pushed diagonally, riding with the current toward the creek bank. My feet slipped. I gasped a breath before going under. Cold magic hissed through the air where only seconds before my head had been. I opened my eyes, peering through the murky water, and kicked my feet. It wasn't so deep that I had to swim, but underwater seemed the safest route.

Black-magic hissed and crackled in the water close on my left, and I veered right, heading downstream as miniature pulsating red lights streaked past me. I winced but kept moving as a few took little nips out of my skin. I'd intentionally bottled my magic away, keeping the wards from touching my skin, funneling everything through my sword to keep as much residue as possible off myself and prevent such love bites. Before my sparring with Brittan, I'd spent a good hour taking the hottest shower I could manage to sweat out every bit of magical residue created by last night's confrontation with Luke. Either I'd missed some, or sparks from our dueling swords had landed on me.

I came up quickly, gasped in one breath, then ducked back down, trying to ignore the icy water pricking my skin like razor-thin needles. As soon as the last boralis flitted by, I turned, staring at the school now circling Titus. Distracted from chasing me, he peppered the rising water with black-magic. That might've worked if he'd thrown the orbs farther out to lead them away. Instead, he was tossing the magic at the fish nipping at his heels. It was like pouring buckets of dead, chopped-up fish into a sea of sharks…without having the luxury of a titanium cage between yourself and the hungry jaws.

Titus was merely whetting their appetites.

With the storm's fury, the light had dimmed. From underneath the murky water I could only distinguish ripples as each blast hit. But I knew what he was doing because with every strike the magical piranha fed, increasing their glow. Although the embryos/embers had moved earlier, they hadn't fully hatched until being submersed. They'd been weak then—another reason they hadn't bothered me as I swam through. But Titus was giving them the power they needed to mature. In essence, he was giving them everything they needed to eat him alive…or, in the case of our unwelcome visitor's walking corpse, to eat him…dead. And this time, he'd stay that way.

I gasped another breath then sank again, edging on my butt through the water to a fallen oak whose roots hung over the creek, never taking my eyes off Titus. If I stood, I was an easy target. One blast, even a graze, could be fatal. The blow might not kill me, but for my pets that was like blood in the water. Protecting myself with magic would have the same result, and I didn't feel like being their aperitif. I made it to the oak and lifted myself from the water. I lay under the roots, using them to slide on my back up the muddy bank.

Once hatched, the boralis would never leave the water. As long as I stayed beyond their jumping range and Titus's line of sight, I'd be okay. I breathed deeply but quietly, watching. If at the very beginning Titus had simply stopped and walked away, he might have made it out. Now, the fish spun around him with such force that he couldn't retreat. But Titus had bigger worries than what was in the water. The whirlpool of magic eaters circling him had never been my intention. Neither was ending up in the creek. That had been a frightening but fortuitous accident.

Titus's fate had been sealed with the one and only blow I'd landed. His expression changed as that realization finally *bit* him. The human body is made up of over ninety percent water. Even decomposing bodies were still mostly H_2O. The embers I'd placed on Titus's back had burrowed into the cut and hatched. They were now eating him from the inside out. I'd intended it as a distraction, a means to siphon off some of his magic until the others could help capture him. I'd only limited my own magical expenditures in the event I cut myself. I hadn't expected embers to fly every time our blades touched.

Titus's mouth opened in a silent scream, his face contorted in horror rather than pain. He dropped to his knees, everything but his head underwater. At this point, I could've left. Titus wouldn't be getting up. The fish would finish the job, and this creek was just a spillover from a neighbor's much larger pond, so the boralis could only go so far upstream before they'd have to turn and flow into our pond. But I continued to watch as I dragged my reclining body farther up the bank. It was a horrible way to go but no less than he deserved.

A tear that had nothing to do with the slowing rain fell. Peter Traylor had been dead for months. His family would never get his body back, but I'd make sure someone told them that he was gone. Peter's family shouldn't have to spend their entire lives wondering if he would ever walk in the door.

My grandmother had once told me that *boralis* meant water-fire. That was why, of all creatures, I'd picked them to keep as pets. That was also what the fish resembled as they fed. Baby fires, seeded in the gel I'd rubbed on my sword hours before, born as my flames sparked against Titus's magic, now a blazing water cyclone.

As the water rose, Titus sank lower. Being a malicious spirit residing within a dead body, he couldn't receive the sweet mercy of a quick death. His essence would live on until every last bit of dark magic was consumed. That would take days, maybe longer. I made no effort to move until his soulless, horrified eyes sank into the frothing, darkened water.

For the first time since landing in the water, the chill in my bones had nothing to do with my wet clothes.

CHAPTER SEVENTEEN

"I'll take you through the looking glass. That is, if you don't mind that the glass is black and that it'll dump you out into the middle of hellhound central. 'Cause if you're okay with that, I'd be happy to punch your ticket."

—Cate Delacy

"CATE?"

I was still half-under the oak's tangled roots, hidden in the sweeping shadow of Spanish moss, when Jacq came for me. I turned my weak head to see her look at the school of teeming fish and the red blood washing onto the creek's sandy shore. My voice caught her just as she set to dive in. "If I have to jump back in that water and save your ass from my man-eating guppies, I'm going to be really pissed."

I sat up, groaning as my sore abdomen, sore arms and sore everything else protested. The little prick had certainly given me a run for my money. Jacq hopped over tree roots and rocks, skidding to a stop by my side. She practically yanked me to my feet before pulling me into a tight embrace, her magic roaming my body, searching for injuries.

For a moment I gloried in her heat, my body feeling warm for the first time in what felt like hours. Then I pushed away, looking down in shame. "I'm getting mud and river gunk all over you." I brushed at a clump of mud that sat where my head had rested against her navy shirt but stopped as my dirty hands simply spread more.

Body shaking with relieved laugher, Jacq pulled me in for another hug. Maybe I had gone crazy because the situation seemed funny to me too, but I was too sore to laugh.

"Forget the clothes. They can be replaced."

I breathed in her tantalizing scent, doubly nice after the smell of Titus's decay. This time I didn't push her away. Jacq was toasty warm, and the sensation of our bodies pressed tight was wonderful. I burrowed closer, tucking my head under her chin. I untucked her shirt, pushing my cold hands against her warm sides. Jacq jumped, and I risked a laugh. The ache across my ribs was worth it. "Sorry, couldn't resist," I murmured, smiling against her neck. For this, I'd dry clean her entire closet.

Jacq spoke softly into my hair, her voice husky with emotion, "What happened? You were supposed to distract him, not drown him." Her words teased, but her body was stiff.

Acting on instinct, I grasped her tighter, pushing my body against hers, reminding her that I was very much still alive, even as I smiled and teased back. "What can I say? I'm an overachiever." Jacq laughed softly, but then my smile slipped. Wellsy knew a great deal about our family. Nicodemus wanted me, which meant that information had been compromised. Biting the bullet, I quietly added, "He was as much here for me as he was for Brittan. It was kill him or let him take me."

Jacq stiffened. I ran my dirty hands up the planes of her back, rubbing at the muscles I knew were as tired as my own. I pulled back. "There's more, but we'll get to it later. Come on, we'd better get back." I pulled my boots off and poured the water out.

Jacq grabbed my hand, helping me over the mass of roots, stones and mud. I didn't let go when we reached smoother ground, carrying my boots in my other hand. Only once did I look over my shoulder at the creek turning black with the setting sun. The glance wasn't necessary. The memory of Titus's face—the face that had once belonged to Peter Traylor—as he sank beneath the waters would be etched into my mind until my last breath. And that was how it was supposed to be.

The day I stopped caring was the day I'd lay my sword down for good.

Jacq squeezed my hand. Could she feel my turmoil over what I'd done? "Risa was hit by the sorcerer's last volley," she said. I'd nearly forgotten my question as to how the others fared. "Her back was turned, and we weren't expecting…" Jacq's voice trailed off. Her set jaw said she blamed herself, though I knew she had been responsible for protecting Becca, not Risa. This time, I was the one squeezing her hand. "She's shifted to heal, but Mynx says the magic's poison is seeping into her system."

At her words, I hurried my steps over the soft pine needles. I could see light from the clearing ahead. "And the nesreterka?" At Jacq's puzzled look, I explained. "The raptors." Rain, now just a drizzle, fell on our heads. I could feel the cool liquid washing trails of mud down the back of my cargo pants, but I didn't feel the chill thanks to the continuous heat streaking from Jacq's hand up my arm and throughout my body.

"Subdued. Mynx said you wanted to wait before taking the heads and hearts?" Jacq's face was in profile, but the question was clear.

"Yes. Serena may be able to read their minds to determine Nicodemus's location. That was my backup plan, and it looks like we're going to need it." I didn't say any more as we entered the open meadow and saw the destruction. It was an instinctual decision to spare the raptors. One I didn't regret when I saw the three carcasses laid out, back-to-back, in a triangular, defensive position.

As if reading my thoughts, Jacq explained, "Near the end the sorcerer's hold slipped and they retreated to that position."

As we passed one, I quickly kneeled, running my hand over the surprisingly soft skin. I could feel the creature's ribs. They'd been starved nearly to death. As promised, everything vital was still intact, but the raptors didn't react to my touch. I looked up.

Jacq shook her head. "Stunned only, but this time we took no chances. I hit them with enough magic to keep them out for half a day."

I knew she was thinking of the hellhound attack and the close call that could've cost me my life. Before kneeling, I'd noted Mynx's green wards circling the bodies. They allowed us to enter but kept the animals contained. Assured that the raptors wouldn't awaken any time soon, I moved to where a white and black striped tiger lay panting in a patch of tall grass dotted with yellow daisies. It was strange to see the tiny beautiful flowers surrounding the large dangerous animal. Rom and Mynx knelt by her side while Fera stood a few steps back, sword still drawn.

"If that weapon's for the sorcerer, you can put it away. He's not coming back."

"All the same. I'll keep an eye on your menagerie over there." Fera tilted her head toward the raptors.

I simply nodded, adding my voice to Mynx's healing chant. I didn't need my powers to see the long black burn streaking from the tiger's right furred shoulder all the way down her muscular back. The burn, in itself, would be painful and damaging, but the tainted magic had to be excruciating…and if not treated quickly… I shook my head, not wanting to consider the possibilities.

Kneeling, I placed one hand on her neck, the other on her side. Just before I left my body, it occurred to me that someone was missing. "Where's Becca?" Under my hand, Risa's damp fur rose and fell as she took short, pained breaths.

Fists clenched at his sides, Rom answered, "She went to call the Clan for more help." I just nodded. Becca was right…almost. We *would* need help, more even than Grey could provide, but that was a talk for later.

I swiftly rose into the mind's eye, surveying the damage. I tried to keep the worry off my face. This was worse than I'd expected. Hurrying, I said, "Romulus Legion, do you give me leave to work the magical arts on your sister of the blood, knowing that it must be done to keep her from falling into the endless sleep?" My voice echoed like a phantom between the physical and metaphysical planes. Of course, I could've just said, "Can I zap your sister till she gets better?" That would've been my preference, but Weres responded best to formality, sugar, and piss-covered walls. And I was fresh out of the last two.

"It's necessary?" Hesitant, his voice was tight with worry.

"Yes." My answer was echoed by the others. Risa whined. In acceptance? In denial?

It didn't matter, because Rom growled, "Do what you have to. I give my consent." And just like that, I unleashed my fire.

I said, "Hold her," and sensed more than saw Mynx and Rom toss themselves across Risa. I whispered, "I'm sorry." Then a half-human, half-animal scream echoed across the planes as my fire, following my will, flooded her, rushing through her veins, racing to burn out any taint that wouldn't be forced out. Cool tears slid down cheeks I no longer possessed.

There was no time for gentleness. No time for a magic less painful. No time to take back my agreement to allow the Weres to assist us in our fight, no matter how much I wished that I could. I'd told Rom this was to prevent Risa from falling into the "endless sleep." And maybe it was. Maybe all the black-magic would do was kill, but I couldn't be sure, especially not with the memory of Peter Traylor's soulless eyes still fresh in my mind.

I dug deep, letting every ounce of magic I could find come to bear against the quickly spreading poisoned darkness, uncaring if my eyes glowed blue with magic or even if flames crawled up my skin, twisting like fiery serpents around my arms, marking me as the demon spawn that I was. I dimly heard a cursing Rom ask if it was necessary to torture his sister, felt Fera's watchful eyes on me, and knew that the body beneath me was becoming dangerously hot. But I ignored it all.

There were worse things in life than pain, worse things than dying. Worse things than exposing to a Council operative the secret that I'd been trying to keep my entire life. Things like being taken— body and soul—by something that could wear another man's face, speak with another man's voice, but never consider the damage it might wreak on another man's heart. I would not stand idly by and watch while this thing…this darkness…claimed yet another victim.

Even if that meant we all died in the process.

* * *

"Gin!" Helena crowed.

"S— Crap." Brittan threw her cards down. They'd played two rounds of Go Fish, followed by three of Texas Hold 'em, and finally four of gin rummy. Brittan had yet to win a game, and her cards had frequently been good. If she didn't know better, she'd suspect Helena of cheating. Brittan folded her cards, looking out the window. The light passing through the swaying crepe myrtles was watery. Thunder rolled, accompanied by a *pat pat* as an occasional raindrop blew against the glass panes. This storm had nearly passed. *But what of the other?*

"I think it's time we go."

At Helena's words, Brit looked up. Helena's eyes had a far-off look, hazy, as if she were lost somewhere inside her mind. The Delacys hadn't mentioned psychic powers. But then, there was a lot they hadn't mentioned. Of course it could simply be the brandy Helena had mixed into her tea. Brit found it humorous that in this world gambling and alcohol were permissible when cursing was not.

Brittan followed as Helena moved through the house piling seemingly random items into a basket, which she passed to Brit. Blanket. Water. Five packs of hamburger meat? Brittan didn't become concerned until Helena grabbed a black bag. Eyes now clear and focused, Helena looked into the bag. "We'll need more bandages." Cate's aunt headed upstairs.

Brit turned and followed, asking, "What's going on?" Before Helena could answer, they heard the front door crash open. Standing on the stairs' midway landing, the two women turned to look at the hall floor where a dripping wet, sandy-haired man with a crew cut stood. Something about him didn't seem right. Helena slowly put down her bag, stepping in front of Brittan, who wanted to protest but kept silent. She was the one with the sword…the one who'd promised Cate to look after her aunt. But it looked like Helena was set on doing the protecting. *They'd see about that.* Brit set down her own basket.

"Luke?" Helena tried to sound casual, but there was an edge to her voice. "What are you doing here?"

Brit stepped up the stairs and pulled her sword, using the ninety-degree turn to hide her movements. As the man Helena had called Luke spoke, she stepped down again, keeping the blade behind her leg.

"I didn't get an invitation to the party, Helena, and I'm real disappointed." His voice was deep and gravelly, but there was a sort of distortion to the sound that made goose bumps prickle her arms. He smiled, sliding a dark tongue over teeth that looked too sharp and rotten to be human. Helena gasped. Yep, this was bad.

"Go to Cate's room," Helena whispered. "You'll be safe there." Then she formed a ball of blue magic and tossed it at the man's head with unbelievable speed and accuracy.

They were both shocked when he swatted the blast away as if it were a fly. It boomed as it landed, blowing out part of the hall wall. Magic. Shit. Brit had no idea how to deal with this. Still, she wouldn't leave Helena to fight alone. Unfortunately, numbers wouldn't matter much. They were sitting ducks on the landing.

"Why Helena, that's no way to treat an old friend."

Brit watched as his features morphed into that of an older, gaunt man. Body frozen in shock Helena gasped, "*Wellsy.*"

"Fortunately for you," he said, "we want you both alive, but only for the night. So Nicodemus won't mind if we play some." He formed a ball of something swirling and black. "As long as I don't damage you *too* badly."

Brit jerked the stunned Helena up the stairs just as he sent his magic toward them. Helena cried out, stumbling. Brit wrapped her arm around Helena's waist, continuing up the stairs, not sparing the injured woman a glance. She could already feel warm blood slicking down Helena's back.

Brit heard a slow *thump, thump* as he moved up the hall. She'd seen the man who'd chased her earlier in the day move quickly, so she knew this one could move faster. He was taking his time, relishing this. Well, that would work to her advantage. There was just one problem.

She didn't know where she was going.

Brit heard closer thuds as his feet began to climb the stairs. They were echoed by a much faster set of thumps as her heart beat loudly in her ears. "Which room?" she hissed. They were nearly to the top now, and he was almost to the landing. Once, just once, she'd like to scrape by on more than the skin of her teeth.

"Third on the left," Helena slurred. Then her body relaxed, becoming dead weight. There was now no choice. Brit dropped the sword, hoisted Helena over her back, and ran for all she was worth. Breathing heavily, she made it up the stairs and to the door before he reached the last step.

Brit could feel his eyes on her, but he made no move to attack, still enjoying the stalking of his prey. She really hoped Helena had been right about this room.

"Doors won't protect you from me, pretty one." His racking, phlegm-filled laugh and the smell drifting her way simply made Brit hurry more. Her fingers fumbled at the knob, suddenly slippery with cold sweat.

The knob turned.

The door opened.

He must have sensed her plan. Or perhaps he saw the shine of silver at the threshold. Brittan heard him shriek and rush toward her. She turned, falling back into the room, trying to ease Helena to the floor as gently as possible.

As his cold bony hand grabbed Brit by the ankle that she was not quick enough to pull back, she knew that at least one of them was safe. If only there had been more time to get to know the infuriating, occasionally sweet and surprisingly shy Risa. She thought that she might have fallen in love a little when the embarrassed tiger had tried to apologize for holding her captive. Brit felt herself being pulled out of the room and was too slow to stop the hand that came toward her throat. She had just enough time to register another woman's alarmed shout ringing up the stairs. Then darkness swallowed her vision, and her mind became blissfully empty of regrets.

* * *

"Who the fuck are you?" Rom's snarl filtered out the open front door.

I stepped through the door and came to a sudden halt. Fera and Mynx, transporting an unconscious, human-shaped Risa, plowed into my back. The house was chaos. Muddy water trailed all the way down the hall. Broken plaster and plaster dust were everywhere. Something had blasted through the hall's Sheetrock and into the dining room.

But the most arresting sight was Rom standing near the kitchen entrance with his blade to the throat of a silver-haired woman who looked ready to disembowel him. I hurried forward, hoping to stop Rom before he got himself killed.

"Sonny, we don't allow that sort of language here. So watch yerself. This may be my granddaughter's house now, but I'm still the head Delacy." My Nana pushed at the blade, causing it to waver in his hands. "And if you don't put that thing up, I'm going to take it away and show you how to use it." She eyed him from head to toe. "You won't like what I cut off first."

I hustled. That was no idle threat. My grandmother was spry and strong, considering she was nearly a hundred. She also still liked to play with sharp things. "Nana!" I rushed forward. Rom dropped his sword, stepping back. The look of shock and confusion on his face would've been comical...had I not been feeling something very similar. "What are you doing here?" I didn't ask how she'd gotten here. Darkmirrors were for more than traveling between worlds.

"Cate!" Jacq yelled from upstairs.

Nana brushed my hug away, briskly walking past myself and the confused Rom. "Come along, dearie. No time for mushiness now." She headed for the stairs, her white gauzy dress flowing around her tall thin frame, and I followed. "I was resting my eyes for a spell and had an overwhelming sense that I was needed here."

I followed her upstairs. At the landing, I hesitated, staring at a cluster of bullet holes. Then I saw the coveted sword I'd given Brit only hours before lying on the stairs along with Aunt Helena's doctor bag and a turned over basket of…food? There was a sudden knot in the bottom of my stomach. It grew as I followed the trail of blood and water up the stairs, down the hall, and into my room.

Jacq knelt by Aunt Helena, her hands glowing silver, her mouth set in a strained line. "I can heal the wound, but you'll need to help with the poison."

I rushed forward, but Nana, kneeling opposite Jacq with her hands resting on my aunt, stopped me. "Child, you're tired, and your magic is low. It'll do Helena no good if you lose yourself." Nana's eyes were closed, her voice overly loud. She was already traveling through my aunt's body, healing Aunt Helena like I'd done Risa. Only this time, Nana was working with her own gentler, much stronger earth-magic. I felt so helpless. *Why now? Why not someone else?* I'd lost my mom. I'd lost Luke. I couldn't lose Aunt Helena, too. I bit my lip, focusing on the small pain, using it to hide my distress.

As I watched, Jacq healed all but a small portion of the wound before moving away.

Nana said, "Detective Slone, I presume?"

"Yes." Jacq's voice was huskier than normal. She looked from me to my aunt then put her thumbs in her pockets, rocking back on her heels.

"Take my granddaughter and you two clean up." Nana gestured toward the bathroom. "And make sure she's fed. That girl never eats enough for my peace of mind."

I blushed but didn't protest, knowing better.

"I can handle this. Helena managed to erect at least one ward, so the poison hadn't yet spread far."

That was a relief. I looked at Jacq. She was covered in sweat, mud, and a good deal of blood that I hoped wasn't her own.

We both ignored my Nana's orders. I couldn't shower until I knew help was on its way, and I could see that Jacq didn't want to leave me. Even from across the room, an occasional *zing* of magic infused my body with healing warmth. If my grandmother sensed the magic passing between us, she didn't comment.

Rom stuck his head in the door, cell in hand, and looked around the room. "Risa's awake and asking for Brittan. And where's Becca? The Alpha says she never reported in."

The minute I'd seen bullet holes in the landing wall and the sword on the stairs, I'd suspected what had happened. Seeing Aunt Helena had confirmed it. And from the amount of blood, I also suspected that Brit had probably saved my aunt's life. I owed her more than a sword. And I owed it to Luke to bring Becca back and give him the future that was laid out for him, whether he realized it or not.

"They're gone. Taken." I kept speaking as my meaning hit Rom. "But we'll bring them home." Stepping to his side, I rescued the fragile phone before his clenched fists turned it to technological dust. "But first, I need to make a call."

We'd get them back. I *always* paid my debts.

CHAPTER EIGHTEEN

"Do unto others as you would…before they do unto you what you know they were wanting to do in the first place."
—From the illusionist once known as Jazmine Manizales

Mirror, mirror on the wall, who's the biggest badass of them all? According to Aunt Helena, who awakened during my calls, it wasn't the spirit inhabiting Wellsy. He wasn't Nicodemus, and we knew from my interaction with Titus and my aunt's with the possessed Wellsy that both dark spirits bowed to Nicky-boy's wishes. That might not make him the biggest badass around, but it definitely put him at the top of my shit list.

While calling in the cavalry, I watched Nana finish her healing. Aunt Helena said the possessed Wellsy had only wanted Brittan and herself for the night, so the ritual was tonight. If they held to schedule, they'd conduct it just before dawn. But even if she'd said the ritual was next week, we were going tonight. I wouldn't have left a roach with Nicodemus for the length of time it would take Rom to put a bullet in his kneecaps. Needless to say, as soon as backup arrived we would be hotfooting it after our friends, Isabella and the kidnapped boys.

But we couldn't barge in and have Nicodemus start the spell, setting up a potential magical meltdown. I rubbed my aching temples and tried to make a plan. We were supposed to have more time. I'd been certain Nicodemus would want to wait for the extra power the upcoming solar eclipse would provide. But something had spooked him. And it wasn't me or our little group. No, Titus had seemed confident that we would be no trouble to them. It had to be something else.

Nana explained how the possessed Wellsy had breached the wards. A family friend for decades, Wellsy had helped lay one of the ward stones. These drew and directed power for the wards from the earth and surrounding ley-lines. Days before, upon suspecting Wellsy's involvement, I'd changed the shield so it was no longer keyed to him. But the thing inhabiting his body had been able to do the impossible and access the deeply buried stone, destroying it and taking out a section of the wards until the other stones could draw enough power to fill in the gap.

After our brief chat, we moved Aunt Helena to her own room. I tried to dissuade Jacq, Mynx and Nana from cleaning the blood and mud off the floor, but they refused, simply working around my dripping body as I made my calls.

My call to the Weres was difficult. It was hard telling Grey that Becca was gone and that the sacrifice of Isabella was tonight. It was even harder when he put on a just awakened Luke.

From the rage and grief in my ex's voice, it was clear he was finally starting to realize what Becca meant to him. Though on some level he probably already knew, I couldn't bring myself to tell Luke that Nicodemus had no reason to keep Becca alive…other than to torture her, and he'd take his time doing it. I told him we would get Becca back. I didn't tell him she might never be the same.

Luke and Grey were coming. Once we knew a final location, they would call some of Kyle's guards to meet us and the others. We had about an hour and a half until everyone got here. One by one, Mynx, Jacq and finally Nana left the room. My grandmother kissed me on a dirty cheek then closed the door behind her. The mirror on its back caught my eye. I looked at the familiar grim expression. The corner of one lip twisted up, a change that would go unnoticed by most.

Mirror, mirror on the wall, who's the biggest badass of all? Well, it certainly wasn't the Wicked Witch of the South. But by the end of the night, she'd be bumped up a notch.

I went into the bathroom. My fingers were fumbling at my cargo pants' drawstring when the door behind me clicked. Even with Jacq's magic, I was still cold and weary. Everything felt stiff. My limbs, my fingers, my clothes. The knotted string was wet and didn't want to cooperate. I was about to give up and find something sharp to cut it when warm hands turned me around.

"Let me." Jacq's strong steady hands covered mine, and I could only nod, closing my eyes.

Swaying with weariness, I moved my hands to her waist, leaning against her. Even covered in blood, raptor gore and mud, she still smelled divine. I lost myself as I grew warm again. My pants loosened, sliding down my hips. She tugged my shirt up.

I was being undressed like a child, and I didn't care. Once I was completely nude, I heard the shower door open and the hot water start. How Jacq had managed that with me resting against her soft, strong body was beyond me. A few tears of pure exhaustion escaped my closed lids. Warm skin slid against my own. I blinked, trying to see through the watery film.

"Wha—"

Jacq placed a finger against my lips, hushing my protests. My eyes widened. She'd removed her own top and was working at her belt. Her hot breasts rubbed against my collarbone, and I sucked in a breath around her finger, my tongue accidentally flicking her salty skin.

"Shh, it's a shower. Nothing more."

That one-dimpled, half-smile returned, and I smiled back. My smile turned into a frown when I saw the faded yellow-green bruise, ugly against her skin's creamy perfection, running across her chest. Jacq healed too quickly for this to be anything but recent… and serious. I tenderly traced the bruise, feeling her pants fall. Soon a warm bare calf was rubbing against my own. It was a wonderful sensation, but she wouldn't distract me so easily.

"What happened?" I looked up. Jacq was gazing down at me. We were both too tired for desire, but there was another sort of hunger in her eyes. Our emotional connection had returned sometime after my dunking, but I didn't need it to know that she'd lied to me—and possibly to herself—when she'd said only one date.

Jacq wanted this for longer. She wanted me for longer. And I was through protesting. I wanted her just as much…and for as long as she'd have me. I'd deal with the ramifications of someday dying on her when I could no longer ignore them. Somewhere along the line, I'd begun to fall in love with this woman. This stubborn, chivalrous woman who'd shower with me and not take advantage. *How crazy was that?*

I pulled back, letting my hungry gaze travel down her strong, lean body, noting the flush on her chest, the dusky nipples and the auburn curls, so dark that they were nearly black, at the apex of her thighs. It wasn't my first time seeing a naked woman, but it was the first time the sight made something burn low and hot in my belly. Jacq's shy look at my perusal made me brave.

"Cate, I—"

This time it was my finger at her lips, halting her words. I looked into Jacq's eyes, once again a stormy gray. I could feel her inhaled breath, her expanding chest pressing softly against my own. The timing could be better, but the woman and the sentiment were right.

"It's okay. It's just a shower, nothing more. Your words, remember?" Smiling, I pulled her by the hand into the shower.

I noticed the heat of it first. Boiling hot, to the point of flaying the skin from your bones. *Just the way I like it.* I sighed in pleasure, letting the steam fill my lungs before stepping under the spray. My body sucked the energy in, filling my cells, reviving me. Remembering suddenly that I was partial to temperatures others found painful, I turned to Jacq in concern, slicking the wet tangled black curls back from my head before reaching for her, leaning forward, shielding her from the spray. "Is this too hot?" I ran my hands over her chest, letting a sliver of magic trail down her skin, making sure its rosy glow wasn't from damage.

Jacq pushed me back until the water sluiced over us both and picked up a shampoo bottle. Groaning softly, I almost forgot my question as her soapy hands moved into my hair, massaging my scalp. "You could never be too hot for me, cher. But as to the water, it's fine. I put out a great deal of heat, so it doesn't bother me." Nimble fingers scratched behind my ears. The pleasure weakening my knees was intense but not as intense as the emotions cascading across her face. "That is how my kind are...*were*."

Jacq paused, and somehow I knew. She wanted to say more but couldn't...or wouldn't. But tonight, I felt similarly afflicted. I couldn't...or wouldn't...press her.

I put orange wash on a loofa and slowly ran it over her skin, paying careful attention to her injuries. I told myself that I just wanted to return the favor and let her experience the pleasure of having someone care for her. Deep down, I was *not* feeling a strange, primal need to paint her in my scent. In denial of my denial, that dark, demon part locked deep within my soul purred its pleasure, something ruffling like the opening and closing of wings inside me. I shut it out, focusing instead on Jacq. "Tell me what happened?" I asked again softly, looking at her bruises.

"One of the raptors got behind me."

The sponge drew soapy swirls across her shoulders. I pressed the tight muscles harder, and Jacq's body relaxed.

I began to wash her breasts, and her voice softened. "Becca blinded it. But there wasn't enough time to move, and it simply barreled me over."

I could almost see it in my mind, somehow knowing there was more. Her words petered out, and I looked up. "Am I distracting you?" I smiled, remembering her previous accusation. I swept the sponge over an erect nipple. My own tightened as Jacq's hands reflexively clutched at my shoulders.

"No." Her strained voice was rougher than usual. I swept the sponge across her other nipple. She cleared her throat. "Not at all." Belying her words, Jacq placed her hand over mine, stilling the sponge over her heart. "I arose quickly, but the beast's tail clipped me, causing this." She guided my sponge-filled hand over her chest. For a moment, neither of us spoke.

My breathing quickened. I couldn't look away from our joined hands. The simple intimacy of my hand in hers, moving together over her body, was overwhelming.

"Cate?" Jacq's voice was hoarse with desire. "I need you to stop me."

Forcing my gaze upward, I placed my other hand against her cheek, watching her eyes darken as I softly said, "I'm not sure I can."

Maybe it was me. Maybe it was Jacq. I wasn't sure which of us began to move the sponge lower. We both watched it move between her breasts and farther, washing her taut abdomen, circling her navel before finally reaching the curls between her legs. We both moaned, teetering at the brink of heaven, seeming to linger there for an eternity. Then Jacq's hand snatched mine away, and her body slammed me roughly against the wet wall.

I gasped. Her hard thigh between my own, Jacq panted, her head bowed, holding herself very still. Silver magic rippled across her skin, and the hot shower grew hotter still. I looked up into eyes gone silver with desire and gulped, lost in that hunger. Her hand reached up, pushing a lock of wet hair off my face before sliding down my neck and over my breast, eliciting a moan. I started to pull her toward me, but she shook her wet head roughly, pulling back.

"No," Jacq said, "when we make love for the first time, it will be in our bed. No rushing. No running off to do battle." She smiled cheekily, tweaking my nipple. Hot magic streaked from her fingertips, and I had to lock my legs to remain standing. "Besides, I read up on these human dating customs. I must first buy you dinner, sing loudly outside your window, and have at least one family member threaten me with firearms."

Warm water dribbled into my mouth as I threw my head back and laughed. There was something about her that made me free to laugh. I looked at her beautiful face.

Our bed. *Our.* The word settled like a weight on my chest—not heavy and suffocating as I'd expected but comfortable, like ballast keeping me upright. How could three letters have such an impact? I didn't know. "Okay." Voice tight with desire, I had to say it twice before the word came out as anything more than a growl. "Don't look so disappointed." Smiling, I poked Jacq in the ribs. "It was your idea to wait." She did look disappointed, but there was also anticipation lurking in her wicked smile. I shivered. Unable to turn from temptation, I turned her instead, in essence to wash her back, and finally saw her tattoo.

I lovingly ran the sponge over every flaming feather, tracing the lines of the beautiful golden phoenix. The fiery bird I'd chosen for my personal totem was etched across the back of my protector. The feeling of déjà vu was strong. I'd been waiting for her for a long time. I ran the soapy sponge down the firm ass, rubbing until Jacq groaned, turned around, and took the sponge away.

"You don't know how you test my resolve." Her eyes nearly glaring, Jacq's voice was low, forceful.

"I bet I do." I placed my hands on her shoulders. "It can't be any more than how I tested my own, considering how hard I fought myself not to give into this." Jacq grinned at my half-amused, half-pained expression. My quick smile froze at the soul-deep longing in her eyes.

"There's still a lot of fighting to come. But this," Jacq laid my hand over her heart, "is something we shouldn't fight. If you believe anything, believe we're meant to be."

Hopefully, she would believe the tears falling from my eyes were water droplets from the shower. She finished washing our bodies, then my hair, and her own. By the time we stepped from the shower, I'd decided to say one last thing, but I had to work my way to it.

"Jacq, how deeply did you research human dating practices?" I asked as she rubbed me down with a white fluffy towel.

Jacq looked up, surprised. I nearly laughed. I could practically see her trying to figure out this conversational turn. It was nice to be able to read her expressions, even nicer still to feel them. Right now, she was curious and just a little wary. Smart woman.

"Not as deeply as I'd like." Jacq gave me an exaggerated come-hither look.

I laughed but sobered quickly. "Maybe I should rephrase that. What do you know about the sexual practices of humans?" I took a deep breath then forged ahead. "Specifically, the one called abstinence?"

All my worries slipped away as Jacq pulled me close, letting our towels drop before whispering against my ear, "All I know, cher, is that we won't be practicing it. And that's all that matters."

My shriek as she picked me up and threw me over her shoulder was loud enough to be heard throughout the entire house, but it didn't matter. I was about thirty years too late to worry about anyone else's sensibilities.

CHAPTER NINETEEN

"Karma's a bitch. Or rather, she's a Southern woman with claws and a bad attitude. There's really not a difference. Trust me on this, and don't say later that you weren't warned."

—Romulus Legion

Jacq carried me out of the bathroom, dumped me on the bed, and gave my nude body a long, steamy look. In turn, I stared at her naked, dripping body. My comparisons to an Amazon, a warrior, lethal elegance? None of them compared to the truth standing before me. She was The Phoenix. Glorious. Bright and shining. And she set me ablaze.

I thought Jacq would change her mind and make some move toward me, but she only wrapped a towel around herself and left the room. I lay there for a few minutes, making no move to shield my wet body from the chilly A/C, digesting what had happened. I should've been panicking, but I felt like the calm eye of a storm. Death and destruction circled me on all sides, but I was at peace. In fact, I was energized and raring to go. I jumped up, dressed in black battle gear—leather pants, black T-shirt and a spare pair of ass-kicker boots—braided my damp hair, then went downstairs to load up on weapons and carbs.

I was suddenly ravenous.

Enlisted by my Nana, Rom had managed to clean up a good portion of the blasted Sheetrock, bloody stairs and wet hall. Perhaps it was his deference to older women—or maybe it was Nana's threat to cut something off—for whatever reason, Rom was being very solicitous. After fixing a stack of sandwiches, I met Mynx and Fera in the training room.

While I put on my harnesses, utility belt and weapons, I confessed to Mynx and Fera what I'd done. They were amused at how I'd gotten a tracker on Brittan. I hadn't planned on her being taken. But for some reason, when I'd passed her the suppression amulet earlier in the day, I'd had the urge to give her the one with the GPS device. Mynx had confirmed that the GPS was working and actively moving toward The Burg. We wouldn't need Serena to read the raptors' minds after all.

Any minute now, the troops would be rushing in. Jacq had come downstairs in her own black clothes. Mynx and Fera were similarly dressed. In fact, we were all dressed for a night run...all except for the woman now entering the room with Rom.

It wasn't the first time I'd seen a woman come to a fight in heels, but the skirt was new. She *had* to work for the Vamps. No one would dress like a maid around the sex-juicing Weres. The Clan would take it as a personal challenge to see who could be quickest to get the lady out of her pantyhose and starched shirt. My mouth was stuffed with turkey and cheese, so I turned around, quickly gobbling my sandwich. But I nearly choked on the last bite when a familiar voice shouted my name.

"Cate Delacy, you *owe* me!"

I spun around, swallowed, and braced for impact.

"Eeepp." I squeaked as Serena barreled into me, picking me up and hugging me hard enough to pop my back. You'd think in the years since we'd met that I would've gotten used to Serena's sometimes enthusiastic moods. Of course it didn't help that she only did this to me. Apparently I was the shortest of the Viking's friends, making me the best for her game of dangle-the-witch. Hopefully one day soon she would find a shorter friend or a lover to run roughshod over her. I nearly snorted in derision. Both options I'd learned over the years were wasted hopes.

"Serena, put me down right this minute." I slapped her shoulder, hissing at the ensuing ache in my hand. It was like pounding steel. My feet were hanging at least a foot off the ground and I was glad none of the Weres other than Rom were here to witness this. I looked around to see Mynx and a confused Fera smirking. The embarrassment I'd survive, but I didn't like the look in Jacq's eyes. Arms crossed, she looked ready to spit fire.

I'd never cared for Luke's possessive streak, but the look on Jacq's face left me a little worried for Serena's welfare...and a lot excited. Would there ever be a time when my reactions to this woman didn't surprise me? Did I even want them to? I looked at Jacq's flushed cheeks. Likely not, but that was a thought for later—Jacq took a step forward—after I kept my favorite law enforcement officer from starting World War IV.

I gulped and looked into gray eyes. "Jacq, meet Serena, Darryl's business partner and good friend."

Serena squeezed harder, letting me know I'd left something important out. Jacq's face darkened, but I waved her away. Serena respected patience, and she had a point to make, though damned if I knew what it was. I hissed out, "The Vampire Queen of Mississippi." She squeezed once more. I added with a *wheeze*, "And my good friend." She let up, and I took a deep breath, turning back to glare at my tenacious friend.

"Jesus H. Kristofferson, Serena. I need those ribs intact." I gave her another scathing look. This was the very reason I hadn't given her a hug when I'd seen her at the House of Delights.

"If that's how she treats her friends," Fera mumbled, "I'd hate to be her enemy."

The room fairly crackled with power, and I wasn't sure which— or if all—of us were leaking magic. All I knew was that my skin was itching, and I suddenly didn't want anyone but Jacq touching me. It was a strangely familiar sensation. I would've kicked Serena in the shins, seeing as my toes were still at the right height, but knew better. I'd have broken a foot.

"Ahem," said the woman in the skirt and heels. Serena set me back on my feet and turned to the woman.

I grabbed Jacq's hand, moving close to her side. Her emotions became clearer with the touch. She'd been somewhat jealous but more concerned by Serena's rough play. My detective had held herself back from staking a claim, and I was proud of her restraint. I wasn't so subtle.

I squeezed Jacq's hand, leaning into her. She had nothing to fear from Serena. But I might, if I was right about the look in the eyes of the woman with her. Noticing our clasped hands and close bodies, the woman's glare dimmed slightly. She held out her hand, "Cate Delacy?"

I recognized the voice and smiled, taking in the woman's wire-rimmed glasses and white-streaked black hair bun. "Miss James?" I shook her hand. "It's good to finally put a face to the name." When I couldn't reach Serena on her cell, I'd called Benito Carmel's office looking for her and gotten Miss James, his paralegal/personal secretary instead. Miss James had said she would relay the message, but I hadn't expected her to join the group. At Miss James' scowl, my happy voice vanished until I realized the dirty look was directed at Serena, who was trying to tug the paralegal's leather bag off her shoulder.

"Miss James, huh? Does no one know your first name?" Serena asked cheerfully.

Miss James' scowl was promptly replaced by a neutral expression. She pushed her glasses up her nose with one finger and, studiously ignoring the vampire, pointed to her bag. "Do you have somewhere I can change? I'm not exactly dressed to fight." She looked around, mentally cataloguing and assessing my companions.

The outfit and demeanor might appear innocent, but it didn't completely hide her shrewd mind. I'd been raised by women who used good graces for the same purpose. I simply smiled and pointed toward the hall. This was a game I knew well. "Certainly, I'll show you the way." I gestured for her to follow, but Serena grabbed her arm.

"Oh, no. You're not in this fight." Serena's fangs flashed a mocking smile as her nostrils flared. "I smell blood in this house. Several people have already been hurt, and I'm sure they were all trained fighters."

The *unlike you* went unsaid, but no doubt Miss James understood, her face getting redder with every word. Magic was so thick in the air—I could nearly smell it as Serena kept digging her grave that much deeper. "The last thing we need is some adventure-hungry novice getting themself or someone else killed."

Miss James shrugged off Serena's restraining hand and cocked her head. "I assure you I am proficient in the defensive arts." Brushing at the wrinkles in her shirt, she turned to walk away then stopped, giving Serena a withering glare. "And I don't care to be touched." She pushed her glasses back up her nose.

Serena should've had icicles hanging from her chin—Miss James' tone was so glacial. The magic in the air fairly rumbled, and I was suddenly aware that it was oozing from Miss James, released by her extreme displeasure. Miss James took another step.

It happened so quickly that at first I stood there trying to make sense of what I'd seen. Serena again reached to stop the paralegal. Without looking, Miss James flicked her wrist. There was a crack like lightning and a flash of gold magic. Then Serena was flying through the air. She hit the side wall with a loud "Uff," hanging there for a moment, suspended, before dropping onto her ass.

Fortunately, Serena's guards were outside. Otherwise either Miss James' head or the guards' would be rolling on the floor beside Serena. At this point, I wasn't sure who I would've bet on. Miss James was hiding more than a sharp wit behind those glasses.

The air in the room went still. Then the raw magic that had been hanging about receded. All that was left was an eerie, emotionless stillness. No satisfaction or gloating. No regret or rebuke. Miss James was one cool number. I changed my mind. I'd take good odds any day that this woman would win if set against a horde of thirsty, sword-swinging, crazed vampires.

Miss James never even looked back. I followed her heels' methodical *click click* as she calmly walked from the room. I just shook my head, grinning as Serena muttered, "What a woman."

I didn't need to see the look on her face to know that had hurt… and more than just her undead body. But I took one last look to confirm suspicions of another nature before turning again to stare at Miss James' receding form. Serena's face said it all. Unknowingly, the prickly paralegal had just released one very curious hound. I had no doubt that Serena would nip at her heels until she unearthed every skeleton in Miss James' Brooks Brothers closet. Serena had found another playmate, and I was just selfish enough to hope this meant an end to certain things and a beginning to others.

A few minutes later, I knew my hoping was not in vain…at least in regard to Miss James. It wasn't a phone booth, but you wouldn't have known it from the super-fast change she made in the downstairs bathroom. Gone were the glasses and bun. Instead, her hair was pulled back into a series of small braids which she'd twisted into a complicated plait at the base of her neck. She was decked out in black cargo pants similar to my own, black boots, and a sleeveless black shirt with thick hammered-gold bracelets around her wrists and small muscular biceps.

My shocked face at the new and improved, battle-ready paralegal's miraculous transformation was nothing compared to Serena's slack-jawed ogle. But neither came close to Miss James' near faint when, a few minutes later, Abigail Gryphon, the Tiger Alpha's very pregnant mate, toddled into the training room (now more a war room).

"JJ!" Abigail shouted, dashing across the room and throwing herself at the unsuspecting Miss James. Abigail's ecstatic voice boomed around the high-ceiling room. Miss James struggled to hold up the pregnant woman, who'd lost her breath and balance.

Jacq, Mynx, Fera, Rom and I stood nearby, going over maps. I leaned my elbows on the paper-strewn table, watching as Abigail's husband, an unamused Grey Gryphon, followed by a worried-looking Luke, entered the room. Grey wrapped his arms around his wife, steadying her. Abigail continued talking from her husband's embrace, shooting out rapid-fire questions, not allowing Miss James to answer.

"JJ, where've you been? And what did you do with your hair?" Abigail leaned forward, gingerly touching the white streak in Miss James' black hair. Miss James opened her mouth but shut it again. "They said you were de…dea…" Abigail started crying.

"Abby." Miss James stepped forward, hugging the pregnant woman, not quite fully encircling her swollen belly. "It's a long story." She gave Serena and Grey a look. "One I'll tell you someday soon… but not tonight."

I thought for sure Grey would erupt over someone making his mate cry. Weres generally removed extremities for that offense. But he merely sighed. "She's been doing this all day. The kits are nearly due, and I cannot leave her." He offered Miss James a hand. "I've heard a great deal about you, lass."

Miss James gave him a dismayed look then shook his hand.

Like a switch being turned, Abby's waterworks stopped, and the flaming redhead hit her husband's shoulder. "You mean I wouldn't let you leave me, you big lout." She gave her husband a watery smile, taking any rebuke from the words. Abby turned to us. "I told him if he didn't bring me, I'd follow him here and have the babies alone on a roadside." Luke and Grey shuddered at that possibility. Abby turned back to her husband, kissing him on the chin. "But if it's okay, I'll stay here and wait for you." She gave him a sweet smile, batting her eyes.

"I don't know, lass," Grey murmured. "What if the kits come?"

"I'll take good care of your mate," Nana said, entering the room with a pale, grim-faced Risa. I wouldn't have cleared her to fight this minute, but with some food and her Were healing, Risa would be fine by the time we made it to The Burg. Nana pointed at me. "I've birthed my share of babies, including that one, who was much bigger than you'd know from how skinny she is now."

Jacq shifted closer, circling her arm behind me beneath the high table. She didn't crack a laugh, but Mynx and Fera muffled snickers. I gave both a tight-lipped smile, and they quieted.

Grey bowed his head. "Your reputation, Gwendolyn, as a healer and midwife is well known. If you will allow me to leave some of my people, then I would trust you with this. In fact, it would ease my mind."

"Agreed." Nana nodded.

I didn't protest. With Aunt Helena still injured, they'd be safer this way. I was sure Nicodemus wouldn't attack, but the extra protection was reassuring. Besides, knowing my grandmother, she'd have them hanging Sheetrock and painting the hall before the rest of us were halfway to the city.

Serena stepped closer to Miss James, who sidled away. "I have a contingent of vampires outside. I'll leave two to patrol the wards." To Miss James, she said softly, "*JJ, huh?* I think someone somewhere knows your first name." She flashed Miss James a fang-filled smile, a curious concentrating look on her face.

Miss James sighed. "*Fine*, call me JJ if you wish. You may all," she looked to us, "call me JJ. Just stay out of my head." She gave Serena a pointed look. "And don't go interrogating my friends."

The Blood-Kin's CPA Bob Rainey had contained an embezzling demonic spirit named Sarkoph. The Virginian coal mine guide Peter Traylor had contained a similar dark spirit named Titus. Our neighbor Wellsy was possessed by yet another unknown spirit. Titus had called Nicodemus his brother, which meant he was probably also a demonic spirit possessing yet another body with yet another name. Now Miss James was JJ. My eyes rolled skyward. Any more of this and I was going to need a list.

The others approached the table, but Luke hung back. He didn't look happy to see Jacq, but he held his tongue, which was more than I'd expected. "Luke?" I patted the table.

He approached hesitantly. There was no lingering anger in his eyes, only awkwardness, which was a relief. "Yeah?" he asked, voice gravelly.

"We'll get Becca back." I looked at the assembled group. "We'll get them all back." I'd asked the others to leave their Vampires and Weres outside. I was going to explain where we were headed and give a plan of action. The fewer who knew the details, the better. "This, my friend," I gestured at the maps, "is the kind of story that ends with a happily ever after." We wouldn't allow it to be any other way.

I looked down, double-checking a portable GPS before resting my finger on a small circled area that wouldn't mean anything to anyone if you weren't from the region and didn't know the tracker's signal had been doggedly moving toward that very spot.

It was JJ who expressed the doubt I could see on Luke's and the other Weres' faces. "Happy endings are for the movies, children and naïve people who think they're in love." She crossed her arms, gold sparks flying as her cuffs knocked against each other.

I grinned, undaunted. "Maybe. But in tonight's case, I can deliver at least two outta three."

Almost everyone wore a perplexed expression as they tried to determine which two they could expect. My smile widened. The night was going to be full of surprises.

It was about time I got to dump one in someone else's lap.

* * *

I was waiting in the hall when Jacq came down from settling Abigail, who had offered to sit with my sleeping aunt in her room. Abby seemed to be full of such courtesies. No wonder Grey's Weres were tripping over themselves to care for her. JJ, having lingered to speak privately with my Nana, walked through the hall, heading toward the door and the long caravan of cars waiting to leave for the battle. I let her pass without a word, never taking my eyes off the woman approaching gracefully from above.

My eyes skimmed Jacq's black trousers, low-heeled boots and black T. Her thumbs were tucked into her pockets. No weapons, no badge, she looked dressed for dinner or clubbing. But her face told a different story. That beautiful, planed face of smooth creamy skin, etched muscle, and one single braid of dark auburn hair passing beside her left eye before the rest fell around her neck...

That was a warrior's face. One that looked at me with hungry, sad eyes.

My mouth was suddenly dry. I tucked my hands into my back pockets and rocked back on my booted heels, waiting. I didn't have to wonder about the sadness. I'd raised my mental shields in preparation for the battle, knowing I couldn't risk Nicodemus or his group reading my thoughts. But raising my barriers had cost us both something. Now, I could only feel a trickle of Jacq's presence in my head. She thought I'd done it to block her. I held out my hand, clasped her warm one, and pulled Jacq to the den.

"Cate, everyone's waiting." There was a question in her voice as I pushed her down into my favorite comfy chair and crouched at her feet.

"They can spare us five minutes." I grabbed Jacq's hands and looked up, my voice soft and low. "I'm keeping secrets." Her face froze. I squeezed her hands. "But not from you." I tweaked my shields, trying to make our connection stronger without letting the others in. It helped a bit. I felt the warmth of her thoughts creep into mine, and we both relaxed. "Besides, after that shower, you've seen most of my secrets."

Jacq smiled and kissed my palm. Her lips lingered. That familiar tingle started at my hand and moved like hot liquid down my arm. I closed my eyes, savoring the sensation. Mentioning our adventure in the bathroom hadn't made me blush, but the look in her eyes as her lips touched my skin made a flush rise to my face, and I found myself once again speechless.

"It wasn't long," Jacq said softly, "but I missed having you with me."

I met her gaze and nodded, enjoying the feeling of my hand in hers. Her presence in my head was so new, but I'd missed it as well. Something had been missing before we'd met. Her presence, both physically and mentally, made me feel whole again. I'd be alone again soon, and I'd welcome knowing she was with me, at least in my thoughts.

I took a deep breath then asked, "Can you promise me something?" I wished for both our sakes that I didn't have to make this request of her.

"Anything," Jacq said.

"Be the last to the fight." Jacq began to pull her hand from mine and I grasped it tightly. "You saw the map. There are houses, apartments, all manner of people in the area where the fight will be. Serena, Grey, Fera and their people won't be worried about keeping the battle from spilling into occupied areas. I'm asking you to bring up the rear, Detective. Keep the battle from the humans. Honor your oath as an officer to protect the innocent."

"And what of you, cher," Jacq asked, worry in her eyes, "who will protect you?"

I stood, tugging her up and behind me toward the door. "It's past time I learned to protect myself." Deep inside me, something dark and hungry echoed the sentiment.

Well past time.

CHAPTER TWENTY

"Temptation: The craving to do something you know you shouldn't. Kind of like opening a gate to hell. It's a real temptation to see what sort of worms will come out of that can. But you don't. That's what makes us the good guys. That, and we generally smell better."

—Evie Delacy

"Hi-O Silverado, away." AC/DC's *Back in Black* was playing loudly over the radio, fighting the engine's roar for dominance, when I jammed the gas pedal and aimed my grandpa's old Chevy toward the charred gates that protected the Cleverly Drive-In from prying eyes. I checked my rearview mirror. No big black SUVs. *No back up.* That was the way I'd wanted it. But it was still disconcerting to realize that I was alone…at least for now.

I crashed through the gates. Wood splintered, hitting the windshield which cracked but thankfully held. I bounced up and down on old shocks, rocketing over the pitted asphalt toward the movie screen's dim outline which was, amazingly, still half-standing. I'd come here with my entire family to see *Gone With the Wind* on the big screen. Ironic really, considering the theater had recently burned, much like the movie's rendition of Civil War Atlanta.

I turned on my headlights. For a moment, nothing happened. Then one bulb flickered to life before heating into a bright torch.

In the light's glare, I saw a raptor move to intercept, but something smaller rushed out of the darkness. They hit and fell back into the shadows. It was too soon for the Weres to be here, but I didn't question my luck.

I could just make out two small herds of raptors running on either side of the truck, escorting me in. I held the wheel steady, ignoring the urge to sideswipe the lot. Not only were they big enough en masse to squash me, but I was banking on the fact that Nicodemus wanted to grab a guardian alive. Hopefully, the nesreterka and any other minions lurking in the shadows had orders not to hurt me. But orders only went so far.

The raptors veered left and right, circling a dark mass ahead. In my rearview, another group moved to block the smashed gate. *No going back.*

I looked ahead just in time to jerk the wheel right as the dark mass coalesced into an unexpectedly large wooden structure. The Chevy, made before the days of power steering, turned too slow for comfort, narrowly swerving to the structure's side. I pumped the old brakes, hearing the tires screech as I finally stopped mere feet from where the structure, a stage, had been erected at the crumbling screen's base.

The sawdust and scrap lumber visible in the headlight's glare explained why there were no scorch marks on the stage. I was right. Nicodemus had picked this location long ago, and someone had been here putting things together. No way had the owners constructed this. I smiled as I listened to the old engine tick in the night air. If someone had decided to reopen the Cleverly, they would've built something more important first. *Like a better gate to keep riff raff such as myself out.* But a stage? No, that theatric was all Nicodemus.

Still, I didn't think Nicodemus's mama-drama was the only reason they'd chosen the Cleverly. Neither was its status as a recently ruined landmark, its destruction a good source of residual magic. No, there were other benefits. The high wooden fence covered in dense overgrown kudzu offered a space where he could gate in an entire army, and no one would know until the mess spilled past the fence. Of course, this could also work in our favor. I knew the sort of people that lived in this neighborhood. They weren't the type to run, even when something as gruesome as a hungry reptilian Otherworld creature was on the prowl. Nope, if the people in this area thought they were under attack, we'd have grandmothers in curlers and house shoes, with pistols, and every Elmer Fudd wannabe in a wife-beater with a shotgun on the lawn before you could say, "The communists're comin'."

Two shadowy figures approached. I rolled the old hand-crank window down and stuck my head out, laying my left arm across the door, hiding the hand that rested on the holstered stun gun under my armpit. I forced my hand to loosen as they neared. Part of me wanted to pull the gun and fire, no questions asked. It was the same part that had wanted to ram the raptors.

Every red-blooded American loves to blow up, smash, or set fire to something. Fortunately, most get their violence-is-entertainment fix vicariously. But this urge I was feeling was well beyond normal. It was the same dark hunger I'd faced down at Lady D's. It wanted to unleash fire until the Cleverly was blazing again or, at the barest minimum, shoot, hack at, and knife any and everything between myself and my friends. The first was not an option. The second? That was yet to be determined.

I'd decided not to use my fire unless things became dire. Unleashing a big bomb of hellfire this near the city (and on the grounds of a landmark, no less) would be like sticking a pair of dirty panties under the top Prime's nose. It would elicit some scrunched noses, a few raised eyebrows, and a swift smack-down upon a Delacy head, presumably my own tender noggin. And as that was on my list of things not to do this evening, I tucked that dark demon part of me into a corner, chained the door shut, and turned my attention to where it belonged: On the two men, now nearly upon me.

"Sorry about the door, boys. Be sure and send me the bill." My joke was met by silence.

The night sounds of crickets and frogs, followed by the two's footfalls, seemed unusually loud as I waited for an attack. I counted to ten then eased my hand off the gun. Their continued silence spoke volumes. These two weren't sorcerers. Their feet were too loud and their mouths too quiet. I'd yet to meet a bad guy that didn't take the opportunity to gloat, and having a guardian deliver herself to your doorstep seemed reason enough for boasting. They stepped into the cab's light, confirming my suspicions.

Dilated pupils. Pale skin. But no telltale smell of decay. They were alive…but just barely. Their young faces were empty, but the bluish lips and cold sweat on their foreheads said plenty. Here were two of the vessels. I corrected myself. Here were two of the missing boys. If

I thought of them as real people—real, indisposable people—maybe we'd get them out alive. But it needed to be soon. I recognized the signs. Their hearts were giving out. The human body wasn't made to hold the sort of power they were carrying around.

And it was a lot of power. I felt it *buzz* against my skin in a way similar to a guardian's magic or the gate's *lira*…but not quite. The magic had been twisted somehow, which might explain why they were hiding it in people. If it was anything like my own powers, which were tied to my life and blood, the magic would go when my life did. It didn't make sense. This sort of power wasn't necessary to open and hold a gate. I had the sudden, unwelcome feeling that I was missing something.

"The Master says you come with us," the smaller of the two said stiffly.

A quick scan of the area didn't show anyone else, not even a stray raptor. But with the limited light, a beastie hoard could be waiting a few yards away in the darkest corners and I wouldn't know until they jumped out, waved their leathery tails hello, and did an Otherworld rendition of Barney's "I Love You" song. I shuddered at the thought.

"Well, I guess the Master would be right. Ain't that always the case?" Again, silence. Apparently sarcasm was as lost to these two as humor.

I sighed, opening the heavy truck door. The hinges I'd been meaning to oil protested. I turned, sliding off the old vinyl seats. Nicodemus had picked well who to send after me. I wouldn't hurt these guys. They looked strong, but it wouldn't take much to overload their hearts, leading to a quick death. I really hoped the cameras Mynx had rigged to the cab's hood hadn't suffered the same fate as my windshield. With any luck, our team was nearby, using the cameras to search for the rest of our missing people.

"Lay on, Macduff." I swept my arm toward the stage, arching a brow as they moved to either side of me but didn't remove my weapons. Not that I was complaining. As my grandpa would have said, "Looking a gift horse in the mouth is a damn fine way to git bit."

They led me to where a set of stairs, hidden just outside the light's reach, led up to the wide stage. The boys stopped at the stairs, waiting. *So much for my gallant escorts.*

Shrugging, I adjusted my guns and stepped onto the first stair, listening. Under the sound of cicadas and other natural life, wood creaked and groaned as heavy bodies moved across the stage's decking. Now would've been a good time to develop a sense of self-preservation.

Too bad my timing had always sucked.

I took one deep breath and headed up, keeping an eye on the two boys below. There was no rail so I stayed close to the wall which held the old white screen's remains. The stage was only chin-high, but falling off would leave me helpless for a few critical seconds. Reaching the top, I took two steps then stopped, leaving the headlight's brightness, allowing my eyes to adjust.

"Lights!" shouted a deep voice I recognized from last Sunday's run as Nicodemus's. The theater's bright security lighting flashed on.

Nearly blinded, I blinked, using a hand to shield my eyes. Two men sat on a dais at the opposite end. Recognizing Wellsy, I turned my gaze to the second man. Domini Roskov, the third "survivor" of the Virginia coal mine cave-in. Or rather, I should say, Nicodemus. I didn't need to see his face to know Nicky-boy inhabited Roskov, but seeing erased my last shred of uncertainty. I'd been expecting the Russian vampire once known as Wall Street's miracle man. First Peter, then Wellsy, now Roskov. It was enough to make a girl wonder what had really happened to the illusionist reported missing, now presumed dead, in that same cave-in.

But that was a quandary for another night when I didn't have two evil-possessed sorcerers decked out in tuxedos and top hats before me. I quickly took in the scene. A silvery looking cage held an unconscious, half-Wered-out Becca. Her clothes and fur were covered with large ugly burns. I sniffed discreetly, not detecting any silver. Maybe the cage was just another ugly prop. Brit's neck and face were bruised, her shirt and jeans ripped in an almost scandalous manner. A collar and chain bound her to the floor at Roskov's feet. Her eyes were bright with defiance, but thankfully she remained silent.

Isabella was there, dressed in a frilly white nightgown that stopped three inches above her knees. Combined with the heels and makeup, it would never be considered old-fashioned. I wasn't sure if she was supposed to look like a Havana cigarette girl or fulfill the virgin sacrifice section of Nicodemus's little drama. The gown went well with the silver cuffs that matched Becca's cage, which Isabella was attached to, and if that wasn't enough, several raptors stood guard around them. Sitting with knees tucked under her, Isabella had pushed her free arm through the bars, touching the motionless Becca.

Inside, my dark side was screaming through the walls of its own cage. And for once I was in complete agreement, but I forced my eyes away, fearing I'd do something stupid—like start a war with only my army of one. I flexed my fingers, forcing open the hands I'd unconsciously fisted.

In true Southern tradition, they'd converted what might've once been La-Z Boy recliners into three thrones. But I was willing to bet the red jewels glittering in the lights weren't rhinestones and the gold wasn't glitter paint. It was stunts like this that gave the South a bad name. At least I could argue that these two and their Graceland-reject décor were transplants, assuming Wellsy's and Roskov's bodies didn't house the ghosts of hillbillies past.

The thrones were garish, tacky, probably expensive, and comfortable—judging from the way Nicodemus was seated in the largest middle chair with chin in hand and one leg thrown over an overstuffed gilded leather arm. I wondered if this was magic wrought...or bought by the Kin's stolen funds. I shook my head. It didn't really matter. Either way, those things were ugly. They could be stuffed with hundred dollar bills, and they'd still be ugly. An expensive ugly, mind you, but ugly nonetheless.

Hiding my concern, I addressed the sorcerers. "I didn't realize the circus was in town." My voice echoed across the expanse of empty parking spaces now visible under the bright lighting. "I've been thinking about a career change." I gestured to the stage. "If you'd told me you were here, I might've joined up."

The lounging Nicodemus stood. His eager, happy expression creeped me out more than the herd of raptors and tuxedo-clad vampires surrounding the stage. With so many here, I couldn't help but wonder who was guarding the dark section behind and at the far corners of the screen.

"No, Miss Delacy. We are no circus but merely humble players upon this stage." At my arched brow, Nicodemus tsked before continuing cajolingly, "Don't judge us so harshly, dear Cate. Oh, yes I know your name. As I'm sure you know mine, so we'll skip the intros."

Wellsy cleared his throat, interrupting from his position in the throne to the far right. "Actually, brother, I believe she doesn't know mine."

Nicodemus clamped his hand on the other man's (corpse's?) shoulder. "You're right, brother. And when it comes to recording history, it's important to get everything just so." He turned to me. "Yes, well, Miss Delacy, as you probably know, I am Nicodemus, and this is my brother, Artus. We are of the House of S'luoth. We'll go over the spelling later."

What in the seven levels of Hell was *this*? I didn't bother to hide my confusion. I'd expected to arrive and have them try to blast me, skewer me, or, at the least, try to slather my blood all over the gate to enhance their ceremony—not be turned into some sort of glorified note-taker.

Before I could comment, Nicodemus continued, "Your presence is such a pleasant surprise." He rubbed his hands together. "And here I had given up on having a guardian to witness this momentous occasion." He waved his arm wide. "But you are here, making the setting perfect. And now we simply wait for the ringmaster, as you might say, to truly begin the ceremonies." Nicodemus gave me a leer that made me want to immediately go home and take another shower. "But believe me, when it's all over, we'll find a position for your many talents."

I made a sound somewhere between a snort and laugh. Good Goddess, they were just a bunch of old letches in new bodies. Or considering that Roskov was over eight hundred years old, that might be young letches in old bodies. If they hadn't been full of an unholy power that buzzed against my senses, making my skin want to crawl off my bones, it might have been funny.

And I suppose, most would have been flattered. My definition of beauty had recently changed, but according to the articles I'd read, many had found Roskov's blond, fit, fortyish-looking body handsome. Nicodemus's white tuxedo shirt was unbuttoned halfway, no doubt as a concession to his vanity, revealing smooth hairless skin and a sculpted chest. Compared to Artus's tall, graying figure, Nicodemus looked like he could pose for the Kin's mag, *VQ*. But though the body looked the same, there was nothing left of Roskov there. One look in the empty black eyes confirmed this.

Nicodemus's voice was the same, but nowhere was the gnarled face I'd first seen in Gulfport. Oddly enough, he looked exactly like his photo. Wellsy, or rather Artus, too, looked as he had the night of the mine collapse. They did smell a little decayed but not to Titus's degree. Only Brittan, Isabella and Becca looked as expected. That is, if one expected a cross between the *Ringling Brothers* and the sci-fi flick *Alien*.

More silent figures stood behind the thrones, half-hidden in shadows. They lacked the vampires' bulk and menace, making them easy to distinguish as the missing college students. Nicodemus looked impatient while Artus looked bored. This was getting stranger and stranger.

My mother had always told me, "When in doubt, tell the truth. If nothing else, it'll confuse the hell out of people." It seemed like a good plan and I knew it worked. I was certainly confused by the shit Nicodemus was shoveling my way. Maybe I could share the wealth.

"That was a nice speech," I said.

Nicodemus smiled wide, flashing his fangs. Finally, something that fit my expectations. His broken, jagged teeth were red-brown, like dried blood. He took a step toward me. Artus shifted uncomfortably in his seat.

I raised a hand. "But it wasn't the best I've heard, and believe me," I rolled my eyes, "I've heard quite a few." Artus smiled at the perceived insult to his brother. Hmm, not everyone was happy with the pecking order.

I filed that information away to use later, rushing to explain in my sweetest I'm-just-a-naïve-Southern-belle-educate-me voice, "So, what is it that makes you two different from all the others set on world domination? I don't need your full résumé." I gestured widely. "A few key points will do." I tucked a stray hair behind my ear and smiled my best Miss America smile, all the while scanning the darkness out of the corner of my eye for my overdue rescuers.

It would be my luck that they were lost. Hopefully, they knew better than to follow one of those electronic navigators. Those things didn't work in the backwoods…unless your goal was to get plugged with buckshot for driving into the wrong driveway at the wrong time of night. If that was the case, then they worked just fine.

Nicodemus nodded, saying with a smile he probably thought was charming, "All will be revealed in good time."

What? I stood there shocked. I finally wanted the bad guys to make a speech, and they'd decided to shut up. Oh, what I wouldn't give for an evil villain that would cooperate.

"Would you care to join us?" Nicodemus patted the empty throne's arm. "It's my understanding that our brother, Titus, will be absent this evening, providing a free seat."

Wow, Titus had said these two were his brothers, but they didn't seem to care that he wouldn't be coming back. Or maybe they didn't realize that I'd literally fed him to the fishes and he wouldn't be rising again to return the favor.

An image flashed through my mind: my blood and utter desolation. I knew on a soul-deep level that it was imperative that they not get me and the power in my blood—not just the guardian power, but also the demon. I'd come here so confident that my big mouth and my status as a guardian would keep me out of trouble until everyone was in position. I'd been wrong.

I could almost hear the I told you so's now.

Okay, plan B: stall and act stupid. The latter suddenly didn't seem too far of a stretch. I made a show of relaxing, easing my feet apart, resting on my heels. But I made no move forward. "Well, far be it from me to be a bad guest, but I do have a few questions before we powwow." I rested my hands on my belted hips, the same belt holding a nice array of spells and amulets. I started to palm a few then decided to keep my hands free. "You see, I'm a curious, cautious sort. It's an odd mixture, I know."

Artus nodded. He didn't know me personally, but he could access Wellsy's memories.

"And I'm a bit concerned that I could be so wrong. You don't look like I expected, which makes you a stranger in my book. And you know what they say about little girls and strangers."

Just then, a raptor strayed away from Becca's cage. "Nice doggie." Eyes widening, I let a little fear leak into my voice, stepping left as it veered too close. I gave the beast a little wave, quickly tucking my hands around my belt as it eyed my wiggling fingers like a hungry toddler eying chicken nuggets. The fear in my voice was real. I was rather fond of my fingers...all ten of them...and I wanted to keep them attached. I gritted my teeth, nails biting into the belt's leather, again suppressing the wave of fire that wanted to surface. If the others didn't arrive soon, I might just start blasting and damn the consequences.

Expecting a reply, I jumped when Artus crossed an ankle over his knee then casually flicked his wrist, throwing a ball of black-magic that blasted the raptor off the stage. It screamed in pain, and I flinched but didn't move, eyes riveted to Artus's face, waiting for a second blast. He'd killed that creature without a glance, without thought, the action almost second nature. *This was one to watch, possibly more so than his brother.* At least Nicodemus showed emotion, no matter how insane, and emotion predicted action.

Artus's cold haughty expression remained unchanged as he said, "I believe this is a question we can answer. These bodies' powers were great before we took them. Combined with our power, they are enough to show these forms as they once were."

"But perhaps you would prefer this," Nicodemus said, gesturing to himself and Artus. They melted away, revealing two men even more horrendous than Titus. At the sudden, overwhelming smell of rotting meat, I gagged. Both men laughed, the sound a deep cold wheezing bark. Artus was bad enough with his broken teeth and purplish skin hanging on bones that had lost most of their flesh. But Nicodemus? The virus that makes the Blood what they are had obviously fought the infusion of dark power. The ensuing battle had twisted his limbs, bloating his skin with baseball-sized whelps in some spots, reversely pitting it in others. Some of the whelps had opened, forming sores with black and green pus oozing out. Bare of skin, the pitted areas revealed pieces of rotting muscle clinging to grisly, gray-colored bones.

And unfortunately, the tuxedos were no illusion. The corpses looked even worse next to the pristine shirts and black jackets. *To hell with vanity, that man needed to button up his shirt.*

As if reading my thoughts, a congenial Nicodemus said, "Brother, I do believe the lady remains...*unimpressed.*" He cocked his head, raising his arm. "We must remedy that. It is truly unsociable to have a guest be uncomfortable."

If those had been my words, they would've been dripping with sarcasm, but Nicodemus sounded sincere. I wasn't sure if I should laugh or drop my mouth open in disbelief. Deciding discretion might be the better part of sanity, I kept my mouth shut.

A boy silently stepped from the darkness behind the thrones to Nicodemus's side. Nicodemus caressed the boy's cheek before pulling his head back by the hair. Nicodemus's fangs almost lovingly slipped into the pale, arching neck. He raised his lips, crimson with blood, and smiled, flashing broken molars. I clamped my lips shut. He gestured again, and their appearances returned to their earlier state. The horrible smell of death decreased drastically. I took a relieved breath.

This time, I felt the circle of dark magic. The missing boys did more than hold power. Nicodemus had linked them all together somehow, and the magic didn't stop at Nicodemus and his brother. I swiveled my head in horror, looking back at Brit.

Somehow, I'd missed seeing the plastic line running into her arm. Dark red blood flowed from another boy behind her, through the line, and into Brit's veins. Her jaw was swollen, her left eye already sporting a nice shiner, explaining why she hadn't tried to pull the line out. Nicodemus or one of his people would simply knock her unconscious and put it in again.

Fortunately, the ceremony hadn't begun, and Brit wasn't holding much power. They'd have to kill Isabella for that, and we wouldn't let things go that far. But little nips of black-magic flowed back and forth with the blood, explaining the occasional flash of pain on Brit's face. She didn't have to hold much to feel the effects.

"Have you figured it out yet, little gate-keeper?"

I looked to Artus. He and Nicodemus smiled at me with those broken teeth. Either their magic didn't hide everything, or they wanted me to see that small detail. I tried to understand but couldn't. They'd turned the missing students into a large, magic superconductor. They'd grabbed Brit for the same purpose and were now about to open the gate. What they'd done to the boys…it was overkill. And if they were about to open a gate, they no longer needed Brit to hold power that could be funneled directly into the darkmirror during the ceremony. With their collected capabilities and stolen bodies, the sorcerers could've opened the gate themselves or with only one or two vessels. They'd laid out a nice jigsaw puzzle for me then put half the pieces through a shredder.

"Wh—" A loud boom cut me off. A massive roaring rumble punctuated by the sharp staccato of more explosions sounded from somewhere far behind the movie screen. The ground shook with each boom, and the stage started to sway. Everyone, including myself and the sorcerers, stumbled as the wooden structure dipped precariously.

I grabbed onto a piece of wood jutting from the screen, uncaring as splinters ripped into my hands, looking in time to see a fleeing raptor knock Brit off her feet. Her shout was drowned out as more raptors rushed from the stage. The wooden planks were barely tilted, but with every shaking thud of the raptors' heavy feet, they bounced, which slid Brit farther and farther down the smooth boards. Her trip was halted by the collar and chain. A fall from the stage wouldn't have been as harmful as the position she was now in. With each jar, her body shifted downward, turning the collar into a noose.

Using the crumbling screen, I tried to make my way to Brit. White-knuckled, she had a death grip on the chain and was using her arms to hold the weight off her neck. But she could only keep that up for so long. Becca's heavy cage appeared unaffected. Isabella gripped the bars with both hands. Most of their tenacious raptor guard had dug their claws in and managed to stay put. Despite the commotion, Becca had yet to awaken, and I was getting concerned.

I made it halfway across before another section of Becca and Isabella's raptor guard left to take up defensive positions on the ground around the stage. I clenched my jaw as their exit forced Brit's body roughly against her constraints time and again. Finally, they were past and the stage stopped swaying. I breathed a sigh of relief as Brittan pulled herself up the planks until there was once again slack in the chain. I halted, uncertain, waiting.

Nicodemus's vampires took to the air, their tuxedo-tails flapping behind them like a swarm of black crows. The security lights flickered then popped, one after another, ever getting closer to Nicodemus's end of the stage. The last thing I saw was Nicodemus and Artus staring at me with those empty black eyes, their smiles growing, sharp teeth seeming to elongate. I knew that look. Growing up, I'd often seen a similar, less twisted one on my Nana's face whenever I'd broken something my allowance wouldn't cover, and payment would be taken out of my hide.

Just then, the last light popped, and I was once again blinking into the dark. *At least I wouldn't have to see my death coming*. Yep, you could say that I was a cup-half-full kinda girl…except my cups always seemed to be half-full of shit…when they weren't completely overflowing, that is. I dropped to my knees, bracing for the blast that I knew was coming. The last thing I did was open my mind, reaching for Jacq. I owed her an apology. I'd promised her one night, and it looked like we wouldn't even get that.

The expected blast never came. Maybe my fairy godmother was looking out for me, because the moon peeked out from behind the clouds. Full and bright, it provided enough light to see Nicodemus and his brother holding council, obviously distracted by whatever was happening behind us, earning me a temporary reprieve. And I had a good idea of what that distraction might be.

I'd connected to Jacq's mind long enough to know she was in the middle of her own fight. Between pushing their way through the raptors, avoiding the gas-fueled inferno that was drawing the humans' attention, and protecting themselves from a group of dive-bombing vampires, the Weres and Immortals had their hands full—even with the last-minute assistance of three of Fera's most trusted Council operatives. I'd pulled back before Jacq became aware of my presence. Her mind was already divided between the battle and worrying about me. She didn't need reason to add to the latter.

Though we couldn't see it directly, the blazing fire reflected off the few remaining clouds, making the sky a strange dark purple. While the sorcerers were otherwise engaged, I allowed my magic to do a brief tentative search. *Funny, I specifically told Rom not to blow anything up.* But there it was, a fire raging out of control in the empty area a few lots back.

We all heard the high-pitched shriek of dying animals at the same time. For a moment, I worried that it was the Weres. Then Artus flinched as his hold over the raptors fed him their pain. Nicodemus jerked Brittan up from where she'd propped herself against a heavy throne. The IV pulled from her arm, splashing bright blood across the wooden planking. Nicodemus disregarded her collar, breaking the chain with one strong yank. He pulled Brit forward roughly, and she whimpered, biting her lip to stifle a cry of pain. Nicodemus took a step then stopped.

He held Brittan in front of him. "Cate, be a dear and get the door." His tone was demanding. Gone was the cajoling charm. He gestured to the movie screen. The explosions had undone the tacking covering it, revealing the smooth black stone that comprised the massive screen.

Only a select few knew that a darkmirror was built into the brick that held up the screen. According to my Nana, it was once a private joke amongst the guardians. So much of the area was extremely religious, thinking movies and TV would steal or corrupt your soul, and so the guardians put a gate to hell right where one was expected to be…just not *how* it was expected to be. The GPS had clued me into Nicodemus's general location. The presence of the gate had given me the specifics. They might not need a gate to do this, but they'd wanted one.

I'd suspected as much when I'd seen how carefully they'd tried to cover their tracks, blocking any attempts to search for Isabella. Why go to so much trouble when they could create a focal point anywhere? Obviously, they didn't want to waste power creating a portal without a gate. But what was the power for, if not that?

Nicodemus continued, "One way or another, the gate will be opened. Then our lord will come through and with him his army. And they'll keep coming until we've overrun this world. Then we'll take the other worlds...one...by..."

I stopped listening to the cliché diatribe. Movement flickered in the darkness behind the stage. I couldn't determine if it was Nicodemus's people or my own, but his next words brought my attention back to him fully. "And you shall mark this history as being brought about by your own kind."

I held my hands out. "Just hold up there a minute, mister. No offense, but I don't need the credit for this." *There it was again.* With Brit in his hands, I didn't dare look past Nicodemus. But this time, I was certain. There had been a flash of gold, and a vampire had fallen from the sky.

Artus had his eyes closed, still trying to mentally coordinate the raptors. More and more nesreterka left to join a fight I still couldn't see, but the sounds of the approaching battle—the growls, the clash of steel, the buzz of spent magic—could already faintly be heard. Oh yeah, my friends had definitely put a bee in these guys' bonnet and were currently in the process of shoving said bonnet up their asses. My internal smile quickly turned to a frown. Of course that didn't mean Brit and I couldn't get killed before the slowpokes got here.

Nicodemus barked out, "Not you, witch whelp." He shook Brittan roughly.

I grimaced as blood began to stain her torn sleeves.

"And not this one." He caressed the shivering Brit's neck with one long, sharp nail, not quite breaking the surface. "Mortals are so fragile...so weak...not worthy of the power we give them." He turned back to me. "Fragile and young...and likely not to live long enough to change that." Nicodemus's look was pointed. Artus gave an evil chuckle, opening one eye briefly, rolling it in my direction. "This was begun by a *half-blood*..." Nicodemus snarled the last word, spat, then continued more loudly, "long before your time. But it will be finished, tonight by *us*, the full-blooded children of Crius."

What a surprise, another –us name. Must've been popular in the Stone Ages.

I moved subtly closer, waiting for my chance and heard Artus murmur angrily as he exited his stupor and turned to his brother. "No doubt the master will want her, his child by that bitch, by his side. A pity."

Who—or what—was the half-blood? And where did the guardians come into this? My mind was running in circles faster than ever, but I'd have to worry about it later. Right now we had bigger fish to fry… like the two who'd finished their conversation and were looking at me like I was the bait on one really large hook.

Nicodemus pulled Brit close, lowering his fangs until they barely grazed her neck before snapping, "Now, Cate, be a good little girl and open the gate." His tongue slowly traced his nail's red mark before smiling back at me with all those broken teeth. "Or your friend will suffer a fate worse than you can possibly imagine." He licked his lips. Neither man hid his excitement. *So much for the plumbing being out of whack.*

Masking my disgust, I stared into Nicodemus's empty eyes. I could feel the others drawing closer. But not close enough. The stress of the moment almost made me laugh and say, "Oh, I don't know. I have a pretty good imagination." But I bit my tongue, forcing the words down. Swallowing my sarcasm left a bitter taste in my mouth, but not as bitter as what I was about to do. If I opened the gate, we were all dead. If I said no, Brit was dead. And I couldn't *not* answer. I silently apologized to Brit for the dangerous game I was about to play.

"Again with the demands. I thought I was here for posterity. Now you spring this? How typical."

Nicodemus and Artus wore identical confused expressions. I'd seen my Nana's steamroller approach a million times. It couldn't be that hard. I picked up speed, getting louder and waving my hands as I continued. "You can't just invite a girl to a party and expect her to walk out the door thirty seconds later. We need time to beautify…to accessorize. This outfit will not do for meeting a demon lord. Why, I didn't even bring your medallion, the one that Sarkoph dropped, which I'm sure you'll need."

At the word "medallion," their faces turned dark.

Artus growled, "That damn spirit was holding out on us."

I tucked Artus's barely discernable words away to mull over later and continued on, not wanting the new nearly fanatical anger shining in their eyes directed at Brit. "And surely men as powerful as yourselves don't need a *little girl* like me for something as simple as this." I smiled sweetly and pretended to wipe something off my shirt, but really I was turning off my guns' safety. I could tell from the dark magic swirling in the air and being drawn into the two sorcerers' bodies that they were out of patience. That was fine with me. I'd given up on playing dumb anyway. It was time to settle for absolute insanity. "Besides," I said, tone suddenly serious, eyes steely, "I don't work for free."

Artus released another wheezing barking laugh. Nicodemus fumed and took a large step forward, jerking Brit along. Pain flashed across her face as Nicodemus's nails sank deeper. Eyes wide, unblinking, holding in sympathetic tears, I flippantly said, "Hey, a girl has to eat." I snapped my fingers. "Cash up front." I held my hand out in the universal "gimme" gesture.

"We don't have time for this," Nicodemus said coldly, looking at my hand. "I could make you." He smiled, his voice soft and slow, then shook his head. "But I won't…since I don't have time to do it *properly*." His lust-filled look made me shudder. "For your disobedience, you'll become my master's new pet. He has a real taste for guardians." Artus snickered. "And when he's done, we'll all have a *nip*." Nicodemus playfully snapped his teeth before shoving Brit into Artus's arms.

I felt the gate's call as Nicodemus pulled more power from the boys. The three from earlier were still behind and between the thrones. Nicodemus turned to his brother. "Finish the ceremony." He gestured to Brit. "Make sure this one survives."

Well, that was pointless. The power they wanted to force into Brittan would eventually be her death. Or was there a way around that? I didn't think so. But if that was their goal, then there was more going on here than your typical kill-the-girl-open-the-gate-demon-hoarde-invasion-world-domination scenario.

Artus dragged Brittan to Becca's cage, shoved her roughly against the silver bars, and bound her and Isabella side by side with magic. I took a quick step forward, pulling up short when the last group of raptors moved into my path. "Ah, ah, ah." Nicodemus wagged his index finger. "Not just yet, Cate. We have big plans for the pretty blond one. You wouldn't want to spoil our surprise."

"Oh, but I would. I really would." Out of options, I took another step and pulled magic into my hands, readying to force a steady stream toward Artus who had begun to chant. "I'm not a fan of surprises. I shot the last person who jumped out of a cake at me." I took a step to the side. The raptors mimicked me, all shuffling sideways. I sighed in frustration. Though gratifying, shooting through the damn things would be ineffective. I'd been practicing the maneuver I'd used on the hellhound that had attacked Jacq. I was confident that I could duplicate it without a sword's conduit…but only once or twice.

No longer caring about appearances, I pulled in more magic, drawing what I could from the blaze still burning far away. It wasn't much, but it might be enough, assuming I got a clear shot.

Artus raised a ceremonial dagger high above Isabella's heart. His chant continued, growing louder. Both bound women thrashed against the cage, crying, but it did no good. Black-magic fairly crackled in the air. My hands began to burn as I concentrated my fire between my palms. Nicodemus joined in the chant. Like a many-armed Indian god, black tendrils of magic sprouted from the possessed vampire's sides, whipping from his body and into the gate. I could almost distinguish similar, smaller black chains linking the boys to Nicodemus and Brit.

Artus's arm tensed. I readied to rush forward, straight into the raptors. Dodging was impossible, but the unexpected headlong approach might buy me enough time for one shot. I'd die, but I'd take Artus with me, saving Isabella and Brit long enough for the others to arrive.

Just as my legs tensed to lunge forward, white flashed in the corner of my eye. It rushed from the shadows, taking my earlier path straight toward the stage.

It seems that while we were all focusing on the battle taking place behind the sorcerers, no one was watching the front door (or rather the wooden gate that I'd smashed to the ground). The white flash coalesced into a wolf, its coat bloody from a series of deep bites and scratches. In one fresh burst of speed, it leapt, hurdling over the few raptors left at the stage's base. The boards under my feet shook as it landed, skidding to a halt mere feet behind me. I heard its snarled growl and felt its overwhelming heat as it moved to my right side.

Easily four times my size, this wolf had enough power to someday be an Alpha. It snarled again, saliva dripping from its jaws as they snapped shut. It stared at Artus with hatred in its eyes, and I was suddenly *very* glad that the Weres were on our side.

Distracted, Nicodemus turned to the wolf. Artus stayed his hand, glancing back at his brother. I didn't know who this wolf was, but he'd just saved our bacon. If we were alive when this was over, I might kiss him…right before I chewed him out. Mynx had assured me that Grey's people would leave the sorcerers to those of us who could defend against them. The white wolf didn't even have the protection of wards like the ones hidden under my clothes, drawn by my grandmother's hand directly on my skin. I let the fire leave my hands. If I started slinging magic, Nicodemus would too. And I could see it in his eyes: The wolf would be the first to die.

From behind Nicodemus, I saw two white tigers rush forward. I pulled my stun guns.

Nicodemus laughed. "Those puny human weapons cannot hurt me." The wolf took a step forward, growling again. "And you?" He turned to the wolf with derision in his voice. "You're not even worth wasting my magic on. Kill him." He waved at the raptors.

Though the raptors were under their masters' control, they approached the wolf with hesitation. One predator recognizes another, and this wolf was definitely one hell of a predator. I smiled grimly. *But sometimes the big bad also came in small packages.*

As the raptors stepped sideways, more power flowed into the gate. A little more, and it would open. With five sources, the power was flowing quickly, and there was still enough left in the boys to hold the gate open for days. I sighed internally, sighting down the barrels. At least the raptors were no longer in my line of sight. But why must everyone be in such a hurry? Didn't they know this was the Land of Cotton? Life moved here at a snail's pace, and death lingered for Sunday dinner. I'd had enough of people rushing to the end. If they were in such a goddamn hurry to get there, they'd get there my way.

With a voice full of resignation, I said, "I'm sorry. You didn't leave me any choice." And I *was* sorry. I really didn't want to do this. Nicodemus only laughed and formed a ball of black-magic. I wasn't sure who it was for and couldn't afford to wait and find out. I checked my aim once more. Without warning, the wolf jumped forward, hurling into the raptors, and I fired both guns. Then I moved to the side nearest the screen in a half-run, half-crouch to reload as the silent tigers bowled into the raptors guarding the ground at Nicodemus's back.

A tiger cleared the fracas, launching itself onto the wooden platform. With another quick bound, it landed atop Becca's cage. The metal bars bent outward with a groan but held. Dagger in hand, Artus looked up. The tiger leaned down and roared, its muzzle only inches from Artus's nose. Artus released Brit's throat, and she slumped to the ground. The dark power in the air moved as Artus drew on it. Before I could shout a warning, the tiger swatted Artus with one massive paw, knocking him end over end off the stage.

Raptors scattered, tipping over the ostentatious thrones. Growls ensued as Artus landed in the midst of a Were pack that had moved around, crouching below our line of sight. Another tiger, led by a brown wolf, landed among the raptors remaining to guard Isabella and Becca. The Weres moved between the women and raptors, while other Weres swatted raptors off the stage into the waiting sword-clad hands of Fera's operatives.

Even with all this, Nicodemus was unfazed, simply laughing harder as my shots whizzed past him. I'd have thought him insane, but I knew why he was laughing. It wouldn't matter how many we set against him, because once the gate opened, demons would pour through. Then we'd be in a whole mess of trouble.

But Nicodemus's laugh died in his throat, turning into a shriek as my stunners hit the two boys standing on either side behind him. My aim was true, and the little propelled batteries landed square in their chests. I didn't need to feel the black-magic dissipating from their bodies to know that the boys' shocked hearts had stopped beating before they'd even crumpled to the ground.

Finished with my reload, I fired once into the confusion. Nicodemus shrieked again, blocking my path seconds too late. My third shot hit the boy who'd given blood to Brit. The power level dropped again, the black arcs of magic shooting from Nicodemus into the gate nearly disappearing. But Nicodemus wasn't finished. There were still two more boys somewhere. And I could feel—nearly see—him pulling magic from them. A rush of fighting Weres and raptors moved between me and Nicodemus. Using magic and brute force, he began to make his way through them toward me.

I looked for Jacq and saw her silver sword flash as she, Mynx and Fera fought their way to the stage. Too bad they couldn't levitate like the vampires currently swooping down upon us. Backlit against the large full moon, Nicodemus's vamps were engaged in an all-out gravity-defying sword fight with Serena's people. Gold flashed, and another corrupt vampire plummeted to the ground. The vampires dove closer, and I shouted, "Serena!" quickly sending a mental image of the downed boys. Then I was again focusing on the fight closer at hand.

"We've got them," Serena shouted over the clamor of snarls, more explosions, and cursing, "Watch yourself, witch!"

I could only hope that they'd be able to save the boys. Otherwise, I'd just taken three innocent lives. And if I didn't stop that gate from opening, many, many more would soon die.

I had one blast left. Too bad I couldn't take my eyes off the really pissed vampire-corpse heading my way and find another vessel. Not that I wanted to shoot another boy, but that was the best option for stopping the gate. I looked at Nicodemus. He'd extracted himself from the fight and was closing in. He'd yet to form a magical sword like Titus's. Maybe like the white wolf, he thought I was a waste of magic. I was leery of pulling my own blade and picking a fight I couldn't win.

And magic was no longer an option. As he approached, black wards began to run like tattoos down his chest and over his face and hands. Anything magical I sent at him would simply bounce back to me. Someone had taken the children's rhyme *I'm rubber and you're glue* to heart.

I searched my pockets for a viable weapon even as a black and white striped tiger rushed to my aid. Nicodemus blasted the Were, and it crumpled at his feet. Nicodemus picked up the unconscious tiger, lifting it high, ready to break its back on an extended knee. The tiger, bulkier than the vamped-out Nicodemus, had to weigh at least a good half-ton, but Nicodemus lifted it like it was nothing. The tiger would heal from that blow, but it would hurt like hell, assuming it didn't get killed while paralyzed.

I lifted my weapon. The charge wasn't doing me any good in my gun. Despite Nicodemus's earlier assertions, I fired, hitting him directly between the eyes. He flinched but didn't stop. Still, it got his attention.

"Yoo-hoo, remember me?" Batting my lashes, I waved my fingers. "I believe the next dance is mine, big boy."

It wasn't very creative, but it worked. Nicodemus blinked twice before contorting his mouth into another grotesque smile.

Once again congenial, he said, "Indeed, dear Cate." He tossed the tiger off the stage and took another deliberate step forward. The tiger hit the hard black tar with a bone-crunching thud, and I winced. Backing away, I threw a collection of razor-sharp discs and spelled-charms pulled from my belt. Most, Nicodemus batted away, the spells fizzing out before even touching him, but one disc sank into his lower belly.

He didn't so much as flinch. "You wound me, Cate. Now's no time to suddenly turn shy."

"Don't take it personally, but I'm rather particular." I took another step back, lifting my boot heels so they didn't catch on the uneven boards. As Nicodemus moved forward, his disguise began to flicker. Maybe Artus had lied, and they didn't rely completely upon their own power to fuel their illusions but used that housed in the boys. That would explain his trouble. With a major chunk gone from the boys I'd killed, the sorcerers didn't have the power to hide. Perhaps it was stupid of me, but I really wanted to gloat over that.

"Why try so hard, Nicky-boy, to keep Roskov's pretty face? Are you afraid Daddy won't like your real one? I can understand that. It's one even a mother couldn't love. Never had a father myself, but I understand they're pickier about those sorts of things, wanting their sons to be a chip off the old demonic block and all."

Almost in sync with my taunt, Nicodemus's illusion fell completely, and with its loss, something in him broke free. Nicodemus had been cautious in his final approach, taking his time, trying to intimidate. But with an unearthly howl, he rushed me.

I dove to the side, nearly striking the screen. But I wasn't quick enough. The smell hit me right before his rotting, pustule-covered flesh did.

I smacked the wooden planking, the two discs I'd been about to throw flying from my hands, my scabbard painfully digging into my back. I lay there, dazed, until cold hands grasped the leather harness running over and under my armpits, lifting me.

"You're more trouble than you're worth, witch." Nicodemus slammed me back down.

There was a loud crack. It took a moment for the pain in my head to register. Warm blood slid down my neck. I spit blood from a cut inside my mouth before saying, "I get that a lot. Personally, I've never considered myself a high-maintenance type of woman." All I got for my lip was a fat one as he slapped my face with enough force to make my ears pop.

"If I weren't so busy trying to hold that gate, I'd savor your death." Nicodemus pulled me toward his horrifying body.

This time, the blood pouring out of my mouth was mixed with bile. Time slowed as I watched his fangs descend toward my neck. I reached downward, fingertips scraping against the rough wood, trying to find something…anything. There was nothing. I wanted to close my eyes. It's hard to watch your own death, but I couldn't give up. I opened my mind fully, searching for Jacq, sending her a desperate mental cry. No words. Only my utter fear.

Just as his teeth pricked my skin, a streaking silver figure flashed in. *Jacq!* Unleashing a war cry, she ran at us, glowing so brightly that it was hard to look at her. She smashed into Nicodemus, and they went down in a tumble of black and silver limbs. I scooted away, realizing suddenly that I was mere feet from the gate, which was about to open and pour a horde of demons into our laps.

Stop the ritual. I heard Jacq clearly, courtesy of my downed shields. I didn't want to leave her, but she was right. If that gate opened, we were all dead. I looked for help, but the entire stage had been cleared of all but us three. The others were in the parking lot surrounded by a contingent of immortals, vampires and Weres. A nude Luke had half-shifted back and was cradling an unconscious Becca in his wolf-man arms. Serena, JJ and another vampire were trying to bring back the boys I'd shocked. Blood flowed down both vampires' arms. Gold magic flowed liberally from JJ's cuffs, the strain evident on her face.

Nearby, Mynx and Fera were fighting to hold Artus within a shimmering, blue-green energy barrier. A striped tiger alternated between nuzzling its downed sibling and Brittan, who were both on the ground. The spirited Brit looked to be out cold, her body convulsing randomly.

Isabella and the white wolf were at the center of the protected area. With my shields open, I recognized Kyle's presence. I wasn't surprised that Kyle had come for his mate, but I was surprised that he'd made it out of Luke's safe house. Knowing Luke, future wolves would not be so lucky.

The only raptors still obeying orders were farther out in the parking lot, surrounding the two other boys, the ones now powering the gate. Grey, in tiger-man form, was leading his Weres against them, but they didn't know the true importance of those two boys. Any action Grey could take would be too late to assist me.

I was on my own. I backed toward the gate. I was never one for obeying orders, so now was probably a bad time to start. Nevertheless, Nicodemus had told me to open a gate. And that's just what I'd do.

CHAPTER TWENTY-ONE

"Panda Imodium: A Chinese Bear shit-fest stopper; also what happens when you put a bunch of Southern belles in the same room with alcohol and they realize that half of them are dating, have slept with, or currently married to the same man."

—Brittan Wessan

For all my big talk, I'd never actually opened a gate. My guardian powers had never been strong enough. I backed toward the darkmirror, keeping an eye on a silver-skinned Jacq. She and Nicodemus had swords now, and the clash of black and silver magical blades was throwing off enough sparks to finish burning down the theater. My body bumped against the gate. My sore head hit the screen, and I groaned.

Then I felt it. The blood on my head had touched the stone. This was a guardian's heritage: the ability to connect with the mirror through a simple smear of blood. It was also what made us targets for sorcerers hell-bent on destruction. Sorcerers, kind of like the one currently trying to remove my sweetie's head from her shoulders. I closed my eyes, focusing on the stone's magic. Best to deal with one world-stopping, pain-in-the-ass problem at a time.

My brow creased. Something was wrong. Nicodemus's dark power should have flowed in and been consumed as it fueled the connection to whatever destination he had in mind. But something was drawing the power away, feeding on it. The dark-magic wasn't all flowing in. And what did wasn't all staying. My eyes popped open. *Brittan. Oh, my goddess bless.*

I should have seen this coming. The magic that I'd forced from the three boys by killing them wasn't natural and wouldn't easily merge with the natural world, and the two remaining boys had been chock-full, incapable of absorbing more. But there was Brittan. The only other living avenue. Tainted by the special infusion of dark-magic-laden blood, she was already primed and ready. And so, like water flowing downstream, the magic had chosen the easiest, most straightforward course.

I could feel it now, flowing into Brittan until she was full to bursting...and then some. By all rights, she should be dead. She was holding more than any of the others, and magic was still flowing in and out of her like the tide. But strangely enough, it wasn't all dark.

Through the gate's connection, I followed the magic back to Brit, careful not to touch the dark power. I could see what had happened. When Nicodemus had tapped the gate, it had tapped Brittan. The shared blood had formed a giant superconductor for Nicodemus's magic, but like all currents, the magic flowed how it chose. The power was flowing from Nicodemus into the gate, but the darkmirror was purifying a portion, pushing that clean power back into my blonde friend. The good and bad powers within her were battling it out. Brit was balanced upon the precipice of a deadly scale, and I wasn't sure how it would all fall.

My hands slapped the cold stone, letting it support my weakening knees. The deaths? The amassing of power? They'd been trying to do more than open a gate. I'd heard of this, but it was supposed to be impossible—a story told by old witches with nothing better to do. Still, maybe I should have expected it. This seemed to be a week for the impossible.

This complicated things. I'd planned to quickly open the gate, extinguishing the magic it had absorbed, then shut it down. That was no longer an option. I couldn't close the gate without killing Brit. Whatever the darkmirror was doing, it was helping her survive the black-magic saturating her body. What we needed was a new destination.

I closed my eyes, reaching out to Serena. It had been so long since I'd needed this skill. I took a breath and focused. *I need something.* I tried to push my words only to the vampire, not wanting to distract Jacq at the wrong moment.

I'm a bit busy here, Cate. Serena strained to hold the connection as she poured her unique magic into the humans I'd shot. I knew from her thoughts that the boys hadn't absorbed enough vamp blood to change, taking only enough to heal their vital organs. Two of them were alive, their hearts shocked back into beating with JJ's help, but the group was still working on the third, the one who'd given blood to Brittan. Serena thought he was lost. This wasn't the time for sadness or regret. Brushing those distracting emotions away, I sent her an image of what I needed along with encouragement and thanks. It wasn't an easy request, but soon the information was tucked away in my head. Just before I dropped our connection, she grunted, *What are you hiding, little witch?*

The better question, vampire, is why do you care? I slammed my shields back down. Serena's laugh echoed in my head but she didn't try to get in. For now we all had better things to do than play peek-a-boo in each other's minds.

I focused on the stone, opening my mind and magic fully to our connection. It was similar to rising in the mind's eye, but whereas that plane was full of life and beauty and endless shades of every color, this place was bleak. We were on the cusp of the void between worlds. Here there was only the cold, black emptiness of oblivion.

Except, my fire brought life. It was a thousand shades of shimmering red that collided with Nicodemus's inky blackness. Nearly as dark as the void, his corruption flowed like an endless ocean in the boundlessness of space, threatening to consume my fire, a lone candle set adrift in the midst of his darkness.

My direct connection to the gate provided me a small advantage. And there was the fact that Nicodemus was fighting on both the physical and magical planes. But let's not bullshit around. No amount of training could have prepared me or any other guardian for going up against this much power, especially not alone, with all my erstwhile backup occupied trying to keep the general population from being overrun by a horde of hungry raptors. So I was on my own. If I'd just been witch or guardian, we'd be lost. But I was, apparently, something more.

I reached down, releasing the locks I'd used to bind my other, darker half—the half that had grown much stronger in the past few weeks. For a moment, I thought I might understand the vampires' unquenchable thirst for blood. My dark side was hungry for it, but not to drink. No, it wanted to spill the precious life-giving fluid. It thrilled for the hunt. The conquest. But there was something it longed for even more. And I understood this need. It drove my own actions, reminding me that, even dark and blood-thirsty, this demon-half was still me. More than anything else, it wanted its freedom, and I shamelessly offered that possibility like a carrot on a stick.

You scratch my back, and I'll scratch yours. And we'll both try not to sink our claws too deep. I nearly laughed aloud—I was talking to myself. But the laughter stuck midway when I felt an answering stir from deep within.

Agreed.

Power surged, like gasoline poured on the flames of my fire. I channeled the magic, pushing it into the gate, never letting a drop spread past my body or the black stone, lest someone knowledgeable, like Fera's operatives, see. The power turned my candle into a small bonfire, then a larger one, until it spread like forest fire, bringing blazing rivers of light to the darkness. *Now we're cooking with gas.* That thought made me snort. My only excuse: the strain on my body was immense. The delirium was obviously setting in.

I focused on the portion of the gate that Nicodemus had sunk his twisted teeth into, carefully avoiding the semi-sentient tendrils reaching out of the void to Brittan. I didn't dare get too close. But while that magic, too, was dark like Nicodemus's, its blackness was natural, rippling like water reflecting the night sky. It was tempting to lean close in hopes of catching a glimpse of some strange and wonderful world that might reside just below the surface, but I resisted. A part of me knew that like the grim mermaids of old that led sailors to their deaths, there would be no return for any who ventured into those waters.

Perhaps it was a moment. Perhaps hours. Our magic fought, forming black and red eddies of pure power. Like giant waterspouts, they pounded each other. For the longest time, it was an even match. Sweat beaded on my head. My limbs weakened, but I stood my ground, never losing my connection with the gate. Dimly, I could hear the clang, hiss and pop as Nicodemus's and Jacq's blades smashed against each other. Then I heard Nicodemus cackle and felt a flash of pain.

My connection slipped, and I scrambled to regain it. He'd winged her! *Oh, he was going to pay for that.* I needed Jacq healthy and whole. The woman had asked me out on a damn date, and there was no way in hell that she was getting out of it. She'd seen me with a snotty nose and red puffy eyes and *still* wanted to date me. She was a keeper.

My sense of urgency tripled. I pushed more fire into the gate, digging for everything I had left, but it wasn't enough. The more I sent against him, the more Nicodemus's darkness spread. My spirits started to flag. Then I remembered—I wasn't alone. I closed my eyes tighter. The others would already be by my side if they could, sharing what magic they had left to give. Still, I sent the call.

More.

Even as it winged away, I realized my mistake. I was too connected to the gate, my mind too deep into the battle. Like a ship on the edge of a black hole, my mental cry floundered, skimming around the void's edge before succumbing to the inevitable and falling in.

I stood between two paths. If I pulled back close enough to the physical plane to call for help, Nicodemus would surge forward. The gate was seconds from opening. Could I hold him those few precious moments if my magic and will weren't completely in the fight? I thought not. But if I stayed here, we would remain locked in this endless stalemate until one of us tired or was killed.

Nicky-boy was drawing magic from others, fueling his fight on both fronts. Jacq and I didn't have the same resources. Her increasing exhaustion paralleled my own. Even my demon-half was quiet now. The beast, asleep in its cage, had shared all it could, or would, for the time being.

Like a general surveying the troops, my mind stood behind the forces of fire. Perhaps it was my imagination, but I almost saw little flaming men racing against those of darkness, heralded on by dragons, mouths spraying red plumes of magic. Whether they were real or only another sign of my flagging energy really wasn't relevant. Any way you cut it, this was a war. And in war, there were casualties. There was only one source of power left. Although I knew no witch that had done this, I now understood why a witch might sacrifice a piece of her soul—and ultimately her entire life—for something. Would I…could I…do the same?

I thought of everyone I loved. My Nana. Aunt Helena. Mynx. *Jacq.* Too great a liability, they would be the first to die under the demons' hands. Without making a conscious decision, I'd found my answer. I reached inside, this time, for a different lock, the one that kept my soul bound inside its earthly cordon.

Something jolted me from behind, causing my magical fingers to slip. Another force flowed into me, into my fire. The most unlikely of allies, the void's shimmering black power flowed around me, pushing with me. I didn't understand why this being, whatever it might be that resided between worlds, was helping. But that was exactly what it was doing. The black ripples of power sank into my fire, but instead of extinguishing it, they turned to molten rivers of lava. Like melted stone, they flowed, racing past my own power, circling Nicodemus's darkness.

Reminiscent of the sphere I'd used to banish Sarkoph, it spiraled inward, ever tightening Nicodemus's noose. Energized by a sudden well of hope, my magic surged forward. Together, we pushed Nicodemus out.

And the gate was mine.

I opened my eyes in time to see Nicodemus spin to stare at me. His gasped "Hell-spawn!" was lost in the chaos, but I read it clearly on his lips. Jacq's glowing sword arced toward his distracted head, and I formed a picture in my mind. *Red skies. Blue grass. Hordes of roaming raptors.* Then I opened the gate, setting the destination.

It was time for all good little demon children to go home.

A loud whistle pierced the night just as Jacq's sword removed Nicodemus's head from his shoulders. Getting distracted at the wrong moment would do that to a man. With no beating heart to pump, there was no gruesome blood spray—which, if you asked me, was a bit anticlimactic. The body fell a few feet away, the severed head rolling until it fell off the stage.

All eyes turned to me, and I lowered my fingers from my lips. No longer under their masters' control, the raptors ran amok, hungry but too weak and scared to attack. Like a passel of extras from an over-budget B movie, I could practically see them spinning in circles, muttering, "What's my motivation? What's my motivation?" Well, since you asked…

"One-way ticket to the Illtrath plane, right here." I jerked my thumb toward the rippling black surface. Like a mirror, it only reflected the chaos around us. But I knew that another world waited on the other side. I'd seen its wild primitive beauty for a millisecond while connecting both gates. At my words, Serena sent the mental command I'd given her, and a multitude of raptors spun as one, heading straight for me.

I scrambled out of the way, only realizing after I'd hustled aside that now the raptors' path separated me from Jacq. The hug I so desperately wanted would have to wait until all our beastie guests had cleared out.

Or not.

With a flash of silver and a lightning quick jump between two raptors, Jacq stood before me. I panicked. What if this thing between us had only been some adrenaline-induced coma that we'd awaken from now that everything was over?

Then Jacq's warm body was against mine, pressing me into the brick, shielding me from the raptors that passed us by, oblivious to anything but their doorway home. Her hand went around my neck, cushioning my head. Familiar magic *zinged*, easing the aching throb and bubbling nausea which were surfacing now that the endorphins were gone.

I opened my mouth, but Jacq placed her forehead against my own. Her words, whispered inches from my lips, silenced me. "I'm not going to tell you the things you want to hear."

I shut my mouth. My aunt would've chided that the way my eyebrows were drawn together would give me wrinkles, but that was the least of my concerns. I wasn't sure if I should object and say I didn't need words...or ask, why not? So I said nothing. "I'm not going to say the words," Jacq continued, "because, eventually, you would doubt them, and I can't bear the thought of that."

My closed eyes misted, but I opened them to gaze into the stormy depths of eyes that looked into me with such determination. Despite the moisture left to freely flow down my cheeks, I couldn't look away. I would have nodded to acknowledge the truth of what Jacq said, but she still held my head, sending healing power into my system. Her grip was gentle, but I couldn't bring myself to pull away...to lose that connection.

"I've said before that I don't understand this," I rasped, "and that scares me. But I meant what I said, I'm not running. It's just..." I closed my eyes, desperate to express what I felt. It seemed too soon to speak of love. And perhaps it was a sign of irrational jealousy, but Jacq was hundreds of years older than me. I couldn't help thinking that in all those centuries at least one other woman had whispered in her ear, "I love you." I wanted what was growing between us unclouded by memories of past loves lost, and maybe a tiny part of me wanted to keep something of myself safe. I couldn't help thinking that someday she'd walk away…whether she wanted to or not.

I tried again. "I never really thought I'd find someone who looks at me like you do. At least, not in this lifetime." I opened my eyes. Jacq's glow had dimmed, but the look in those two orbs had not. "Part of me fears that I'll get used to that." I sucked in a lungful of air before taking the plunge. "And part of me hopes for it with every breath." I flooded our mental connection with the truest essence of what I felt for her.

Jacq gasped, her body thrumming with heat as my emotions hit her. Sure, there was lust and the unrelenting attraction we had for each other. But more, there was my amazement at how gentle she was, my joy at seeing the little considerate things she had done, my respect for the times (even before we'd met) that she'd consistently acted to protect others, going so far as leaving a powerful post with the Council to work with human law enforcement. And above it all was my love, shining bright. Which was how she made me feel: radiant, as if someone saw me, even the secrets I'd yet to share. I felt both cherished and desired simply for being me, for being Cate.

That was the most exhilarating, most frightening thing I'd ever felt.

"Cate." This time it was Jacq's turn to close her eyes.

"Yes, Detective Slone?" I put my arms around her, doing a fair imitation of her single eyebrow arch. Her eyes opened, lips twitching into that familiar, heart-stopping half-grin. I couldn't help but echo her smile.

But Jacq's voice was all seriousness as she said, "I may have misled you."

My heart dropped, my arms sliding away. Her hands stopped my retreat.

"I want much more than the one date you promised me."

Jacq yelped as I elbowed her in the ribs, but I was smiling as I limped down the stairs. She followed close behind. I might've bruised a hip when Nicodemus had sacked me, but my heart was whole and overflowing. Still, as I stepped into the stage's shadows, that didn't stop me from ribbing her one last time. "We'll have to see about that."

As we moved off the stage, I glimpsed, between the moving raptors, a vampire, silhouetted in the moon's glow, lay a tarp over the third boy. My good humor quickly faded. Jacq gave me an inquiring look. I shook my head. There was blood on my hands. Maybe not literally, though if I dared to look closely enough, there was probably plenty of that, too. It's not as if I hadn't killed before, but never had the blood been so innocent, the brief life so undeserving of an end.

I had killed a boy…a man really. Some might argue that he was dead either way, but I didn't see it like that. I'd made the decision to sacrifice one, possibly three, to save millions. I'd crossed a line and would have to live with the consequences. Most of me wanted to be with Jacq. To burrow into her heat and forget what I'd done. But there was a small part that wanted to be alone, to digest this. The raptors pouring through the parking lot's middle made the decision easy.

My limp slowed me. Jacq offered to carry me through the raptors to our friends, but I waved her away. Jacq wanted me by her side to speed my healing with magic she didn't have to spare. I pointed out that the others needed her, and I could stay on this side and do what I did best: Issue orders.

Jacq turned to go. I grabbed her shirt and pulled her back, saying sternly, "Before you do anything, see Fera's healers about that slash on your thigh." It looked shallow but inside I still burned with fury that Nicodemus had wounded her. It hurt that I couldn't be her healer, but until I closed the gate such magic was beyond me.

"As my lady commands." Eyes flashing silver with desire, Jacq laughed but quickly turned serious. "And what of your injuries, cher?"

There was another warm *zing* as she sent more magic to my aching head. "I'll join you once I close the gate. Until then it must be my main focus." I didn't need to say how disastrous it could be if I let the connection slip. I smoothed her shirt before reluctantly letting it go.

Concern in her eyes, Jacq caressed my cheek. "I'll come for you the moment the gate is closed." She zipped away.

Worries momentarily forgotten, the heat of her touch burning in my chest, I watched the creatures that now separated me from my love. The raptors were a temporary inconvenience, but I couldn't begrudge them their path home. They'd been beaten and starved on this plane. It was little wonder that they were in such a hurry to leave. As I watched, the sea of fighters parted, making paths for the raptors that flooded in from all directions. Blue reptiles leapt onto the stage, rushing to the open darkmirror. At first I wondered how so many could be here. Then I remembered. Like the hounds, certain lower-level creatures could be called from their homes without a darkmirror. In truth, anything or anyone could be called, if the wielder had enough power. But gates linked the paths between worlds for a reason. Without at least one, the chance of being lost to the void was great. Knowing Nicky-boy, he wouldn't have cared if some raptors had been lost so long as he could call enough to meet his needs.

I leaned against my truck door. With Jacq's care, my bleeding had stopped, but now that I had a moment, my body made me very aware that my stomach was upside-down and a polka band was doing their all-time favorites between my ears. Translation: I had a concussion.

I closed my eyes, doing nothing but breathing in and out, willing the nausea to go away. Once the pain lessened, I opened my eyes and began counting heads as best I could in the moonlight. I realized one thing right away. There was nothing and no one that needed my immediate attention, which was good. At the moment I couldn't do anything more magically strenuous than pull a hankie from my sleeve.

Nicodemus had supplied the power for opening the gate, but it took a great deal of concentration to keep it open and linked to the other side. I could walk and talk—and probably even chew gum—but part of me was still there, keeping things together. Between my roving mind and my tired body, it was all I could do to remain standing.

So, despite my disregard for the Council, I found it fortuitous that the three magic-wielders Fera had brought were capable healers as well as fighters. Even from a distance, I could feel the healing energy they wove around Becca, Brit and our other injured fighters. Or rather, the fighters who would submit to magical assistance. More than one Were was doggedly limping as they dragged the downed raptors toward the stage.

Like I'd known they would, the Council had given orders that no evidence be left behind. That meant the raptors had to go. And for a change, their purposes aligned with my own. Maybe it was my demon-half, but I didn't want to be responsible, if indirectly, for the raptors' deaths, which was the only outcome if they stayed. On the other side, they would regenerate, coming back to life. Here, they would be burned in the name of damage-control—a permanent death even for demons.

Someone, likely my ever perceptive Jacq, had pointed out that throwing the raptors into the gate was the easiest and less attention-grabbing option. (Creating a bonfire of roasting demons was not a good idea when fire crews were already close by and on alert.) Serena and Grey had ordered their people to retrieve every single raptor and toss them through. Still, from the way the Weres and Vamps were carelessly tugging the beasts along, it looked like the big kahunas had left out a few details, like the fact that those overgrown reptiles weren't dead. They'd be waking up soon, ravenous, and in a piss-poor mood. And if I was the wolf unloading one of the raptors Mynx had loaded on my truck, I wouldn't place my hand in its mouth for leverage.

I stopped the Were and gave him a quick, descriptive lecture about the regenerative powers of demon creatures and their love for small fleshy pieces of meat that protruded from their prey's body. I, of course, was referring to fingers and toes. But when I was done, the much paler Were hauled his burden off with a greater sense of caution. *Now what to do with our sorcerers?*

Artus was by far the most pressing issue. Nicodemus's body would wait, or rather Roskov's corpse could. Although it would need to be fully incinerated. A prickle of unease lingered at the back of my brain, but it slipped away every time I tried to form it into a solid thought.

Mynx and Fera still had Artus circled. Blue and black sparks flew as he tested his prison. The illusion of a whole and hearty Wellsy was gone. Although I knew Wellsy's soul was as well, the body only a grotesque shadow of the man I'd once thought of as a pseudo-uncle, a small part of me continued to see bits of him in that decayed corrupted form. And it was that part that needed to stay and watch whatever destructive thing we'd have to do to Wellsy's body to remove Artus's spirit. It wouldn't be pretty, but I owed my family's old friend that much. In truth, I owed him much more but had nothing more to give.

All but one of Nicodemus's vampires had been killed. The last one Serena had taken prisoner. The raptors, including those previously guarding the two remaining boys, had completely abandoned their masters, fleeing into the gate. The fight was over but there was still much to do. Starting with closing the darkmirror.

I limped up the stairs and watched as the grunting Weres and Vamps tossed the last raptors through. Once they were finished, I headed for the gate. Jacq moved toward me from the parking lot, looking none too happy as she eyed my continued limp and the blood drying on the neck of my shirt. I simply shrugged, wincing at the movement. Wiped out, I couldn't even strengthen our mental connection enough to send her reassurance. Besides being physically and magically empty, I was still holding the gate, making it hard to focus when part of me was watching the raptors descending home through the darkmirror.

Out of the corner of my eye I saw Grey walking the last two boys forward, toward the stage's base where his tigers had gathered. The black-magic still shrouding both boys must have repelled the Weres, because none would touch them. Grey gestured for me to examine them, and I mouthed, "Three minutes." I was exhausted. The gate needed to be shut down before it tried to take something I wasn't willing to give. If Brit wasn't stable by now, keeping it open wouldn't change that.

The stage was empty of all but me and a headless body, so I shouldn't have gotten a bad feeling when the last boy continued past Grey. He looked dazed. I frowned. Something was off. I'd been too busy thinking about reconnecting to Jacq and worrying about my friends to notice that the cold place in the pit of my stomach hadn't vanished with the battle's end.

The boy climbed the stairs woodenly and stepped past me. At the same time, a last group of raptors darted out of the shadows, moved across the asphalt, and rammed a surprised Mynx and Fera into their circle, breaking it, before rushing onto the unsteady stage and into the darkmirror. Artus leapt onto the stage, running toward the gate. I should have been watching him, but I was staring in dread at the black mist forming around Roskov's corpse. The same corpse between me and Jacq, who'd rushed onto the wooden platform's other end. And the very same corpse that our last, zoned-out college student was heading for.

Coming to my senses, I lunged for the boy, narrowly missing his collar and stumbling right into Artus's arms. The mist came toward me.

"Not the guardian," Artus barked. "We need her alive." The mist switched course, climbing up the boy. The young man's pale face contorted in pain. His locked jaw bulged. The darkness that could only be Nicodemus wouldn't even allow his prize the relief of screaming. Jacq stepped toward us, and my mind shouted, *NO!* Nicodemus would take her, because with me as a hostage, she would be too noble to resist. She halted, uncertain. Her expression was heartbreaking.

I stumbled, my feet dragging as Artus's clawed hands towed me and the boy, whose legs no longer seemed to work, toward the gate. As I was forced into the darkmirror's rippling blackness, I looked at Jacq helplessly. Then my body dissolved, traveling on the path between worlds, heading toward Illtrath and blue fields overflowing with hungry raptors. I wasn't sure if the resounding scream in my head was hers or mine.

* * *

I landed on my face, as usual. What was new was the location. I'd landed on a nice, soft and very warm body. A body that I was intimately familiar with...or nearly so. One whose strong arms held me so tightly that I couldn't have moved if I'd wanted to, though I definitely didn't want to. I couldn't see anything, as my nose was resting between said body's breasts, but I was pretty sure that—while we weren't in Kansas—neither was this Illtrath. I'd never been so happy to hear the distant sound of a blaring car alarm.

"What happened?" Jacq's soft words rumbled under my ear. My head rose and fell with the rhythm of her breath.

"We...I..." Voice hoarse, I lifted up, looking at her worried face before allowing my body to sink again into her warmth. I was aware of the others watching from the parking lot, but I didn't move away, enjoying the moment alone with Jacq. "How long was I gone?"

"Seconds. I was about to follow when you were tossed out like a sack of potatoes." At my frown, she kissed my head, adding, "A very beautiful sack of potatoes."

I looked up, seeing that one-dimpled, half-smile, and tried to smile back, but her comment about my not-so-graceful landing wasn't my concern. My memories were scattered, pieces missing, but it felt like I'd been gone much longer. I'd never heard of a gate being rerouted mid-jump. Yet, I was certain that I'd never made it to the other side.

"I think…" I cleared my throat and rolled to the side, keeping my hand in hers as I stared at the now silent gate. "I think maybe the mirror did something, or maybe it was the void. There was something there earlier…" I didn't understand what had happened to Brittan, but I was certain that, if I allowed my blood to sink into the smooth, ebony stone and connected again to the darkmirror, I'd remember. I'd understand. But I was too weak and more than a little frightened by the possibility of what I might find. "I just have this feeling that Nicodemus and his brother won't be back. Something happened as we passed through."

I take exception to the ill-treatment of my daughters. I clutched my head as the memory of that cold, bodiless voice struck like lightning. I got to my feet, leaning against the now solid blackness, trying to breathe evenly as the pain receded. For some odd reason, I found the cool surface comforting.

"Cate?" Jacq rubbed my arms.

I looked into her concerned gray eyes. "I don't know." I suppressed the bitter urge to laugh. That answer was getting old with me. I was sure Jacq didn't appreciate it any better. "Maybe a memory." I looked at the darkmirror, seeing a hazy image of myself reflected back. I was pretty sure it had just saved my life. Twice. I let my fingers briefly caress its surface, wiping away dried blood as I said quietly, "Just a voice in the darkness." I shook my head, remembering with a fresh flash of pain my wound. I tore my gaze from the mirrored woman's face—for once, she didn't seem to know any more than I—and took one last look at the headless body. It was against my nature, but this was one time when I would leave it to someone else to clean up. I was going to make sure my friends were okay and the last boy was purged of dark magic. Then we were going home.

I grabbed Jacq's hand and pulled her to the edge nearest our injured friends. There were no stairs, but I was gratified to see those garish thrones had been chucked off. I sat on the wooden planks and lowered myself down. I thought to land on my feet, but my auburn-haired phoenix was quicker. Jacq was there to catch my fall, and I was just weak enough to hope that it would always be so.

* * *

Day Nine

The sun would be rising soon. It had been an exhausting night, and I longed to find a soft bed, climb between the cool covers, and snuggle with the warm woman currently sitting by my side. But Jacq and I would have to settle for an old throw and the den's lumpy couch, as all the beds, other than the one in the Agency's upstairs bedroom, were already taken. And while it was probably safe to sleep outside the wards tonight, I felt the need to be close to my family. My trip through the darkmirror had left me unsettled.

After my examination of our friends, we'd transported Brittan and Rom, who were the most injured, home. I'd been surprised to be greeted upon entry by three crying newborns. But not as surprised as Grey, who'd rushed to see his mate and kits. The third baby, a little girl they'd named Alecé in honor of my Nana, had been a surprise to all.

It had been too close to dawn for the vampires to travel far, so the lot of them, including Serena, tugging along a vampire hostage and extremely peeved JJ, had headed to Lady D's. The patrons at the House of Delights wouldn't blink an eye at a group of bloody, hungry vampires rushing in before daybreak. Serena had extended an invitation to the wolves, but Luke had declined, instead taking his pack-mates to his safe house. Luke was unlikely to forget his first and last visit to Lady D's any time soon. Still, I'd made him promise to bring Becca by soon for an examination. I trusted Fera's healers, but at some point Becca had become a friend and knowing she had been alone for hours with Nicodemus, Artus, and their raptors made me uneasy.

We'd lodged Rom and Brit in my room for the night. Risa wouldn't leave either, so we'd placed Brit in my bed and a man-sized Rom on a temporary cot against the wall. When I'd left, Risa had been pacing between the two. I'd kept my family from telling her what Brit had become. Considering the events immediately after Jacq and I had left the stage, it might be for the best.

We bedded Grey and his newly expanded family down in the guest room, which I'd begun to think of as Jacq's. Grey's people had filled the other rooms. My Nana had confirmed that I indeed had a concussion. I was supposed to stay awake a bit longer to allow my heightened healing to somewhat repair the damage, but I wasn't so sure I could remain awake.

And Jacq wasn't helping any by being so cuddly. The damn chivalrous woman had a body that was made to sprawl across.

"Cate?"

Jacq's voice brought me back to myself. "Hmmm?" Eyes closed, I burrowed deeper into her side.

"What does your great-grandmother have to do with you leaving your marriage?"

"Shhh." Remembering that I'd been explaining how my Grams saw the future in her dreams, I put my finger to my lips to forestall more questions. Or rather, that was my intention. I was already half-asleep against Jacq's shoulder. When her warm breath tickled my skin, I realized with a start that I'd put my finger over her mouth. I popped one eye open, craned my head back to look at Jacq, and waggled my finger, making her eyes cross as it danced too close to her nose. "Patience. I'm getting there."

She snorted, making me smile. She'd been here long enough to know just how long it could take a Southerner to tell a story. I closed my eyes again, collecting my thoughts.

"I've always had dreams, too. Not as clear as my Grams', but I always knew they were possibilities for the future." I lost my train of thought.

"Cher?" Jacq's hand over mine brought me back to the point. Well, almost back. The accent that came out on that single word was as sexy as hell and always pointed my mind in less practical directions. Jacq's husky laugh in my ear reminded me of our strengthening mental connection.

"Oh…yes…well, I've had these dreams." I felt the belated flush in my cheeks. Sheesh, even my blush was tired. It was about a minute late. I cleared my throat. "Sometimes they're of love. Sometimes other things. Something happened on the day of my wedding to Luke, and I ended up getting a longer, clearer look."

I felt her thumb softly trace my cheekbone, but my eyelids were too heavy to open. "The dreams were fuzzy, but they felt right in here. It was clear that Luke was meant for another." I tried to move my hand over my heart to demonstrate, but my limbs were so heavy. I yawned, my jaw cracking. Or maybe that was the old couch protesting as our weight shifted.

"I loved Luke…still love Luke…but it wasn't…" My heart and breathing slowed. There was something important I needed to say. Or was that see? I remembered then. I needed her to understand…

to not be hurt. I was too tired to search our mental bond…to share the feelings I had for a man who would always be part of my life but not my love. But I didn't need the bond to know Jacq's reaction. One look in her eyes would be enough.

I could see everything in her eyes.

If only I could open mine. My forehead stretched into a frown. Lips pressed gently to the creased skin. There was a brief tug then strong arms surrounded me. Already drifting, I rested my head on a soft pillow and heard Jacq say in her thickest accent yet, "Sleep, beauty, there will be other days to finish your stories…" much quieter, "and other dreams yet to live."

I'd never told her about how Luke had been there for me when my mother went missing. Or how, in my grief, I'd mistaken friendship and comfort for love and agreed to marriage. I'd wanted my mother at my wedding so badly that after the ceremony I'd tried a desperate spell. It didn't matter that I'd tried to take the spell's cost upon myself. I couldn't tell her that. Or that I'd nearly died when it had backfired. At least I couldn't tell her those things without some preparation.

Jacq was already a bit protective. The woman would keep me in her sight twenty-four-seven if she thought I'd do that again, which I wouldn't. I'd been fortunate to only end up in that coma, spending those six days dreaming. I'd seen countless futures and gained a great deal, including unlocking a level of magic that I now thought was tied to my demon-half. But I'd also lost a great deal. When I awoke, the dream of Luke and me had ended.

Darryl had friends in high places. With his help, my marriage was annulled within a day. Luke had been by my side every sleeping moment. He hadn't understood why I would undo what had just been done, and I'd felt like a shit for hurting him.

As a child, I'd believed that there was someone for everyone, a soul *amore*. I wish I could say there'd also been a great love for me in my dreams. But I couldn't remember my future, only a mixture of feelings from anticipation to dread. I'd walked away from Luke, knowing that there was a great love for him…but maybe not for me. Don't make me something I'm not—I acted out of selfishness. That childhood belief, which I'd given up to be a practical adult, had been reaffirmed. There could also be a soul-deep love out there for me, and that was worth waiting forever for.

As I drifted to sleep in Jacq's arms, I couldn't help but wonder if the one thing that I had been too scared to look for, even in my own dreams, had actually found me instead. It was a simultaneously harrowing and thrilling thought.

* * *

"Mmmm…" The contented hum began in my chest and moved all the way to my heart. I was having that dream again, and it felt wonderful. I snuggled deeper into my pillow, hearing it grunt as I stretched my legs and arched my back. *Pillows don't grunt.* This thought finally made it through to my sleep-fogged brain. *Neither do they rise and fall.*

I slowly blinked open my eyes, squinting. The light was all wrong. My bedroom faced the setting sun, not this gloriously bright glare. That's when I realized where I was lying. Or rather, on whom. We were on the den's old couch. I dimly remembered sitting beside Jacq and talking after we'd returned from the battle. I winced in preemptive embarrassment. I'd been known to talk in my sleep. There was no telling what my conniving (yet wonderful) detective had wormed out of me. Then I remembered. *We have a date tonight.* Okay, so maybe it wasn't such a bad thing that we'd talked. But I would've liked to have been conscious for it.

My *pillow* was still asleep. Somehow, Jacq had ended up lying across the couch with me spread over her. A throw covered our entwined legs. My head was resting on her unexpectedly comfortable breasts.

Double wowza. I'd thought she was stunning before, but this sleep-tousled look was just…mmm…wow. Long, lush lashes resting against pale, rosy skin. Deep auburn hair mussed. Lips, full and slightly parted. I pushed up to get a better look. Jacq groaned again, and I fell back with a whimper. Her legs were spread, cradling my knee, which pressed high to her center. And our pants were missing. I had a moment to think, *How had the sneaky woman managed that?* Then our clothing was forgotten.

My wandering eyes stopped on Jacq's lips. Were they as soft as they looked? Would the breath from her mouth tingle as it flowed down my throat? Fire began to slide beneath my skin, and I locked it down tight. I needed to know if this would work…if we could work when it was only *us*. Just two women. No magic. No interfering, evil forces with bad fashion sense out to conquer the world.

Again, I pressed upward, careful not to move my knee further into the heat between her thighs. Jacq's eyes fluttered open, locking with mine before drifting to my lips as they drew inescapably closer. The moment before we touched seemed to hang in the air for an eternity. Then she leaned forward, closing the distance.

A line from the *Princess Bride* passed through my head, "Since the invention of the kiss, there have only been two such…" Then I was no longer capable of thought. Her lips were softer than expected. They opened as she nipped my lower lip. I gasped in surprised pleasure, and she slid her tongue over and into. I drank her down, my body flaming, shifting closer.

"Cate," Jacq groaned into my mouth as we parted for breath. *Breathing was overrated.* I pressed her lips again. She tasted like an exotic spiced tea, and I was dying of thirst. I returned the favor, gently biting her lip, soothing the hurt with a sweep of my tongue.

"Cate." Jacq's voice was sleep-roughened.

Disoriented, I pulled away, gazing into silver, desire-filled eyes. A bolt of heat shot through my veins straight to my groin, and I shuddered.

"Your grandmother," Jacq said, "is in the next room, fixing breakfast. If you press that leg any higher, I won't be held responsible when she finds us in here bare as the day we were born." She rubbed a smooth leg against mine, accenting her words.

I blinked. "But we're not naked." I admit, my mind wasn't working quite yet.

"But we will be." Jacq again brought her mouth to mine.

"Okay." I was panting when we finally separated. From desire? From lack of breath? I was beyond caring. But the thought of my Nana finding us in our unmentionables sobered me. "I just have one, very important question. Then I'll let you off this couch."

I put my finger to Jacq's lips, stopping any comments. The gesture seemed familiar.

She nipped my fingertip.

"Cut that out." I mock scowled. It felt so exquisitely comfortable to simply play. "Keep in mind that your answer determines where we go from here…" Her body tensed. I leaned down, whispering in her ear, "The one thing I want most to know in the whole world," I let my breath blow in her ear, punctuating each following word by tugging on her delectable earlobe, "is...where...are...my...pants?"

Laughing at Jacq's bemused expression, I jumped from the couch, grabbed the cover, and ran. I had just enough time to admire the blue shorts with little green dragons plastered to her muscular body before I was out of the room and bounding up the stairs, two at a time. "Dibs on the shower!"

We had plans to make, injured friends to check on, and a house full of people (including a set of baby tigers, whom I could hear making their presence known) to see on their way home. Later I would focus on what Wellsy and the others had been doing in that mine, how they had been possessed by Nicodemus and his brothers, and where the Kin's embezzled funds were. But for now, my mind lingered on only one thought as I headed into my room, trying not to disturb Risa, or Brittan who was cradled in the other woman's arms. It was the same thought that repeated in my head as the warm water from our guest shower cascaded over my skin. *Boxers? Really?*

My elegant phoenix was full of surprises.

Continue Reading for a Preview of
The next in the Darkmirror Series:
The Devil You Know…

All heads turned to watch the white limo slowly roll down Bourbon Street. All heads but mine. Considering the barricades had been raised hours ago, converting the street and surrounding avenues into touristy walkways, it was an unusual sight to see. But it was probably the small squadron of muscle-bound, gun-toting suits accompanying the vehicle that drew the eye. If they hadn't been of the vampire variety, they could have been mistaken for Secret Service.

But despite all the hoopla my eyes were elsewhere, watching Jacq return from changing into the new jeans I'd bought her. She gave me a smile, and my heart fluttered. Once it settled, I noted the way the light denim and white shirt fit her tall muscular frame. My mind wandered to another time and place, one where that body had been substantially less dressed. Suddenly, more than my heart was beating double-time. A gruff laugh brought me back to my senses. Embarrassed, I felt my cheeks flush.

"Baby girl, that there's your trouble," Jupiter rumbled. I'd been telling him that the "trouble" he asked Luke to warn me about had been dealt with. He'd simply shaken his head. I'd started to ask why but was distracted by the return of the first person I'd ever wanted to play dress-up with. Fortunately, my brain cells focused long enough to realize that Jup had not been referring to Nicodemus and his group. Which begged the question: What was more "trouble" than a group of dark sorcerers running around killing, kidnapping, and trying to unleash a demon army to take over the world? Whatever it was, Jup was pointing right at it.

I followed the line of Jupiter's dark, knotted finger, and my heart dropped. I saw only Jacq.

The trumpeter is never wrong. The phrase, known to everyone from witch to moon-howler, echoed in my head. *No.* I clenched my fists. It didn't matter what Jup saw coming. We'd deal with it. Jacq moved into the street, stepping around a group of drunken sailors who'd stopped to watch the limo. But Jup's finger didn't follow. My lungs filled with sorely overdue air. Jup pointed to the limo and its entourage. Not that I didn't think Detective Jacqueline Slone was trouble. While I'd yet to have the pleasure, I was of the personal opinion that she was of the more earth-shattering rather than earth-ending distinction.

The limo crept closer, only yards behind my returning date. Jupiter propped his old silver trumpet on his knee and wiped the sweat off his forehead with a faded handkerchief. Though it was nearly midnight, the day's heat was only now fading. My friend turned his head toward the limo. "You best be getting on." Jup picked up his dusty fedora and began to pocket the tips collected therein.

There was no point in asking the trumpeter what he meant. He'd donned his I'm-just-an-old-man-ignore-me expression. "That act, Mr. Jones," I shook my finger at him, "may fool the tourists, but one day, real soon, me and you are going to have a sit-down."

Jup just harrumphed at my half-playful, half-earnest scolding. He dusted his hat against his knee before setting it on his head. I looked from him to my auburn-haired love as she stepped near.

The smile on my face slipped away.

A stranger would've seen a calm, carefree woman-about-town. But Jacq's normally gray eyes, so often dark with passion, were a much lighter gray-blue. And in them was a grieving woman preparing for some inevitable loss. Jacq was working hard to hide her emotions. But our mental bond had grown stronger over the past twenty-four hours, giving me a good idea of *what* she was feeling…if not precisely *why*.

She stopped before me, looking at me with those cloudy eyes. With one hand taking hers and the other on her white belt buckle, I tugged her onto the sidewalk and out of the approaching limo's path, not dropping her hand even as we stood together. I was still puzzling over her strange turn of emotions as the car pulled to the curb feet

away. Disturbed by the magic rolling off the white stretch limo, my demon-half began to pace in its cage, pushing my fire to the surface.

I let it rise.

I couldn't imagine what Jupiter considered worse than Nicodemus. But whatever it was, it had to be bad. Jacq moved subtly, angling her body so we could both watch the car, leaving a portion of her larger frame between myself and the vamp-suits now fanning out around us. I really hoped that this was not one of those moments where the stupid chivalrous woman got hurt on my account.

Thoughts of injuries forced me to look around. The streets were packed. If there was going to be a fight, it needed to be elsewhere.

The bulkiest of the vampires removed his shades. I buried my urge to roll my eyes. Like people wouldn't know he was Kin just because they didn't see the glowing irises. Puleeze, the fact that he wasn't breathing was a dead giveaway.

"Miss Delacy." He opened the long car's rear door. "Her Majesty requests your presence."

The car's crest belonged to Seth, NOLA's Master Vamp, King of the Louisiana Vampires, and head of the Southern States. (Yeah, I know, he had way too many titles.) But when the Kin said "Her Majesty," he wasn't referring to Seth's sister, Serena, who also happened to be my friend. Serena preferred to travel alone, in more low-key vehicles (to her brother's continued ire). I ignored the waiting vampire, simply looking at my gray-eyed protector in question.

Jacq shook her head. "If you decide to go, I won't hold you here." She gripped my hand a fraction tighter, her actions belying her words. "It's your decision." Her voice, as whiskey-smooth as ever, was pitched low, though we both knew it offered only the illusion of privacy. The Kin, with their sharp ears, could've heard us from a block over, much less their position only a few feet away.

Jacq caressed my cheek. I closed my eyes briefly, savoring the hot magic trailing over my skin. But cutting off my sight also helped me focus on our mental bond. If I didn't know better, I'd think she was saying goodbye. I could almost hear the words *I thought we'd have more time* ringing through our ever-deepening connection. The silly woman had been dogging my steps for days, going so far as to sleep on my lumpy, too short couch. Why she thought tonight would be any different, me getting in that car without her, was beyond me.

I opened my eyes, searching Jacq's face for clues as she continued, "Whatever you decide, do it without regrets. I don't want anything to come between us." She cut her eyes to the waiting car, her speech becoming more formal as an icy curtain fell over her expression, hiding her heart from everyone but me. "But if something must, I'd rather it be a distance I can travel or a wall I can climb, rather than a past I cannot undo."

I looked from the vampire's stoic face to the idling limo's open door to Jacq. With the donning of her cold mask, I could feel Jacq gently but steadily pulling away from our emotional link. In my mind, I grabbed the bond, not forcing her to stay, but showing her I'd fight with power and determination to keep her there. As I wrestled with her internally, wielding hope and love like psychic chains to bind her tighter still, I rushed to add my words to the battle.

"There are a lot of things in life I regret." I spoke softly, raising my hand to hold hers against my cheek, laying my fingers in the creases between hers, fitting our hands together. "But not this. Not now. Not you and me."

I lifted my chin, meeting the eyes of the woman who'd become the living embodiment of my totem, my bright phoenix, and forged ahead. "But I live with the wrong choices, the paths untraveled, the lives lost, and I never hold those regrets against anyone but myself. So, if you have some reason that you think I'll regret getting in that car or not getting in that car, then tell me. Because I won't have anything between us, either." My mind flashed to an hourglass, grains of sand trickling away, carrying my life with them. "At least, nothing that we can avoid...like the fear of unspoken words."

I blinked once, keeping my eyes wide. This was not goodbye, damn it. And there was no way I was going to get all misty-eyed in front of a vampire wearing wingtips. No longer even pretending not to listen, the vamp looked from us to his watch. Don't get me wrong. The undead could take a long walk off a short pier into a bright pool of sunshine for all I cared. I was not ashamed of what Jacq made me feel. But I'd never live it down if I started crying and it got back to Serena. That bloody Vampire Queen had a mind like a magical mousetrap. If she ever heard I'd so much as sniffled in public, she'd tease me until I was dead, reanimate my corpse, and do it all over again.

It was Jacq's turn to close her eyes. I held my breath, feeling blind without that gray window into her thoughts. An infinitely long moment passed before she sighed and blinked. As her gaze once again locked with mine, something in her shifted, and I breathed deep. Her body relaxed, as if a decision had been made, and with it, a demon exorcised. The icy curtain lifted and she stopped fighting our bond, letting it flow back into place like the river of love it had become to the dry bed of my heart. Before her husky words even began, I wanted to kiss her. And kiss her I would. Soon. But not the kiss goodbye she expected. No, this would be a kiss hello. Because, little-by-little, this woman was showing me pieces of her soul. And, in that moment, I might have fallen in love with her all over again.

"You, cher, are a curiously honest woman. You keep secrets. Yet, you hide nothing of yourself. But the things that you don't know about yourself, the secrets that have been kept from you, tear at your heart. I can feel it in here." She brought our joined hands to rest over her breast. "And your pain is mine."

I blinked again, restraining that dreaded sniffle. A public corner in the heart of the city beneath the sea, with more than one nosy eavesdropper, was not the place for this talk. But there was no way in hell I was going to stop her now.

Jacq continued, "And maybe there's a good reason for that hurt. There's so much you don't know, probably won't ever know." She swallowed, her voice unnaturally calm as she added, "unless you go now." In my heart, I knew what she was saying: *I don't want you to go, but I can't ask you to stay.*

The truth was evident in her eyes. Jacq believed the answers she spoke of would decide my decision. And maybe she was right. Maybe the answers I'd been seeking were waiting inside that limo. My gut seemed to think so. And part of me wondered if it wasn't that possibility, more than the aura of powerful magic rolling out of the car, pushing through my shields, that had my demon-half clawing the walls to be released from its cage—before it was forced to reveal itself in the full moon's light.

Questions. Answers. Power. Demons and Blood. All should matter. But they didn't. Not as much as this moment. Not as much as what I felt for Jacq. Not as much as what she felt for me in return.

I raised our joined hands to cup her face before pulling her down for a brief but no less passionate kiss—my previous reticence to public displays of affection having been thrown out the proverbial window… along with my sanity. I held her face close to mine as I said, "There's only one answer I'm interested in right now: Would you go with me? Because if not, we'll both walk away." I smiled, adding sweetly for the benefit of the oh-so-serious suits surrounding the car, "And whoever's in the over-polished tin can can go find another runner to dig them out of whatever hole they've landed themselves into."

Jacq's eyes registered shock then pleasure before she laughed quietly. Her warm breath brushed my still tingling lips. Her arm wrapped around my waist for a tight hug. Up until now I'd been a loner, so I could understand why she'd think I'd go it alone. But a little understanding and her current half-smile's delectable dimple wouldn't get her out of a lecture later.

The happiness quickly faded from her eyes. "If I'm right about who's waiting, then I won't be welcome, and my presence might do more harm than good."

Meaning I might not get my answers.

I didn't have to think about it. But I did, looking at Jacq, seeing her. Her loveliness. Her courage. Her strong, selfless heart. And I answered with the honest surety garnered from a lifetime of gauging people by their actions. "My question still stands."

She nodded just once, her smile returning. "As my lady commands." At my arched brow, she added, "It's your show, darlin'."

I bit my lip, hiding a smile. I found it irresistibly cute when her badass immortal self tried to talk all modern. But from the twinkle in her eye I knew that she knew...and that she was going to milk my reaction for all it was worth.

I turned to face the vampire. Leaning back against Jacq, I wrapped her hands around my waist. My statement was clear, even before I said, "Where I go, she goes. And I'll have your blood oath upon your loyalty to your Master that we won't be harmed—in any way."

He started to flash his fangs in a practiced smile but stopped as I added, "And that includes mind and magic games, along with the usual physical promises of good health." My look was pointed. At the vampire's scowl, I felt Jacq's silent laughter against my back. There was a quick conference as he murmured into his headset before opening the door further with a bow.

The Kin's eyes flickered red before resuming their normal, nearly black stare. In a tone surprisingly mellow for such a broad-chested man, he said, "You have my vow. More notably, you have the Queen's." I started to move forward. He raised his hand. "But a warning, little witch. Seth is my Master, but Serena's my friend. And the friend of my friend is my own."

My expression remained neutral. He'd said a warning, and his tone implied it. But heck if I knew what it was. Still, if it delayed climbing in the limo, I'd listen.

He smiled again, this time fully, showing a set of glistening white fangs before continuing in a much deeper, more serious voice. "But a vampire's loyalties always lie first with his Master. As they say, so the blood flows, so the Kin goes." He slipped his shades back on and moved to stand behind the door, opening it further. He continued, more drolly. "I'd suggest you hurry. Once you reach a certain point, patience often decreases with age."

Though it seemed he was referring to the car's occupants, I had a feeling that the vamp's warning had everything to do with someone else. Someone who wouldn't tell me himself that he was running out of patience.

I stared into the shadowy interior, trying to pierce the darkness. That extra sense—the one that sometimes felt like an Alpine skier, skis half-hanging off the edge of a steep cliff, anticipating and fearing the plunge—said that this was one of those moments that would define my life. Did I stay or go?

With little to lose and much to gain (or so I hoped), I chose the latter. Just before I ducked to enter the car's doorway, I saw our reflection in the limo's windows. Jacq looked the same, but the mirrored Cate's eyes held an eagerness I didn't feel. Keeping my hand in Jacq's, I moved into the car, sliding across the cool, light-tan leather. Not that I thought my detective would back out. But for all my attitude with the vamp, I was still nervous. Her touch and the increased clarity of her mind in mine that it afforded soothed me. We were barely settled before the car started moving. Jupiter's trumpet trilled as a clock somewhere began to chime.

Midnight. The witching hour. *How appropriate.*

As the car moved forward, I couldn't help but wonder if our coach would turn into a pumpkin. Although, considering my once black, now a more faded dark-blue jeans and similarly faded dark-blue shirt, perhaps I was the scruffy mouse and they would hitch me up to pull the damn thing. Jacq didn't say a word, but I could feel her amusement in my head. She had obviously caught something of my thoughts. Maybe my elegant warrior liked the scruffy look. But that was an experiment for later. Much later.

We sat there, unspeaking. Behind tinted windows the sights of New Orleans slowly passed. Like the dim glow of a flickering bulb, streetlights flashed in and out, painting Jacq and me in a wash of shadows. The ever-changing light made it impossible for my eyes to adjust. Facing us, two figures sat just outside the light's reach. No doubt the Kin, with their heightened senses, had no need for the light and had disengaged the bulb. I was certain that Jacq, with her own enhanced eyesight, could see our hosts, but her thoughts were unworried. She was waiting for me to speak. And I was waiting on our hosts, not ready to announce my limitations, though they likely already knew or would remember soon.

So I relaxed, letting my magic do what my eyes could not. For anything else, I'd have to wait until we reached an area where the light didn't constantly shift. Or until some courteous soul remembered how shortsighted we mortals be and sent up a flare. Although with a magical wake flowing behind us big enough to swamp a double-decker full of Japanese tourists, anyone in NOLA with an ounce of magic would know where we were without the additional help.

I began the process of lowering my magical shielding and felt the almost undetectable touch of a power-probe as the car's other occupants, too, took our measure. Offended, my demon-half rattled its cage, testing the bars. Until I eased my protections, I couldn't return the favor, having shielded tightly all night, not wanting anything, including the jumble of magic flowing through the city's epicenter, to distract me from the woman now seated beside me.

Jacq squeezed my hand. Though it went against her nature, she was hanging back, letting me take the lead. She'd said it was my show and was honoring her word. I flashed her a small, tight smile. She winked at me. Jacqueline Slone was racking up some major brownie points, and she darn well knew it.

There was a smile on my face as I peeked past my shields, careful to keep my fire leashed and the beast that was my demon-half confined. But I didn't have far to look as my search stopped short, striking a wall of breath-stealing power. It permeated the air, pressing into every available crack. *Holy shit.* Or was that unholy shit? I didn't know who, but I knew what they were.

Demons.

The word echoed in my head, even as Jacq stiffened, her grip tightening. I knew without asking that she'd suspected as much. But thinking and knowing were often two very different things.

Like a thousand pounds of water forcing its way through a cracked dam, the demon magic pounded into me, threatening to wash away my shields and drown my mind in the process. I should have expected this. Even when fully shielded on Bourbon Street's sidewalk, I'd sensed this power's outer edges. I'd been confident that I could handle whatever they were packing. I was wrong. I hadn't expected the magic to be so invasive…so aggressive. Now I was in the middle of it, and there was an ever-widening opening in my protection. The wolves were at the door, and I'd just opened it, saying, "Oh, do please come in an' sit a spell." And in case you need a translation, let me say it again in simpler words. I was completely. And utterly. Screwed.

I threw everything I had into shoring up my shields, temporarily patching the hole, leaning a great deal of magic against it to hold the alien force at bay. Jacq squeezed my hand, and I felt her concern and added strength in my mind. Her hot magic pooled between our palms, a reserve offered to help me, but I resisted drawing on it. Something within me said this was a challenge, one I had to resist on my own.

The worst part was that the demons didn't even seem aware of the harm their magic had done. In fact, the magic became more concentrated. It was like a man with halitosis not understanding why the room had suddenly cleared.

Or maybe they only played the fool. The latter seemed more likely as one of the figures leaned forward. With a barely audible electric buzz, a set of muted lights popped to life. Still softly panting from the magical gauntlet I'd just run, I blinked several times, forcing my eyes to adjust faster.

"There, that's better. We can't have you frying your brain simply to get a quick peek, now can we?"

The cheerful tenor with no noticeable accent came from the man seated directly across from Jacq. His black hair, streaked like JJ's with a white forelock, and dark charcoal Armani suit could've belonged to anyone. (Well, anyone with a big enough roll of C-notes.) But the blue eyes were shockingly familiar, as were the matching eyes of the silver-haired woman seated at his side. Unlike my Nana, whose hair was more salt and pepper, this woman's short, elegant do was so silver it was nearly white. The color implied extreme age, but the face was wrinkled in a minimal, graceful manner that attested to either amazing genes or the world's best plastic surgeon.

My gaze met amused eyes. Caught staring, I blushed but didn't look away. The silver-haired woman said, "You flatter me, Miss Delacy. I hope you'll believe me when I say, it must be as you say 'good genes,' since this face has been altered only by time."

I didn't care if Serena or Jacq took an occasional rummage around my mind, but I didn't appreciate a stranger's intrusion. As if synchronized, my shields went into place as Jacq battened down her own hatches. All that was left open was the mental bond connecting us.

The silver-haired woman turned, shrewdly eyeing my elegant warrior, whose hand was still in mine. "Genes, I like this human word. Apt, considering the circumstances. What do you think, Miss Delacy?"

The silence lengthened as the car slowed, waiting for the vampires, who were keeping pace outside, to lower the barricades. Distracted by the magic still pushing against my mind, I realized, belatedly, that they awaited my response. I watched the two demons, trying to focus on anything but the magic buzzing in my ears, singing to my blood, calling forth something in me that I didn't presently want to deal with. "Honestly," I said, "I don't have a friggin' clue." I cut my eyes from the demoness's eerily familiar light blue ones to her companion, who was trying, unsuccessfully, to strangle a laugh. I shifted closer to Jacq, letting my thigh rest against hers.

Waving my hand, I tried again, hoping to hide my weariness with politeness. "Please, excuse me. My patience with all this cloak and dagger sh…stuff has worn thin this week. I'm certain you didn't invite us here to expand your vocabulary, so maybe you could explain what it is that I can do for you—" I searched for a proper title, finally saying, "Ma'am." She wasn't my majesty. Heck, I didn't even know what she was Queen of. But since she was a demon, I had a sinking suspicion she wasn't something as benign as the Queen of Hearts looking for her tarts. It didn't seem right to call a woman wearing a nearly white silk top and skirt that probably cost more than my Jeep, "Miss." And I didn't think she would appreciate my impression of Jerry Lee Lewis's, "Hey laaay-deeeee." So, ma'am it was.

The male demon cleared his throat. "May I?"

The silver-haired woman patted his knee. "Be my guest." She folded her hands, crossing her legs in an elegant move I envied. I couldn't hold that pose for more than a minute without fidgeting.

"Maybe an introduction first. We know you, Miss Delacy, as well as the good Detective Slone." He gestured with a hand much darker than my own. At Jacq's icy expression, he added, "By reputation only, of course."

Since I hadn't been alive long enough to garner the sort of reputation that attracted a demon's attention, *that* was obviously directed at the woman by my side. "I'm Vanguard—bodyguard, jester, and whatever else my aunt here should require."

With an arch look, the silver-haired woman muttered, "The last is questionable."

Not missing a beat, he grinned. "And this is—well, we'll skip all the long, dreadfully dull titles. This is Her Majesty, Queen of Denoir."

I froze. Denoir? Where my mother had been trapped, met and loved my demon father, only to leave when she'd found herself pregnant with me? That same Denoir? *Well, there certainly isn't more than one*. I was pretty sure that sarcastic thought came from my demon-half. Too bad I couldn't blame her for all the sarcasm that came out of my mouth. The knot in my gut was growing. And my demon-half was nearly frantic (when she wasn't being a smart-ass), suspecting as I did what was coming. I jumped to listen as the man, Vanguard, kept talking.

"Genes, Miss Delacy...er Cate. May I call you Cate?"

I nodded woodenly, barely comprehending the question.

"Like I was saying, genes. My aunt was correct when she said this is about them. Or maybe you would prefer the term biological material?" There was a teasing note in his voice. Slowly emerging from my stupor, I didn't react to his rhetorical question. "The fact is that you, dear Cate, are carrying a portion of our family's biological material, specifically my cousin's." He smiled briefly, flashing white teeth in a tan face before saying in a decidedly deeper tone, "And we want it back."

I didn't have to pick my jaw up from the floor, but only because it didn't reach that far.

With the cold clarity of a slap to the face, I came to my senses. I was being played. No longer able to read our minds, this one was trying to elicit a reaction. For what purpose, I was unsure. Part of me wanted to fly across the limo, jerk the demon up by his outrageously expensive lapels, and shake a sensible sentence out of him. But I suppressed the urge. I wasn't going to play a game when I didn't know the rules.

"Really, Van, could you be more obtuse?" The silver-haired woman turned to me. "What my melodramatic nephew is trying to say, Cate, is welcome to the family." She patted the empty seat on her left. "Now, come...give your grandmother a kiss hello."

I shot from my seat, remembering at the last second the car's low ceiling. "Wha...What—" My loud stutter was cut off as the limo's driver, another demon if I was sensing his magic correctly, lowered the partition. I eased my ramrod body back into the seat, leaning heavily against Jacq's side. Her arm pulled me close. Maybe the interruption was fortuitous. My vocabulary was currently limited to a series of four-letter words.

The driver's quiet, "Your Majesty?" was tense. There was the sound of a commotion outside the car. As the Queen and Van conferred with the driver, I turned to the dark glass. Several of the Kin, including the one we'd spoken with earlier, flitted away. A cold fist gripped my heart.

Riding in cars with demons was *such* a bad idea.

Sharing my unease, Jacq pulled me closer. "Cate." The limo decelerated quickly, jostling us nearly out of our seats.

Several things happened at once, the combination of which is my excuse for the transgression that followed. The limo turned quickly, screeching to a halt as a midnight funeral procession, singing a sad spiritual and bearing a pine casket on its shoulders, blocked the way. At the same time, my magical guard dropped.

Maybe it was a subconscious attempt to delay giving the demoness an answer. Maybe it was a knee-jerk reaction to their words. No matter the cause, I slipped, loosening the temporary shield I'd so hastily erected to protect myself from the demon magic that hissed like a strong electrical current around us. It would take only seconds to plug the breech. But as was typical for my luck, it was during those few critical moments that the shit decided to quarterback-sack the fan.

The car was still rolling to a stop when two quick successive blasts of raw uncontrolled demon magic slammed into its four-ton frame, tossing Jacq into the side door and me halfway across her body, knocking the breath from us both. There was a slew of grunts as the demons were tossed willy-nilly.

Everything happened in slow motion. The demons reacted defensively, unleashing their magic fully, forcing it outward, shielding us from the unseen attackers. The magic in the car increased a hundred-fold, snapping against my body with the force of a high-wire power line, breeching my weakened defenses effortlessly. In horror, I watched as their magic brought mine to the surface. The control I'd worked for years to gain over my fire? The chains, the cage, the locks containing my beast—each painstaking constructed consciously and unconsciously? All demolished in a heartbeat.

My demon-half, driven senseless by the magical assault from without and within, was unleashed to fight for its own survival. Sparks danced in the air as our magics reacted. My reaction time was dulled from hearing the word "grandmother" and then being tossed like a rag doll across the vehicle, leaving me too stunned to reel my magic in before another's slapped it down. My body jerked as my inner demon was literally and forcefully pushed back into its cage. Like a wrecking-ball to the chin, the raging tide of invading magic scorched through me, physically throwing me backward. Everything went dark as my eyes snapped shut.

My still slightly fractured skull slammed into the door's window with a loud crack, but I felt no pain. The foreign magic receded, leaving behind a trail of burned-out nerves, making it impossible to force my eyes open. The magic's sudden absence, like a wash of cold water, cleared my mind enough to focus on just one thing.

Jacq. Had the demons seen my unleashing of magic as just cause to break their vow? Their reasons, whatever they might be, weren't important, but the possibility that they might see their oath as void and turn on my love was.

I could hear Jacq's roar and feel magic flying. Possibly the most concerning—the expected sound of gunfire was missing. The Queen's undead allies were the shoot-first-ask-questions-later kind of folks. If they weren't shooting, they were probably dead-twice. I fought to stay by my love's side, fearing what the devil we knew and the devil we didn't might do to her.

Jacq pulled my body to hers, cradling me in strong arms. I felt the warm, familiar *zing* of her healing magic and wanted to protest. She needed her power to protect us, but I couldn't make my mouth move. Her voice, urgent in my ear, called my name over and over. I managed to briefly force my eyes open. As she pulled me closer, my head turned, my face sliding across spider-webbed glass, leaving a trail of crimson blood behind. Through the red haze, I saw the mourners, somehow unaware of the battle raging around them, marching through the wrought-iron gates of an ancient, willow-bordered cemetery. As I slipped into unconsciousness, I could hear the spiritual, "There Will Come a Day," echoing to us.

I'd never ascribed to the belief that fainting made a lady delicate, ethereal, or whatever other bullshit word you wanted to use. Nope, I was pretty sure it was a liability. But my body refused to obey my order to stay away from the darkness. As I drifted away to Jacq's voice accompanied by the mourners' dark melody about war and lost innocence, my last thought was that sometimes it really sucked to be a mortal hanging with immortals.

They never knew when to pull their punches.

Bella Books, Inc.

Women. Books. Even Better Together.

P.O. Box 10543
Tallahassee, FL 32302

Phone: 800-729-4992
www.bellabooks.com